First Farmer in Space

Phoenix Phoenix

Published by Phoenix Phoenix (04/27/2016)

ISBN: 978-1-9995408-0-7 (sc)

ISBN: 978-1-9995408-1-4 (hc)

ISBN: 978-1-9995408-2-1 (e)

This story takes place in an alternative world and is a work of fiction. Some historical facts are used fictitiously. This is not a biography of any person. The characters depicted are fictional and do not represent real persons.

All characters and most events are fictional and are not related to any person, living or dead. This book does not divulge personal information about any person, nor does it defame any person or group. The author does not claim the title of "first man in space" for himself nor for his characters. It rightfully belongs to the true heroes to whom the author owes a page of tribute.

Cast of Characters

Yezh Kalinin: A farmer and an inventor in his heart. Though he tends to get distracted from working quite easily, he is nonetheless a hard worker.

Marushka: Yezh's pitiful wife, who can't stop worrying about everything. A woman of conservative reputation.

Ivan: The jealous neighbor that Marushka cannot stand. He harbors secret hateful feelings toward Yezh and always tries to find a way to prove himself better than his unearthly neighbor.

Katenka: Ivan's wife. Very materialistic and no less jealous than Ivan.

Maksimilian: Yezh's son, who supports his father in his dreams.

Sputnik: The loyal dog and companion of the road. No one travels without this little barker.

Aleksei: The rich brother-in-law. Somewhat egotistical by nature but respectful. Has more money than he could count.

Tatjana: The woman who is fascinated by Yezh's invention. Close friends with Marushka. She is an outgoing woman who likes to go around the village. She will have a favor to ask, which will contribute to Yezh's greatest invention of all time.

Igor: A big, tall guy who is silly and autistic. He is the trash man who comes by every Friday—but someone keeps forgetting about that. Don't forget to throw your trash out in time!

Joseph: The only blacksmith in Leninsk. He helped Yezh in great ways when it came to make his dreams a reality. There's nothing that this man of hot steel can't fix or melt!

Georgiy: The mayor of Leninsk. Short and fat and full of kindness. For twenty years, he's been trying to make Leninsk a tourist attraction but to no avail. Will he succeed one day?

Boris: The radio announcer of the Red Star station. Always announcing the most unusual events throughout every day.

Nikolai: Maks' best friend from his class, whose random lingering around played a huge role in Yezh's dream inspiration.

Sgt. Heartlock: A retired British ex-military captain and policeman. He had come to vacation in Russia in search of some entertaining sightseeing. He had no idea that his randomly picked village in the world's largest nation would bear him a surprise that he would never forget.

Sergei: The director of the national soviet space agency. He had launched Luna 2 in space and is believed to have been the man who did the incredible, but had no idea that some clever competitor out-braved him.

Oleg: The minister of defense and intelligence. Also short and fat. Good thing he wasn't the type to shoot first and think later!

Natalya: Maks' and Nikolai's teacher, whose class inspired not only sons but also parents.

Anastasia: The interviewer. Her employer sent her to investigate the climate and lifestyle in the backward village of Leninsk. Her career gets shifted around by a strange flying object in the sky.

Jovani: The cameraman who assists Anastasia for interview.

Sasha: The local flower merchant. A unique hairdresser. Her hairstyles are so beautiful that people say they grow like flowers and vines.

Radomir: A great neighbor down the street. But has a tendency to get drunk easily.

Four Cossack musicians: They travel from village to village to sing their popular ballads. Their fate becomes intertwined with Yezh.

Rodion: A mustachioed man under a Cossack hat. He wields his lifelong friend, his balalaika, and his main instrument, which is an accordion. The youngest of the group.

Makar: A mustachioed gusli player. He never fails to display flamboyance with his unique style and his warm, thin leather. The oldest in the group and the shortest as well.

Kiril: A balalaika player, by far the most colorful musician. He attracts many eyes with his folkloric uniform.

Bogdan: A professional svirel and buban player.

Chapter 1
Old Habits Die Hard

Once upon a time, in the great Soviet Union, a farmer named Yezh lived in annoying boredom with his wife, Marushka, and his son, Maksimilian, in the countryside of Leninsk. It had been this way as long as he could remember. His descent from a long line of farmers had somewhat sealed his fate as a man who lived in a poor family.

He was like any other farmer: strong like a horse and hardworking like a humblebee. But unlike others, he was also an inventor who loved ideas and never grew short of imagination. And unlike others, Yezh had dreams of "somedays." The range of dreams that a farmer could conjure up is boundless.

And what could a man dream so much about?

Yezh had lived in boredom and poverty, and he worked days after day in his field, preparing and producing crops. Days turned into weeks, weeks turned into months, and months into years. Yezh had lots of reasons to feel bored in his straight, unflavored lifestyle. A farmer could have plenty of dreams in his lifetime, such as owning a house and a large field and having children. Though inventions were only a means of adding variety to his boring way of life, Yezh regarded it always as a privilege to have something more in life.

Yezh was a hard worker but grew tired of doing endless hard work just so that he could eat. He tried countless times to invent something that he could use to crop his field with less effort.

You see—a poor farmer can't afford a new tractor or any technological machines, so the use of muscle is inevitable, but Yezh refused to accept that. Thus far in his inventor's career, he had invented countless techniques. But today he had something new: a mechanical device that he would use to plow the soil. The device was a simple structure of wood materials. It had a pair of wheels to help it move on the soil while curved blades sliced the soil. With a little help from some weight, the blades went deeper in the soil for a better furrow.

One fine morning, Yezh was eager to start using the new tool he had invented. He had completed it the day before, but it was too late to try it in the field. So, on this morning, he awoke earlier just to try it in service.

First Farmer In Space

At first the work was good, but he quickly realized how hard it was to push it with his hands.

Yezh had a neighbor—a hard worker like himself who nonetheless had an unquenchable jealousy and competitive outlook toward Yezh. Despite this, they didn't hate each other and had shared a lot of black coffee at the table together. Ivan viewed Yezh as a competitor and constantly tried to prove himself superior by having better crops, more field, more tools, and better results.

Yezh didn't bear quite the same feeling for his neighbor but did notice his strange behavior. Whenever Yezh would buy a new tool or piece of equipment, you'd see Ivan running off to the nearest city to fetch for himself the identical product—sometimes more enhanced. Whenever Yezh would work an acre, Ivan would double it just prove himself a better, harder-working farmer. But Yezh did not do or say anything about it. He would just simply do it for himself. Yezh had the feeling that no matter what he did, his neighbor would have his eyes over the fence between them.

In the early hours of that day, Ivan came out of his house when he began to hear noises that came from Yezh's side. Yezh was having a hard time pushing and pulling his new invention.

Ivan leisurely put his arms on the fence and paid close attention to what he was doing. Every day he got to see his neighbor's new inventions but witnessed only failures and flaws.

When Yezh encountered difficulties with his plow, he decided to use his horses. So, he brought out his three lucky horses, which he called *"Troika."* They were of three different colors and personalities. He attached them to the wooden machine. All the while, Ivan watched carefully, but Yezh did not notice his presence.

When it was ready, the horses began to pull, and the plow seemed to dig deeper. Ivan was furious about how those blades plowed his soil better than he ever did by hand. His jealousy exploded inside, though he didn't show it. He told himself that something was bound to happen to the Yezh's invention. Even Yezh knew that such misfortune could happen whenever Ivan threw an evil eye over the fence—a dark gaze imbued with malicious intent.

Easy work gave Yezh a smile as he encouraged the horses to keep pulling with shouts of "Hoy!" Everything started well and went well, and the field slowly got plowed—until some screws unexpectedly loosened. Soon the machine broke down. As the screws came out, the wood began to crack from the extremely unstable force, splintering the wood until plowing was no longer possible.

"This can't be happening! What could have gone wrong?" Yezh asked himself in an angry tone, and like a true Russian, Yezh would not let this go without a good cursing.

Ivan had a devious smile on his face. It seemed almost like he knew this would happen and that he enjoyed watching another of Yezh`s inventions break down. He could almost see the despair in Yezh's face and couldn't resist making one of his annoying remarks about what he witnessed.

"Good day, neighbor!" yelled Ivan from afar to gain his attention. Yezh didn't feel like seeing him in this early morning, but he showed good manners and temper in his reply.

"Good day to you as well!" he said as he approached the fence.

"I see it didn't turn out too good," said Ivan, trying to show empathy, only to add more to his remark. "Bad luck. You've put so many hours into it, and for it to break like that was a shame." Ivan presented the comment with tact in order to be as polite and empathic as possible.

Yezh looked at his wrecked machine with pity and dismay.

"It will cost even more hours to repair it." complained Yezh.

"The life of a farmer isn't like a god's life," said Ivan, but he quickly moved onto his own story. "On my side, I have almost finished plowing everything. We'll be planting our sprouts soon, perhaps tomorrow, if heaven doesn't urinate on us."

As much as Ivan wanted to make Yezh sad about his performance, Yezh felt that he wouldn't be able to plant anything anytime soon. Yezh assumed from the advanced state of his neighbor's agricultural work that he was late as he still must finish plowing everything—half an acre.

"My tomato and pepper sprouts are growing fine every day—this big." Ivan showed the height of them with his hands. "You should see how big they are."

First Farmer In Space

"My sprouts are growing, too, but the lack of sun inside the house is hindering their growth."

"That's why you have to hurry up and plow that field if you don't want them to die on you."

Yezh threw a look at his field that was bringing him shame and anger. It reminded him only of his lack of progress because of spending too much time on tool inventions.

"I was busy for these last few days. I think I will have to catch up with the plowing."

He didn't know how he'd do that, and Ivan wasn't too sure about that promise.

Sputnik was growling at something through the window. Marushka caught a glimpse from the window when she passed through the kitchen, wondering why Sputnik was growling. She had caught Yezh talking to that neighbor, but they had just finished talking, and Yezh was moving away from the fence.

What could he have told him now? she wondered.

She hated when other people meddled in her private life and that Ivan was the worst neighbor in the area. Sputnik's doggy growls were tenacious but unsurprising. Sputnik had always been a growler and a barker, sometimes acting as a guardian of Marushka's garden or warding off unwanted visitors. Often Marushka would let him out to chase them off. It was unusual for animal thieves to appear in daytime.

Breakfast was ready, and she had to call Yezh to come in or else he'd continue to work in his *secret headquarters*—the barn. She reached the door and let the sweet spring morning breezy aroma enter the house. At the first gap of the opening sliding door, Sputnik shot himself like a bullet into the backyard while barking madly. He went straight to the fence and barked at what appeared to be a squirrel among the branches above, where it looked down at the silly little dog.

"Sputnik," Marushka said to make him stop. "Don't bother the neighbors."

Sputnik was used to barking at anything he saw moving, big or small. Despite the relentless intimidation of his barks, Sputnik was still an inoffensive, gentle, and friendly pup.

Damn those squirrels! Always around to cause sabotage! she thought.

Marushka cursed in a low tone. She moved her attention to Yezh, announced breakfast, and slipped back inside. She couldn't look anymore at the fence between them and their nosy neighbors.

Yezh couldn't stand being outside anymore, now that he had nothing to work with, so he went back inside to console himself with his wife or a bottle of vodka. He wasn't feeling for eating anything. Sputnik was hungry, too, and followed Yezh inside. His entrance was quite dramatic because to Yezh, his inventions were like children. Marushka, who witnessed the breakdown through the window, saw him entering in a bad mood, and she was worried, seeing him like this.

"Did something bad happen?" asked Marushka.

"The machine broke," said Yezh, who tried to find some physical explanation. "The wood wasn't strong enough for the screws, and the weight of it did not help it at all. It might have been a bad idea that couldn't work out because of the laws of physics."

"Again?" said Marushka, surprised by the bad news.

Yezh's wife did not understand well the scientific facts that he learned from his bad experience, but as a decent woman who couldn't understand science, she understood quite well the law of nature. She just had to show him how to approach the hard work.

"It didn't work out the way you wanted," said Marushka. "Maybe we should be like the other farmers and begin to work it the old-fashioned way. Winter is coming, and if things continue as they have been, we'll starve in winter!"

Yezh knows he has accumulated a lot of lateness. "I need to rebuild it! I have no idea how long it'll take me to do it again."

"Oh, but the field cannot wait! What about our survival?" Marushka replied anxiously.

"I know, but I can't let go an existing possibility," said Yezh with regret.

First Farmer In Space

"Alright. How about we make a deal?" She gained Yezh's complete attention, who wondered what she was about to say. "If you work another square of land in the field, then you can go back to work on your invention. How's that?" said his wife.

Yezh thought about it. "That seems to be a good idea."

"Each day you do a little bit of field work, then you can do some more invention so that both jobs get done at a reasonable rate," his wife added, hoping to completely convince her husband.

Marushka had her own work to do such as laundry and caring for sprouts that were stored in a warm, well-lit room that got only half a day of sun. But even she believed that it was inevitable that she should also join in the hard labor.

"To make it easier, I will try to finish the work inside the house. Then I'll come and join you outside," said Marushka.

But Yezh felt bad because she had a lot to do inside the house. Well—they both had their own little interests. Yezh showed sorrowful agreement and decided to retry his luck later on.

Just as Yezh was about to walk away to the washroom, Marushka mentioned some of her dissatisfaction.

"I've seen you talking to that Ivan again. I hope you weren't telling him anything."

"Telling him anything?" said Yezh. "What did I say? I just exchanged greetings. That's all!"

Marushka turned herself away. She had to finish preparing the table. "You know that man never thinks well about us."

Yezh agreed but assured her that he'd never say any such things.

"For now, the breakfast is ready. You have to eat before going back out."

The table was ready. Yezh was about to sit down when his son came down the stairs in his school uniform.

"Good morning, son. Breakfast is ready," said Marushka.

Phoenix Phoenix

The boy showed his manners by returning a proper morning greeting.

"Going to school today?" asked the father.

"Yes," said Maksimilian with a dejected tone that showed he wasn't too excited about it.

As they prepared to dig into their food, the boy asked with sudden interest: "How was your new invention?"

"Bad. I had no luck with it. It went belly up even before it broke a sweat."

"I can stay home to help fix your machine."

"No, Maks. You have to go to school," said his mother.

"But I don't want to go to school. I want to stay home to help Father in the field."

"No, Son. School is very important. You have to be good at school and study hard, so you won't end up being like your father," said Marushka. Yezh raised his eyebrows; the comment hit him over the head. "Working in the field isn't the best work. I want you to find a better job," Marushka explained.

"Oh, but school is boring."

Yezh understood such feeling of boredom, and he had words for that.

"I know. I feel the same about field farming. Trust me: it may be boring, but the fruit of your hard work at school will be more fun."

Marushka came to the table to put the plates before her son and husband.

"We want you to become like your uncle—not like your father," said Marushka, placing the plates of breakfast in front of them.

Yezh didn't know if that was a compliment to make the boy feel better or an insult to him.

"Father likes to invent new things. That's fun work, right?"

First Farmer In Space

Yezh didn't know how to respond to it. Marushka wasn't shy to speak her mind.

"It's fun, but it doesn't bring us money or put food on the table."

She looked at the clock and reminded Maks that he'll have to hurry up if he doesn't wish to be late.

After breakfast, the boy walked to the front door to leave. His mother and Sputnik accompanied him to say good-bye.

"Alright son, have a great day at school, and please study hard."

"Yeah, don't worry."

He slowly opened the door after putting his shoes on. Sputnik barked at him once.

"Even Sputnik says bye-bye," said Marushka.

The boy regarded the dog as his best friend and greeted him in return. After patting the dog, the boy walked out of the house and onto the streets. Sputnik went to accompany the boy until the gate. Marushka had to restrain Sputnik with fierce commands to keep him from marching off with Maks like he was used to doing.

Now that the boy was gone, Marushka had another childlike person to take care of. Yezh tended to doodle with his toys, which he considered to be like his children. She wasn't opposed to a man's dream or hobby, but a profitable end was what mattered to her.

She waved to Maksimilian before picking up the newspaper sitting in the box by the door. With a single peek on the right side of the fence, she saw the neighbors had already picked up their copy, which didn't surprise her.

She called Sputnik back inside, went back to the kitchen, and offered Yezh the newspaper, but the man rejected it, barely casting an eye on its cover but without any will to read it. He didn't care. He didn't hang on to it long before it found the edge of the table, Yezh wanted to eat fast so he could get to work faster.

Marushka remembered that she was supposed to go to the cold chamber to take out some cauliflower. A cold chamber is a storage room for fruits and vegetables that saves food from summer's heat. In the suburbs, where no refrigerators are available, cold chambers are indispensable and an affordable way to preserve perishable items naturally.

Yezh finished his breakfast, and just before he could get outside to work, Marushka appeared to let him know that he needed to throw a piece of junk outside.

"Yezh, the barrel of cauliflower is finished. It's leaking a little bit, too. The barrel is old. I think we have to throw it out."

"Leaking?" said Yezh, surprised.

"It's making a mess in the cold chamber."

"Where is it? I'll take it out now."

He got up and walked to the door of the cold chamber. All his wife's nagging about winter provisions now slapped him on the face: He could see less in the storage room now with all the vegetables being almost gone. They were short on food. The previous year wasn't a good one— their crops weren't that great. They had quite a few barrels filled with different crops, but the one that had cauliflowers was empty.

He grabbed the barrel, closed it tight, and rolled it out of the room and through the house to the pile of junk on the side of the house. While he rolled it, he thought about how pitiful it was to throw out a useful item. He knew it could be used for something else but couldn't tell what use it could be. He looked through the pile of junk. If he'd had time, he could fix it, but that wasn't the case anymore.

Marushka was waiting at the door. The pile was big. Stacks of various objects made it impossible for Yezh to throw it above the rest, making stacking any higher impossible. Due to its growing height, many objects were falling on the side, and each new object they threw could only be pushed to the side. The pile of junk grew, and Marushka was worried about it. She no longer could endure watching the pile growing skyward. Every day she had the pain of seeing the junk pile sitting inertly in their backyard.

"That pile of junk is growing each time I look at it. It's taking a lot of space."

Yezh sighed. He saw the problem but couldn't do anything about it. Igor the trash man seldom passed in wintertime, and the latest renovation they had to do inside their home took its toll of junk, especially the old water heater that he had to change, still sitting there. Not to mention that Yezh was also a forgetful person and tended to forget when Igor was passing by.

"Maybe I'll need to call Igor the trash man for this. I don't know when he will be coming."

He could only scratch his head as he pondered the heaviest pieces of the trash: long thick wood, large broken branches, and the thermal tank that began to rust and break down from the snow and rain. He just hoped that Igor was strong enough to haul this junk.

"He passes every Friday. How can you forget that each time?"

"Ah! I can't remember everything in life. I've got enough to remember in my brain," complained Yezh, who seemed to be as affected by anger as she was. Yezh moved away, all the while thinking about what to do with the scraps from his creations.

Yezh was about to walk away when suddenly a chant rang his ears from afar, from somewhere in front of his house. He looked around but couldn't see its origin.

Who's singing so early in the morning? thought Yezh.

Then a man appeared, walking on the sidewalk, his legs wobbling and uncoordinated. A bottle in his hand, and with the help of a little dose of its wonders, Radomir sang an unearthly song. Yezh knew that the man hadn't forgotten how to walk properly, and Yezh knew who it was, too. It was Radomir, and he was drunk—again!

Radomir halted in his tracks and raised his bottle high above his head. A long gulp of whatever remained in it followed and coursed deep inside of him.

Yezh only stared from his backyard at what was happening. The long gulp ingested, Radomir flung the bottle violently to his side but couldn't throw it any farther than Yezh's yard. The man went off on his drunken march to wherever he was headed.

Yezh walked to the front yard, picked up the bottle, and read the description on the label.

"Vodka—45 percent" it read.

He shook his head and threw another look at Radomir, who was strutting far down the sidewalk by this time, his singing barely audible by now. At least the bottle was made of hard plastic rather than glass. He would keep it as a lucky gift.

Chapter 2
Another Day of Work

It was time to work. And so Yezh went to gather all his tools—his plow, his shovels, his homemade compost made of autumn leaves and vegetable leftovers. Sensing he was behind schedule, Yezh had to go back to his field.

By this date he was supposed to have done plowing like his neighbor, who was currently sowing his sprouts of pumpkin, tomatoes, peppers, and cucumbers from his well-insulated warm shelter for farming. Ivan indeed had something to be proud of. While Yezh was carried away by his inventions, the man could have had a chance to produce a bit more. Plowing would be the hardest and most boring work, but it had to be done. If one can eat easily, one can also work easily. Yezh still had a long way to go, but if he would give his best today, he could finish it.

Each time he felt dismay over the difficulty and sweat, or whenever he reminded himself of his broken machine patiently waiting to be repaired, Yezh would throw a look at it, cursing it for all the world's misfortune, for his work would have been easier and faster with it if it hadn't broken down. His body was working, but his mind was also involved in another kind of mental work.

***

Sgt. Heartlock, an old, retired soldier from the British army, had come to Russia for a vacation. After visiting Leningrad, Moscow, and Stalingrad, his next stop was Leninsk. His vacation to Russia was motivated by his desire to learn new culture. When he arrived with an expensive-looking car, everybody knew that he couldn't be a Russian but must be a foreigner.

The first thing he did was to visit the local merchants. Heartlock was tired of the popular big cities, being more of a nature lover. After gathering some food from the local market, he was able to rest at a cozy apartment. He would continue to enjoy his vacation, this time in the countryside. What could he learn from his trip to Leninsk? What wonders would it share with him? Heartlock couldn't tell but felt deep within him that this would be the best place of all, the right place at the right time, and a worthy place for a vacation.

***

Phoenix Phoenix

Georgiy the mayor was taking a ride in his old car. His driver, a militarily dressed man with a cap, drove him down the street. He rolled down his window, and when the car wasn't traveling fast, people from all corners and different professions waved at him. Georgiy returned the wave, accompanied by his big smile. Greetings poured from his mouth like water from a pitcher. The baker, the blacksmith, the flower merchant—everybody loved the great leader of this backward village in the middle of nowhere. He visited Leninsk daily, busily planning something that would attract tourists. Recently he had built an attractive park with a Ferris wheel. Upon investigation, he learned from the park manager that people were indeed coming to have a great time—mostly children. But those people were already citizens of Leninsk. Georgiy sighed in depression because no tourists visited it yet. He had been trying for a while to boost his village's appeal but could think of no idea that might make people fall in love with Leninsk. Not much could be done here as Leninsk was a tiny little place, far away from any big city.

Later, he visited the only hotel in the village, and for the first time he realized how small and underrated it was. It wasn't even crowded. The rooms were mostly empty all year long. The owner complained about his business going dark. Georgiy planned to offer more money to build new hotels. But building hotels would not help them.

How could he attract tourists?

Coincidentally, Heartlock had reserved a room in the hotel, and when Georgiy spotted an unknown face walking toward the hotel, he couldn't stop himself from asking. Heartlock barely knew Russian, and the mayor was surprised to hear his British accent.

His very first tourist! He was overwhelmed by joy: At last he managed to capture one of them! Georgiy managed to have a conversation with the man. The two men grew fond of each other quickly as if they had been friends since childhood. For Heartlock, it was almost an honor to be Leninsk's very first tourist.

***

A group of four musicians, great travelers and wanderers, took on a soul-searching journey with their instruments to seek inspiration and fortune. Their journey led them to this village. They were:

First Farmer In Space

Rodion, a young, mustachioed man under a Cossack hat, wielding his lifelong friends, his balalaika and his accordion.

Makar, an old but short mustachioed *gusli* player who never failed to display flamboyance with his unique style.

Kiril, a *balalaika* player, by far the most colorful of these musicians, a man who attracted many eyes with his folkloric uniform.

Finally, Bogdan, a professional *svirel* and *buban* player.

They travelled locally from city to city, gaining people's hearts with their soul-touching music. Their last march was from a city nearly several kilometers north of Leninsk. These musicians, who are from Stalingrad, finally arrived, all of them weary.

"This was a long trip!" said Kiril.

"We haven't earned anything for nearly a day now. My pockets are empty," complained Makar about their lack of economic fortune, but Rodion expressed assurance that this city would offer them much glory in return for their songs.

"I can feel this would be a fine city to visit. People say that Leninsk is a folklore-loving village," said Rodion.

The musicians dropped their instruments on the ground as if they weighed a ton and sat down near a tree overshadowing the area. Bogdan sat down, his weight too hard to carry. His long sleeves, flying in the wind, elegantly swirled around his sides like wings.

"My feet hurt all day. We have walked all the way from Stalingrad," said Bogdan.

They complained about their long walk and what they have seen on the road. They listened to the summer cicadas singing and enjoyed the cool, long grass. It was a quick short but leisurely rest.

"There should be some tavern in this city. Should we go have a look around the place?" asked Bogdan, looking at Kiril first. The latter agreed with a grin on his face.

"Why not?" replied Makar. "Let's go, comrades, to see what there is!"

Phoenix Phoenix

After a good short rest, their curiosity to visit around awakened. So, the four musicians stood up and walked around Leninsk in search of taverns to listen to their masterpieces.

***

I've finally arrived home, thought Aleksei. The flight from America had been long and fatiguing. His big house in Russia was not as great as the one he resided in in the West. It made him feel nostalgic, a feeling from his childhood that he did not like. Aleksei was a businessman, but he needed to get away from his work sometimes. Despite the lifestyle in the Soviet Union being not his own preference, he got used to these last years, and he loved his second home.

He dropped his keys on the wooden table, which was cheap-looking to the eye but heavy on the wallet for a mere peasant in Russia. He sat on his couch and sighed deeply. His uniquely fashioned hair fit only him. It had been styled before the flight and was still slick and shiny, everything still in place despite the sweat and wind from this warm southern climate.

Taking a short rest, he reminded himself of his sister, whom he hadn't seen in a long time. He thought it was time to give her a call to see how she had fared all these months without him.

***

Every day the boy needed to walk three kilometers to his school located at the other end of the village. It was a fun trip for all kids. Walking with effort through forests along the side of the road, they went to meet many friends with whom they make adventure with.

The school itself was small and uncrowded due to the small population of Leninsk. It was easy for students to know each other at school, like their parents did around the village.

Today the teacher had a special subject to introduce to children, something that for many generations never failed to fascinate the youngsters.

"Today we will be doing something interesting that is causing modern technology to grow."

Finally, a fun class, thought Maks.

15

First Farmer In Space

"Can someone take a guess?" asked Natalya.

"Are we going to watch a movie?" asked one student.

"No. But if it wasn't for what we will be learning, you couldn't watch anything like a movie today."

The children wondered at the riddle.

"It is science! Believe it or not, our everyday life is constantly changing due to it and depends heavily on it. But that's not the real big topic of today's lesson, of course. That would be too vague. We will be studying the forces of energy with the help of science. I will demonstrate to you an example of what you can do with a single item—or with many—starting with just one."

She presented a bottle to the class. "A bottle!" The mention of a bottle raised some brows.

"We will see a show of brute force. But not all energy is the same. Here in the box behind my table we have some examples of each different type of energy, this being only one of them."

Natalya exhibited all her different gadgets that she had personally made from various objects—a Newton's cradle among them. Others like solar panels, charcoal, elastics, and magnets were displayed on the table, each representing different types of energy that this universe exhibits.

After an hour of presentation of each of the gadgets and the explanation of some theory, she was able to conclude one part of the class. She had showed how each of them worked, but the one that intrigued Maks was the bottle, which had yet to show its potential.

"Now we will do some demonstrations. I hope I haven't made you all sleepy. The fun is yet to start, but for that we will have to go outside."

Natalya held her breath to see their reaction. Some eyes were bulging out of interest, others were half-way hidden behind their lids. Everybody lacked a reaction or expression on their faces. Either they were still asleep since this morning or her long-winded explanation had been like singing a lullaby. This was understandable. The class spent several hours on this topic, and now it was afternoon.

"So, are we ready, children?"

"I am!" answered one of them.

"Is that all? Only one? I can't hear all of you."

"We're ready!" replied the class.

"Off to schoolyard we go, then. Come on."

Once outside, it was easy to gain the attention of the kids. She started a demonstration of one of the easiest and most fun examples. She had even brought a pump. First the bottle was filled with water and a few carbonating pills she had put inside. With a pump, she charged the pressure inside the bottle until it could no longer take any more. The gases that built up inside were making it even more charged. Then it launched the bottle maybe fifty meters up. It brought excitement to the young audience.

At last she ended the experiments and soon the class after giving the children their assignment for the night.

"This is it for today. For homework, I need each of your teams to make your own bottle rocket at home. Please be careful and ask permission from your parents since they must assist you with your experiments."

Soon afterward the students were dismissed for the day. Maksimilian walked to home from school. He was alone but not for long. When Nikolai saw him walking alone in his direction, he joined him from behind.

"Hey Maks. What's up?"

"Nothing much."

"That thing in class was so awesome. I never thought that it was possible to blast something so high like that."

"Yeah. I'm planning on finding a bigger bottle and breaking records with it."

"Wow, really? That's crazy!" Nikolai became excited by Maks' bold ideas. "I was thinking about doing that cool bottle thing with you."

"Really?"

"Yeah. My parents are lame. They never want to do anything with me, and they're always busy."

Maks thought about his father, who also seemed to never have time for him. Adults are always busy—that's their lame excuse. There's always something that must be done. They never have any fun. He knew how Nikolai felt about lame parents. But Maks' lack of response got Nikolai to repeat himself, this time with a question. He was hoping for a positive reply.

"Do you want to do it?"

"Sure. Why not?"

Now he was walking home with a friend and having a conversation about their future experiment. For a little while, they felt like young scientists on a mission to a great wonder of discovery.

***

As promised, Yezh did a huge chunk of work on his field. He had to be sure to have made Marushka happy. Tired, he came back to his chair by the house for a quick rest. Suddenly all his tiredness got washed away when he looked at his broken plow machine. Anger and disappointment flooded back to his mind, and he decided not to take any rest yet. He had another job to do. He looked over the machine, standing by it, trying to see what went wrong. Hopefully he could find a way to fix it.

The problem had to be due to weight. And the wood was too thin. Perhaps a second round would make things right.

In the house, Marushka was doing the laundry. She had dirty clothes in a bowl of soap. While the clothes were being washed, she had wet clothes that she was hanging outside on the balcony. She would then go back inside to keep washing the rest in the bowl, where her hands scrubbed clothing within the soapy water for nearly an hour of her day.

Just then, the phone rang, echoing throughout the house. Marushka was busy doing her duty with her hands full. Of course, she fast-paced her work to get rid of it. The phone rang for a second time, and she still couldn't get out of the place as the baskets and clothes were around her, covering the floors and table.

Even Yezh heard it from outside, but even though his mind was preoccupied with fixing and examining his broken machine, he couldn't ignore the phone ringing. On the third ring, he grew impatient and yelled to his wife to pick up.

"Marushka! Pick up that phone!"

Phoenix Phoenix

She heard him as loud as the annoying ringing.

"I'm getting there!" returned the wife with a shout, desperately trying to find a way out of the messy room. Eventually she got to the phone on time and answered.

"Hello?!"

"Marushka! It's me, Aleksei!" said a voice that she quickly identified. "How are you doing today?"

"Oh, Aleksei. We are doing fine," replied Marushka with a tone of surprise and joy in her voice. "Long time no see you. How have you been doing?"

"Very good, actually, always making a bit of money you know," said Aleksei.

Marushka couldn't comment on such a response, but she showed a bit of empathy for him, though she didn't care too much about it. Bragging became fancy tittle-tattle in this village.

"How's Yezh doing?" Aleksei asked again.

"He's working hard as always."

"Still inventing something every day, is he?"

"Yes, he is."

And trying to make him understand he needs to expend serious work in the right place, thought Marushka.

"Ah, you can't take away the man's favorite thing in life," said Aleksei. "That's good!" Aleksei then came to the bottom line to his call: "I have come back to the Soviet Union for a few days to see my family."

"Oh, you did?" The news lifted her spirit. "That's wonderful news."

"I haven't seen you in a while. I'd like to see you soon. So, I was wondering if you and Yezh would want to come over to my house tonight, and we could talk a little bit. Are you up for it?"

"That would be good, but I can't decide for Yezh. I'll go ask him and see if we will be coming."

"That's fine by me. You are always welcome to ring my doorbell. Got to go now, but I hope I'll see you tonight. Alright, Marushka, have a good one."

"Same to you, Aleksei. Bye!" She hung up.

Wonderful—her brother came back from the West. More friendly faces finally; they needed that for a while. She'd had enough with these hostile neighbors who never quit peeking over the fence, always talking propaganda against them and whose evil eyes always bring them bad luck.

Change of plan, she thought. Just when she managed to make Yezh work harder in the field, she was forced to interrupt him with this news. She stepped out and saw him still lingering around that broken wooden machine that now was only mere wreckage.

Yezh, who heard the door sliding and a few steps coming his way, was interested in the phone call.

"Who was it?"

"Aleksei." She paused a few steps closer. "He's back from America and he's inviting us to come over to his place tonight."

Another distraction, thought Yezh. To the point, he felt like not going to her brother's place, but he restrained himself this time, considering their family relations, which was an important thing in this village. Because Aleksei would seldom come back to the Soviet Union after leaving for the United States and being away for months and months—nearly a year, he felt the need for a family visit. Aleksei had come back here for his family, and that was something that Yezh could respect someone for. In any case, he was quite happy about the goals he accomplished today.

"The job is done as you requested."

"Yeah, I can see that. You've made a big improvement."

"I'm trying to fix this thing to get it up and running. If I can manage to get it running, then the plowing will be a piece of cake."

"Don't go crazy with it or your brain will break down. Be sure to change your clothes before going, too!"

"Yeah, just put some clean clothes on the bed, I'll come later to change."

Phoenix Phoenix

"Well then, we'll be going to Aleksei's after Maks comes back from school."

"Fine. Meanwhile I'll be doing some more work around my wreck here."

***

After a long day of work and waiting, the boy returned home. He was happy with whatever was on his mind. He simply couldn't wait to see his parents. His friend was also coming over.

"Father! My friend is here," spoke the son in greeting.

Yezh brightened upon his son's arrival. He hadn't heard him mention the visit.

"Oh hey, how was school today?"

"Very good."

"Strange, I thought you didn't like school at all."

"Today we were doing experiments at school."

"Experiments?" repeated Yezh. That sounded like something about himself.

"Yeah, we built some water and air projects—something about energy and force."

"That's …" said Yezh, who was searching for the right word, "very interesting."

Yezh shifted his attention to the guest.

"So, you came to play with him, huh?"

"No sir! I came because we have a teamwork project to do for school."

Great, thought Yezh, *something to keep the kids busy.* Though he knew his son wouldn't spare him.

"Father, can you help us make a bottle missile?"

He thought about it shortly and was about to say no to the request, thinking that he didn't want to waste his time, when Nikolai spoke out.

"Yeah, that would be fun if you could help us, Mister Yezh," Nikolai pursued.

"I actually have a lot of work to do …"

"Come on, please?" pushed Maks, cutting off his father as if he anticipated the *no* answer.

Yezh hesitated a bit and finally changed his mind. After all, Maks had been nagging him for a few days about when he could play with him. His son wanted to spend more time with his father, and being a serious inventor, he couldn't find any time for that.

"Alright then. Let's go make a bottle missile."

They had acquired a stainless bottle. It was the only kind of bottle they had around, and that was thanks to Radomir. If it wasn't due to his drunkenness, they probably wouldn't have had any bottle to play with.

Yezh brought his air pump that he used to pump flat tires. Maks filled the bottle with water and more carbonation pills than what his teacher had used in class. And no experiment was without their best friend and fourth tester, Sputnik. The bottle was tightly attached to the tip of the pump, and Yezh pumped. It was brewing a chemical reaction in it and all four of the amateur scientists prepared for the worst.

Sputnik ran to hide when he heard a loud hissing noise, and when the water in fumes was escaping the bottle, Sputnik ran to their side and barked like a mad dog. The boys laughed at the poor little dog, who had no idea what just happened.

The bottle blasted upward to the sky like a missile, startling everybody. The water dispersed into thin droplets that resembled to smoke. The intense pressure in the bottle took it very high. The laughter was followed by eyes on the clouds above.

"Where did it go?" asked Maksimilian. "Wow, it went high. I can't see it."

A few seconds after the blast, Maksimilian walked forward to see, thinking maybe it had fallen somewhere without them noticing. A big blast of water had fogged the area.

Phoenix Phoenix

"It's not on the ground. It's still up there."

All three heads gazed under the intense sunlight. Squinting for a long time wasn't helping them.

"How high do you think it went up? A hundred meters?"

Maksimilian's eyes hurt from sunlight and he couldn't stand watching it anymore for the sake of his neck and eyes.

"Where is it?"

The bottle landed on his head, hitting him before falling on the ground.

"There it was!" exclaimed Nikolai with laughter.

Maksimilian found that awkward, but he was sure that the bottle must have gone really high. He just didn't know precisely how far.

"It would have been better if we'd picked a tinted bottle," said Yezh with a chuckle.

"That was fun. I haven't done anything like that for a very long time," said Yezh.

He felt good being able to laugh sometimes. All the field work gave him only stress. This was exactly what he needed to decompress.

"Do we know how far it went up?" asked Maks, hoping that maybe they knew the answer.

"We don't know for now," replied his father. "But we know how long it took to fall on your head. It took it about seven seconds."

"That's not in meters."

"No, but I'm sure you learned mathematics at school, right?"

Maksimilian couldn't recall any theory about this that he had learned.

"Is there any formula for that?" replied Maks.

"Well yes. Let's see," said Yezh, preparing his mind to jump into work. "Distance can be found if time squared is multiplied by meters per second squared, which is known to be 9.81, which in this case gets multiplied by half a unit," Yezh explained. "Which means the height should be around 240 meters."

Yezh showed a face of doubt. Feeling like taking it back, he thought perhaps there was a better equation for it. He didn't know, quite frankly, and let it go.

"That's ingenious," said Nikolai, who then said to Maks, "Your father is so smart!"

Maks didn't catch any number or equation his father used but he was more focused on praising his own father as someone intelligently talented.

Their moments together were interrupted by Marushka stepping onto the scene, her hair well-arranged and wearing a clean outfit. She let her family know that it was time to go. Nikolai was politely sent home. Their school project was completed, and both had lots of fun.

It was time to go see his uncle. Maks was excited to see his uncle as he hasn't seen him for quite a while. Finally—another activity to break his boring routine.

Chapter 3
The Sun of Inspiration

Yezh's family rarely went out to visit a relative or friend. Whenever they did, Maksimilian would be the first one to reach for the door. When they traveled around, they drove a small car that was about thirty years old. It had belonged to Yezh's father, and Yezh kept it in good shape after so long. His family had always been poor, and although he couldn't afford a tractor, he had a car that was precious to him. His father had a tractor, but it broke down a decade ago.

Sighting the house where Aleksei lived was awe-inspiring, no matter how many times they'd seen it. When Yezh turned the corner of a street where the foliage was sparse, and a clear view was available, Marushka saw bricks through the thick foliage. "We have arrived," she said.

It was a large house, with white bricks piled higher than any walls they have ever seen.

"The house is very big."

"Wow, I'd love to live in that big house."

Yezh wondered how many acres of labor this house was worth. He guessed he'd probably need to work for fifty more years to buy this house. Yezh despaired at the thought of it. Banishing the idea from his head, he could only consider how lucky his brother-in-law really was in life. He had a private business in the United States and a personal income, something impossible in the Soviet Union. They would never become rich but could rest assured they would never become too poor, with nothing in life. For that they had the Communist Party to watch over their welfare. He wasn't complaining about his lifestyle in that way.

Yezh could only wish that dreams had nothing to do with economy.

Maksimilian was the first one to reach the doorstep; he proudly rang the bell. It wasn't long before they saw Aleksei's face for the first time in a year.

"Uncle!"

"Maks!" exclaimed Aleksei. "Yezh, Marushka, come in."

Everybody gathered around the long table. After they got comfortable for some casual talk, the rich man began interrogating his family.

"How is the work going along?" asked Aleksei.

"There is a lot of work to be done. It's going slowly but surely."

"Have you finished plowing the fields? It's getting hot. I remember when our parents used to start planting sprouts in early May."

Yezh couldn't find any words for it and didn't answer but tilted his head as if he wasn't sure what to say. Marushka feared shame and felt the need to interrupt.

"Our sprouts are big; they're almost ready to be planted. We're working hard, but a lot remains to be done." At last she threw a look at Yezh. She disliked this kind of situation, but she was sure that she turned the discussion to their favor.

"Ah!" exclaimed her brother. "That's good to know. You must be working really hard in that boring environment, something that I praise and respect."

"How are you faring in the West? Business still growing?" asked Marushka.

"My company has increased in size. New positions have opened in the last few months. Money's flowing in alright."

All the talking about money put Yezh into a malaise.

"Are you still inventing new farming devices?"

"Yes I am."

"What could it be this time?"

"A machine that plows soil with blades."

Aleksei was impressed until Yezh let him know that it broke down easily. Aleksei had always been interested in Yezh's inventive imagination.

"That's lame. You have a good artistic mind for that. You know, if you put it to good use, you could make some money with it."

Such an idea probed Yezh's mind as something new, something he hadn't thought about … well, not much—he never knew how to make money with it. For probably a decade he'd been thinking about how to make more money, but never did his inventions come consciously to mind.

"Everybody dreams of making more money," explained Aleksei. "People try different things in life to make a greater fortune. I remember when I left my family and the farm, leaving behind a miserable lifestyle with only four cents in my pocket. If it wasn't for my dream, I wouldn't have had all of this now. It just goes to show how important dreams are."

Yezh listened carefully, hoping to extract helpful advice from this businessman who came from a farm with only a few coins in his pocket.

"Do you have any dream?" asked Aleksei.

Yezh snapped out of his bubble. He gurgled at the question. "Well I—uh. I'm not quite sure anymore. I never put much time into thinking deeply about it."

Aleksei remained quiet to provoke more feedback from his brother-in-law.

"Well, I would like to invent something new."

"That's great!" exclaimed Aleksei with enthusiasm. "You know that if you invent something really good you could patent it. Who knows, fortune sometimes strikes talented inventors."

Marushka didn't like that comment. It was like a dagger in the achievements she had been trying to make with her field and with Yezh. She wanted to push him to work harder in the field, but her brother wasn't helping at all with that comment. Aleksei moved his conversation to someone smaller in the room. They'd been so much into adult talking that they'd forgotten about the little boy.

"Hey Maks. How are you doing, little one?"

"Fine, actually. Today I did some experiments with my father for a school project."

"Oh really?" Aleksei threw a look at Yezh who seemed to blush a little bit. "What could it be?"

"We blasted a bottle to the sky. It was so cool! We pumped the bottle with water and air until it couldn't hold any more. It blew like a missile."

"That's interesting. How high did it go?"

"We even added some kind of pills in it to make it blast higher. We couldn't see but it took a long time for it fall down again."

"I like that. You're learning to be bad boys at school."

The adults looked at each other.

"Well, it was a school project." Marushka blushed under an awkward smile.

"It's good to know that life in the class isn't as boring as on the field."

A "ting" sounded its way from the kitchen in the silence that followed the end of conversation.

"Turkey is ready, who wants some?"

That night they feasted on good food and drinks and had some good conversation that hadn't taken place for a whole year. Yezh remained thoughtful as their speech on that night had a significant influence on him, one that had yet to change his life forever. Invention could definitely be used for making money. But the question was what and how?

Chapter 4
Birth of a New Invention

The next day Yezh went back to work on his field. He had promised himself that he was going to work harder from now on to improve his lifestyle. Enough playing around, enough distraction. He had to be more serious. Otherwise he'd have more trouble than what he already has.

This wasn't the first time he told himself that he'd change himself and his action but betrayed his words by breaking his promises. He didn't know what to do. Marushka had been insistent about finishing the labor so she could start planting. For a while he did that, concentrating and keeping his eyes away from his broken machine in the corner of his yard.

*****

The night before had been busy for the four musicians. They had played around the village privately in local taverns for a few coins. When tavern owners witnessed their flamboyant folkloric uniforms, they did not turn these musicians away. Their songs played sonorities that these people never heard prior to their meeting.

Today they traveled only around the village. Spending most of their time outdoors, they had walked kilometers around Leninsk. Makar did not show tiredness, despite being the oldest. He was ahead of everybody. They had used a little trail off the main roads that only farmers use.

Makar had to step aside to let a herd of cows accompanied by a herdsman pass by. Makar looked behind at the cows. Their moo sounds were fresh and tasty to their ear. Makar was thirsty for some good milk.

"I'd like to ask for some milk from these farmers later on. I'm kind of thirsty now."

"We should sit down somewhere and relax a bit. My legs are hurting me again," complained Bogdan.

"Yeah. I think that's what we'll do," said Rodion, wishing to give his neck a rest. The weight of the accordion, carried since Stalingrad, was starting to have an effect on him.

Then came silence, and on the dusty trail only cows and their footsteps could be heard. After sweeping his eyes around the environment,

First Farmer In Space

Makar raised his finger and exclaimed: "There! We could take a rest on that hill over there!"

Everybody looked where he pointed, a small, friendly green hill where only one single tree lived peacefully.

"Makar," started Rodion, "you've always had good eyes to pick a good spot to rest."

Makar let out a short, enthusiastic laugh.

They moved to the hill and dropped their instruments down. It was silent while they caught their breath and examined the surroundings for a bit.

"Nice view here," said Kiril.

"Anywhere is good as long as we have a tree," replied Bogdan.

It was somewhere past the edge of the village. A great forest was behind them, and in front they could see a few houses and fields soon to be yellow with wheat. By coincidence, Yezh's house was ahead, directly across from them, maybe a kilometer away. Yezh could be seen plowing his field.

"People work hard here."

Everybody knew what Makar was talking about. All their eyes fell on the same person plowing in the distance. They sat there for a long time, enjoying nature's voice and Yezh's display of hard work.

***

It couldn't wait: Katenka was well ahead in her gardening. Meanwhile Marushka wasn't improving at all, and she felt the need to prepare her garden earlier because she couldn't face the shame of her unproductive garden. When she watered her sprouts, she observed their dangerous growth. She had to start planting something today, at least as much as Yezh had already plowed. She took a few foil plates where she had planted sprouts, tomatoes, and peppers that were getting too tall for the plates. Outside she took a small portion of plowed field and began planting, tackling the field with her green army.

***

Katenka saw Marushka on her knees and wondered if they'd push their planting because of them. "Those neighbors are trying to catch up to us," she said.

"They must have seen that we were getting too far ahead of them," responded Ivan, who was listening to the radio in his living room.

Every once in a while, they'd throw a peek through the window at the miserable neighbors who struggle to compete with them. Ivan always kept an eye out not to let Yezh surpass him in the work done. Ivan was always measuring his moves.

***

A thousand-square-meter field was enough to drain his energy for all day. Sweeping the sweat from his forehead, Yezh could see that he had a lot more to do, but he had no more motivation. When he turned, he didn't see Marushka working in her garden anymore, but sprouts of various plants had been carefully sown. She must have gone back in the house for something.

He planted his shovel and retreated. Ivan came out to start to work because he felt bad that Yezh was working too hard; it made him sick. He had to do something; he couldn't lose his title of hard worker even if he wanted to because Yezh was hardly a competition.

"You've decided to plant your sprouts today I can see," said Ivan to Yezh while looking on their first sprouts.

Yezh moved his tired body to the fence.

He said, "My wife was eager to do so. She was pestering me to finish plowing. I've done quite a lot but more needs to be done." He let out a sigh of relief, enough to catch his breath. "Before you'll know it, we'll catch up to you in no time."

"Ah! I can hardly wish for that. You have accumulated too much lateness. For that, you'll have to put more time in your garden and less on your inventions."

Yezh understood that was his greatest weakness, but he had no intention of forfeiting either one.

"You never know, neighbor. A man can do incredible things in life," responded Yezh.

First Farmer In Space

Another chitchat ended quickly. If it wasn't due to Marushka, it would be because Ivan had better things to do.

Many leaves from the previous autumn were scattered around. But Yezh had been using his homemade compost made of shredded dead organic substitutes such as fruits and vegetables and leftovers from the long, harsh winter. He had bags of it stored and had been using it in conjunction with the plowing.

When Ivan saw over the fence that Yezh was pulling out his bags of compost, Ivan quickly had an idea. He went to his old barn located deep in his backyard and which is placed at an angle opposite to Yezh's barn. He slid the bar upward to open the door and hopped onto his tractor after warming the engine.

Yezh heard the engine roaring closer, and he saw his neighbor on his tractor—something that he never had a chance to have in his life. It was okay. Yezh believed he could fare without one, as he had all these years. It seemed to Yezh that Ivan was going somewhere. Perfect, nobody likes him anyway. They'll have peace of mind for a little bit.

The tractor heavily traversed the bumpy soil. It hadn't even reached the front yard before the tractor stopped in its track. The engine choked, and no life was seen or heard from it shortly after.

"What is this?"

Ivan thought it might have been because he forgot to add water, but he remembered he did that yesterday. He climbed down and went in front of the engine where he could open the hatch to see the quantity of water. Nope, it was full of water like he clearly remembered. That meant there was a problem with the engine.

"Curses! What happened to the engine?"

Ivan walked around the tractor to see for any visible damage.

Katenka, who heard the tractor shutting down and curses escaping from Ivan's mouth, came out of curiosity to ask him what happened to their thousands-of-coins-worth decade-old tractor.

Ivan had always been the careless type who couldn't own anything for more than a year. When something gets into his hands, something must happen to it. The tractor never used to break down like that previously.

Phoenix Phoenix

Ivan could only stare and wonder. He investigated different parts but couldn't find the problem. Up to a point, when they both figured out that the tractor had reached its expiry date, they believed nothing could be done. The cost would be tremendous to repair it. It would be less to buy a new one even if it costs an arm and a leg. As long as it doesn't cost a head, they will survive.

"What are we going to do with it now?"

"It's too expensive to repair it, so we might as well throw it away."

Katenka was dissatisfied with this inevitable idea.

"Oh, what a shame. How are we going to farm the grain field?"

"We'll figure something out."

Yezh heard curses, low-toned voices, and an awful silence from Ivan's side, which was unusual. It was silent in a suspicious way—almost like they were trying to hide something. It was obvious. Yezh wasn't stupid; he knew it had to do with their tractor. It must have broken down on them.

Yezh went to their front yard by the fence and appeared with a smile—the same way Ivan does to him whenever something breaks down on his side.

"Is everything fine on your side neighbor?" inquired Yezh, still keeping his cool diplomatic manners.

Ivan was already having a difficult time.

"My tractor is dead, I think. Nothing much we can do."

"I see," answered Yezh suavely, using all his most sarcastic badinage. "I guess nothing lives on forever."

"Right," said Ivan in good-humored yet awkward agreement.

Yezh came over to their terrain as if wanting to help somehow.

"What brings you here, neighbor?" asked Katenka.

"I heard your tractor shutting down suddenly, so I came to see what happened."

"Do you think you can help us to fix it?" demanded Katenka casually.

"Well, it won't hurt to have a look."

Yezh slowly approached and examined the tractor. It took only a blink of an eye to see the problem after opening the hood. It was somewhere near the pistons and the end of the cylinders, in a component within the engine that couldn't possibly be fixed without dismantling everything.

"Do you think it can be fixed?"

"I'm afraid not."

"Well then, that's that!" replied Ivan. "Can you help me to push it? I want to throw it out. I'm going to call Igor to come and tow it away."

"Sure!"

And just like that, they decided to push it off their property. Yezh helped them to push the tractor off their land when suddenly Yezh had an idea.

"Hey! I'd take it in my yard if you don't mind?"

"You said you can't fix it."

"No," started Yezh. "But I can use some of its parts. Not everything is garbage to someone who has a good eye."

"A good eye, right," said Ivan, finding it almost funny. "I don't mind if you take my junk. It's going to save me some coins in my pocket."

"So, will I!" replied Yezh. As Ivan thought about his remark, they pushed it into Yezh's backyard.

Marushka was the first one to complain about it, but only when the neighbors left.

"What do you think you are doing?"

"This is a wonderful piece here."

"It's junk, Yezh. Junk! It's not a junkyard here."

"Don't worry, this won't stay here too long. I need some of its body parts."

Phoenix Phoenix

She waved her hand in disagreement and turned away toward her house.

Ivan, on the other hand, had to go by car to buy whatever he needed—something better than what Yezh was putting on his soil.

Despite his shamming generosity over the dead tractor, Yezh knew that all Ivan wanted was to get rid of the junk from his yard. This served them mutually, for it was the sole reason for his acquisition, even if he knew it would get Marushka's dander up. After that, Yezh had had enough talking with his unfriendly neighbor, and thought he deserved a bit of rest. So, he sat on a chair in his backyard and heaved a sigh of relief from the intense physical activity.

He was able to see the good work that Marushka did on a small part of the land. His tomato and pepper sprouts were standing gloriously. He just hoped that his peppers wouldn't suffocate under the overwhelming talkative sprouts on the other side of the fence. Maybe Ivan's sprouts were annoying like their master.

With a sigh he looked up and saw that the moon was still lingering in the late morning sky. The sky was blue, and the sun wasn't strong yet but was climbing on the other side of the house. This gave sweaty Yezh a chance to enjoy the last breeze of the day in the shade.

He tried to find a good rest despite all this negativity that his day was giving him. Then the poor farmer remembered the conversation they had over dinner at Aleksei's place. He thought hard about it. As he looked to the sky for inspiration, the blue sky was clearing away room in his head for deep thoughts.   His eyes went back to the moon involuntarily. The moon nagged him with its majestic appearance. No matter how hard he thought about it, he couldn't answer a simple question that Aleksei asked him: What dream does he have? Nothing came to his mind. It was blank. It was like he had exhausted his imagination and energy on his inventions all these years. It was frustrating him to believe that was the reason why they were living such a terrible lifestyle.

There was a reason why Aleksei ran away from it, and Yezh believed it was time for him to make that kind of change in his life as well.

"A dream?" he whispered to himself. "If I had a dream, I'd fly to the moon if I could."

First Farmer In Space

That was all he could say sarcastically to himself in his frustration. He knocked the vexing idea away. He sighed, his eyes falling on the thin lawn and dusty soil.

He looked around, his eyes trying to catch anything interesting to look at. He spotted an aluminum plate next to his chair, one of the plates that Marushka used for her plants. It must have fallen from the table and been carried over by the wind. He took it in his hand and had a good look at it as it wasn't every day that a farmer would see aluminum-based foils. He looked at it from every angle. Its reflection was intriguing to the eye. It reflected light brightly. Aluminum was like silver or gold to farmers out here. Its appearance in everyday life was rare and attracted the attention of people. It had numerous properties that were advantageous to the farmers.

Now that he thought about it, he did realize how hard it was to see something made of aluminum foil. He touched the center with his finger, and its malleable property gave him a variety of new ideas for possible inventions.

Why was Yezh still thinking of invention, even in his leisure time? It was like an obsession. What could be made of aluminum? He wondered what he could build with aluminum.

Such weird material seemed almost like something he had read in the paper about future and alien technology. They have spotted this material in the United States that had this weird shape of a saucer, like a giant plate flying in the sky. Some books also depict a man made of tin, having the same kind of glossiness as these materials. For these reasons, Yezh, like any other person, related aluminum and tin to science and the future. Suddenly, foggy ideas started to form in his mind.

Curious about his dreams, Yezh looked above his head at the moon, which was still present in the morning sky even though it would soon be noon.

"I wonder if people from the outside world are using aluminum for future technology?" he asked himself, barely audibly.

Aluminum is reliable but rare, and since it is bound up with future technology, it reminded Yezh of how successful humanity would produce a material of great value. He thought about what he told himself earlier about the moon. It had always been in a farmer's life as something that was present but never to be reached or obtained from the sky.

Just as a pleasurable thought, Yezh wondered how great it'd be to walk on the moon. He wondered about its landscapes, about its riches, and if it had life of its own, so apparent yet underrated. Like any other farmer, Yezh paid little attention to this celestial body. Could aluminum be connected to it? Could there be an invention that combines both objects?

"I wonder how I will be able to fly myself to the moon?"

Oops, it was time for him to go back to his work. All this thinking about the moon and dreams nearly derailed him.

He grabbed his plowing tool with dismay and started to plow. He had a few thousand square meters more to work and it would be done, but nothing could convince Yezh to think about it. Plowing began. After a while, ideas start to appear in his mind.

Moon … aluminum … invention … dreams: they all echoed in his mind as distractions. He was physically plowing alright, but he was seeing something else than himself plowing. He was seeing again those rare visions of the possible, visions that were once thought to be impossible.

Flying to the moon—is that feasible? Could it be done by something like a flying plate in the sky? Was the flying plate something people truly saw in the sky or just some elaborate figment of imagination? And what about this strange location where the stars dwell? What kind of place is it? Does the sky extend infinitely as he always believed it does? Does such a place have a name? What does the outer sky look like? If such worlds exist, could there be life above their heads?

He thought how great it would be to see himself soaring to the horizon in incredible heights. But there must be some way to fly. That is, if only he could find a way to fly.

This idea spawned a memory of the bottle that they had blasted yesterday.

That's it! thought Yezh.

The bottle—how did it travel so high so easily? It would take a lot of water pressure and a lot of carbonation pills to launch a big bottle where he'd comfortably embrace himself for the ride of a lifetime.

First Farmer In Space

Yes, it would be a ship, his very own ship that would help him to reach that dream.

A bottle ship?

The Wright brothers proved to the skeptical world that it is possible for men to fly like a bird. So, could Yezh prove to the world that launching to some beyond-the-sky location would be possible? If there was a ship to travel on water and another to soar the skies, then it should be possible to make one to aim for the stars.

His mind was set on what he believed to be his new and unique dream. The moon was patiently waiting to be explored by an adventurer. The jigsaw pieces were fitting in his mental image.

Yezh would be the first farmer to reach the moon.

All this thinking pumped him up, making him smile. The adrenaline caused by pleasurable thoughts produced energy, and Yezh plowed faster.

It would be made of tin, but what shape would his ship have? The way he would launch it was another challenge. Yezh lit up when the image of the broken tractor came to his mind. Could he use the tractor for its engine? It might be a possibility, but he needed to fix it. In worse case, he was sure he could make his very own engine that would imitate water pressure and carbonation pills.

Yezh continued to gather jigsaw pieces mentally, and when he snapped out of his thought, he was astonished to see he had accomplished a hard job. Behind him was a large portion of plowed field.

Marushka slid the door open and yelled afar to her husband.

"Lunch is ready! Come to eat now!"

"I'm coming!" Yezh yelled back.

She witnessed the end of the hard labor that took nearly two whole weeks. She had never expected to see Yezh finish it.

It was lunchtime, and Marushka had just finished preparing the food for her hungry husband. Over the table, Yezh's mood seemed upbeat. His great efforts in the field deserved praise.

"You have finished plowing the field?" Marushka asked with a spark of joy in her voice. "That was very fast."

He was quite proud of himself as even he did not know how he did it, but all that dreaming made him work fast and continuously.

"Yes. It is finally done. I couldn't wait to start to invent again. I must say that those hours of nonstop work were painful."

Painful indeed, but the moon dream transformed a painful work into a fun one. It wasn't as painful now, he thought.

"Now we can start to plant all of our remaining sprouts. I already started a little bit. Our neighbor has already started long ago."

"Finally, we can catch up with him. How are the sprouts doing?" asked Yezh, remembering how good Ivan's sprouts looked.

"Very beautiful. I think this year the crop will be very good. We haven't had a good crop for two consecutive years." said Marushka.

Yezh took a few tasty sips of the soup, providing a short pause to the talking.

"I had this very special vision earlier," said Yezh, who tried to put it in words carefully. "About what your brother said last night—about the dream." Yezh paused and Marushka looked at him patiently as she could see the contentment in his face. Something was making him happier than usual. *Could he have realized something finally?* thought Marushka. *Could he have found a way to become rich like her brother?* Everything came out in a sudden breath.

"I think I found it at last," he said, eager to get to the next sentence. "I wish to fly to the moon one day."

Marushka almost choked with a full spoon in her mouth. She couldn't find a thing to say to the ridiculous idea. She felt like she had been mentally knocked to the floor.

"The moon?" Trying to find any reason to accept what she heard, but to no avail, she finally asked politely: "Why did that come to your mind?"

"I always dreamed of doing the impossible, I always wanted to do something that nobody had ever experienced, going to a place where nobody has ever been. The thought is exciting me deeply!"

"That's good, Yezh, but no man has *ever* gone to the moon. That sounds ridiculous. You know that's impossible. What made you to believe you can do that?"

"A man with a dream," said Yezh while looking in his soup. "That would be the ultimate dream that a man can have in his life. And I believe that when there's a will, there's a way!"

To convince her, he came up with a fact. "Remember what comrade Stalin used to say?"

Marushka thought about it and she could imagine what he tried to make her understand.

"Humanity's will can achieve many things. Just imagine what we have done so far: building machines, making paper, using medicine to save lives. Think about how technology has come so far because of humanity's great will!"

Marushka was proud of Yezh's words, and she believed him in a way. Her only concern was what the neighbors and the people around Leninsk would think about them. They already laughed many times about Yezh's odd behavior and inventions. She was afraid to be laughed at by everybody. What would they think about them if they learned about this odd dream of Yezh? She couldn't leave her house for a century from embarrassment, but she said nothing to Yezh about it.

With passion in his voice, Yezh said, "I had this good idea for an invention. I thought of building something big, something impossible, something that nobody had ever built before!" Marushka could only wonder. "I want to build something that can fly to the moon."

"What could you possibly build to fly up there?" said Marushka with curiosity, since she never heard of anything like that in all human history.

"I decided to make a beyond-the-sky ship."

"A what?" she repeated in confusion.

"An airplane but for whatever is beyond our sky above our heads."

It was hard for Marushka to imagine a beyond-the-sky airplane because she couldn't give it a shape. An airplane was the only shape she could think. What Yezh was thinking was impossible to guess, but she knew that Yezh could think complexly. He had a mind for such concepts.

"How are you going to build that?" asked Marushka.

This idea had sparked an innovative spirit within Yezh. He slid his eyes up toward her, and something was born inside of him.

"I think I know how," said Yezh with a low tone of voice as though responding a question in his head. And with that, he got up from his dinner and headed outside, leaving Marushka lost in the same old everyday lunch.

There he goes again! Off to his inventions again.

Chapter 5
Building a Dream

Yezh went to his shack accompanied by Sputnik, who wagged his tail. His shack had all his tools. Whenever he opened the door, a blast of bewilderment would sweep him off his feet. Nearly every time it started with "tch" and a grumble.

The shack was small but crammed with all kinds of utility tools: blades of various sorts; hammers; shovels; picks; a mowing machine he got for his birthday, which is one of his most valued objects around his farm; along with his old, smoky car. It was the kind of stuff that gets accumulated after years of dumping within the shack. His session of wonders—which is meant in a sarcastic way—always ends up with a few curses. The shack resembled a cross between a junkyard and a butcher's shop. He considered it the most dangerous place around his house due to the many sharp objects hanging from walls and even from the ceiling. And it was running out of space. The mess came from his bad habit of collecting litter and junk among the years.

Yezh was well equipped and had almost all he needed in there. He found a wood-cutting saw and some nails in a pot. Even Sputnik was in the shack, wagging his tail and sniffing everything what Yezh touched. It was like if the dog wanted to help.

"You want to help, Sputnik?" He patted the dog's head. "Good boy. You want to fly to the moon, do you?" The dog barked once.

Yezh gathered tools from the storage shack in the backyard. He picked some wood bars and nails and prepared to build the foundation of what would become the skeleton of his future invention, a beyond-the-sky shuttle.

He chose a solid but naked part of soil, far from anything organic. At first, he thought of building it inside his barn, away from his nasty neighbor with the evil eye, but he wasn't sure how big it would be, so maximizing the space allotted to this project might save him some pain later. For that reason, he picked somewhere outside with no roof above.

He did not know what it would look like, and when the time came to visualize it and to drive some screws, he couldn't get a feel for it. The inspirational sun had clouded away. It all seemed foggy in his mind, and he could picture only a silhouette of what he dreamed about. But when he remembered the bottle that he skyrocketed, it gave him a clear base shape: it demanded to be long and high. Perhaps it needed to look like a bottle. He had been astonished by the performance of the water-driven bottle. The secret must lie somewhere with the water. Suddenly Yezh was drawn into his imaginative world, ready to explore new limits of dreaming.

*****

"Looks like that peasant over there is building something," said Makar.

The four Cossack musicians didn't move from the hill. They had been studying Yezh for a while.

"Yes. We are witnessing a natural inventor. A peasant different from the other folks indeed," said Rodion. "I am becoming fond of this one."

Their eyes locked on the skeletal big box Yezh was building behind his house.

"What do you think he's building?" asked Makar.

"I don't know; I can't say," said Bogdan, who took a long gaze but couldn't make out what it was.

"Maybe a new tractor that could plow the field in five minutes," said Kiril in a quick guess.

"That can't be it," corrected Bogdan. "It could be a new barn or a shack."

They saw only a pointy-looking shape. What could be made in a pointy shape?

"It looks more like a bomb," mocked Makar with a short little laugh.

"Let's keep watching him, maybe we'll see more clues later on," said Rodion, who concluded the debate. Rodion soon learned to admire this peculiar peasant. This one had to be a very special one, he could feel it. It was a simple Cossack feeling.

Chapter 6
Helping Tatjana

All in a hurry, one of their neighbors who lived a few streets away came to their door. She was hoping that Yezh was home.

Someone knocked on the door. Marushka felt excited for a moment because she loved visitors. Since they lived in a small village in the countryside, it was easy to know the neighbors, making the world seem smaller than it was. At the door was Tatjana, who showed her a big, friendly smile.

"Marushka! How are you? Did I bother you somehow?"

"No, no you haven't. I just finished watering the sprouts."

"Oh, you haven't planted them yet? You are working so hard; it's strange that you haven't planted anything."

"I've started but haven't planted everything—they will all be planted soon if the clouds don't find it too sorrowful."

"I see your neighbor is doing quite fine. His garden is already growing green."

"Yes, the weather has been better lately. Summer is beginning." Marushka managed to speak the words, but the notion of thinking about that nasty neighbor wasn't easy on her nerves.

"Where is Yezh? I saw something in the backyard. Still building some things, isn't he?" asked Tatjana with curiosity.

"He's always busy with those things. I sometimes must fight with him. He spends more time with his invention than with me or the field."

"Understandable. We all have problems with our husbands," said Tatjana as if she knew quite well about men. "What's he building this time?"

Marushka hesitated to answer as she didn't know what to say. All this moon traveling, and sky science made her uneasy, but she would have to say something untruthfully—until that thing is completed and resembles something everybody knows about, and she won't be able to hide the truth anymore. People are not blind. She hoped that Yezh was only joking with such an idea.

"Well, he's … huh … building a windmill—I think. I have to ask him."

Tatjana nodded. Marushka wouldn't wait for her to ask any risky questions. She had to talk fast.

"What are you doing here? Is everything going good on your side?" asked Marushka, hoping to change the subject.

"Not so good. My oven just now broke. I don't know what is wrong with it. I can't make anything right now and I am worried I won't be able to cook anymore." Tatjana looked ever so worried.

"That is very unfortunate, Tatjana!"

"Say Marushka—can you ask Yezh if he could come and fix it? I know that he knows quite a lot about those things," said Tatjana with a smile. "If he has time, of course."

Her sympathy was hard to resist, and she really didn't mind helping a good old friend. After all, everybody in this village was trying to help each other as much as they can. Otherwise, it's for nothing that this country is named Soviet Union.

"I could ask him, but he's struggling in his work," said Marushka, trying to prove a point. "You see, I've been arguing with him to spend more time on the field work, but he seems to be more and more into his invention work than ever before." It was the smile and intonation of her voice that led Tatjana to believe it was a vague expression.

"I see," said Tatjana in worried doubt. "Well, only if he has time, dear. I will greatly appreciate it."

"Don't mention it. I will let him know."

"Thank you so much, and sorry once more for the trouble," said Tatjana with a hand movement indicating that she was going away. Marushka sighed as she closed the door as now, she had someone else's problem to worry about.

The wood bars were holding solid. Yezh had built its foundation but had no idea how it would work yet. The first hour of his work had been fruitful and inspirational. He had conceived it with each internal space allotted to a special compartment. He backed away for a better view. There would be a cockpit and an engine motor that would take up some space.

His heart beat faster, as he was suddenly sure that he had finally found the invention that might make him a legend.

Marushka came to him with the news, but she felt bad to interrupt him when he was hidden inside of the giant box, where only the knocking of his hammer could be heard.

"Yezh!" she cried out loud. She had to shout two times for him to appear, peeking out from that sketchy box.

"What is it?" inquired Yezh.

"Come over here!"

Yezh came out and demanded answers.

"Tatjana just came here. She said that her oven just broke down and asked me to ask you if you want to go and fix it for her."

Yezh couldn't believe it. He had been so busy working, and he still had lots more to do. He threw a look at his work in progress. He really didn't feel like going, but he didn't want to show no interest in other people.

"I don't feel like going anywhere. I'm into my work. If I stop now, I will lose the feeling of it."

"If you don't help her, then everybody will think of us as unsociable."

"I know that," said Yezh, who hated admitting she had a point about that.

"Maybe you should go. Who knows, perhaps you will do better after getting some air."

After thinking about it, Yezh finally agreed to go over to Tatjana's place. "Alright, I'll go see her now."

Yezh hurried to leave everything behind and departed to Tatjana's house, which wasn't too far down the street. It was a fairly small village, so the walking distance wasn't great, and horses are not needed for this situation.

While he walked, looking at various houses and gardens, especially paying attention to what people had in their backyards, Yezh saw how poor and simple the place he was living in was. Perhaps he was asking too much of life, but he refused to let the idea linger in his head another second more because Yezh was a person who, though not very spiritual, believed in hope and will. With it he felt mighty and that nothing could stop him. But the second thought came back to his head, one that reminded him that he was a mere farmer. Yezh grew fearful of future success—or failure—that was bound to the fate of being a farmer.

And all the way to his destination, he thought about his beyond-the-sky airplane, about its various components, and began to understand how difficult it would become. He found it amusing that all his best ideas came rushing to him when he was far from his hammer, but none dared to show themselves when he was standing ready to net them like fish. He still had no idea how his device was going to propel itself into the air, but Yezh constantly thought about the bottle and the physics of such energy. He also disliked seeing himself and his work being interrupted by little mindless troubles such as this.

In this small village, many trades were represented: carpenter, mailman, tractor mechanic, doctor, and seamster. But nobody was like Yezh, who was a skilled freelancer. Nobody else knew electricity and machinery with a keen eye for originality like him. That's what he saw in his neighbors, and in himself.

***

Tatjana was happy to see him arrive in her yard. She was just sweeping the dust from off the front of her house, and she greeted him to her house with a big smile. Inside, she showed him the oven she had difficulty fixing.

He inspected it carefully. It was a very old oven, and Yezh was impressed by how long this thing had lasted. That's one beauty about Russian inventions, he thought. They always last longer than any foreign product. They're cheap, easy to repair, easy to clean, easy to use, and have the life span of an elephant.

"I couldn't understand why this had to happen. I've been kind to it for many years. And right today it had to break. It never did this before," complained Tatjana.

First Farmer In Space

Yezh inspected the oven thoroughly after opening it, and when he did, he realized for the first time how simple and easy and empty it was inside and understood that such a small system could make a big, useful heating device. Because of this, the time that he took to spot the problem was short.

Yezh informed Tatjana with regret of the defect that infiltrated her oven: "One of the cables burned out," he said, backing off from the oven.

"Really? Oh, curse that! Don't tell me that it's a dead oven!"

"Unfortunately, it is unusable in this state."

"Curses! How will I cook from now on?" said Tatjana, who had her hand on her mouth and cheek while she thought deeply, puzzled by what to do with the oven. "So, what should we do about it?"

"You will have to throw it away," answered Yezh. "If I try to fix it, it might cause accidental fire in the future."

At first Tatjana couldn't accept the fate of her oven and walked around in circles from intense stress. Yezh stood up with his sore back. He was getting old. He knew no other way to help Tatjana other than to comfort her for her loss. In Russia, because some objects last as long as your grandmothers, many people get so used to their personal belongings that they feel sad when one breaks. It's easy to get attached to an object.

After a while, Tatjana finally accepted the reality and kindly asked Yezh another favor.

"Fine. I guess I will have to find another oven. Could you please throw it outside for me? It's very heavy."

"Sure, I could."

Yezh grabbed it from the side and tried to balance it from side to side to move it around the room. Alone in the struggle, Yezh took the oven out from her house.

"Thank you so much for your time, Yezh. I feel bad for my oven, but I really appreciate it."

"Helping others is the cultural way in the Soviet Union. What would comrade Stalin say if he were to see us being selfish among each other?"

Phoenix Phoenix

"Agreed, comrade! How can we not help each other when we all know each other since childhood?" said Tatjana in her own words, and with some greetings they parted ways.

But the oven stayed there outside on the street, waiting for the trash collector to pass by and take it away, which was to be the next day. It reminded Yezh that his own trash needed to be collected. Yezh departed for his home to work on his beyond-the-sky shuttle, and he wondered to himself along the way. Would a beyond-the-sky shuttle burn and break down, too?

Such is a terrible fate for machines.

Chapter 7
A Weasel Neighbor

Yezh went straight back to work when he arrived. Marushka was already on her knees planting her sprouts when Yezh asked her how much she had planted. There were nearly twenty plates, and the empty plates were all still lying around, so he went around collecting them.

When she saw him picking them up, she knew he was hiding something.

"What are you doing with those plates?"

"I need them for something," replied Yezh. "Save them on the side for me, will you?"

She grew suspicious of him for leaving so fast with the plates without saying anything. She knew him too well and that it always meant trouble.

***

Ivan was just arriving home from his errands. Now that he had no tractor, he had to use his small car. He looked tired to Katenka, and when she asked him, he simply brushed the question off with a hand wave.

The hammer knocking attracted unwanted ears, and right away Ivan guessed that Yezh was building something new. Mockery was the only thing that put him in a good mood. Nothing is healthier than having a good laugh at his neighbor.

Well then, why not go have another look? thought Ivan.

A good laugh once in a while is good for the nerves. What he saw was these wood stubs standing high and that they were interconnected with each other, making a foundation.

At the same time, Yezh grew thirsty and decided to come down and go have a sip of water that was on the table nearby. Inevitably, he saw Ivan gazing by the fence on his side.

"Neighbor. What could you be building there this time? That looks big. What is it?" inquired Ivan.

"It is what it is! It's still incomplete," said Yezh, who grabbed his bottle and had a drink.

"Is it a new barn?" guessed Ivan.

"No!"

Ivan took a second guess. "Is it a windmill?"

"No!" said Yezh, almost enjoying it.

Ivan felt like giving up guessing but was too curious to quit.

"What could it be?"

"It won't be a secret if I tell you."

Ivan was hoping not to hear that.

"What secret could it be? You are building it in front of people. It can't be a secret forever, can it?"

"It won't be forever, but for now it is, and not until I finish building it will anyone know what it is."

Ivan became saddened not to be able to hear what it was. And as for Yezh's stubbornness, he gave up asking. Instead he changed the subject to something else.

"I just arrived from the market down the road in the next city. Look what I bought." Ivan showed the bags behind him with his thumb. "Compost. Fresh earth from fertile lands far away they said, sure to give good crops in autumn."

Ha! So that's why he ran off so hot-headedly, thought Yezh. There isn't any race that this man wouldn't willingly lose. No man was shrewder and dangerously cunning than Ivan.

"Really? It didn't take you more than a blink of an eye for you to buy those bags even before I finished composting my field."

"You need a good eye for that, neighbor."

Yezh didn't know what that meant, but he always had his own opinion about this man.

"Sure. I don't think you'll run short on that," said Yezh sarcastically, but Ivan didn't get the humor.

***

Ivan went in his house and was interrupted by his wife, who was placing all the new items he bought in their respective places along with the compost. She had seen from the window only a moment ago that Yezh was building something, and she had to know what it was.

"What is he building out there?" inquired Katenka.

"I don't know. He didn't want to say anything. He said it was a *secret.*" It was Ivan's sarcastic emphasis on "secret" that had a provocative effect on her.

"Oh … oh what a ridiculous man he is! His fantasies have left the realm of reality," Katenka said with great sarcasm and mockery. "I don't know what he was thinking, but I wonder what he could be building for it to be such a secret?"

"I don't know either," replied Ivan. "It has to be something very special. He's scared that someone might steal his stupid, worthless ideas."

Ivan did not stress himself over the matter. All truth has feet, and sooner or later, it would be known to him. Nobody would be keeping a secret from Ivan. Nobody!

Chapter 8
An Adventure in Collection

Marushka reminded Yezh of the trash day which was the next day and urged him to move the junk out of their backyard. He surely would have forgotten it if she hadn't mentioned it.

Yezh moved everything in front of the house. That took him nearly half an hour. The branches, the wood planks, the water heater—he got rid of everything. He could finally return peacefully to his ship. The rest was up to Igor.

What better time could there be for Aleksei to drop a visit? He arrived in his expensive car that he stores in his garage all year long. He parked his car in front, between Yezh's and Ivan's house.

Ivan hated him because of what he worth. He even called him "fresh boy" and found the young man's brags to be provocative. He estimated Aleksei to be an overrated rich man.

Aleksei stepped out from his car and looked toward the house, knowing already where to find Yezh. His sunglasses made him look cool; the only thing warm on his complexion was his slight smile.

Aleksei was curious when he saw Yezh on a large object. Both Yezh and Marushka were surprised to see him here. Another distraction for Yezh. Aleksei was asking a lot of questions—too many in Yezh's opinion. He felt bad hiding a secret from his brother-in-law, and so they spoke of how he wanted to fly high in the sky. Aleksei raised his eyebrows when the moon was mentioned. Yezh explained how he was inspired by the dinner they had at Aleksei's place the other night. Aleksei was proud of him but promised that he wouldn't be telling it to anyone. Of course, Marushka pulled him away with her chatting about sprouts, and Yezh sighed when he left. At least Marushka kept him company for a while.

The brother-in-law stayed for a while until he decided to leave. It was with sorrow that they learned that Aleksei was departing for the USA again. He'd leave after he paid Moscow a visit for a meeting. Some Russian industrial businessmen awaited him for a speech. His business should be coming to Russia soon. His flight was tomorrow, and he didn't want to leave without saying his farewells to his sister and to his good old friend.

First Farmer In Space

Aleksei was a talkative one. Yezh sighed in relief now that he could return to his work. So many things had happened this day that impeded his progress.

Yezh had been dead serious about his dreams. He had given his ship a basic but original shape that he believed would be perfect for launching upward. It had to be upward, not sideways. The skeleton was completed, and it looked sturdy. It was nearly time to start skinning his ship. The key material was missing, though.

Yezh casually descended from his ladder and approached the table where Marushka put her plates on. He took what remained of Marushka's leftover plates, but without telling her anything of his true intentions. She was further down in her garden, still planting some sprouts. Then he went inside to take shade from the rising sun and to think about how to find the material he needed.

The master had been so busy that even Sputnik felt discarded, he had grown hungry and barked ceaselessly when he entered the house. Yezh had forgotten about poor little Sputnik. Yezh picked a dog food can from the armoire, opened it, and poured all of it on his plate on the floor. Sputnik dug in his food as if he hadn't eaten for weeks.

Yezh hadn't thought too much late, before throwing the can in the trash, that what he had in his hands was a piece of aluminum. He examined it carefully. The way it was cleaned from the inside was as if cats had licked it clean. It was made of aluminum, and Yezh had yet to discover a way to find aluminum in raw form. If this was a lucky find, how many times would he need to feed Sputnik in order to skin his ship?

He had seen aluminum in various forms. It was the right material, just not the right form. How could he melt it? The only thing he could think of now was Joseph the blacksmith: he had all the equipment to melt and make metal pure. There was no other way. He peeked through the window at Marushka working in her garden. He grabbed one of those thick garbage bags and put the plate and the can in it. Without questions or attention, he left the house discreetly. It won't be a long visit he told himself.

He carried the black bag all the way to the village blacksmith. It was quite a big workshop that Joseph had, and when Yezh stepped in it, a blast of heat struck his face and made him sweat instantly. The hammer clinking onto iron indicated Joseph's location within this blazing hellfire. He was smithing an iron plate. Yezh couldn't come too close due to the intense heat, which he wasn't used to, but all the while, he saw Joseph handling it easily. Joseph knew of Yezh's presence and he abandoned his smithing to see what Yezh wanted.

"Busy, are you?"

"Busy?" said Joseph to reconfirm what he heard among the gushing noise of fire and iron. "Not really. Is there something you need?"

"I'll need something as a favor from you," said Yezh, who looked briefly at the raging flame inside the pit. "I was wondering if you can melt this tin can?"

He showed the tin can to Joseph, but he thought it was a joke and answered back with a jolly voice: "If that's what you need, of course I can melt a piece of tin. Why do you need that?"

"I'm building something, but I was wondering if you could melt these for me. I will, of course, need a lot of them. Do you have any spare aluminum here?"

"No, I don't have much aluminum here. It's all been used for various things."

"Would you care to show me some examples of work?" asked Yezh.

"Sure, leave it to me. How thick do you want it to be?"

"Um, how about something that is thin just for a try?" said Yezh.

"Right on, comrade."

Joseph took it in his hands and went to melt it right away. The bag gave up all its contents. The way he made it was simple and fast, and Yezh was impressed by the techniques he used. He heated a pot with aluminum inside, and within a brief time, Joseph poured the melted tin onto a cold, solid, heat-resistant plate where the aluminum spread across it and froze immediately. A minute passed, and Joseph presented an aluminum leaf to Yezh.

Joseph grabbed it boldly in his hands. Thinking about how many times he must have burned himself with such hot molten, Yezh guessed he must have become used to the pain. Yezh examined the leaf. It was large for a single bag of tin and was thin, as he requested, just a few millimeters thick, and it still appeared to be malleable when Yezh bent it slightly. Yezh looked at Joseph to show he was impressed.

"That's what you wanted, right? I gave it a few millimeters of thickness. It was very easy to make—you just need a lot of them to make plenty of papers."

"I don't know where to find so many tin cans!" said Yezh, who showed in his face a mixture of surprise and desperation.

"You could ask people, or just take a simple walk every day around the village. You'd be surprised how many cans you'll find on the ground."

Yezh showed thoughts on his face. "How many should I need, for example"—Yezh licked his lips— "if I were making a roundish windmill eight meters high and a diameter of five meters?"

Joseph did the calculation in his mind, and it was clear to him how much Yezh would need for that windmill.

"You'd probably need a several thousands of them."

"Several thousand!" Yezh repeated in surprise. There was no way that he could ever find so many tin cans. He felt depressed.

"I wish I could help you, but I don't have any aluminum," said Joseph, who wondered again what he could possibly be building to need so much aluminum. "What are you building again?"

"A … A windmill," said Yezh, who lied about it.

Joseph thought that it could be done with simple bricks and didn't understand why Yezh needed this amount of aluminum, but he didn't say anything against the idea.

Yezh left Joseph with the belief that he would try to come back with as much of that material as possible. Joseph was left with confusion.

***

While Marushka was working hard on planting the sprouts in the field, Yezh was out walking the streets and asking whoever he met about tin cans. Occasionally he'd search in trash cans when no eyes were on him.

People around the village witnessed the man roaming the land and searching for what seemed to them to be tin cans. He even knocked on a few houses where he asked for any aluminum-based objects, and people did offer him what they didn't have use for. Plates, boxes, and foils were given away, and each of them made Yezh feel that he was getting closer to his dreams. People did ask him what he was trying to build, but Yezh did not want to reveal the idea yet, claiming that it was too early to speak. This was one thing that he hated about Russian people: they need to know everything about everything. But his plan had to be secret, and there was no way that anybody would know it from his own mouth.

Just before he'd had enough for the day, he looked in his bag. The amount of his effort did not reflect in numbers in the bag. He spent a good hour for that and could only find a mere two hundred tin cans of various sizes and shapes. He was as puzzled as he was desperate. Getting the materials was harder than he thought, and what he had was not nearly enough to skin his spaceship.

Where would he go to look? Where would he find more aluminum? He concluded that finding this "silver gold" was not as easy as he thought earlier.

Chapter 9
A Party Not to Miss

After an hour, Yezh came back home. Marushka wondered where he was all day, but the bag caught her eye.

"Where were you? What did you bring home?"

"I collected some tin cans from people." He showed her the bag's contents, but when she saw what resembled scrap and useless junk, she grew dismayed.

"Did you search in the trash or something?"

"It's not trash. It will be useful. It will be recycled, and it'll become good as new."

"So, you went everywhere just to collect this garbage?" recapitulated Marushka in her own words.

"It's not garbage I said. I will use this to build my void-flying ship." explained Yezh who didn't know how to explain what the sky looked like in infinity.

She found the idea weird and couldn't imagine how it would look like with that trash hanging on it. Once again, this nonsensical idea made her uncomfortable.

"Did you finish with the sprouts?" asked Yezh, hoping to hear more about her aluminum plates.

"I did a lot but not all," said Marushka, happy with her work when she looked at her garden.

"How many aluminum plates did you empty?"

"A couple dozen."

"Perfect, I think I'll need them. Where are they?"

"So that's why you were collecting them!" said Marushka with questioning humor. "I've piled them up in one place outside."

She also had news for him. Before he could step outside again, she mentioned what Katenka told her earlier: "There is a party tonight."

Phoenix Phoenix

"Where?"

"At the peasants' square. Everybody will be there, and they will roast a pig, said to be for Workers' Day."

"Why did it have to be tonight when I am busy?" said Yezh, complaining about the date of the party.

"Let's go and see how it turns out. Changing your mind a little bit will be good."

"What are you going to bring?"

They had no idea what they could bring since they hadn't prepared anything.

"I don't know yet," Marushka said anxiously, looking the other way. "I'll find something for the celebration."

Their reserves cried out from emptiness. They were afraid they didn't even have enough for themselves, let alone to bring something to the celebration. Yezh didn't like the way things were turning out: being unable to keep working on his beyond-the-sky shuttle for a decent span of time, with there always being something to do, always something happening somewhere.

"I know what we could do!" said Yezh, whose voice brought hope to her. "I can go hunt something and bring our own meat."

"That's a great idea; they'd love it. But do you have enough time? It's already two o'clock in the afternoon, and Maks is about to return from school."

"I'll see what I can do about that."

***

Before long, Maks dropped his bag in the living room. His mother met him when she heard noise. They quickly let him know that they would be going to the party that night. Being a kid, his heart must have raced at the news.

Yezh was in his safe room, where he'd locked his most precious items. He came out of it with his SVD Sniper in hand.

First Farmer In Space

Maks didn't have to guess twice to know why the sniper appeared in his father's hands. When Yezh had told him that he was going to hunt game for the party, the boy pleaded to assist him. The kid had nagged him countless times to spend more quality time with him, so Yezh didn't refuse his assistance.

Just like that, they departed onto the trail at the back of their yard that led to a nearby wood. It was a good chance for the boy to be with his father. They hadn't had many chances like this to do things together. Even Sputnik decided to walk with them. With a bark from the dog, the father and son looked back to see who was speaking up.

"You want to come too, Sputnik? Come then!" said Yezh.

The boy waved his hand toward the dog, inviting him to come. Now the three of them were walking in the wilderness in search for a small rodent. This did not happen every day, so the boy wished that this moment would last forever. Even Sputnik was in a good mood. His tail wagging high and proudly inspired happiness on their trip. Sputnik loved playing in the field where dandelion grew aplenty, so most of the time, the dog would stray from the road on the side to have a few rolls on the patches of yellow flowers.

Yezh used to hunt quite often in his younger days in this area, and he knew this part of the woods like his own backyard.

They halted at a spot when he found it quiet. Their eyes investigated every corner of the foliage, their ears like antennas, ready to detect any signal of disturbance among the leaves.

Maksimilian tried hard to find anything alive, but for Yezh it was evidently easier to depend on Sputnik, freeing himself of the trouble.

Sputnik moved to a corner and began to growl quietly toward a particular direction. Maksimilian believed Sputnik would growl at anything alive or moving, even a dead leaf caught in the wind. Maks didn't pay attention to what it could be as Yezh did, who shifted his attention to the dog.

"I think Sputnik found something," whispered Maks.

They took their hiding spot and peeked around, trying to spot something small and furry. Sputnik's growl grew, and the boy had to pat him to calm him down to keep from losing their game.

Phoenix Phoenix

Maks stared in fascination at his father in action, also for the awesome high-caliber SVD—an item that would typically spark interest among small kids.

Yezh took aim, and a loud bang echoed through the woods. There was no movement in the corner where the game was located. As they approached, Sputnik rushed to meet the kill before his masters.

It was a hare!

Yezh picked it up and held it like a trophy. It impressed Maks so greatly that he forgot to feel bad for the hare.

The trio marched back, now with a rabbit among them. They were noisy this time. Yezh bragged about his skills, and the boy demanded more explanation about hunting. He asked if he would have a chance one day to hunt for himself, and Yezh replied that he would—when he grows up.

***

It had been an hour since they left. Marushka was growing lonely and worried as a mother and wife but kept on doing her duty and trying to prepare herself for that night's party.

Picking the right clothes and dressing her hair were necessary. When she was finished, she peeked at the back window and saw them coming back from the field. She greeted them and let them know that she was ready. A smile appeared on her face—they had caught something.

Maks ran forward with Sputnik to reach his mother.

"Mother, we caught a rabbit!"

"That's great!"

Yezh caught up. "How about you go prepare yourself with Mother while I go to skin this rabbit?"

The hunter found himself sitting on a chair and skinning the hide off his game. After that he went to change his clothes in his room. It was still a little bit too early, so they had to wait for half an hour more before the celebration would start.

***

First Farmer In Space

The sky grew darker, and the streets became noisier. Yezh's family took to the road toward the square. Yezh and Marushka arrived, but there were already people aplenty. Everybody was there, even Ivan and his wife, whom they tried to avoid contacting. It was noisy, and lanterns were seen burning oil in every corner, well prepared for the nightfall. Maks run off to meet his friends. Though familiar faces were already starting to speak to them, they'd first have to sit down a bit to catch their breath.

The mayor was talking to one of his subordinates who helped him to plan for this party. At this moment, the mayor noticed the newly-arrived guests, still confused about where to go and what to do next.

"Oh, oh! What do we have here!" exclaimed Georgiy with joy hard to be contained. "Isn't it my favorite inventor of the century?" said the mayor, who hugged Yezh heartily. "I'm very glad to see you both here. Come, let me show you where to sit."

The mayor is a friendly man, always the type to greet others with a big warm smile on his face. A little short and fat, perhaps, but a great man nonetheless.

Georgiy accompanied the visitors to their table. Being a talkative man, he couldn't restrain his long-windedness.

"We have so many people tonight. I have a feeling it's going to be a long night for us," said the mayor, who turned hastily back to them, nearly forgetting something. "We are having roasted pig at the end."

"I was afraid you'd forget that this year," said Yezh, who caught a smile on mayor's face.

Their table was reserved by the mayor himself, who called a waiter to come and serve them. "Brother! Serve two glasses of vodka here to my guests!" said the mayor, who forgot his manners. "Please have a seat over here!"

They sat at a long table where a few of the guest were already sitting. People were talking, walking around, getting food to eat over the counter, and some were even playing card games and such.

By coincidence, on the same location, Tatjana was bathing them in words of friendship, just to prove that she was there, you know, to make known her presence.

"I see you managed to come; we were just thinking about you," said Tatjana with a smile. "It's good that we still sit like neighbors."

"Ah, ah, well you know what we say—it's a small world we live in!" said the mayor with another bright smile like he had just proven a point.

"Whenever we hear that there is pork being roasted somewhere, we always charge headfirst," said Tatjana's husband with laughter.

"A party is not a party without a pig," said Yezh.

"That is true!" said the mayor. "You have come just at the right moment for that. We have some snacks and small appetizers if you want some—you can find them at the table over there. The government has even offered a donation of food."

It is a custom for the government to fund the national party. The mayor is sympathetic to the idea of a celebration every year at Leninsk. Thinking of all the food, Yezh was hungry and did not hesitate to set off for that table.

"I'll let you have some fun. Talk to you later," said the mayor, who had to attend other duties within the party.

They found their way among the crowds. At the table where drinks were served, Marushka gasped when she saw a familiar face in bad shape. It was Radomir behind a table, and he was drunk. A bottle of vodka entirely for himself hadn't left his hand for half an hour.

"God! What are you doing there?" asked Marushka.

"Drinking!" Radomir hiccupped once, brandished the bottle in the air. "It's time to drink well. Celebration has come to town."

"See what you look like, Radomir!" said Marushka with a punitive tone. "You are in bad shape."

"What? Can't a man have a nice drink once in a year?"

Radomir was a neighbor from a bit further down the street. He was the careless type. Something always had to happen to him. Many people considered him a curse or a devil because if you were to cross him on the road, something bad was bound to happen to you. Still the man looked innocent. A great neighbor.

"If you drink everything now, there won't be anything left for everybody in the party!" said Yezh, who tried to talk it out more reasonably.

"You're right." He hiccupped another time and offered the bottle to Yezh. "You want some?"

"You were doing a good job," said Yezh with a grin. "I'm sure you can handle it alone."

The four musicians arrived an hour ago and had been rehearsing the tunes they would be playing at the party. They got comfortably set up in their corner. They did not expect to see Yezh here, as they knew him well as the man who would prefer to stay home working on his invention.

"Hey comrades, it seems our hero Yezh has decided to come to the party," said Bogdan.

"Oh, look at that—he did!" answered Makar. His head bobbed as he tried to get a better view.

"That Yezh always seems to be at the right place at right time," said Kiril.

"Indeed, comrade," replied Bogdan. "But he has no idea yet how the outcome will turn to his favor."

"Ha, that Yezh is lucky. It seems that luck strikes him, but he has no clue yet," said Makar.

"Yes, it's a strange fate that he has to be present where destiny calls him to be," said Kiril.

"Don't you think he deserves merit for coming to the party?" said Bogdan.

"Why not?" replied Makar. "I think we have a song for this man who is about to change the history of this great nation that we are celebrating tonight."

"Let's sing him a song to his wonder," said Bogdan.

"Yes, comrade, let's play a song!" said Rodion, raising his accordion higher. "For Yezh and the Soviet Union!"

"*Korobeiniki?*!"

Phoenix Phoenix

And to the request, their music started to sooth the ears of the guests with home-inspiring reminiscence, pleasant music that they haven't heard in a while to please them! Something to remind them of why tonight they were around good food and drinks.

"*Korobeiniki*," or "*Korobushka*" in a different interpretation, is a folk song that today is seen as *the* main theme of Russia in the eyes of the Western world. *Korobeiniki* simply means "peddlers," a story that romances about a promising love between a young girl and a peddler. The young peddler promises her goods and fortune if she becomes his and embarks on a journey for selling his extensive goods to convince her.

Strangely, our hero is ready to give everything he owns just to fulfill his dreams, to meet the sky along with his new lover, his new ship that aims for the stars.

There was music, there was food and lots of drink. After filling their plates with their favorite food, they went back to their table. Good long conversations were aplenty here. Nobody grew short on words. It was a good time for rumors. And the usual question that they asked Yezh whenever they saw him was about his inventions.

One of the people nearby was having a long debate about his business: how it was going badly and how he was struggling. Yezh listened to him because he spoke loudly. Yezh knew the man was speaking truth, unlike Ivan. It was hard to open a business in the USSR. The long speech gave the man a dry throat, so he drank more than others. He finished his drink the quickest. He dropped his empty can aside on the table somewhere in front of but far from Yezh, who spotted it and became fixated on it for a long time. He didn't understand why, but it was as if the can was calling to him.

Yezh turned his eyes and thought about it. *This can can be recycled for its aluminum material, perfect for Joseph's melting,* thought Yezh. Then he saw another man with a drink at hand, and another one by the other corner of table. Everybody was having the same canned drink. At one point, Yezh considered drinking some canned drinks but couldn't tell where they could be found. He hadn't seen them yet.

This might be a chance to collect more aluminum than he could another way. Why couldn't he have thought about this earlier? Just to think that he almost didn't want to come here. Good thing that Marushka pressured him. He'd get a lot more of tin cans.

First Farmer In Space

Yezh's eyes were locked on the tin can on the table, and he could feel it calling. He couldn't let it linger there in front of him. He got up and went by the man, putting an arm out to fetch the can from the table. The man looked at him with confusion.

"I believe you're done with this? I'll throw it away for you," said Yezh with a smile.

Marushka saw him coming and wished to see him not bringing shame to the table. He found a litter bag on a table and used it to keep his can in.

"You're still collecting trash?" whispered Marushka.

"Sorry, my habit!" said Yezh, quickly shifting his attention to the topics being discussed at table.

Yezh pretended to be having a good time, to be listening to people's gossip, but in truth he was looking at everyone else's drink. He had his own little drink after he fetched one over the counter, which he drank occasionally to mask his side gazes.

A man who walked with his tin can in hand threw it in the garbage before heading away.

Yezh dropped his drink on the table. He stood up and went to the trash after seeing no eyes were watching him. What a pity that someone would throw away such useful material! Then Yezh approached casually and took the tin can out and dropped it in his bag. Yezh saw there was more in the trash.

He looked left and right around him to see if someone was looking at him, and he quickly dove into the trash can, hands shuffling through junk in search for the tin cans.

"Yezh what are you doing there?" asked Georgiy out loud, startling Yezh and almost making him jump. Turning quickly to face the interlocutor, he saw it was the mayor himself with his undying smile on his face.

"Mayor, I … uh …"

"Tin cans?" said Georgiy, seeing the can slipping from Yezh's hand into the bag. Yezh didn't know how to respond to that, feeling almost ashamed.

Phoenix Phoenix

"Are you collecting tin cans?"

Yezh looked at the bag in his hand and thought of something quickly.

"Well yes, I'm recycling these tin cans. I see people are throwing them into the trash, but I thought that the perfect citizen would think about the environment." It was the certainty in his last sentence that made him feel like he'd saved himself from embarrassment.

"Our dear Yezh, inventor and environmentalist! You never cease to impress me, Yezh!" Georgiy cheered up in a flash.

The mayor exploded with enthusiasm. Yezh couldn't wish for more than that. He had just avoided a potentially shameful moment. Or did he? He didn't want to be seen as a junk collector.

"You are doing a very good thing you know, Yezh," said Georgiy, who approached to talk to him in a low tone of voice, his arm behind Yezh's back.

He remained speechless but waved his hand to show a sign that it wasn't important.

"Let's show your great deed to everybody," said the mayor, fetching Yezh's arm.

"Ah. It's really not necessary to do that …" said Yezh, but a bit too late. Instead of hearing Yezh, Georgiy already clapped his hands to gain the full attention of the crowd.

He demanded silence, his arm wide open in the air, moving his body from left to right as if trying to have all eyes on him. The musicians interrupted their ballad. Guests redirected their attention to their mayor.

"Dear people of this great nation: Tonight we are having a great deal of food and roasted pork. It is on this celebration day that we shall see only happiness and food for everyone. Many of us are drinking like madmen at a tea party and creating a big mess around this place." A smile appeared on his face that demanded some laughter from people.

"Regarding that manner, I have a great announcement to make about our dear Yezh, who is doing a great deed for our nation and Mother Nature by collecting the tin cans that were opened and thrown in the trash.

First Farmer In Space

Yezh is a great contributor in the fight against pollution!"

This is not what Yezh wanted to happen, but he tried not to turn red. He could see the face of Marushka, who felt like hiding under the table. Instead of receiving the expected shame, everybody showed good heart toward the kind words of the mayor and applause was raining on Yezh.

Even Ivan and Katenka applauded in their corner—forcibly, that is. You'd never see that from them usually.

"I always knew he was a junk collector!" whispered Ivan to his wife behind his fake applause.

Applause rose above all else for Yezh, who became somewhat vainly shy. Most people had no idea what Yezh's true intention was and why he was collecting cans, but folks did find him weirder every day and with every invention he pulls out of his sleeve.

"Yes. Let's drink a lot like Radomir and celebrate like real people."

Radomir, completely drunk over in his corner, raised his drink high above his head as if to show off his pride in being drunk. Tin cans were raised above heads in cheers.

That's right. Keep on gulping while I'm collecting! thought Yezh.

Truly, he wanted only to gather more tin cans, but he wouldn't be able to drink everything from the basket to empty the cans. With a cheerful smile, he went to sit down by Marushka again, who looked at him oddly.

"Since when do you care about the environment?" asked Marushka.

"Since I found profit from that."

She turned away, trying to solve the puzzle of his words. One more gulp from his can for his soul. This would be a good party, one that he nearly skipped if it hadn't been for Marushka. By tomorrow, nobody would be able to recall what truly happened at the party, nor what Yezh did with the tin cans. They'd be too hung over to remember anything.

Chapter 10
Unwanted Attention

Feeling somewhat confident, Yezh went to see Joseph early the next day, and he offered his bags of tin cans. The man left his flames for his guest.

"Did you bring them?" asked Joseph.

"I did. Last night I was at the party, and I collected many tin cans. I haven't counted them, but there's a lot, that's for sure."

Yezh handed over the bag to Joseph, who calculated with his eye.

"That's a lot of tin. This is madness. I don't know what you're going to do with this much, but in my opinion, you may have to find a bit more if you intend to build a windmill or something."

"What? You think it won't be enough?" said Yezh.

"It might not be enough," answered Joseph. "It depends on how many thick sheets of aluminum you want."

Yezh didn't know how to obtain any more. He refused to wait an entire year doing nothing but collecting tin cans, which would stagnate the progress of his beyond-the-sky ship. It would be insane. By that time, he could have finished his ship a hundred times.

"I don't know where to find any more without losing too much time looking," said Yezh, expressing his desperation in action and voice.

"You may have to buy some materials. I think you're forgetting about the market—not very trustworthy, but worth trying. Or you may have to find bigger objects that contain more aluminum."

"Bigger?" repeated Yezh. "But what could be made of aluminum?"

What item could be so big? Yezh wondered, looking at Joseph's face like he knew the answer.

"If you look closely, you'll be able to find many things," said Joseph, who then planned to move forward with his work. "I'll start making these sheets for you, and meanwhile you search for more material. Before you go away, tell me one final time what dimension you want them to be."

Joseph grabbed his bag from the ground.

"Let's see. I want them to be thin enough to be malleable but thick enough to be resistant to scratch or puncture."

Yezh provided the dimension of the sheets, and there was nothing more that he needed from him other than some more of the raw materials. With what he had, Joseph was able to start.

After some hard thinking, Yezh remembered something with a great enlightened face.

"Oh! I got something. You're right! I forgot about that one!" Yezh showed surprise in his voice, his face enlightened.

Joseph had no idea what he was talking about, but he felt convince that the smart Yezh did find a cure to his problems. Yezh started to depart hastily with no word, but Joseph, called him once more with a smile on his face.

"Hey Yezh!" the man wheeled around to meet with his eyes. "You haven't told me yet what you are building!"

The slight smile on his face was a sign of great enthusiasm, one that someone would see on his best friend. Yezh smiled back with a friendly reply.

"You will love it!" And so, he bounded off for another place.

Joseph carried his bag over to the furnace to prepare the meltdown.

***

Yezh ran as fast as he could to reach Tatjana's place. If it weren't for the trash bags and containers sitting aligned on the corners of properties, he wouldn't have remembered it was trash collecting day, which meant that big Igor was bringing his garbage truck around, driving down the streets, and collecting junk to take to the junkyard. The oven was in his mind, and he clung to the hope that nobody had taken it away.

And when Yezh arrived at the corner and saw the truck standing there with Igor manipulating the oven, he screamed with all his might. Igor heard him yell and stopped to have a look.

The half-witted man did not understand what was going on but gave a chance for Yezh to take a breath and to explain to him.

Phoenix Phoenix

"Igor!" said Yezh, breathlessly. "I'll need that oven!"

Igor looked at the dead oven where there couldn't possibly be any life remained in it anymore and asked himself some questions.

"Why Yezh need this garbage?"

"No, that's not garbage," Yezh replied, brandishing a finger at Igor. "I want to keep this oven. I'm going to have to take this item to the blacksmith."

Igor seemed to understand him better now, and Yezh took a breath of relief. The guarantee of ownership of this broken oven was now assured: He had the oven for good now. Igor did not argue over it. Instead he offered him the honor of taking it out of the street.

"Yezh can take it. Igor don't mind at all. Less work for Igor."

"Thank you," said Yezh, who looked for a way to grab it.

"Why Yezh need it? This is broken oven," asked Igor.

"Yes … well …" said Yezh who, with his hands showing signs of letting pass such a question, tried to say something. "Recycling!" He let out a small short laugh, still a little bit breathless.

To prevent any more questions from Igor, Yezh asked for some help. "Say, can you help me to take this to Joseph's smithing shop?"

Igor was a kind man. Though he didn't have much brain power, his heart was full of kindness, and he had lots of muscles to support that.

He offered to help Yezh, though he was afraid of the mayor if he accumulated a lot of lateness in his work. Igor was currently working and had so many properties with junk laying around in the street, it was imperative for him to collect them all in a single day. But he was willing to take that chance for Yezh, since he had always been a good guy to him.

"Igor not sure if mayor will like this, but Igor will help Yezh to carry this."

"Thank you so much, Igor."

They grabbed it on each side and threw it in the back of the truck. Yezh hopped in the truck and they drove to the blacksmith.

First Farmer In Space

Whoever saw them dragging the machine in the street must have found them weird. Even Joseph barely kept himself from sniggering upon their arrival. But the poor Yezh, a brilliant man as always, was anxious to carry out his wishes. No matter how heavy it was, or how awkward, Yezh did not stray from his ambitious path, but he didn't quite know for sure what it was.

"What is this?" inquired Joseph, who looked at it to see if he could guess.

"It's an oven," said Yezh.

But Yezh did not want to say too much in front of Igor, so he thanked him gratefully, and Igor left to go back to his truck.

"It's made of aluminum. Think you can melt this thing?" said Yezh.

"It will be harder, but it can be done. I will need some time to break the material from what's junk, and it'll take some strong pliers to do that."

"Do you have such pliers?" asked Yezh, a little bit worried.

"Of course, I have. You never know when you'll need them in a blacksmith shop."

"Will this be enough do you think?"

"This will provide only a bit more aluminum. I will need more of this."

Yezh did not know where to search for any more.

"The good news is that I have successfully made your sheets."

"That fast?"

"Yes," said Joseph with self-confidence. "Want to see them?"

On the table was a pile of thick aluminum sheets.

"Here are your aluminum sheets, a total of five sheets, each with a thickness of a centimeter, and with a dimension of three meters by three meters."

Yezh calculated their dimensions, going through the numbers in his head. He wondered if he had reached a right amount.

Phoenix Phoenix

"This will be enough to cover only half my ship," Yezh whispered quietly to himself.

"Your … *what* …?" inquired Joseph, who misunderstood Yezh's whisper. But Yezh tried to correct his mistake. He'd always been a man who moaned a lot and got carried easily away by his complicated thoughts.

"Oh … uh … my windmill!"

"You're building a windmill? With aluminum?" said the confused Joseph.

"Ah you know, it gives a new look to it," replied Yezh, sweeping his hand.

Joseph grew wary of him, but he wouldn't dare disrespect him by saying that he suspects him of lying. He understood that whatever he was building was a secret. But it was harder to help him if he didn't know exactly what he was building.

"Will this be enough do you think?"

"I don't know for sure," replied Yezh. "I will need to find more, I think. Do you think I can buy raw aluminum?"

"Sure; it isn't that expensive, either. I won't speak for any villager here, but if you have a decent amount of money, you might put your hands on a fine amount of aluminum."

Cash has always been a worry for every villager in this poor village. With a government that collects a lot of wealth for communal security, and a country that barely escaped the starvation of a corrupt tsarist regime, people simply couldn't become rich with all these misfortunes of the past weighing on their shoulders. Apart from those who join the military or security forces, or a millionaire with a serious business outside Russia, for example in the case of Aleksei, a person can only become a bit better off than poor in Russia. No matter what Yezh did for his invention or lifestyle, he had challenges to overcome that took the best out of him.

Joseph could see the pain in Yezh's face from thinking about those wretched coins that he didn't possess. But Joseph found an argument to make him feel better, an undeniable fact.

"You have already collected a serious amount of aluminum. Which means that you saved a lot of money. Because of your hard work, you won't need to buy as much as you would have needed."

Yezh felt somewhat convinced and wouldn't lose any time going to the nearest shop to buy raw aluminum. But only if he had enough in economy.

"I will go back home to see if I can gather enough coins. Then I'll go buy some materials."

"While you're gone to find more of this, I will melt this oven carcass, and before you know it, you'll have another sheet or two."

***

Yezh arrived home with quiet feet.

His son was home. He didn't have school today but was doing his homework on a table, and Marushka wasn't around, which was kind of good for Yezh.

"Hey Father, what are you doing?"

"Nothing much."

Maks found his father very quiet, and that always meant that he was hiding something from his mother.

Yezh retreated inside his room, where he reached out for his bottle that he used to store his coins. It wasn't much, but he hoped that it'd be enough to buy whatever amount of aluminum he could carry. He collected good amount of his coins and aimed for the streets once more.

Maksimilian knew that it was shopping time. He could hear the coins clicking in his pocket.

"Where are you going?"

"I'm going to buy something at the corner."

"Can I come, too?"

"Nah, you don't have to. Keep doing your homework."

"Oh no, I'm done with homework. I want to come with you."

Sputnik wagged his tail for Yezh, being agitated too. He had enjoyed a nap on the chair next to where Maks was doing his homework. Sputnik had his fill of napping and playing with Maks and was up again, ready to tackle more activities.

"Even Sputnik wants to come with you," Maks insisted in his effort to persuade his father.

Yezh thought perhaps Maks could come; he could help carry the bags.

"Alright. Let's go!"

***

Makar loved his apple. He just bought it from a merchant and he could affirm that Leninsk produces the best apples in the Soviet Union.

"This apple tastes really good. I haven't eaten one like this for a very long time."

Rodion strolled by his side, studying the markets beneath tents placed all in a row. His accordion still put weight around his neck, but the man had gotten used to it.

The four musicians had been traveling around the village for two hours. They had good food and had good conversation with good people but hadn't heard any good music that would challenge theirs. They hadn't heard a note for a while now and grew weary of its absence. Life is truly boring without music.

Bogdan was up ahead from them, a little bit faster, and he saw a familiar person walking down the street—no—it was *three* familiar people, one of them being not so much of a person.

"Hey, it's Yezh!" said Bogdan.

"He must be going to the market, too," said Kiril.

"Looks like he brought his friends," said Makar.

"Look at that dog wagging his tail next to that boy. They must be happy to walk with their father," said Bogdan, pointing his finger.

"Now that you mention it, we rarely see those three together. The boy has been nagging his father for quite a while to do something with him," replied Kiril.

"I wish I had a good father like that," said Makar.

"I believe there is a song that reminds us of something that goes by three," said Rodion.

A short silence lasted between them as they thought about it.

"You're absolutely right, comrade," said Makar.

"Do you know what I'm thinking?" asked Rodion.

Everybody took up their instruments at same time Rodion spoke. They didn't need to be reminded what to do, nor which song Rodion had in mind. It was obvious!

On the count of three, they played another folklore song, all the while walking down the road following the three walkers.

"*Troika*?"

Probably the saddest song in Russian folklore, "*Troika*" starts off as a traditional Russian harness-driving combination of three horses used to pull a sleigh. The triplets, all with unique traits and personality, were harnessed abreast. It also was a peasant song related to the harshness of wintertime. In fairy tales, a farmer was said to have used three horses to gallop across frigid plains, which helped the peasant to reach his home before freezing to death. Soon after, it became a song that would bring one good luck when traveling by horses.

Afterward, it was used to describe the three leaders in the Soviet Union. Until today, a song that speaks of three is used to describe the legendary walk of these three identities.

***

The inseparable trio marched down the street, strolling along as the man who was lost in his thoughts, the boy who enjoyed spending every moment with his father, and the dog who never wants to let his master walk any road alone.

In front of the store, Yezh instructed Maksimilian to wait outside with Sputnik. Yezh entered, and the two friends sat down near the edge of the road, waiting for Yezh.

Phoenix Phoenix

Yezh had no idea what to look for but took a visit around the store. Too many things to see, no idea what was where in there—a typical Russian retailer store.

Luckily the clerk, a lovely lady in her twenties wearing an elegant scarf on her head, recognized him and offered him help.

"Yezh? Is that you?"

He knew who she was; theirs was a small village!

"Ilya! Good thing you are around."

She offered him guidance when he asked about aluminum foil. She mentioned that she wasn't sure if they have any. They ventured deep inside the store for quite a few minutes.

Maks was growing tired of waiting. Sputnik growled at passersby, and Maks had to hush him. If it wasn't for Sputnik's funny spectacle, he would have fallen asleep long ago—or died of boredom.

After a good while, Yezh came outside with a long roll of shiny material. With the roll in hand, Yezh did not risk his hide by showing himself back at home with that roll in his possession. Instead he went to drop it at Joseph's place. Recycling of the oven took more time than Joseph expected. Although the sheets were ready, Yezh would have to come back with his car to pick them up.

After that detour, they headed back home, where Marushka grounded them grumpily for having vanished from home all of a sudden with a devil or something.

***

Nobody was as eager as Yezh to work when he came back home. By the time Yezh returned to Joseph with his vehicle, more sheets were ready. What was prepared Yezh took home, which barely fit since Yezh didn't have any way to carry them for quick transportation, but his vehicle did the job right. Yezh believed that this was it—he had just acquired enough aluminum to skin his ship. Now he was ready to work.

At first, he took a moment to visualize what he wanted. Then he started to attach the sheet onto the wood planks with a hammer and some nails. Maksimilian and Sputnik decided to help him. Maks held the sheets while his father punctured them with nails and sealed them with a blow torch. Nearly half of the ship was covered, and Yezh was seeing it becoming something that looked like a machine.

They were very busy when suddenly a roaming engine neared their residence. It was a truck. Yezh immediately knew it was Igor, who came for trash. So, he interrupted his work and told Maks to be careful around his ship and not to touch anything while he was gone.

Yezh went in front of house. Igor was viewing the piles and piles waiting to be picked up. Igor's facial expression was priceless, and when Yezh neared him, the poor half-wit man gave his opinion.

"Yezh have a lot of garbage here."

"Well yes," laughed Yezh. "You know—accumulation over the winter."

Igor put his muscles to work, but Yezh, who felt pity for the man, couldn't let him work alone.

"I will help you," said Yezh. "It will be faster."

The two men had spent nearly ten minutes picking up the trash when suddenly Igor spotted a problem that his low-intelligence mind couldn't have realized earlier.

"Igor don't think this will fit in truck," said Igor. "Too much garbage. Sorry, Yezh. Truck is full."

"Oh, that's too bad!" said Yezh. He looked behind and saw that only half of his trash had been loaded. Some big pieces were still lying around: the water heater and more old, rotten wood planks.

"Igor must come back another day for the rest. Forgive Igor!"

"Ah, it's fine, Igor. Don't blame yourself. I'm the one to blame. When do you think you could come back?"

"Maybe tomorrow or next day," replied Igor. "If mayor is okay with it."

"That will do, my friend. Whenever you can," said Yezh. "I will try not to forget next time. Thank you for your hard work today, comrade."

Phoenix Phoenix

Igor left, and Yezh cursed the rest of the trash that littered the front yard. What would people think if they knew that the trash he had filled up the truck? People would start to call his residence a junkyard, and Marushka would turn even more red and angry!

Nothing could be done now. Yezh returned to his ship, where Maks and Sputnik were sniffling inside the ship. And so, the work continued from where he left it. The aluminum was nailed down and then slightly bent without much effort. These aluminum sheets, though they were thick, were very easy to bend. Almost all the superficies of the shuttle were covered within a few hours.

When Yezh went inside it, with the walls making it dark inside, Yezh could see that the ship was still spacious. There was still more to do in this machine. With Maks and Sputnik by his side, he didn't need to worry about time or hard tasks.

Next step was the wiring—the electronic part. Yezh had made the wiring and decided which part would be his cockpit. Lastly, he installed the aluminums walls around his ship from within. That was his procedure.

They worked until they were exhausted, but Maks had enjoyed every moment with his father. For him, inventing was just having fun. The ship was well developed, but a lot remained to be done.

They had worked enough for that day and decided to call it a day. To avoid rain or unwanted attention, Yezh had blanketed the ship. He regretted building it so exposed to the public, but even though the barn offered privacy, it couldn't have been done. There would have been no way to blast it through the ceiling, and it would have been extremely heavy to move around. What he needed to think about now was how to hide it, how to make a wall to protect his privacy. For today, enough progress had been made. A blanket would surely suffice for now.

***

The next morning, Maksimilian had a class like any other time, all boring, long, and hard to endure. They rarely did something fun in those walls, which he found to be torture. Their last exam was a disaster for all students. To counter that problem, Natalya chose to take a few minutes of their time to talk about employment, and she couldn't stress enough how important it was to study.

First Farmer In Space

"School is what makes a person who he is when he becomes an adult," said Natalya. "Since we all have parents who have jobs, how about we all present to the class what our fathers do for a living?"

She stared at faces who wondered who she would pick to speak first.

"Who wants to go first?"

After a long silence, one student raised his hand. Natalya offered him the spotlight.

"My father is a lawyer."

"Very good," replied Natalya, who forced her tone of voice to be pleasant. "That's a rewarding job. Without lawyers, people wouldn't know how to defend themselves in a court of law. What about you Valery?"

"My father works as a doctor," said Valery with some pride.

"Oh, that's great," said Natalya. "He must work hard to cure sick people in the hospital."

She randomly picked another student, scanning faces for who might present something unique.

"And you Maks? What does your father do in life?"

Maks only gurgled quietly, edgy about speaking up. But that didn't last long.

"My father is an inventor!"

"Inventor? Now that's something interesting," said Natalya. "What is he inventing?"

"Anything, really. Lately he has been inventing a new machine to fly!"

What he said raised snickering around the class—not necessarily mocking. It was just odd, an answer that nobody had expected to hear. Maks himself didn't anticipate such a reaction from other classmates because he found nothing funny about being an inventor.

"Well your father sure has a good sense of imagination," said Natalya behind a smile with a small giggle. "We all have interesting things to say about our fathers, don't we?"

Natalya next made her point. Some faces were pensive while other only remained attentive.

"As you see, our parents work hard every day to help us stay alive. Work is not easy, and finding a job is even harder. Therefore, studying well in class is imperative to earning a good living."

Natalya pursued her tutorial, an exhortation meant to stimulate their motivation: What you do in life dictates how you will live it.

Maksimilian thought what his mother told him about the hard, boring work his father didn't like. Should work be fun to do? It was something hard for a child like Maks to fathom. His father loved inventing more than anything else, and recently he got into sky exploration. That made his father happy, but what would Maks like to do one day? He'd probably need to figure something out because it seemed to him like age changes fast. Maks could only wish that his adulthood would never arrive to drag him into misery because what he hated the most in the world was to work.

***

"Comrades, I'm telling you it is a barn that he's making," said Bogdan, taking the first guess.

They were on the same old hill because they liked what they were seeing. Yezh's serious work was compelling to witness. They had been watching him for quite a while, and since the day before they'd witnessed huge improvements. Despite Bogdan's opinion, others rejected it with their own.

"Nah, it couldn't be that big," said Kiril. "It's something smaller."

"Smaller?" replied Bogdan, startled. "Like what?"

"I don't know. Maybe it's a tractor," replied Kiril with a grimace on his face.

"I bet it is a vegetable factory!" said Makar from a leisurely position, "something that will replace all the sweaty work in the field."

Makar's response raised great opposition. They talked it over, being loud as if they were having an argument. It was a silly idea. They knew that Yezh disliked hard labor, and that it would be something to serve him better, something to replace him in the field. But the purpose of it remained a mystery.

"No, you can't be serious, Makar," said Bogdan. "How much do you want to bet on that?"

"Hah!" Makar took out his wallet and threw paper money on the grass. "A hundred rubles!"

"You want to bet, Bogdan?" asked Makar defiantly.

"You think I'm going to chicken out on the offer?" said Bogdan, pulling out his wallet and throwing in his share—the same amount. "There you go. This is for the barn."

Makar mocked Bogdan's bravado. They both looked at Kiril who remained quiet, hesitant to bet what he had left in his pocket.

"I don't have much to bet." He took coins out and threw them down. "Fifty rubles!"

"That's it?" said Makar.

"I'm not going to bet my whole wallet."

"Rodion?" Makar turned to their last member.

"It's a machine of some sort. But what it is, I couldn't say." Rodion took a moment to muse.

He sensed that it would be something that would change the course of history; he could feel it but remained oblivious to its origin.

"I don't know," started Rodion. "I'll go for an airplane."

Rodion fetched his wallet and made it even for all. "There. Let's make it three times!"

Suddenly, Kiril got an idea.

"Oh, wait!" Kiril's face brightened. "It could be a tank!"

"Oh, come on, Kiril," mocked Makar with loud laughter.

Bogdan expressed his opposition, not believing what came out of Kiril's mouth.

Phoenix Phoenix

"Kiril, you silly Cossack!" Makar couldn't control his laughter. "Why would he need a tank in the countryside?"

Kiril reconsidered his options, his fingers on his chin. He could use it to fight off his neighbor—or simply to be the Hero of the Soviet Union by defending it from future invasions. "Perhaps that's a bit exaggerated," concluded Kiril.

"I'm staying with my vegetable factory," said Makar, completely positive about it.

"Same here. You will see that it will be a barn!"

"You're all like children. Let's just wait and see what it will grow into," concluded Rodion.

***

When Maks came back home, he caught his father near his ship—of course. He joined in his passion. The next few hours, Yezh showed his son various parts of the ship he had installed while he was at school. It was mostly electrical parts that fascinated Maks as great wonders.

Yezh had to build and rebuild some parts but nothing too hard. He'd finish building something only when he had a feel for it, a feeling that it was right.

Maks even had the honor of being shown his father's cockpit. Maks liked the ladder he used to climb to the cockpit. There were still some cables hanging around, unconnected to devices. Each device on his ship was to have a specific role, but many of them were not assigned. Yezh still had no idea about one important device that his ship should be equipped with.

Yezh spotted something wrong on the wall while inspecting it with his son: a small corner of aluminum was bent because a screw wasn't placed properly. He took a hammer and knocked it straight and tightened the screw. Occasionally, whenever he saw a flaw on his ship, he tightened something up, or aligned it. It was very technical and advanced for little Maks, but he liked it. The precious moment between them was engraved in his mind.

A boy who passed by Yezh's house was attracted by the banging of the hammer. Seeing something shiny and big in the backyard, the boy carefully approached the fence and peeked without being seen. He could imagine the object, but its odd features clearly shocked him. Roundish shape, shiny walls, pointy roof—it was something he had never seen before. The kid was awed by it, whispering out loud some words of amazement.

It was big, and he knew it had to be something important. So, he ran off into the streets, mindlessly running into people along the way, making a neighbor fall when he stormed a corner that led directly to the peasants' square.

Quick on his feet, the boy ran to the streets and into the peasants' square and reached for his mother, who was talking with several other women where merchants bargain with clients.

"Everybody!" said the breathless kid. "Yezh is building something new this time."

The women, who were deep in conversation, were bothered by the agitated boy. Other merchants nearby gave a look at the boy.

"Oh child, that man is always building something," said his mother.

"It's big—very big!"

A few people did not care what Yezh could be building. Others focused their attention on the news. Since it was a small town where everybody knew each other like a family, they felt the need to know more about Yezh and his inventions. Only a few people knew the potential in that man's handicraft.

"Big?" said the woman. "What could he be creating so big?"

"Could it be an electrical windmill?" said a woman with long, curly black hair.

"Maybe a floating car?" said a short, blonde-haired woman.

By now their curiosity had grown into interest.

"I definitely need a new windmill with electrical upgrades," said the long, curly black-haired woman.

"I have always dreamed of taking a ride in a flying car," said the next.

"If he's building a new oven for my pastries, then I'll be damned," said a baker who overheard the loud ones.

"Or a new machine that slices meat for me!" said a butcher who was cutting a slice for one of his customers.

They talked among each other, questioning the purpose of the invention. It wasn't every day that Yezh built something as huge as the boy claimed. They let their imaginations gain control of their minds, each finding their own dream machine to help them in their lifestyle.

Their change of heart convinced the people to go for a walk.

"I want to go see it now," said the mother, who thought about it and boldly made up her mind to go see.

"Yeah. Let's go see Yezh."

Soon, one by one they were convinced enough to march down the road to Yezh's house.

***

Yezh and Maks had been working like ants. Maks helped him finish skinning it outside after his father connected a few cables and moved inside to build its interior. All the while, they were oblivious to a crowd gathering by the fence. The loud gossip disturbed the neighbors within their houses—meaning Marushka and Katenka.

When Katenka alarmed Ivan about the newcomers, he quickly jumped to his feet and tackled the back door. There was no time to rest. This was something for which to skip his fifteen-minute break, something he had to inspect.

It had been a while since anybody looked at the shuttle which Yezh was building. Even Ivan, who finished his field work long ago, had taken some moments of rest after flea market visits. All these hours he was away from home, he also missed information on Yezh's side.

At noon, when the day became warmer and the people started walking to their work and shopping, many of them gathered curiously at the front fence of Yezh's residence to see what they could see of something large and flashing the sunlight's mighty rays. A big object made of aluminum captured their sight. They could see it was in progress.

The people—men and women—were pointing fingers and talking

among each other about what this mysterious object could be.

"What is that over there?"

"I don't know."

"It's nothing like I've seen before."

"It looks like a missile of some sort."

"It could be a radio station or a satellite."

"I don't think so. It appears to have wings down there. You see?"

That was important information they had witnessed. It had to be something made to be mobile.

Marushka, who spent her time inside doing housework after doing intense physical work in the field the day before, wasn't paying too much attention to the outside world. The commotion outside drew her to the windows. She followed everybody's pointing fingers and stares.

This is bad, thought the woman, exactly what she had feared.

Yezh stood outside of the shuttle after hours of dedication to it. Its general appearance was satisfying. The ship was nearly completed, and various components were already attached to it. The boy was glad to have nearly finished building the ship with his father. It was genuinely majestic. Yezh thought of blanketing it again and hiding it from the world.

Voices caught their attention from their rear. The people around their fence were another problem they needed to deal with. Were they envoys of Ivan, seeking to know more about his invention? Yezh expected such things from his neighbor. It would happen just when he was about to blanket it again to hide it from sight. He approached his fence with diplomatic manners, like he had nothing to hide.

"Yezh, what are you building there? Is that some kind of machine?"

"Yes, it is!"

"It's really big this time. It has to be something very important."

"What is it for? It looks like it can fly. It has wings," asked a man holding a pitchfork.

Yezh peeked behind him. Indeed, those small wings at the base of the ship were giving away clues. Yezh hoped it wouldn't be that obvious.

"Is it a new machine that flies?"

Was it a lucky guess or some kind of quest for knowledge? How would they behave if they knew it would be a beyond-the-sky travelling machine? Yezh could only hold his breath when he thought of Marushka's face. He blushed.

That's when Maks came in. The boy spoke out boldly to their visitors.

"Yeah, it is. My father is planning to fly in that machine to the sky where stars live!"

Yezh was too slow to prevent his son from speaking up, but it was too late. He could only squint as his mouth closed.

"A ship for the stars' dwelling place?"

"That's something new."

Unexpectedly, people remained almost indifferent to the news, as if it were normal to create a star ship. It was like they had been waiting all this time to hear when a star ship would be built.

"Unfortunately, it's not yet finished, so talking about it would be premature," responded Yezh to reassure the crowd. "Not to mention that it hasn't been tested yet."

"But it is good to know that you are tackling something challenging," said the woman. "Just let us know when it will be finished. I really want to see you flying off."

Yezh didn't know what to say because he wasn't listening closely, being afraid of his wife. Yezh hoped to see this conversation and crowd dissipate into the streets and occasionally peeked at the windows of his house, smiling as if he had no other things to hide.

"Well, I don't mind …"

"Yeah that would be fun if you let us know, sir," said another man who interrupted his reply.

First Farmer In Space

These pleas made Yezh accept they were praising and had a good opinion of him. Where was the mockery?

Yezh walked away with Maksimilian by his side. The crowd wouldn't dissipate by itself.

"You shouldn't have said that. It was supposed to be a secret."

The ship was blanketed for the night. The stress almost made him forget about it, and they went inside their home. Yezh didn't know if he'd be working again later, but the darkness dampened his ambition.

***

"I knew it," said Rodion. "I knew it was something to fly." He nearly jumped for joy. His fist whipped the air above him.

"Misery! It turned out to be a ship!" said Kiril.

"Ah, I was wrong," said Bogdan.

"It's not even a vegetable factory," said Makar, who threw the rest of his money on the grass. He was disappointed at the choice he made.

"Good thing that I bet only fifty rubles," commented Kiril.

"You mean that's all you had in your pocket? You couldn't have lost much anyway," replied Makar.

There was still money on the grass. All but one guessed wrong, leaving only one victor—and a sole acclaimer. "That means I won," said Rodion.

"Yeah, but you said a new airplane. You didn't give the right answer, so that means you don't keep the money," replied Makar.

"Yes, he's right!" Bogdan said in support.

"Argh!" Rodion pounded his fist into the ground. "I almost had the right answer. Almost!"

"That means we get to keep our money."

All four of them collected back what was rightfully theirs before the bet.

***

Phoenix Phoenix

It was time to rest inside their home, partly because Yezh wanted to shake off a little bit of the attention, but he knew he owned Marushka an explanation when he saw her coming away from the front windows.

"What was that all about?"

"They wanted to know what I was building."

"I knew this would happen," said Marushka with worry in her voice. "Your idea is going to get us laughed at for as long as we live."

"They seemed interested in a good way, I must admit," said Yezh, trying to show optimistic belief.

"They're all wearing faces of innocence until you turn your back on them." She walked away, unable to make that thought sink into his mind.

Meanwhile, Ivan was also peeking from his windows, watching as the gathered crowd dissipated from the front yard of Yezh's domicile. He knew all along that his secret wouldn't remain a secret for too long. He enjoyed the way Yezh was dealing with his fame, for the good or for the bad, Ivan knew only negative things would come from that strange neighbor that he seemed not to have laughed enough at.

Chapter 11
A Name for a Legend

After consoling Marushka from worrying too much about their reputation in the village for the next few hours, it was time to go to sleep.

Yezh accompanied Maksimilian to his bed and tucked him in under his blankets.

"Father, are you really going to the moon when the ship is completed?" asked Maks in the silence of the night, but a faint whistling roars came from the window.

"That's a dream, Maks. Dreams stay only dreams. What you do and how you do it is what makes a change."

"People say that nobody ever went to the moon," said the boy. "Are you going to be the first person to walk on the moon?"

Yezh had the feeling that he'd be forced to chat a bit with Maks, and so he sat on the bed. He searched his words.

It was a good question that even Yezh wasn't sure of. "Who knows? I hope that it'll be me."

"What kind of place is beyond-the-sky?"

Yezh structured his idea with a small pause, and he told him everything he knew about the enigmatic far-fetched environment being a mysterious, endless height of some sort as the sky continues to spread to the horizon of existence. Though he didn't know much himself, it nonetheless fascinated the kid.

"Does the sky really go to infinity?" asked Maks, his eyes big from interest.

"There's only one way to find out. Someone will have to fly up there to see it for himself."

Yezh smiled to Maks and told him to go to sleep. Tomorrow would be a big day. He got up, went to the door, and was about to turn off the light when is son spoke again: "I hope you'll fly to the moon very soon."

With another smile, he turned off the light then closed the door.

Phoenix Phoenix

Maks took his comfortable position for sleep. The night became slightly windier. He heard the howling winds near his window. Although scary to his ears, it brought him his slumber like a lullaby.

Yezh went to his bedroom where Marushka was already prepared to sleep if it wasn't for the lamp still turned on.

"Don't make him believe anything that will never happen," his wife warned.

"I haven't. The boy already believes in me. I simply told him good night."

Everybody went to bed, but Yezh desperately tried to find sleep.

***

He wasn't sure what time it was, but he had awakened in the middle of the night. At this point there would be no sleep for the daydreaming Yezh, and he knew it all too well. He was fully awake and already dreaming. After endlessly turning sideways in his bed, lost on his road to the land of dreams, he left the bed for the back door where the large window gave him the pleasure of looking at the moonlight. The old floor cracked with each of his steps.

The first thing he saw about his wonder in the backyard was that the blanket was on the ground. The wind must have blown it off the ship, revealing the shiny properties of its bottle-like shape. It was a clear sky, and the stars were scintillating high above the sky ship patiently waiting on the ground for its first liftoff. The night was quiet and dark, but the moonlight silhouetting the shapes and edges made it all look mystical.

Yezh's eyes were fixated on the ship, but the bright shining properties of the stars drew his eyes like a magnet. *They are beautiful*, thought Yezh. Looking back at his shuttle, he could almost recall seeing stars reflecting on the aluminum body. The moonlight added only a shiny edge where it overwhelmed all other lights. He knew at that moment that they both—he and the ship—had the same vision and dream. They were both talking the same language that no one else understood. They spoke the star language and were meant to fly to the stars until the stars start to cry with showers.

Then Yezh thought of something: Why has he been referring to it as *beyond-the-sky?* Shouldn't it have a name? He didn't like referring to something nameless, so he thought of giving it a name. Did someone already give it a name? Yezh, who learned to speak Greek at a young age, decided to fetch it a Greek or Latin name.

Maksimilian heard noises in the kitchen and woke up. He knew it was his father who had walked by his room, and he got up to have a look. His footsteps, quiet as the night, took him to witness the same beauty as his father. He stood by the large window where the moonlight cast a hue over his face and front body while the rest remained shadowed by the darkness of the room.

"Aren't you sleeping, Father?"

Yezh tilted his head to see who was talking but returned to his primary attention.

"I'm not sleepy tonight," said Yezh, who showed weariness in his tone. "How can I sleep when a dream is boiling inside my mind?"

Maksimilian understood what he meant and walked by his father to look at the ship where a long silence was established. Yezh asked his son to share the reasons for his own insomnia.

"Why did you get up? You should be sleeping."

"I heard noises, so I wanted to see what it was."

"I just came to look at the ship."

Maks also took a moment to observe what his father was. And at the time he never imagined that this moment would be engraved in his mind for the rest of his life until he became old and reminisced about his beloved father.

"I just can't believe it—that I am just a few days away from reaching my dreams if everything goes as planned."

Maks did not interrupt him as he believed that his father had many interesting things to say. Their conversation paused for a while.

"In a few days, I'll be flying up high," said Yezh, who didn't take his eyes off the moon, his deep thoughts still in an oasis in his mind. "And I'll be walking on that moon up there."

Maks grew sad from the words that made his father happy, as the young boy saw the situation differently. He couldn't imagine his father gone for a moment. For each of those seconds he would be thinking about him. From his class and the culture of other people he learned that beyond-the-sky was a frightening place with no flight and no return.

"Say Father—are you going to leave us soon?" said the boy as if he would be leaving him for good.

"I'm going to see what it looks like out there, and then I'll come back here. I won't stay there for too long. Just a few steps on the moon won't hurt," said Yezh, not without a moral reason. "You see, that is my dream. Every man has a dream in his life."

Yezh looked back at his ship, and Maks couldn't take his eyes away from his father, still fearing the possibilities.

"The other day, I read from the newspaper that a scientific research lab found out that beyond-the-sky is an uncharted location. That there is no north or east, that there is no up and down, left or right."

Maks was puzzled by this discovery. The boy simply had no idea how someone could travel somewhere if there is no direction.

"So where is the moon? How do you know where to go when there are no directions?" asked Maks.

"That's silly," said Yezh, who gave him a friendly pat on the head, "but still a good question. You see, the moon is up there." He pinpointed the moon with his finger. "I just have to go straight with the ship until I bump into the moon."

"Bump into the moon?" repeated Maks.

Maks started to imagine the ship bumping into the moon, and it seemed goofy the way he had imagined it, like something that he'd seen in a cartoon on television.

It was the lack of direction that frightened Maks. Imagine a world with no direction whatsoever. How could a person find his way home if there is no north? How many people would be lost every day if it weren't for direction? Even the compass wouldn't work if there was no north. What would it point at?

As much as he wanted to see his father walk on the moon, it scared him a lot to think how he'd find his way back if the beyond-the-sky is an uncharted place and anyone can get lost out there!

"How are you going to come back then if there is no direction?"

"I don't know yet for sure, but I suppose that I have to go straight toward the earth. Perhaps that will be easier than I thought."

The notion of finding his way back struck his mind like a meteorite: a problem that he hadn't thought about yet.

"Or harder than I thought: Is earth a bright, shiny planet at night?" Yezh started to talk to himself, asking question a bit too scientific for little Maks. How would he see where the earth is if it isn't a bright object in the sky at night? He even came to wonder how the lunar people see the earth at night, and this greatly puzzled him even more. Indeed, this would be a problem for his return.

Maks saw only worry on his father's face.

"I'm scared, Father. I don't want you to get lost in the sky." Maks snuggled his face in Yezh's pajamas. His sobs could be heard drowning him in sorrow. "How can you come back if you can't even know where earth will be in the sky?" Yezh barely heard his words coming out from his pajamas.

"Don't be sad, Maks. Father will come back to you. It's a promise!"

This comforted his son's spirit.

"That's a dangerous job you are undertaking! Do you have to do it?"

Yezh didn't know how to respond to him without making him sad. He understood the risk that he was running but was not willing to abandon what he believed to be an opportunity.

"That's a risk that a man must take for a dream," said Yezh with great serenity. "Every man has a dream. Should he be deterred by fear, he will never have a chance to grasp it. It may be a perilous journey, but I will have to devote my entire life to this machine. I'm definitely sure that this machine will help me to fulfill my dreams!" Yezh said the last sentence with great pride as if by doing so he was assured of success.

Maks didn't know what Yezh was trying to prove to the world.

What could the moon have to attract his father's attention? Could there be treasure? A new field to farm?

"What happens if you do walk on the moon? What could be there worth going there for?"

"Son," Yezh started, "could you imagine yourself in a world, probably in twenty years from now, in a time where everybody would know and talk about your father and how he was the first farmer to go beyond the sky?"

Maks looked him deeply in the eyes, moonlight glittering in his dark eyes as if he were already seeing him as a superstar.

"I am trying to be the first person in history to prove to the world that it is possible to do the impossible," said Yezh. "Who knows, if I manage to prove to everybody that we can fly among stars, maybe you'll be able to walk on the moon one day too, son."

Maks tried to find solace in that reasoning, but nothing seemed more important than his father.

"Would you like to go to the moon too?" asked Yezh.

Maks nodded his head positively. The boy thought his father had a strange dream, a very dangerous one. Would his own dream one day be as dangerous? Would it be as big as his father's? Today Maks did learn something about dreams—about their size and shape and the intensity they emit, that it is at time exciting and frightening.

He asked himself a question and then said it out loud: "I wonder what kind of dream I will have one day?"

"You'll eventually find it, and when you do, you'll have to fight for it. Dreams don't come by themselves. They are like the moon: you must come to them—to reach for them. Remember what I did. If I manage to do this, perhaps I will finally prove to the entire world—to everybody—that dreams can come true."

Yezh cuddled his son to comfort him. He hoped Maks would forgive him for being the kind of father he was and that he would always love him no matter what. Yezh could only hope that everything he was going to do would have only a significant positive effect on Maks, to stir up some dream or inspiration.

First Farmer In Space

"You could have plenty of dreams. There are"—Yezh tried to find a number, but any number was unrealistic, so he had to express the amount indefinitely— "plenty of dreams out there, waiting to be grasped by someone."

Maks watched as Yezh did an imitation with his fist as if he was grasping something tightly.

"It depends who's going to be first. No matter what kind of dream you undertake, no matter what happens, you must believe in your dreams. But most importantly, you must believe in yourself." Maks started to see what his father was seeing in his mind and began to think about his own dream. One thing Yezh did that inspired Maks was to talk about the unlimited, infinite possibilities of dreams. But Maks seemed a bit lost in his father's long-winded exhortations about dreams. Yezh knew he had spoken too much already. Maks seemed lost, but for Yezh there was something fundamental concerning his son that he needed to be assured of.

"Promise me that you'll never give up on your dreams."

Maks agreed to his kind words of wisdom, and then they both continued gazing through the window, enjoying the priceless moment as father and son.

Yezh looked at the peak of his shuttle until he could no longer see the ground. As he stared at what he saw as the ship swimming among the ocean of stars, he felt as if he was seeing it in action, in a dimension where time stood still. It was a timeless and motionless sight of the stars and dark sky. Everything fitted perfectly. Such a wonderful combination of themes. Even Maks found it magical the way the ship shined brightly with stars surrounding it.

"The stars," said Maks with amazement, "they're beautiful."

Yezh had been calling it a beyond-the-sky shuttle or a star ship, and sometimes he'd forget what to call it. Maks found it hard to talk about something that has no identifying name.

"Father," said Maks.

"Yes, what is it?"

"What do you call this machine?" asked Maks.

"A star ship!" replied Yezh.

"I know it's a ship. I meant—what's its name?" Maks reformulated. Yezh was puzzled by his question and didn't understand what he wanted to know.

"What do you mean by a name? I think star ship explains it just fine," said Yezh.

"This ship must have a name like any of us, a name that makes it different from any other star ship."

Now Yezh understood the question and quickly shuffled the letters in the words.

"I think I'm going to call it ..." He paused as if he wanted to think about it one last time. "Soyuz."

Maks did not respond yet, but Yezh was curious to know his opinion.

"What do you say about Soyuz?" He threw a look at Maks, who didn't know any reason for picking that name. To him it was an unoriginal name, a name that only old people would give to something.

"Why Soyuz?" asked Maks.

"Why, it is a dignified glorification of our country," said Yezh, but he found another reason just to make them aplenty. "Because Soyuz means unity, and that name would make all humans around the world feel united as one. Science is a tough subject, and I believe that two heads are better than one. We live in a world that is divided between east and west. If the world can't be united in politics, then it should be united in science. Just imagine how far we'd go as united people. Perhaps Soyuz will be that inspiration and the connection."

"Yes, Father, sure it will, but the name sounds a bit too serious and boring."

"It needs to be serious, lad. Science is a serious thing." Yezh switched his attention to the second defaming adjective that he heard. "And boring? Since when a name can be boring?"

Maks hadn't thought of it that way. Because of his youth, he didn't know how to say it in other words.

"It should have a fun name that is beautiful to hear," he added to his explanation.

"Like what?" asked Yezh.

Maks searched for a name in the silence between them. The silence of the night was pronounced, and one more thing that was pronounced in the contrast was Sputnik's loud snore. It seemed so abnormal that Maks had to see where it was coming from, but all he could see was Sputnik sleeping sweetly in his doghouse. Maks adored the dog and couldn't resist its cuteness. Even when he went back to the idea of naming the star ship, he couldn't ditch the image of the dog from his mind. Then the idea came to him.

"We could call it … *Sputnik*," said Maks in a low tone.

"Why would you give such a great thing a dog's name?"

"It's a good name. What's wrong? Don't you like Sputnik?"

"Of course. I love him."

"Then why would you break his heart by saying such a thing?" asked Maks. "Besides, the ship will be your only companion in space. Naming it *Sputnik* might be a name that would bring you good luck."

A good luck-bringing name interested Yezh, and the kid did make sense. In a hostile place such as beyond-the-sky, since he'd said that he would devote his life and security to his ship, seeing it as a companion might make him feel less lonely.

"*Sputnik* …" whispered Yezh. "Fine. *Sputnik* it shall be!"

Yezh looked in Maks' eyes and, with a smile, hugged him closer to him. The father and son continued to enjoy the quiet night.

Chapter 12
A Problematic Truth

Mornings were cold, but Yezh was getting used to it. Being an early bird because of his invention, he was up from bed and into his ship. The big part of the ship was done. What remained were only small components that he felt that his ship needed. His eyes never had enough of the aluminum beauty of it. He was simply proud of his new invention.

Every morning Ivan took a walk around his garden to see how his new sprouts were faring. But Yezh doubted that was his true intent, thinking that he was doing it for propaganda, for a hungry curiosity for news. That man only wanted to know everything: everything that you do, everything that you say, everything that you think—and in bad ways. It seemed that only bad news interested Ivan. He'd collect information only to divulge it to others. If you turned your back on him, he would start to talk about you. That's who Ivan was: a propaganda lover.

Coincidentally, the two men met outside over the fence.

"So, it ended up being a ship to fly?" inquired Ivan over the fence. It was as if he had been waiting for Yezh to appear. Was it that hard to have a rough, easy guess? In any case, Yezh sighed at his futile efforts. He tried to keep his cool intact from provocation. There was no need to hide it from him. He only needed to deal with him boldly. Sooner or later, everyone had to know. You couldn't really hide anything from people in this village—even if he had built his ship in the barn.

"Yes. It's my new dream."

"I must say you've done a very big job there," remarked Ivan with an expression on his face, being everything but truly impressed.

Yezh wasn't sure if that was a compliment. It was unusual to hear one coming from that man.

"Is it a new type of flying machine? Its looks quite different from an airplane. Do you think it's going to work?" asked Ivan.

"There's only one way to find out."

"Neighbor, you know that's what the Greek believed until he fell down and realized men aren't meant to fly. He built a pair of wings and took flight. They said that the sun was so hot that all the oil melted away from his feathers. The poor Greek found himself on the ground again." Ivan then switched his attention to Yezh's version of the birdman challenge. "What I don't understand is why you haven't made it the same shape as the original ones?"

"Ah, I'm going to give it a different type of flight."

"What kind of flight?"

"One that will take me someplace where nobody has ever flown."

"Where are you thinking of going? That thing is aiming directly up to the sky. You aren't planning on going straight up, are you?"

"I'm planning on going as far as the sky reaches above us," said Yezh. "I want to break that record. I want to fly beyond the sky!" Yezh pointed at his ship with his thumb.

"Beyond what? What did you call it?" asked Ivan who began laughing. "Neighbor, we call it space. That's the universal name. As for a proper name, it doesn't have any. You can call it the universe if you like, too."

Space ... whispered Yezh in thoughts. How could he have not thought about that one before? But that wasn't really a name. He still needed to give it a name. Anyway, that wasn't his main concern here.

"It's almost completed," Yezh continued. "I just need to attach some components and it'll be ready to fly. I'm still thinking over the engine matter."

"Neighbor!" Ivan started, who didn't know how to put it. "Even if you manage to build whatever you need to add, you have no idea what *beyond the sky* looks like."

Normally, Yezh would never lend an ear to Ivan for anything. But this time—today—he found himself obliged to listen to this man's story.

"It was a talk they had on the radio. Of course, you don't have one, so I know you couldn't know anything about that, but I've heard what some scientists have claimed it to be."

Yezh knew he didn't have a radio and being reminded of that wasn't proving anything that Ivan said. All it did was to provoke Yezh. Instead of continuing to feel dismay toward the man, his mind quickly cooled down when he thought about what scientists had discovered about the sky.

"What did you hear from scientists?" asked Yezh, his anger controlled.

"That it is a very dangerous place. They tried to do research on it with some machines and discovered that where the sky ends there no more atmosphere. They say it's the end of the world and nothing exists on the outside."

"You mean there's no air?"

"We aren't too sure about that, but the test confirmed that the sky isn't endless. They say that space is also a very dark place at night. "

Yezh tried to digest the knowledge. He couldn't have guessed anything of that sort.

"Really? All my life I have believed that the sky is endless."

"We all believed that. And you know what? Believe it or not, many people still believe it is like that. What do you expect from farmers? We are stupider than a pig."

The sky proved to be more mysterious than Yezh thought. So-called *space* is an uncharted place, and nobody truly knows what it looks like: that much he was able to understand by himself. Yezh knew nothing about space, but this only fueled his will to fly so he could witness something new.

Could Ivan be right about it? What if there is no air to breathe? How is it possible to fly a machine in an airless place, not to mention that he also needs air to breathe?

"That is worth taking into consideration. You really believe those stories to be correct?" asked Yezh.

"I've never been there myself, but I heard some philosophers claiming space is a void of some sort. Most of them were inaccurate, so I don't really believe in science and philosophy anymore."

Great, now we must be concerned about what philosophers believe in their scientific, curious, rebellious minds. Could there be more to space than meets the imagination? Yezh took solace in the fact that nobody has ever seen it before and contemplated that he needed to see it in person to understand it. To the hatred he had of admitting that Ivan was right, he added willingness to tackle any hardship that space might throw at him.

"If that is true, then I'll need a reservoir of air," he said, nodding to the spaceship behind him.

"You see, you can't fly up there if there is no air! You'll run out of air. It's like if you try to explore the bottom of an ocean without an air supply," said Ivan, still not finished with supplying facts. "Maybe it's even impossible to fly where air is nonexistent."

"Maybe you are right," said Yezh. "Thanks for teaching me about space."

Yezh walked away from the fence with a sad expression on his face.

Ivan thought maybe he finally brought some sense to that crazy old man. There was no way he was competent enough to invent such a smart idea. He was just dreaming. If Ivan couldn't do it, neither could Yezh!

Yezh strolled around his ship, his hand on his chin, thinking hard about this new problem. He found it funny to think about how to contain air in a reservoir. You can't just hold onto air somewhere. Having to contain it elevated the bar of complication. How could he do it? The idea of some sort of tank for air popped into his head. What object could he use as a tank?

As he walked toward his house while desperately trying to think of what he could use as a container, he sighted his junk pile.

Damn, that junk pile is still standing in front of our house.

His anger flared up again. The junk reminded him of Igor's promise. He would be back soon to finish the job. Then his eyes caught something. Standing on top of the trash, the white aluminum tank shone under the sun.

"That's it! The water heater would be perfect for the purpose!" whispered Yezh.

He hurried to the front of the house and thoroughly studied the tank. Upon inspection, the water tank seemed thick and resistant to pressure, solidly built, and multipurposed. Yezh was proud of his nation for inventing reliable standard objects.

Yezh pulled the tank away from the pile of junk. He first thought it had to be cleaned thoroughly until it sparkled. It would be used for an air supply, so Yezh thought that it needed to be sanitary, disinfected. He had a bottle of disinfectant somewhere but couldn't remember where. Maybe Marushka moved it when she cleaned the house a few weeks ago.

He turned to call for her. "Marushka!" The woman arrived at the back door.

"Do you know where the disinfectant is?"

"Disinfectant?" Marushka wondered what purpose he'd need it for. "It should be in the kitchen's armoires. It was in the bathroom. I had to move it, so it wouldn't get lost."

"Good. Can you bring it?" asked Yezh. "I need it now."

She hurried to the armoires, opened them one after another, and grabbed the bottle that sat inside. She returned to Yezh in wonderment. Handing over the half-filled bottle, she saw the useless broken water tank. She remembered it had been thrown in the trash.

"What are you doing with that junk? I thought you threw it away."

"I did. And took it back."

"What use do you have for it? It won't work for to supply water anymore."

"It may not work for that purpose, but I've found it a new one."

She was puzzled as to what purpose he was talking about but left him to play whatever game he wanted. As long as he did his work in the field, she was passive about the rest.

The tank was big and almost too heavy for a single person to lift, but with a little support from tables and ladders, he was able to attach it onto the ship. He had made sure that no leak would come from the tank. Among the objects he had thought of using, this tank was by far the most closed and resistant. He installed a psi gauge that he had sitting in his shack. Then came the job for the air compressor to pump it up to maximum capacity. He spent the next hour testing it for leaks and potential problems. The inner ship was receiving its air supply. It was working.

Yezh stepped down and back from the ship for a general view. The sight of it holding on was charming. It fitted the ship perfectly as if it was meant to be part of it.

The ship was completed. Ivan needed to see this!

Chapter 13
A Flawed Ship

Once more Yezh approached the fence with a smile on his face, thinking that he had finally solved the most challenging problem. He saw Ivan in his barn, shoveling straw anew.

"Neighbor," said Yezh to gain his attention so he would come near the fence to talk. "Sorry to bother you in your work. Look at my ship this time!" said Yezh happily. "I've improved it."

Ivan was able to see what was different with the ship—the tank on the side.

"You attached an air supply tank to it?" He peeked at it and could clearly see a white tank on the back of the ship. "You *did* attach an air supply!"

Look at that; this guy really did something to solve the air problem, Ivan thought. How Yezh pulled that one off was a mystery.

"You attached a tank … Wait a minute …" Taking a second look at it, Ivan said, "Is that a water tank you have there?"

"Brilliant, isn't it?" exclaimed Yezh. "I solved the air problem. Now I'll be able to fly up."

"Wait, wait, wait a minute!" said Ivan harshly. "You don't think that putting some old broken water tank for an air supply is going to solve everything?"

"What do you mean?" asked Yezh, his confusion renewed. "It looks perfect in my opinion."

"Because it's your opinion. Your ship has too many flaws, I'll bet."

"What kind of flaws do you see?"

"Well look at it!" Ivan pointed at something, and Yezh followed the gesture. "You have holes on it everywhere. Even if you do have a tank, you haven't welded it carefully. All the air will escape from it."

How Ivan saw holes on his ship from that distance Yezh didn't known. He couldn't force his eyes to see any better. This man has the eyes of a hawk or maybe like a wolf. He has many eyes, even behind his head, deadly eyes, Yezh thought as he gulped.

"Look at that; I hadn't noticed that."

But he did understand what Ivan meant by holes. The joints he'd attached weren't completely sealed. Yezh left the fence with an idea in his head. To that, Ivan shook his head. He walked away to his barn again to add some more new straw for his livestock.

As usual, Yezh went to work right away. He improved the skin layer, covering any gaps left previously for a solid seal by welding. He got the job done with a blowtorch and some leftover aluminum.

A better way popped into his head. Yezh had the brilliant idea to release the air within the ship. With the hatched closed, he stood outside and approached with his ears and hands to feel any air leak or sounds. It worked like a charm since it was easier to find where they were. It took a long time to inspect for small gaps until he was sure it was completely sealed.

Yezh believed this would handle the atmospheric problem. He thought about what Ivan said, and wondered if there were more hidden problems that he was not aware of. He couldn't think of anything yet because of his intense excitement. He wanted only to go back to Ivan to show him his newly improved ship.

His neighbor did, after all, see good points despite being so negative about it. Yezh tried to think what other flaw he might have missed. His eyes weren't trained for that, and he couldn't see any flaws. Ivan surely had his own skills of sight. After failing to find any new hidden flaws, he had the marvelous idea of going back to Ivan to ask him again about his ship. He saw that this ship was getting on Ivan's nerves and that Ivan was constantly trying to hinder him. He didn't want Yezh to fly, which was why he was trying to find flaws. So, the smart Yezh had the idea to use his criticisms as a method for finding all the flaws.

Good thinking, Yezh. Now let's go see your horrible, pessimistic neighbor, thought Yezh.

Chapter 14
A Guiding Light

Yezh went back to the fence. Ivan had just finished shoveling straw in his barn, and once again the duo met up.

"Neighbor, I can't see any more holes," said Yezh with subtle sarcasm, his hand on his chin, trying to hide his smile. "Can you see any?"

Ivan looked from top to bottom, scanning every bit of the ship.

"You did a good job there I can see." Ivan responded.

Ivan couldn't believe it. Again, Yezh prevailed in solving a problem. His face was saddened for a moment. Then he thought he found another flaw on the ship that he hoped would discourage Yezh from continuing with his dream. A devious smile appeared on his face.

"You think that solving the problem of air by attaching a tank on your ship and sealing holes is going to make you fly up there? You don't see the problem, do you?"

"Like what? Why you think my ship won't be able to fly?"

"Well look at it," said Ivan, still pointing his hand at the ship. "How can you see where you are going up there when I don't see any light anywhere?"

Ivan's head moved left and right, trying to see a light, but Yezh looked behind and saw his point.

"Space is a dark place at night. If you stay more than twelve hours up there, you'll run into darkness. What then?"

"I see, what a pity. That is a problem isn't it?"

"That's why the best way to get up there is when it is daytime. That's when the way is lit up."

"That's a very good idea!" said Yezh. "Well then, sorry to bother you in your work. I guess I'm not going to fly in darkness."

Yezh departed to his ship, leaving Ivan behind by the fence like he'd been discarded. Ivan shook his head. With his pitchfork in hand he walked away, thinking he would be better off finishing his work around his field than listening to a madman's ramblings.

It cost Yezh another half an hour or so to find an operational lantern, which he used for construction purposes. It had been sitting in his shack for many years but looked brand new.

What can't I find in this butcher shack? I've been able to find everything that I need in there! thought Yezh.

Yezh was impressed by his lucky find. The lantern was attached to an upper part of the ship where it would be sheltered beneath thick glass and where heat wouldn't damage it.

It was another successful attachment. He had to try it to test its operation. The light was bright as the sun, and he could rotate it with a mechanism onboard. He shifted the light toward his neighbor. It blinded him when he was fetching water from the well. He nearly dropped it back inside trying to shield his face with his hand. He knew that Yezh did that on purpose. Yezh stepped down from his ladder and walked toward the fence again.

"Hey, neighbor!" called out Yezh, this time with enthusiasm and a degree of assurance in his voice. "Look at my ship now. I have installed a light. Now I can see where I'm going. What do you think of it now?"

Ivan looked over the fence, his head darting left and right for a better look at the ship.

"Look at that—you actually did it," said Ivan with awe in his voice.

He pulled back his head and came back to Yezh's question.

Yezh carefully examined Ivan's face for any emotional clues, but the farmer was cunning enough to hide any feeling.

"You may have succeeded in doing that, but you still don't get the point, do you?"

Yezh showed a face of interest, ready to hear what he had to say next.

"You think that it's only about air? Problems come aplenty around the world. Imagine outside of it."

"What other problems might there be?" said Yezh, this time with worry in his low tone. He was sure he had crushed it brilliantly.

"Well, there's temperature to think about. What if it's too hot up there? You know it's hot up there because of the sun. If you get too close to it, your ship will melt down. What then?"

Yezh thought about it. It was a good point.

"I suppose I just have to go further away from the sun. The sun couldn't be so big that it can catch the entire sky."

"If you do that, then you'll reach places where there is no sun and you'll freeze to death. You'll be a drifting, shooting ice cube!"

Yezh saw what he meant. The sun could be a killer. What if his ship melts even before he reaches that infamous void?

"I see!" was the only comment Yezh could offer, and it somewhat satisfied Ivan.

"Now you understand that you can never travel high to the stars. Otherwise someone among us would have done it long ago."

"Thank you, Ivan, for helping me understand such unfortunate possibilities."

Yezh walked away in thoughts and sadness. Ivan grumbled in his corner.

"Space travel," whispered Ivan to himself. "Yeah, right! As if a farmer would be the one to fly up there! Nonsense!"

Ivan walked away again to fill up his bottles with water from the well, hoping that would be the last of Yezh's stupid attempts.

Chapter 15
New and Improved

A new inspection had to be done. All the patching up was one problem solved in case the ship needed to go through an airless area. But now another one rose. Yezh stood near his ship, his hands on his waist, and he sighed.

Still more troubles. This is getting harder and more complicated than I thought.

What about cold and heat? Ivan said that it was a place of incredible heat due to its proximity to the sun. If it ends up being cold, then that's the other side of the coin on the temperature problem. Coincidentally, that shouldn't be a big problem for aluminum because it is highly resistant to both high and low temperatures. His ship was nearly covered by that material, but just in case, he'd be prepared for the cold, arid weather.

Something told Yezh that space isn't very hot, and that Ivan was wrong about that, or perhaps he was listening too much to his farmer's gut feeling. He thought about how earth's altitude brings coldness. What is higher still should be colder. Otherwise, why would tall mountains have snow and ice on them? Aren't they supposed to be closer to the sun than we on the ground are?

Probably Ivan didn't know that because he didn't have a mountain in his backyard. He probably never even saw one!

That was one good theory but not the only one. It would be dangerous to draw conclusions based on it, but just in case, he'd do something about it.

Regarding the pressure backed by coldness issues, what he did with adding another layer of aluminum and sealing the gaps had contributed greatly in keeping air stable in it. Also, a layer of insulating material covered the interior of the ship. To install the insulation, he needed to open inner walls to work. That cost him another hour, but he finally finished it. Then with unused cable ends, Yezh installed a heater. Now the ship provided air and heat. He felt he had made an important improvement, one that could have been missed if it had not been for his neighbor's somewhat weird accusations. No matter how bad the weather or uncomfortable the environment might be surrounding his spaceship, he was sure that none of it would affect him now.

Everything looked stiff and steady on the ship. The tank, the light, the walls, the screws. Then just as things were getting better, he heard a loud noise outside that demanded his attention.

"What could that be now?" he asked himself in an annoyed tone.

It sounded like a metal squeal, and knew it had to come from his ship. And suddenly his balance was off.

He stepped out of his ship. One of the legs that held the ship from touching the ground had detached itself and fallen. It was a good thing that it broke here on earth rather than somewhere far away in the sky.

"So even that happened," he said quietly, in speech that was surprisingly curse free. The first thing that he thought of was the weight must have caused it. Obviously, the new tank must have added more weight on one side.

Luckily it wasn't the wing—or a fin. Yezh didn't know which term would be the best for naming the thin, triangular plate that protruded from the bottom near the boosters would be. The legs were used as shock absorbers, which seemed to be holding the weight.

What would he have done if the wing squealed? He didn't know if this malfunction could cause a major failure in its operation. But he guessed that every body part is useful, just like a human body. He had created a design that would imitate the design of an aircraft. If the fin breaks on an airplane, it causes problems, because fins are used for navigation and have value in air support.

No big deal! He could repair it easily. But the sudden shifting of weight was causing a dangerous problem on his ship.

All these spins around the ship, trying to fix this and that, made Yezh dead on his feet. He inserted some support beneath where the leg was supposed to be. It held good, and the ship will not crash down. He went back into his house, where he sat next to Marushka, who was knitting a new hat for next winter.

"Tired?"

"Is it worth it to talk about extra energy?"

"I suppose not," said Marushka. "I can see you are dead tired.

You've been out there nearly the entire day." But Yezh wasn't inclined to reply.

"What did you speak to Ivan about this time?" asked Marushka, who didn't take her eyes off her knitting. "Still bragging about his sprouts?"

"Not this time. He actually discovered the secret about what I've been building."

"I told you," said Marushka, "you can't keep anything secret from that hunter. He's shrewd like a fox."

"More like a hungry wolf," complained Yezh, who thought about the positive side—or so it seemed.

He understood why she opposed his talking to that neighbor. Though he'd only banter with his neighbor, a game of wordplay was Yezh's counter-tactic.

They engaged in badinage about anything at all, and Yezh would try to squeeze a couple of that spiteful man's nerves.

"We had a little talk about space."

Yezh explained to her what he learned about the mysterious void. Even she was surprised to hear how much a farmer like Ivan knows about it. She claimed later that he was only trying to scare him with his "lie-tales." But Yezh admitted that it was because Ivan pointed out flaws that he was able to perfect his ship.

After a half an hour of rest, he decided to go back to work on his spaceship. Once outside, he concentrated on the broken leg. He'd make something more solid yet flexible to handle the weight. That job cost him maybe another half an hour.

Even if he repaired the broken body part, Yezh feared that more parts would eventually break in his uncertain journey through the unknown. What would he do if it reoccurs?

He won't be able to come out of his spaceship to fix any damage on the shell. This was indeed another challenge: The cold, the lack of air, the damages. His body wouldn't stand a chance in the extremities—if the rumors are true. Probably Ivan will try to get him killed up there.

"If my ship needs to be properly dressed for up there, so must I be!"

There must be a way he could wear something to keep him warm and offer some reserve of air. The question of what he should look like also came to mind.

What should a space traveler look like? Should there be some special way of dressing? He didn't know why this came to his mind, but he quickly connected it to the challenging problems he faced.

Marushka could help with this clothing problem. Perhaps he'd have another job for her.

Chapter 16
A New Look for a Star Traveler

Yezh hurried to Marushka in the house with a new idea. She saw him excited about something but a little bit worried.

"Marushka, I had this great idea of having special clothing for my trip up there!"

She had no idea what he meant by that, but she was curious to know what he demanded.

"What do you want to wear?" said Marushka and offering a bit of advice. "I find the clothes you're wearing fine."

"No, no, I thought about that as well, and … you know that space is very cold, right?" said Yezh, and Marushka agreed with her head. "And you know there is no air out there, right?" Marushka agreed again. "Which means that I will need a better outfit than this farmer one. I can't go out there like this." Yezh showed his dirty, torn clothes. "It's probably always winter out there, the worst of them, too. I'll freeze to death if I don't dress appropriately."

Or I could burn on my hand-made grill, thought Yezh.

He wasn't too sure anymore what was true about space. For all he knew, it could be like always being on vacation up there.

"If you want, we have hats and mitts."

Yezh tilted his head sideways slowly and gazed upon her.

"Marushka," said Yezh earnestly, "that's not the kind of winter I was talking about."

"Isn't your ship … shuttle … rocket …" Marushka blocked on the name because she couldn't remember what he called it.

"Ship," said Yezh several times to correct her, and to imprint it for good in her mind.

"Isn't it supposed to give you protection from that?" asked Marushka.

"Yes, it does," replied Yezh with worries, "but what happens if something breaks around the ship? I will have to get out of it to repair it, right?"

Their previous talk about the void had made Marushka worried. Now she became even more worried. "You're not going to plan to play with your life, are you? If you get out of your tin ship, you'll fall down in space. You'd fall back to the planet and onto the ground. Or worst case, you'd just fall in space, down … into that … void." She was forming her own hypothesis about space.

He thought badly about such a humorous idea.

"People don't fall from space into the endless void! Don't tell me you've been listening too much to that Ivan next door."

"You're the one who listened to him!" exclaimed Marushka. "What if he's right about it? What made you think suddenly he is wrong?"

Yezh appreciated for her caring, but even though he didn't quite understand space himself since he had never seen it personally, he still couldn't agree with that theory.

"Oh, Marushka! That's such a farmer-like mentality, a stupid way of thinking from silly, uneducated people like us who know nothing in life. There could be more to it. There are plenty of unexplained theories. If I don't see it myself, we will never know the truth of whether it's a cold or hot place."

Marushka did find that somewhat interesting for a man. But she did not need to learn any truth for herself about such a thing. Space and its dark secret remain meaningless for a farmer's life. It was nothing that would help them in any way: not in field work, nor in money. It could very well bring death and misfortune. What could a place so little known hold so great that a man would desire? But she would never say anything harsh to break Yezh's dreams. His morale was important to her because that's what puts a smile on his face. Still, to make him even happier, she agreed to make him new clothes for whichever winter he was talking about.

"Let me see what material I have. You choose what suits you the best."

She had no idea what space clothes should look like as she had never seen a model before.

First Farmer In Space

They went to the cloth storage room where drawers and tables were covered with all kinds of material with different colors and textures. Yezh was a man of the field, and he felt unfamiliar with this kind of place he wasn't used to lurking around. As for Marushka, she knew every corner, every bit of cloth lying around.

Yezh didn't know where to start looking, and Marushka couldn't help it either when she had no example to follow.

"What color do you want?"

"Something preferably in the theme of space, something in contrast to space," said Yezh, who thought to pick a color. "Something light-colored, like white!" Marushka searched and shuffled through the piles of cloth until she found something white, and she showed it to Yezh for his opinion. He touched it with the tip of his finger. It had a soft texture and was warm, but he realized there was a problem.

"This one is ventilating through. It's letting air come in and out!" he said, looking thoroughly at the textures. Marushka had to agree with him.

"Then let me see if I have something better, something that seals air better, but it may not be white."

She shuffled more through the pile. Yezh helped, and he found some weird and funny fabrics. There was a dark blue blanket with moon patterns on it that seemed interesting. He had to show it to Marushka.

"Look at this one. There are cute little moon and star motifs on it, and it's dark blue like the night sky—so fitting for the space theme."

"Yeah it is! But that looks childish. You're not going to wrap yourself in a children's blanket up there, are you?" said Marushka.

"No, that won't do," Yezh agreed, dropping the material back on the table. "It needs to be serious and professional-looking. But it's still a nice design!" Yezh felt sad to put it back.

She picked up another white-colored tissue, but this one was very rigid and harsh to the touch.

"There's another white one here."

Yezh grabbed it as only his star-traveler finger could tell if it was really a good one, but he found a problem with it.

"It's too hard," said Yezh. After grabbing it, he tried to move his hand in it where it was hard to fold. "I wouldn't be able to move in there."

Marushka put it away and continued searching. Then she came to one that was the right texture for what was needed.

"I think I found something." She showed it and Yezh took it from her hand. "It's somewhat softer and it doesn't let air inside. It has a gleaming texture."

It was a bright color, warm material, tear-resistant, and sealed air. Yezh used his sense of touch to decide and had to agree on this one, this particular one caught his interest.

"Not bad, I think this should be something that could be used for a spacesuit."

"I just hope that I will have enough of this material to make it for you."

"Let's take your measurements, shall we?" she requested.

Yezh stood on a small chair. She took a ribbon to do the measurement and a piece of paper and a pencil to write down the size. She started with his height, and as Yezh was a tall, middle-aged man, she had a little bit of difficulty reaching all the way up. Then she asked him to stretch out his arm where she took his length and width. Yezh had no idea how to hold himself and only obeyed her commands. The woman knew this stuff better, he believed.

"I'll make it a few inches wider to let you move your arm easily," said his wife, and she wrote down the numbers on the piece of paper.

Next up were his legs and then his waist, and Yezh grew dizzy seeing her spinning around him like a moon. When she took the inches for his waist, she had to comment on his skinniness.

"You ought to eat more; you barely have a waist. You better eat before you go up there or else, you'll come back as a skeleton."

Yezh wasn't sure if that was a sarcastic comment or just a plaintive one.

"It's better than being too fat to travel. You don't want me to end up rotating on myself like a planet, do you?" replied Yezh, trying to maintain the same level of sarcasm.

"If that's so, you'll be scaring everybody on earth like a *Babaroga* from space. Are you trying to look like those creatures from the newspaper?"

Yezh knew he wasn't ugly enough to scare people, but he'd eat enough before leaving home so perhaps the fatter he would be, the more days he could spend up there without food.

In due time, Marushka collected all the information for his clothes, and Yezh went back to continue working on his space ship.

He walked in the hallway thinking now he had clothes to cover his body, but what about his head? Hats wouldn't do; his face needs to be covered as well. But what could be used as a helmet? He turned his head to the right as he passed through the living room, a comfy place crammed with shelves, sofas, a table, and an aquarium with a fish—Boko, as Maksimilian called him—who, in his little own world, swam meaninglessly left and right all day—comfortably.

That's it! thought Yezh.

The idea revolved around the aquarium. Its transparent glass could provide sight and cover his entire head. How could he recreate it? Where could he find a material with the same properties and advantages as this aquarium? Among all things he could create in life, a perfectly shaped glass was something he couldn't make. The search would be hard. He doubted that Joseph could help him there, either.

With a little thought, Yezh went for the obvious. Why should he make it complicated?

"Sorry, Boko!" Yezh grabbed the big aquarium in his hand. "You'll have to move away from your comfort zone."

He took a glass of water and poured water and Boko in it. The poor little fish, all confused and frightened, found little space to swim free. The poor little thing could only spin around in the glass of water. His castle turned into a small shack with only a single sip of water.

"Don't worry, we'll buy you a new home—a bigger one, too."

With the stolen home of the inoffensive little creature who didn't get a chance to speak his mind about anything that happened to him, Yezh retreated to his workspace—or laboratory—or whatever it's called. His barn and his shack were the ideal place to build something, and sometimes it had to be secret from Marushka.

It took Marushka a good long hour to finish sewing and attaching various parts of the clothes. She made sure that nothing could easily come in or out of this garment. But nothing could be confirmed without consulting with Yezh about the matter.

She searched for him all over the place, but he was nowhere to be found: living room, bedroom, backyard, or front yard.

Where could that man be? thought Marushka.

She always hated when she had to chase him around or search for him, but from experience, she knew it always meant something bad. Especially when she saw what happened to Boko, she knew Yezh had another diabolical plan.

Finally, she tried the shack. The noise from inside spoke for his location, but when she turned in and saw Yezh standing there with something that resembled a …

"Yezh! What are you doing there?"

He had a glass sphere on his head.

"Oh, Marushka, look at my new helmet."

"What is that on your …" She paused, taking another second to look at it.

No, he couldn't have …

"Is that what I think it is?"

"A helmet. I just told you that," replied Yezh.

"I know it's a helmet. I'm just afraid to ask if that's the aquarium that you took from the living room."

"Yeah, it's the aquarium. Smart isn't it? It's going to give me maximum protection." He had completely transformed it into something that no longer looked anything close to an aquarium.

"And what happened to Boko?" she asked, recalling what she saw in a glass of water.

"Yeah, well I kind of owe him a new home after this project," he said apologetically.

"Couldn't you have found him a bigger glass of water?"

"I was in a hurry. I feel bad for the little guy."

Yezh tried his helmet on. It was thick and glossy on one side. She couldn't tell which other material he had sacrificed to use for it. But enough of side distraction.

"I have finished sewing your clothes. I want to know if everything is done correctly to your taste."

"Ah, great! I can try them both now to see how I fit in my new space suit."

He went to his house to try on his outfit right away. It fitted him well, and it was warm, but Yezh believed that he had to see its effects as a temperature moderator. For that he went out into the sun. His large, unfamiliar size was hard to pass through the kitchen's door. Ivan was outside at the time, having a nice beer near his cheap wooden table not too far from the fence when he heard noise and saw something terrifying coming out from Yezh's house.

The reddish orange reflected some rays of light. He stood in the open and noticed that his body temperature rose after a few minutes out in the bright sunlight. He raised his head to the sky. For a while he wasn't sure if his suit could keep him safe from high temperature. Anyway, it was almost the end of the day—around one or two o'clock, but the heat still lingered.

Ivan peeked over the fence and nearly toppled over from either fear or awkwardness when he saw someone dressed up in a funny, warm colorful outfit that resembled to those people from the sky—the ones we see in the newspaper whenever a cow goes missing from a barn. He could hear him breathing very loudly inside that getup.

Ivan's eyes bulged out. He couldn't believe what he was seeing: a terror from the sky unfolding before his weary, drunken eyes? When the creature seemed to turn away, it waved its hand to Ivan, but Ivan simply lowered himself below to hide behind the fence, with only his bulging eyes peeking above the top, ever watchful.

The next few minutes Yezh spent testing his new suit in the sun, and Ivan was only gazing, studying carefully the nature of the disturbing suit. It lasted enough long to make him realize that it wasn't what it seemed to be. It couldn't be anybody but the silly Yezh himself. What he found scary turned out to be something awkwardly funny. Readopting his old cool, diplomatic matter, he called out to the man in the ridiculous suit.

"Neighbor! What are you wearing there?"

The sky traveler approached the fence.

"It's my new outfit for space."

Ivan dropped his smile. There'd been enough playing around. Someone needed to tell this guy straight what is wrong.

"Don't you think you're taking this space traveling thing a bit too seriously?"

"Well, someone has to be serious if he wants his dreams to come true."

"I thought your dream was only a way of talking, of expressing a wish," said Ivan. "Seeing you build that ship seemed like a crazy idea, but now that I see you in that outfit, I don't know what to think anymore."

"What would be the purpose of a dream if you had no intention of making it happen?"

"I do understand that, but this," said Ivan, pointing out with his both hands, "is just some crazy fantasy! You look ridiculous in that costume."

"What do you mean by ridiculous?" Yezh replied with a questioning tone. "This is supposed to protect me from heat and cold and give me an air supply. It's my life support armor."

"Life support armor," repeated Ivan with disappointed-sounding sarcasm. "There are more things that you need to understand about that *beyond-the-sky*," said Ivan. "I bet there will be harder complications."

"Like what?" asked Yezh. "I mean—I have solved the air problem, the heat problem, I have a light to guide me, my ship couldn't get any better than this."

"I still think it won't work. This is not good."

Ivan's mind desperately tried to catch a flaw on the ship, any little speck of flaw.

"Why is that? There has to be a problem somewhere again?"

"Well! It's … it's …" said Ivan, still searching for any flaws, but he ran out of excuses. "It's just not good, Yezh. That thing can never fly up there. It's nonsense. You still don't have your engine."

Yezh tried very hard not to show a smirk on his face.

"Well then, if you can't tell me any flaws you think you see, then I will suppose that my ship is in perfect condition to fly up in *beyond-the-sky*. The engine will come in due time."

Ivan felt his sarcasm being returned by the man he hated the most in the entire universe.

"If that's what you really think," said Ivan, who tried to sound most earnest, "I'm sure there are flaws that even I'm not aware of."

"Oh, come on, Ivan, what could you possibly not be aware of?" said Yezh with a spark of sarcasm in his voice—a friendly one, of course. "I thought being aware was your specialty."

And with that comment, Yezh turned his back and walked away from the fence. Ivan tried not to look angry but was becoming increasingly red and uncomfortable with the way Yezh responded to him, and about this—ship—he was building. Its existence annoyed him.

Ivan lowered himself down by the fence, his fist tightened from frustration, and he blew a breath of anger. His nerves were eating him alive.

Yezh went inside his house like nothing happened, and when he was no longer in Ivan's staring gaze, he jumped for joy, both his fists closed, ready to cheer for glory.

This is it, thought Yezh. My ship is good to go, and Ivan is finally biting on his fingers.

Chapter 17
How to Fly This Thing?

Yezh took extra care when he took off his armor and placed it on a stand. This is the kind of job he always dreamed of: a job to die for with passion—not hard work. This was certainly going somewhere.

He forced himself to take a quick nap on the couch because his excitement was overwhelming him emotionally. In his quick rest, he dreamt about the bottle they blasted. Upon awaking, Yezh thought about the engine, which he briefly thought about at the beginning of his journey of building a spaceship.

He looked to his right, and nobody was in sight. Marushka must be busy. A glass of water with Boko was on the table where the aquarium had been. He pitied the fish. Of course, as promised, he did find Boko a new temporary home that was bigger than a glass of water, and the fish was more than happy for that thoughtfulness. Though it wasn't all that Yezh thought for Boko. It remained to buy a larger aquarium for him. Yezh was a man of his word.

Marushka came down from the second floor and told him that she was going to visit a friend around the corner and would come back shortly. He had rested well and felt like doing some hard work on his *Sputnik*. He stepped out of his house.

He had conceived it, built its bones and skin, gathered all the components, even applied all of Ivan's criticisms. But for the first time now, Yezh wondered how he'd make it fly. He knew he should have thought about it more as the first thing since beginning but remained confident in his skills.

Steam was his initial choice—his *only* choice, actually—and for that he had Ivan's dead tractor to deal with. Now that he thought about it, it was a beautiful coincidence. Yezh always could find all kinds of uses for old, broken, dead objects. He postponed finishing his ship's design so he could switch over to the steam engine, which would take its own toll of work hours.

His ship's mass climbed quickly with each component attached, and he feared that it might be a bit too heavy. He thought about the airplane—about its shape, its components, and its mass—and tried to adopt similarities and reject differences. This ship was turning out very different—too different to compare to its cousin that had ruled the skies for many decades.

This ship, suited best for altitude rather than longitude, would use the laws of physics differently. It depended heavily on raw energy to pull it airborne against gravity, unlike its cousin the plane, which depended more on gliding along with gravity, using wings for air support over the force of gravity.

He disassembled the tractor into pieces, leaving only the steam engine. Luckily, the defect had taken place elsewhere in the engine's vital parts, and he was able to fix the minor damage that demanded the entire dismantling of the vehicle. The fate of the tractor was inevitable. It was heavy indeed, but he managed to pull it near the ship, and with equipment around him and the assistance of a rope, he lifted it up so he could attach it. With proper connection, he was able to complete it. This part took the longest to make. The ship looked more balanced.

***

Now all that remained was to find proper fuel. In Leninsk, many machines work with either electricity or steam, which makes them the most common due to their cheap cost. Oil was too luxurious. How much oil would he need to fill up those barrels? Yezh wouldn't even bother to think of it as an option. Since he had a steam engine, he had to use water, although other resources were highly competitive in the market.

No—it had to be water for this project.

His new steam engine was properly installed, so now it was time for him to fill it up. Wiping the oil off his hands with a handkerchief, Yezh did a little bit of mental work.

Even the water was sparse in this village. Where would he gather water from? There were no rivers nearby. What a shame that he hadn't lived or built his ship near a river somewhere. Where else could water be found?

He got a bright idea: Of course—the well!

He leaned over his worn-out well, and amidst the darkness, he could see sparkling light on the surface of water deep down. There wasn't a lot of water for his ship, but it was worth a try. The water from this well served various purposes: for drinking, washing clothes, taking a shower, and watering flowers. Yezh found another purpose for it.

Grabbing his bucket by the corner, Yezh reconsidered his options but then thought that he'd go all or nothing.

Would it work? Could water do the same job as oil? He could only try it. Like when cars started using water before moving to oil, ships will share the same evolution, thought Yezh.

Without any shame, he collected water in a bucket from his well and poured it into the big tank reservoir on the side of the ship. Every bucket led his ship's tank to fill slowly up. He grew impatient each passing moment at the effort demanded to do all the pulling and walking.

*****

Ivan chopped his wood for a quite a while, an activity that cost the life of one of his nearby oak trees. The few wood stubs he had in stock he sharpened into shapes of his liking. Though Ivan was a persistent worker when it came to competition with his neighbor, he couldn't resist taking a peek over the fence. Katenka came to inspect her husband's work. She had ornamental design preferences of that she wanted to see on her future new armoire.

Yezh was absorbed in his work and didn't realize that Ivan was staring at him, wondering what he was doing. Katenka approached Ivan closer to whisper to him. She saw the buckets but had no idea what they contained that Yezh was pouring into his tank.

"Is that water he's putting in?"

"Yeah."

"Really?"

"Yeah!"

What in the blue world? This man is going well above the clouds. What Ivan wanted to see more than anything was what Yezh will do once his well becomes drained from water. Katenka soon after went back in her house. Still, Ivan was somewhat interested in watching what his neighbor was doing to his broken tractor, but only after a while did he realize it had been dismantled. Ivan made a "tch" sound of disapproval.

If it didn't work as a tractor, it won't work for a spaceship!

First Farmer In Space

But Yezh remained focused. He drained the well, bucket after bucket, and there still wasn't enough water to fill it up, probably not even enough for the launch.

Yezh had the wonderful idea of sewing drapery to use as a parachute. To his surprise, Marushka had already arrived from her friends, and Yezh found this to be an opportunity to ask her to find draperies for this project. When she wondered why, he dared not explain the reason he believed it would be necessary.

She found the material and sewed it easily, but because of the size of what he needed, it took her several hours. Night would soon fall, and he had no choice but to continue it tomorrow. He helped with the draperies in the basement. Nightfall arrived while they were lost in their work, and the parachute was not yet finished.

In addition, he did not speak of the water he used from the well.

***

It wasn't until the next morning that he continued to work on it, but not before breakfast when he undertook only minor examinations. He tested the engine and it worked fine. He checked the electrical circuits and lit up the cockpit. Yezh almost danced from joy when he saw that *Sputnik* was operating.

Marushka prepared Maks for school, and when her hands were free, she went back to work on the parachute. Yezh helped her to finish. While they were hidden in their basement, the world flourished with life outside.

The parachute was huge and multilayered, which made it resistant to tearing. Finally, Marushka exclaimed that the parachute had been completed. Yezh rejoiced and departed with it, leaving her to wonder what it was. She still couldn't understand what purpose it would have for his ship.

With the help of a ladder, he installed the parachute into the tip of the ship's muzzle.

***

After a while, Yezh came inside his house in a high mood. He was grinning, and he was rubbing his hands together briskly. Luckily the house had some water quantities unused. Marushka was washing dishes and was curious to know what made him so cheerful. He looked agitated, and

Marushka could only guess what it could be.

"The ship is ready now. I'm ready to launch anytime now!"

"Finished?"

She wasn't sure if that was for the better or worse. He had put so much effort into it. Skepticism messed up her thoughts.

"What will happen now?"

"I just have to decide when to start the launch. The day has come for my dream to come true."

"How ready can you be? We don't even know if this is going to work at all."

"I have made important improvements. I can feel it. It's going to work."

No improvements or attachments to the ship would suffice to soften her worries. This was still a very dangerous activity.

"What happens if something goes wrong? How are we supposed to help you? How will I know about your whereabouts up there? Will I ever hear from you again?"

Another idea flashed in his mind too late, something he hadn't thought about.

"You are right. I have not thought about that. That's a very good idea," he said, raising his finger to his head. "There has to be a way to keep in contact with the earth."

Yezh puzzled over this new obstacle. He obviously needed another electronic device of some sort. So far all of what he used on his ship came from broken or malfunctioning trash. He hadn't given much thought to it, but he now began to fear that the once-broken status of those materials might show consequences in the near future. Attaching broken electrical devices without repairs and double-checking them would only increase the risk of misfortune. He dared not think nor admit the possibility of such a thing, but definitely wouldn't want to ignore it either.

But without money, how was he supposed to acquire them in first place?

Chapter 18
First Launch!

Security became his first concern. An untested ship could be dangerous. And he needed to have an action plan to increase his security and experience. Yezh knew what to do. This required a test plan.

He quietly went to dress himself. With his armor and helmet on, he went out. He tried to accustom himself to his suit, moving his joints and walking around the mud.

His test had only begun when Sputnik came running, barking madly. Yezh could tell that it even excited the dog.

"Do you want to join me in a test of my moon project, Sput?"

It was almost as if the dog agreed with his bark. This dog was like if he'd start to speak at any moment now—so understanding and obedient.

The space traveler walked around the backyard as if he were on the moon with Sputnik assisting on his mission. Plunging his mind into an imaginary world, he saw himself surrounded by no air but lots of rocks lying around the cold plains of the moon.

Ivan had just come out with his plate to have his lunch outside. As he thought about how proud he was of his garden, his eyes looked over to the other side of the fence. His spoon, halfway toward his mouth, stopped in motion. Ivan was unable to comprehend what he was seeing. He approached the fence with quiet steps to peek.

Yezh was slowly strolling around unintelligently. He carefully picked up a stone that was in front of him and threw it not too far ahead of him.

"Mission accomplished, Sputnik."

What is he doing?

Ivan couldn't fathom anything. This was madness, getting creepier every day. He had made an expression of dismay and confusion when he had to duck upon seeing Marushka come to the door. Ivan wasn't stupid. He knew that Marushka didn't like him much.

"What are you doing in that suit?" asked the woman.

She thought it might be dangerous to walk around in that suit. Unintentionally attracting a crowd is dangerous.

"Oh … I … we were testing our project," replied Yezh, his voice barely audible from within his armor.

Marushka found it weird to be planning a test. Yezh assured her that it is essential for a space traveler to know what he's doing once up there on a mission. But it was frustrating her to see him playing around like a kid.

***

Ivan went back to his house after finishing his lunch. When Katenka met him, he said that Yezh was playing in his backyard like a small child. They had a laugh, for the man was a grown-up, too old for such fantasies.

When she demanded to know about the progress in his armoire construction, he reminded himself that he needed to go fetch some paint from local stores. With that goal in mind, he departed for business far smarter and more important than his neighbor's ridiculous, unorthodox hobby.

Katenka also joined him as she wanted to pick her paint color by herself.

***

Yezh's spacesuit was malleable enough to allow him various exercises. After he had tested his movement on soil, he moved inside his ship— still with Sputnik. Since the dog couldn't climb a ladder, Yezh took him in his hand and climbed up with him. He had a seat, and Sputnik was on his garment. The world seemed different in its dimension now. He put on his belt. He felt a force dragging him from behind the chair, and from Sputnik. Being perpendicular from his world of sense made him somewhat nauseated from confusion of gravity. It wasn't every day that he sat on a chair placed facing the sky. Sputnik was kind of standing on his chest to be more precisely, his tail occasionally slapping him on his face. This wasn't very comfortable.

It was time to play with some buttons.

All buttons should be operational with equipment it was related to. He turned on his ship, and lights began to flash. Sputnik was barking at the colorful lights. The first switch was the light, and the cabin was lit behind him.

"Light operational."

The second switch he activated was heating. The nearly silent humming behind him was promising.

"Heating operational."

"Everything seems in good shape, Sputnik," confirmed Yezh. "Are you excited?"

Sputnik barked once, agitated by the lights. Yezh had to hold him tighter so he wouldn't slip behind or fall—he couldn't say which direction was what anymore. At a moment when Sputnik caught Yezh off guard, he jumped onto the panel and onto the joystick-like maneuvering system. Yezh screamed his name, but it was too late. He heard a loud roaring sound behind him and the ship began to shake.

"Sputnik! What have you done now?"

The dog trembled in fear of the roars. Yezh hesitated to react, having no idea what to press this time, but the joystick was going mad in all directions and Yezh had to hold it steady.

"The jet turbos are running," guessed Yezh in a stressed tone.

A sudden force struck him, making him sink harder into his chair. He felt heavier somehow. He held onto Sputnik tightly. It was only then he realized from a blank point in his windshield that they were actually mobile. The numbers on the panel were going crazy, telling him that they were climbing in altitude. Could it be a defect, or could this be something else? No, they were moving alright. This must mean one thing. Could it be?

"The ship has been launched skyward," said Yezh, who couldn't fathom the situation from skepticism. "The ship is flying."

***

"Oh! Oh! Look at that!" Makar's voice erupted on the hill. Everybody else had their eyes on the mysterious machine departing the soil.

"He managed to fly," said Bogdan quietly.

"I'm telling you, this is the person we've been waiting to meet one day," said Rodion.

Phoenix Phoenix

***

Yezh tried to look around for any hint of what was going on. It was lasting for a while now. *The ship is truly airborne*, thought Yezh, still not believing it. With the sudden increase of excitement and a feeling of success, he burst into laughter. Yezh was more absorbed in the flight than in trying to make things better. He forgot to punish Sputnik. Instead, he expressed his joy to his companion.

"Sputnik. We are flying, friend!"

He was so happy that he could jump to the moon. Why would he need a ship then? Yezh forced himself to control his excitement.

Sputnik's fear was increased by the roaring and shaking.

***

People from all over the village, whatever they were doing at that moment, had to stop to have a look at the sky. An object, a sound, and bright light caught eyes from all corners of Leninsk. A merchant lost the attention of his clients, who were pointing their fingers up, forcing him to look. A farmer dropped his shovel, not believing what he was witnessing. Children at school were awed by the mysterious flash of light in the sky. One of them was Maks. It took him a few seconds to understand what it could be. It had to be the work of his father.

***

Nothing flashed redder than the screen at the minister of defense's military headquarters. An agent witnessed signals from their satellite. Panic-stricken and sure it was a surprise attack from the West, he called out to his superior.

"Commander. We have received a signal from an unidentified object that flies at incredible speed."

The man in a decorated suit hurried to his side.

"What is it? Can you acquire more information?"

"The signal came from the south, somewhere around the rural parts. It appears to be some kind of rocket moving at a speed of hundreds of kilometers per hour—and still climbing."

131

First Farmer In Space

"That's impossible!" whispered the minister of defense, unable to recall any Soviet activities that were planned this day. "Moscow did not tell us of any plans. Not to mention that nothing in the world that can travel in the sky that fast."

They both looked at the red dot climbing in altitude at a demonic speed.

"It could be a terrorist attack," said the agent. "Should I send a command to shoot it down, sir?"

"No!" said the minister hastily. It was nothing like he had ever seen. "Let's see what it is first."

The minister turned and shouted at another agent in the back upper rows: "Contact Moscow about this."

"Yes, sir."

The man then plunged into deep thought away from the screen, trying to recall any known vehicle of such potential. He didn't dare take any action without the opinion of Moscow.

Could the United States have finally managed to create something of advanced technology that the Soviets did not possess?

***

Jovani and Anastasia came to Leninsk to report on natural resources and how people in Leninsk fare the weather conditions. They had mingled in this backward village for too long where nothing happened. It was getting hot in this barren, quiet location.

"We have been out here for several days now, and nothing have been happening. The boss will be angry if we don't come up with a report on something," complained Jovani.

"We have been searching all the while, not slacking," said Anastasia with a breathless voice, drained from the spring heat. "Nothing ever happens out here."

"What do we have to sum up? Do we have anything at all?"

"Well," Anastasia started off, "we know that the climate is arid in summer, which means it's a near-desert climate."

Phoenix Phoenix

Anastasia shuffled through her papers where she had written about biology and the natural resources. What a mess! She always had trouble making her workplace organized; it isn't any easier when you're a nomad.

Jovani, the driver, spotted something in the sky. He flapped his lips soundlessly at Anastasia, who was absorbed in her messed-up documents. She went through what they had gathered as information about the fauna and flora.

"Anastasia," said Jovani, his eyes locked in the sky as if he'd seen a ghost, "you'd better take a look up in the sky."

"What is it?" Anastasia asked, but quickly turned mute like her partner. "What is that thing?"

A long vertical streak of white fume escaped whatever was flying so high.

"Is that an airplane?" guessed Jovani.

"Come on, Jovani, airplanes don't fly like that."

They were silent for a few seconds, and then both had the same idea.

"Do you know what I'm thinking?" asked Jovani, this time somewhat more lost in his thoughts. "I think we just found ourselves something that is worthy for a newspaper."

"Go! Go, Jovani! Track it down!" Anastasia said urgently, her hands in frenzied motion.

Jovani lost no time turning on the engine and hit the gas, following the object in the sky with the distinctive flight pattern.

Their old white truck, which resembled a box with a satellite antenna on the roof, lifted a cloud of dirt on the road.

***

It had been a while that the boosters were roaring and the ship shaking, and Yezh wondered where they were in altitude. He tried to fight the gravity to throw a peek at the narrow windows.

He could confirm it. He was truly flying. Yezh knew he could not go back down yet, even if it was all a mistake. He couldn't put the blame on Sputnik, who felt the same about flying in space. Yezh was set on continuing this journey while his mind frantically tried to concoct a logical move. He needed to grasp this moment professionally, not letting it deteriorate. He was eager to meet the void; the moment of truth was about to …

The sound of the roars changed, and upon listening to it, Yezh grew scared. This had to mean something bad. He looked at his gauges on the panel and saw that the fuel—the water—was low. The gauge was red.

"No, no, this can't be happening. We're running low on water."

The engine shut down, and in his stomach, he felt the gravity pull changing direction after the roaring stopped. When he checked the altimeter, it said his maximum height had been fifty kilometers. The number was meaningless.

"We're falling! Hold on, Sputnik!"

He looked to see if there was anything he could press to save them. Only one button would help, which he had cleverly thought about, anticipating this situation. Suddenly his doubts about using old, broken electronics and rushing too fast were causing him anxiety.

He lifted the cap that kept the red button safe and after pressing it he felt a little bump. Then the gravity pulled less violently, which meant they weren't falling as quickly as they were. The parachute had opened.

***

"Aww. The ship is falling down," said Makar, disappointment in his voice.

Their eyes followed the ship gliding down.

"Argh!" Bogdan swept his arm in the air with a fist. "Almost!"

Kiril was making continuous "tch" sounds at what he was seeing.

Rodion was disappointed but was still convinced that this man had some potential. He knew that this mere peasant wouldn't be giving up that easily.

***

Phoenix Phoenix

The minister waited for the phone call to be delivered, and when it was, he was told that the head of state knew nothing of such activity and asked for more information.

Soon afterward, the agent spoke again: "Sir! The object has changed its course."

The minister returned to the screen, staring carefully.

"What is it doing?"

"It's going straight down toward the ground but at a much slower speed than it went up."

"Is it falling?"

"It appears to be so."

The minister's mind froze, a sudden burst of adrenaline taking over his body.

"Could it be a bomb?"

It was only seconds before it would be too late to react to it. The minister felt a shiver in his bones.

***

Before long a loud crash was heard outside that startled Marushka in the living room.

Marushka immediately went out to see. Smoke and heat were in her face. The sight was cloudy for a while. Then she saw the hatch open. Sputnik jumped out, shaken. Marushka hurried to the ship to assist and saw Yezh exiting. Her heart skipped a beat.

"What happened?"

"The ship flew into the sky."

"I told you not to try that risky game. Look what you have done. You might have killed yourself."

"I didn't mean to do it today. It was a mistake." Yezh took off his helmet. "Sputnik pressed a few buttons."

"What was the dog doing in your ship?" asked Marushka, but Yezh didn't answer. He was in bad shape. The hissing noise of steam was drowning out her voice. It wasn't time for questions, so she helped Yezh to get away from the ship. She needed to know if he was all right.

"Are you injured?" She waved the smoky air away from her face. "Come on, let's get in the house."

Neighbors from all sides gathered around the fence, staring at the smoking ship in the backyard. They all arrived too late to witness anything. Only evidence was left behind to explain the story, veiled in mystery.

***

It did not explode. The entire crew at the defense department were unable to draw any conclusion about what they'd seen.

A dreadful silence was in the big room, where screens and flashes of light were on the walls. Many were expecting a disaster but remained dumbfounded by the absence of such a threat.

The dwindling speed was convincing enough that it was intended to fall purposely and for a specific reason that the minister of defense needed to know—and fast. He owed Moscow some explanation.

***

Marushka told Yezh to lay down on the couch for a while. He was shaking a little bit, and she didn't want to overstress him with questions. She suggested that he take off the suit and helped him to undress.

Sputnik had his share of stress, too. He didn't even say hello to anybody but immediately retreated to his doghouse. Even the doghouse shook from the dog's fear.

***

Jovani and Anastasia arrived too late but not alone, encountering many local peasants gathered around the fence. They forced their way through the crowd; they never would have found the location without them.

"Sweet virgin mother of a cow! What is that thing?" said Jovani, who looked in the backyard. Something was smoking fresh snakes of steam.

They were all trying to gather information, but the smoke was veiling the strange object. They took pictures and interviewed witnesses. At last, Anastasia tried the door, but when Marushka opened it, she made a grumpy reply. She explained that her husband was hurt and needed to rest. Then she closed the door in her face.

Anastasia returned without success to her partner in the truck. At least they got some pictures that they were eager to show to their employer. The crowd scattered after a while, and Marushka could finally breathe a sigh of relief that nothing worse went wrong.

Marushka went to the well to draw some water for poor Yezh. She threw the bucket in and scooped, but when she pulled it out, realized the bucket had not picked up any liquid on its journey to the bottom.

What?

She peeked deep inside, witnessed a summer solstice horror, and grasped her hands in a prayer.

"What has he done to the well?" cried out the wife. She cried out all the miseries and misfortune of the world for the disturbing discovery. She would have to have a serious discussion with Yezh tonight.

***

The table tonight was quiet with Yezh being withdrawn into his miserable bubble of thoughts. His head inclined to his plate with his spoon stirring the soup into an endless vortex. They had a short discussion about his action regarding the well. She nearly punished him like a child, and that made him feel even gloomier than from his injury.

Marushka saw he was in a bad mood, and nothing she could find to say helped him. She did believe that Yezh needed to be left alone to expend his thinking on personal matters. They now had a serious problem with the water drained from their only source. Shock and fear were in the air.

Even Sputnik had the scare of his life. That would surely be the last time he'd ever touch any buttons. She found him more frightened than before that failure nearly cost two lives.

The child arrived in a hurry to the table, hungry and excited to hear about his father's early launch. He was at school, and when he heard a buzzing in the air and something rising, he knew immediately that it was his father.

First Farmer In Space

"What's to eat?" asked Maks, taking a seat.

"Vegetable soup with carrots and a cheese pie."

The boy saw that his father was different from his usual self. As he joined them for dinner, he was curious to ask a few questions.

"What happened to *Sputnik*?"

"He's eating in his doghouse," said Marushka scooping her soup.

"No, not that Sputnik. The spaceship!"

"The ship?" She was confused. "You gave it a name?"

"Yeah. The other night, Father and I named his spaceship *Sputnik*."

Well look at that, they even gave it a name.

Marushka thought there'd been enough playing around. It was time to talk seriously about this matter of space travelling.

"Your father had a bad time there. Maybe it's better if you start to eat your soup."

Maks felt sad for his father but was optimistic about the ship. Nearly everybody ignored the possibility that his project might actually work.

"Well, at least it worked. You managed to fly. You proved to everybody that you can fly."

"I haven't proven anything to anybody," replied Yezh after a long silence. "That was an epic failure."

Yezh's dark feeling drowned the conversation in silence.

"It was so close—so close!" Yezh made a fist, as he felt he almost had his dreams in his grip. "I really thought it would work. I flew really high. I must have been about fifty kilometers according to my altimeter when it had to crash down."

Yezh felt like hiding in this soup.

"What happened?" inquired Maks.

"It ran out of water," Yezh responded.

"Could it be that the heat evaporated all the water?" asked Maks.

Phoenix Phoenix

"No. It needed more water. There wasn't enough. For this kind of launch it needed an enormous amount of water."

Maks wondered how many liters of water he would need to blast that giant bottle. They ended up talking about *Sputnik* while eating until a silence drowned the conversation again. Dinner was eaten with shallow spoon scoops, making it tasteless and quiet.

***

Ivan returned home when everything cooled down. All that was left were rumors, neighbors feeding him news of Yezh's trial that took place that evening. He did raise his eyebrows, but again he wasn't very surprised for he knew the outcome before anybody else. It was a surprise that he missed the launch and the fall. Now that it had happened, this would surely be the last of Yezh's crazy imagination of space flight. Now Ivan knew that he was always right after all.

Chapter 19
Backfire

The next day, Yezh woke up at his usual time only to remind himself that nothing special would happen today. His good night's sleep, somewhat painful, nearly made him forget about his broken dreams. From the epic failure of yesterday, and the damage it had caused to the ship, he knew he'd have work to do around it.

Rejecting a cup of coffee, with what little water they had left, and a loaf of bread so early, Yezh went out. He inspected *Sputnik* angrily. Every broken bit frustrated him. It wasn't bad, and it might have been worse were it not for the excellent idea of a parachute. There were just some dented parts here and there, nothing too hard to fix.

Yezh stepped outside, sighed deeply, and couldn't even keep his eyes on it. It was too painful. The way *Sputnik* looked, he'd have plenty of work to do on it. How long would that take? He reminded himself of the harsh winter and realized how desperately he needed to finish this work, so he could pass on to his farming duties. His wheat would start soon, and the windmill needed to have something to grind on.

Yezh sighed deeply.

***

When Ivan was outside, he noticed Yezh's bad mood from not speaking to him, not even throwing a peek at him. Ivan was still wondering about yesterday's event.

Ivan was not fascinated by his neighbor. Ivan had cursed the heaven that led *Sputnik* ignominiously back to the ground. He enjoyed hearing about the spectacle as if it were entertainment and was sorry that he wasn't present to see it. Now that his evil eye and curses had had an effect on his nemesis, Ivan was able to return to his work, retreating to his basement for the next few hours to finish the armoire that Katenka had demanded for so long.

***

The news about the unpredicted launch of the mysterious object that Yezh had built spread through the village like a plague. Even the school's walls had echoed the rumors. Children are like parents: what they hear they retell a hundred times. What people saw in the sky yesterday of Yezh's first flight was the main topic in the class—a failure that turned into a joke.

Maksimilian could only stay in his corner while others talked endlessly and laughed about his father. Everybody knew whose father he was, and Maksimilian knew he couldn't hide his head under the sand for long.

"Hey Maks, was that your father who built a flying machine?"

Maks shrugged with an apologetic smile that lasted no longer than a blink. But soon another student nearby spoke up.

"It's impossible. I saw that machine in his backyard the other day," said one of them.

"Didn't he say a few days ago that his father is an inventor? Nobody else would have flown with a machine," said a third boy.

"That's true. Good point, Gori. So, it was Maks' father: He really did fly up."

"What goes up must come down." replied Gori.

"Yeah. I forgot about that, too. He didn't last long."

Laughter burst out in the class, putting Maksimilian in an awkward spot. That his desk was in the middle of the class only made things worse. Natalya had left the class temporarily, leaving the students with the sole instruction to prepare their exercise book. Maks hoped that she'd return faster. That period felt like an eternity of torture.

Even teachers heard about the missed launch. Miss Natalya commented that it was a nice try that demanded a lot of courage. She praised Maks' father as someone brave and smart to pull that trick off. She expressed her worries for his safety, understanding the complicated danger invoked in such action. Of course, Natalya corrected mockery from others on that question. Her words, wise as could be, made no sense to skeptical hearts.

***

Nobody felt worse than Marushka, who felt pain looking at her husband through the window in the backyard for the way he fared after all that happened to him. He was clearly having a bad day; it was visible. The man offered every bit of his strength, knowledge, and commitment to make it happen, only to have it come back and slap him in the face. She watched him as he scratched his head, trying to fix broken parts with a wrench. She still couldn't believe what happened the day before, still in awe and shock.

She had to admit, though, that the boy was right. Yezh did manage to make it fly, even if it lasted only a few minutes. But Yezh wasn't satisfied with that accomplishment. That's not what he wanted. He dreamed of something bigger, more than just an ordinary flight.

Then she thought more about it, about the violent crash and the loud noise that nearly scared her to death. She had wondered whether Yezh had been killed, if by chance she lost him in the accident.

She was confused, not knowing what to think anymore. She feared for Yezh's safety but did not have the heart to tell him straight out of her belief and worry about the danger that lurks in his adventure. Should she convince him to quit that dream? Is Yezh flying toward fate instead of toward glory?

After repairing a lot of what was wrecked around *Sputnik*, it was time for Yezh to go back in the house. He had given every spark of energy he had for nearly three hours straight. His physical tiredness was visible, and Marushka invited him to sit down for a while. He let out a big sigh, his mouth wide open and dry.

"I'm thirsty. Can you make me some tea?"

"We are low on water. We don't have enough for anything anymore. We need some for tomorrow and for the rest of summer."

"Oh damn! That's right. I forgot about the well."

He had used nearly every drop of water from the well, and it was not even enough to reach space. Unfortunately, now there was not even enough to make him tea or coffee. This was bad.

"I told you to be careful what you were doing. I don't know what moved you to empty our well like that."

"A flight for nothing," answered Yezh, disappointed, his gaze locked onto the ground.

She didn't mean to bring his mood down. Enough of negativity;

she needed to think productively. Troubles seemed to strike them from all directions.

"What are we going to do about this?"

It took him a few moments to think of an idea.

"We need to find another source. We'll dig a new well somewhere else."

"How long will that take? We'd better be digging as soon as possible, before hard and hot days come."

Just great—this is what Yezh hated the most. Instead of inventing something to make his life easier, his imagination backfired and caused him to have to work a few more days in the field. But Marushka was right, and he was ready to accept any punishment for his mistakes. After all, this situation was something that he had created with his poor judgment.

"I'll be up to do that as soon I rest a little bit."

Yezh aimed for the couch, his only consolation for all his miseries. His mind was preoccupied with the work remaining on his ship. The wrecked body parts—the engine, the wings, the jets—caused chaos in his mind, but Yezh shoved it all away and restored order to his spirit. Enough thinking about mechanics, which constantly popped into his mind. Enough thinking, period! He'd never been able to rest since this madness started.

The door opened. Maksimilian was arriving home from school. His parents turned toward the door to see their son coming in with a sad expression on his face, his head lowered. Yezh knew something was going on with him after a long look at his face.

"Hey, Maks, welcome home."

The child didn't answer but dropped his bag, his face expressionless.

"How was school today?" Yezh's voice was enthusiastic once more, trying to shake off his negativity.

Maks sat down on one of the sofas but not next to his father.

"Not so good."

"I can see that. Your face is miserable. What happened?"

No response came from Maks, his face still expressionless and his gaze on the ground. Was it fatigue that caused him to be like this? Yezh tried to find out.

"Leave the child, Yezh. He's just come back from school. Maybe he had a bad day like you did."

Yezh was tired of all the negative things happening to his family. All the hardship he went through to help them seemed to ruin their happiness.

"Oh, come on, Maks. How can we know what happened if you don't speak up?"

Still no response from the child.

"Did someone steal something from you? Did somebody say or do something bad?"

In a sudden outburst, in a grating voice that epitomized sorrow, the child answered harshly.

"The whole class knows how you tried to fly to the sky and failed. Now everybody is laughing at me."

He got up and walked to the stairs. Yezh was speechless and saddened to hear that. He never thought it'd have such a big effect on Maks' life at school.

"At least if you really flew to the sky," he said one last time before tromping up the stairs and he was no longer with them.

Having witnessed her son's outrage, Marushka understood her child and could only hope that it would never happen to any of them ever again.

"Even the child is having problems at school because of you. I told you it would be detrimental to let everybody nose around your machine," said Marushka.

"What am I supposed to do?" Yezh defended himself with a little shrug. He couldn't bind their eyes up, couldn't gag them, either. He certainly couldn't build a wall all around them that would be impervious to any evil eye. What could he do to keep evil eyes off their property?

He could do nothing to make things better now other than going back to work. A hole was waiting to be dug and he didn't have too much time. Summer wasn't going to wait for him any more than winter for his crops.

Right after taking a little nap, that is. He needed to be recharged to build stamina for the field.

Maks went to sleep soon afterward. But his sheep counting turned into a spaceship launching countdown. Maks flew to the world of dreams, where he peacefully dreamed about how his father could have been walking on the moon, and how his classmates could have become jealous of such a great deed by such a unique father as only he had.

Chapter 20
Luck Strikes

That half an hour leaked out from the hourglass so quickly it brought Yezh to a cynical perception of time. As he stepped out, he took a moment to feel nature around him. The wind moved the trees. The soft heat touched his face. The cicadas' song—a lullaby in the springtime that felt like summer. Then he saw the progress in their field: the sprouts were growing at slow rate and more had to be done. The wheat had to be cultivated soon.

He took a few steps down the field. He had been so busy with work and stress that he rarely enjoyed nature, never had time to appreciate its songs and beauty.

***

"Poor Yezh," said Makar. "He has to go back working in his field."

"Still more and more digging," said Kiril.

"Are you telling me that he won't be working on his inventions anymore?" said Bogdan.

"When you have to work, you've got to work," Kiril commented. "The field cannot wait."

They compared his field with his neighbors'—not much to be proud of. He had accumulated enough lateness.

"There's still a lot to do in the field, more to plow, to prepare sprouts, to attend to their needs," said Rodion. He sighed deeply. "The field is a big place."

"So small yet so big," replied Kiril absently.

"That's true. At least his field to be worked is growing smaller with every bit of sweat," replied Rodion. "It reminds me of a good song."

"A song to cheer him up?" replied Makar, throwing a look at Rodion.

"Ready to sing for the field, comrades?" asked Rodion.

"Sure," replied Makar, who picked up his gusli, "a song for the big field."

Phoenix Phoenix

Rodion waited behind his accordion and when the last one, Bogdan, was ready they started their song.

"'Polyushko Polye'!"

And so, the four Cossacks began to play a folklore song, and a sad song it was! It was originally sung to tell a story of a young Red Army soldier going out to the field to keep watch for the enemies' possible invasion.

Russia is a big country, the largest in the world. The farmers who live here depend solely on good crops, but the fields in Russia make a vast territory to cover. Big fields inevitably bring big work, but such work isn't easy in Russia—recalling the famines in the past. Farmers used to sing a wish that would make their field smaller to work on. Or when they wished it to be bigger to produce more food, it would not respond to their efforts. Some see it as a Russian soliloquy that curses the vastness of troubles that it brought them. But even as winter falls, the snow takes its place and their lands grow smaller nonetheless.

Little field, you never seem to dwindle!

Now, with Yezh out there, his brows furrowed, ready to dig dirt, he seemed to be fighting the invasion of all misfortune on his field and simultaneously the evil eye of the spiteful neighbors.

***

He analyzed his backyard, and the hunt for a well began. He heaved another sigh as the only thing his mood could muster. Yezh knew some spots where rainy days used to create a pond of water, a shallow, deep crater that easily accumulates any rainfall onto its surface. It was a place far behind his courtyard still visible from his windows and near the windmill. Shovel in hand, Yezh was into dirt again. This would have to be deep, probably deeper than his first to accumulate more water.

***

Marushka had been absorbed in cleaning the rooms upstairs. Later, she decided to go collect some provision of water. She went to her room to pay the pink pig a visit—or in this case, a mere bottle. She collected some of the rainy-day funds.

Wait a minute!

First Farmer In Space

She believed she had seen more coins than this. The idea of Yezh sneaking around came to her. She took some coins that were left in the bottle bank and she went searching for Yezh until she spotted him far behind in the backyard, digging his new well.

As she stood by the sliding door, she watched carefully in silence. *Poor Yezh*, thought the woman, *this man is trying hard to work like any other men.* She hoped he wasn't pushing himself too hard. It looked like he was like digging his own grave, inflicting so much pain on himself for nothing. She still loved him even though he had been behaving recklessly. Her frustration over the lack of coins in her pig bank turned into a sorrowful pity. What was done was done, there's no need to cry over spilled milk. She needed to go buy water while they still had it in stock. Russian markets were unreliable in quantity of stock. There might not be enough water for everybody! She'd better get her share.

She went out to let Yezh know that she was going to buy water. Yezh hoped it wouldn't drain their funds, what was left after his last purchase. Marushka did realize the shortage and wondered what could have happened as Yezh remained silent in his shallow hole that promised a hard hour of solid work. He couldn't disagree with that investment. His water was much needed. Marushka bounded off, leaving Yezh to continue digging in uncertainty.

Please make it already filled with water, don't make us wait for the next rainy or foggy day, thought Yezh.

***

She walked to the store with a fast pace. Contrary to her wishes, the store was crowded. Marushka felt like hiding her face from the crowd, and it could only get worse when Tatjana coincidentally appeared. The first topic was about Yezh just as she had anticipated. She tried to avoid discussing useless details. She lied about being in a hurry, but Tatjana's long-windedness knew no restraints. She refused to reveal any more information than what had already circulated. She barely shook off her mouthy neighbor and aimed for the bottles, so she could hurry out of there before anybody else asked too many questions.

***

Anastasia finally found a perfect time to catch Yezh for an interview. She had tried several times since yesterday's failed launch, but they never had a chance to interview the man who undertook that dangerous challenge. She took her chance another time and went to the backyard with Jovani.

Her fragile, skinny legs found walking on the ragged farm soil to be harsh. Jovani was right behind her with a camera. The ship was still unmoved since yesterday's events but did look slightly damaged. She swept the land with her blue-eyed gaze and found Yezh all the way in the back. She hurried along.

He had been digging for quite a while. With some persistence and in the coolness that the pit offered him, he was able to get to a great depth. When he came back up to rest a little bit after pulling buckets of earth out, his muscles were hurting him. That's when a voice distracted him from his duty. He wondered what could be happening now. By the looks of it, he had guessed her to be one of those propaganda makers, one of Ivan's most trusted scouts. Beside her was this man who was taller and a little bit more built than himself, holding a camera.

Don't be rude. Act normal. She's not Ivan. thought Yezh.

They exchanged greetings.

"I'm sorry to bother you like this, mister. We tried to get in contact with you since yesterday but were unable to find you. I know you are busy, but I have a request."

He planted his shovel, hands on the handle, ready to listen to her story.

"We wanted to have an interview with you ever since you flew up. Could you have some minutes to spare for us?"

He thought about Marushka again and didn't know if that was a subject she'd be willing for him to discuss.

"Not quite sure what my wife would say about that."

"Oh, is that the problem?" said Anastasia. "There is nothing to worry about. It'll be only a few questions about your ship and your story with it. Not many have done that. You could become famous for what you have done, you know."

First Farmer In Space

"It depends in which way I'll become famous," said Yezh, a little bit more than doubtful.

Anastasia didn't understand what that meant. She tilted her head slightly, expecting more details, but Yezh did not follow through. He thought about it and concluded there was nothing about it that could invade their private life.

"Sure. Fine. I don't think it's going to hurt me in any way."

"Trust me, it won't take long," said Anastasia. "Can we move near your ship for the interview?"

Yezh agreed, and Anastasia went in front of *Sputnik* to shoot to show the world what a great invention was standing behind her. They rolled the interview in front of *Sputnik*, the first ship of its kind in existence.

"This is Anastasia from your local Red Star news report station, and here we are here with Yezh, a mysterious man who has made one of the most intriguing things in the world." She moved to her side to give Yezh a chance to speak up. "We have seen a bizarre flying machine in your backyard. What is this machine behind me?"

"That's my ship."

"Could you tell me what kind of ship it is? Yesterday we saw that machine in action, but many have been left to wonder about it."

"It was made to fly very high; it was made to fly in space."

"Interesting," said Anastasia, who thought this should be the biggest news story of all time, and that they were at the right time and place.

"How did it go yesterday when you tested it?"

"Not so good." Yezh expressed dissatisfaction on his face. "It didn't perform the way I wanted it."

"No? What went wrong?"

"It ran out of water."

"That's unfortunate," said Anastasia, "but still it was something unseen in the history of mankind. You still managed to fly with it to some point. How do you feel about that?"

Yezh couldn't find the word for his dark opinion. "Well, it's an all-or-nothing situation. If it doesn't accomplish what I meant for it to do, then it's a failure."

"I understand that point of view," responded Anastasia. "Will you try again?"

"If I can find better way to upgrade it."

"What did you use to launch it?"

"Water."

"That's it?" exclaimed the interviewer. "Wow, that's interesting to hear. I never thought I'd hear that water could launch a machine in the sky. As we all know, planes don't run on water."

"Yes, I know that," responded Yezh. "I tried to go with something unique and affordable."

"Now that you used water and it didn't work out too well, what will you use next? Are you still going to go with water next time? It seemed to do a good job though."

"Yes, it did at first, but it wasn't enough for the rest of journey. I'll have to find another kind of fuel maybe—or make a bigger tank."

"I see. There's always a way for everything. Wish you good luck, master Yezh!"

Anastasia moved back to the invisible audience from the camera's eye where she concluded the news report: "… wonderful invention of the twentieth century. And this was Anastasia from your Red Star news report station!"

It lasted barely a few minutes, and Yezh saw the camera cut off. *Finally, it's over.* It must be said that he felt awfully insecure in front of it. That was his very first interview in his life. Anastasia thanked him and told him about another part of the story.

"I received a notice from my employer earlier. He asked me to ask you if you could come for an interview at the radio station. Would you be interested in that offer?"

"Another one?"

"Yeah. Well, this is truly a marvelous, historical phenomenon. You have done a remarkable work, Yezh. You deserve to be known for it."

"But it's a failure. I don't feel like sharing failures with anybody."

"Even from failure people learn. Everybody makes mistakes, and that's how we get better. I trust you will try again, and next time could be the real thing. Don't you think?"

Those were inspiring words for Yezh.

"You're right." Yezh showed a face recovered from shame and fear. "Perhaps there will be another way; I am sure of it. I think I can come to your interview."

"That's great. You can come tomorrow around midday. How is that?"

"I'll make sure not to forget that hour."

"Alright, mister Yezh. We'll be seeing you soon. Have a great day of work!"

Anastasia departed, leaving behind Yezh, who didn't know whether he should be regretting his hasty decision. Perhaps the mention of fame is what drove him to say such rubbish. He looked at *Sputnik's* towering height with a reconciled, woeful stare.

Sputnik, why did you have to be famous in negative ways?

***

Later that hour, Marushka arrived home with plenty of bottles for drinking. Since she knew that Yezh would be thirsty as a stray dog, she went to give him a cold bottle.

She was surprised and happy to see how deep Yezh was able to dig in less than two hours. It was incredible how hard this man works when he is motivated. Not many motivational things had happened lately, though. He probably did it because he realized that he had no other choice.

In return, Yezh told her about the interview he will have tomorrow. She didn't argue much, which he didn't expect. Just the same old warning that she always gives, even reminding him of what effect it could have on their future. After that, she let him be for the next few hours.

Phoenix Phoenix

***

Katenka was annoyed to see Ivan spending so many hours outside rather than building that armoire, and whenever he was inside, she'd see him nosing in a newspaper. When Ivan learned about the failed launch that he missed yesterday, he tried to catch up on the story. When Katenka came out from the kitchen, she saw Ivan in front of the television.

"Are you going to finish that armoire?"

He watched for any news about Yezh. The reporters he saw yesterday must have spread some viral information, but all he could hear was the Kremlin talking about their scientific research and then the activities of the Americans who wished to surpass the technology of the Soviet Union. The latest launch of Luna, the world's first satellite, had inspired criticism and paranoia from the West. Ivan could smell a war coming along.

"I chopped wood and cut it for hours yesterday, and this morning I was assembling the wood frames. I need some rest."

For a while Katenka nagged him to build an armoire, so Ivan remained in his basement for hours. It was almost done. The wood cut was done earlier, and the pieces were jigsawed together.

"Don't be a slowpoke like your neighbor, Ivan. You should finish it soon like you promised."

"It's almost done, it's almost done," said Ivan with a spark of annoyance in his voice. "Can a man have some rest? I'm going right now into the basement."

With no time to rest, read a newspaper, or watch his television, he headed to his workplace. It wouldn't be long before he'd start to paint it.

***

Every strike of his shovel hitting the ground brought a curse to his lips. He had dug for several hours or more, what seemed then like an eternity of pain. Every level of depth that he excavated had to be thrown out with a bucket that was heavy and had to be pulled out with a cord. He did this to the point that he nearly got *too* tired—tired of everything.

He swept the sweat from his forehead. He had to persevere in digging for a new well or he'd be digging through solid ice in frigid tem-

153

peratures. Despite his wishes, he saw no water pooled underground. He was disappointed by the rotten luck he always had.

He took a gulp out of his bottle. It was almost empty, and he was still thirsty. The sun was still strong in the sky.

Come on Yezh, you can do it, he assured himself before picking up his shovel again.

He went down into the hole and kept digging. He plunged the shovel mightily to make bigger holes for the work to go faster. This last stroke wasn't a soft one. It seemed he had hit another rock.

Cursed stones!

It was too dark down there to see any rocks. When he raised his shovel, something was coming out of the hole—something black, something liquid, but it was so dark he could barely see anything. All he could see was its dark textures and glossiness from dim sunlight.

"What is this?" whispered Yezh in astonishment.

Whatever it was, it was leaking out and invading the small space he had for stepping, making him step aside. It was staining his boot. This couldn't be happening. He knew what this liquid was all about, but he wouldn't dare to believe too much, couldn't give it too much hope. He didn't want to fool himself in case it turned out to be dark water. But no, this was really something unusual; this could be only one thing. A shaky smile appeared on his face in the darkness.

He was forced to climb up the ladder quickly as the liquid was catching up in height. When he came out, he peeked in. It was still climbing quickly in elevation. Yes, he could confirm it now.

"Marushka!" yelled Yezh from afar. It took several shouts for her to appear at the back door and to come running to him—all the way back. The poor woman thought that Yezh got injured, and her heart beat faster.

Oh, spirits of misfortune, what could have happened now? thought Marushka.

"Marushka!" said Yezh when she arrived, so happy, it almost terrified her to see such extreme excitement. "Look at this!"

The hole with more than several meters deep that she remembered was now gone, completely covered with this black fluid.

"What in the world is this?" demanded Marushka with a shaky voice.

"Can you believe it? Please tell me I'm not imagining it!"

"It's something black—black as coal, Yezh," confirmed the wife on the verge of laughing out in joy. "What did you discover?"

"It's oil!" yelled Yezh with uncontained joy. "We found oil!"

One or two gazes at it wasn't convincing enough. It was too hard to believe it.

"Blessings of nature," said Marushka as she peeked in the pit of coal-colored liquid, something she had never seen, at least not in natural state.

"This is truly wonderful." She too couldn't hold herself from shaking and exploding in tearful happiness.

"Do you know what this means?" said Yezh with undying excitement. "We're going to be rich! Rich, you hear me?" repeated Yezh, who obliged himself to bring her to believe this.

If she wouldn't believe it, then he didn't know what to do with her skepticism.

He jumped high from joy. Marushka offered her prayers before joining him in the dance of madness.

***

It was Katenka who first saw them after she heard wild cries of what she thought was her cattle. But it was just their neighbor. She took a better look and understood that something had happened.

"Ivan, I think our neighbors are finally losing their minds," Katenka said loudly. "We can finally confirm that today. Come look at them!"

Ivan was busy in the basement, finishing what he started yesterday, the armoire, which was yet nowhere close to looking like one. Much parts needed to be attached after the paint would dry.

"What are they doing?" asked Ivan, who felt lazy about going back up the stairs. He already knew that Yezh had lost his mind, and if his wife lost hers today, he wouldn't be surprised, nor would he care much.

"They're dancing!"

"What?"

"They're dancing like a wild pack of wolves after a kill."

Who cares about the armoire? He rushed to thunder up the stairs just to see through the window, abandoning what he had started doing. His laziness was suddenly murdered by the great joy of more bad news from Yezh's side—sarcastically speaking, of course. He caught up with her.

"What are they doing?"

"I don't know," Said Katenka.

Unable to see well what was going on, Ivan was curious to see up close and personally.

"There's only one way to find out."

He took his leave for the far corners of the backyard and moved along the fence with careful, quiet steps.

They had jumped, danced, and screamed, and all of that hadn't calmed down their excitement.

"This is truly the best day of our life," said Yezh. "Do you know what we can do with this? We can sell it for a fortune." His voice changed to a mere whisper.

"We can become like Aleksei, don't you think!?" asked Marushka, unsure how to measure their joy and luck under conditions of fortune.

"Of course, but even better. We won't need to do field work any-more."

"And no more sprouts. And lots of water supply," continued Marushka, the sentence guessing what Yezh wanted to say. The larger the list the merrier.

"Yes. We could even have enough money to repair my ship, to make it bigger and more advanced than it is now," he said, going on with his enu-meration. "And the rest of it can be used as fuel for my ship. There's lots of it everywhere! Enough to go back and forth around the moon."

Their excitement became suppressed when a terrible realization dawned on Yezh. "Let's not tell anyone," said Yezh in a low tone. "Be sure that Ivan doesn't know this."

Marushka showed a face of surprise and understanding because she had forgotten about their nasty neighbor.

"He will die of worries about this," said Yezh, who finally believed he had the upper hand over his neighbor.

Ivan, who arrived by the fence, did not risk being spotted when he heard his name being mentioned by Yezh, quickly taking a low profile behind the fence. He had arrived casually to have another neighborly talk, but this one was quickly turned into a sneaky approach. They hadn't seen him yet. It was a good thing he hadn't spoken anything, which he intended to do when he got there. It looked like they didn't want him to know about this.

What did they find? What was their secret that they absolutely wanted to hide from him? He was all ears, all very attentive.

"Oh, how fortunate we became today, Yezh!" exclaimed Marushka, her hands in prayers.

"And we have lots of it."

"What are we going to do with all this oil?" asked Marushka absent-mindedly.

It took Ivan a while to understand what they were talking about. Yezh found oil.

Ivan didn't know what to think as anger and confusion washed over him. It seemed that luck had struck Yezh finally. As for luck, only Ivan could be affected, no one else. A smile appeared on his face after he gave a little thought.

If Yezh found oil in his backyard, there is a chance that there could be oil under his yard as well.

Yezh peeked around the place, making sure that nobody saw him, especially not Ivan. They weren't around, not peeking through any window like owls from a tree hole at night.

"Go fetch some buckets somewhere. Hurry!" It was the haste in his voice that Marushka obeyed immediately.

And she departed first. After Yezh studied the stagnant state of the oil pool, he also went to assist her. He wanted to contain this spill, prevent any loss, hide it from any eye, and prepare some batches for sales.

"Oil, isn't it, Yezh?" whispered Ivan with a devious smile. "You thought of hiding that from me, but there's nothing that Ivan doesn't know."

Ivan slowly sneaked back, staying close to the fence, his steps quiet like a mouse until he reached his house to let Katenka know of the situation.

Chapter 21
Spring of Gold

Yezh hid well the dark pit from any eye. He managed to fill many buckets and store them somewhere safely. But he didn't have enough buckets, so he had to let the pit be for now, for what had plentifully remained. It's wasn't like it was going anywhere.

Yezh knew that the next step would be to find a way to sell the oil in massive quantity but had no idea how and to whom. He asked Marushka to call her friends to see if they were interested in buying some oil since it was black gold that was indispensable in this village. The overstressed woman went to start the calls. The first ones would be her closest neighbors around the corners.

That's when Yezh thought of changing his engine. The steam engine would not work with oil, and he had to find or buy a new one that would run on oil. He hurried to his ship. Shaping ideas and measuring his plans, he began to dismantle the engine.

***

After counseling his wife, Ivan thought of digging in the backyard to see if he also had oil. He had to know, as every second he didn't was killing him. Katenka advised him to hide his intention from their neighbors. It was better to let them wonder, to think that they didn't know anything of the oil discovery.

Casually, Ivan left his house, pretending to have another regular day. And why not have an ordinary conversation with Yezh?

"What could you be building this time?" said Ivan, who then corrected himself to maximize his deception. "Or un-building, since that's what I see you are doing right now."

Yezh had already taken out the heavy engine with little effort. The levitators did their job, pulled it out easily, which had been attached to the ship's wall.

"Oh, neighbor," he said, expressing his fake surprise. "I was just about to change my engine here."

"I told you it wouldn't be able to fly."

First Farmer In Space

"We all make mistakes, and every mistake makes us stronger next time."

When Yezh asked Ivan what he would be doing today, Ivan lied about his intentions. He told Yezh that he'd labor some more in the field. In return, Yezh said that he would be going shopping soon, an excuse for his imminent disappearance in an hour or so. Ivan then walked away from the fence. Both men were unaware of each other's foolishness, both lying, and both fooled.

He hadn't gotten too far in his work when Marushka finished calling some of her friends who agreed to buy some oil from them. The work around the engine could wait; he didn't have time for that now. Hiding the pit with a wooden board, his ship half-way disassembled, they made their final preparations. In any case, they were well prepared, and started off with a few buckets as test that they carefully placed in their small car and drove around the city in search of potential customers.

***

Ivan used that opportunity to start digging his hole. He had peeked subtly over the fence, and when the choking red car left his sight, he concluded that it was time to do something about the oil while their foolish neighbor went shopping. They wouldn't be back for another hour or so. No matter how long it would take him to dig, Ivan was already convinced he would find oil in his backyard. Even Katenka agreed to help a little bit with a shovel.

He chose a good spot and began digging.

"If Yezh found oil, so can I," said Ivan after his first shovelful. "We'll see who's going to have the last laugh at the end."

***

Discreetly, Yezh and Marushka managed to sell some buckets privately to some local merchants and neighbors. At a fair price, people bought it. When the people asked them about the origin of the oil, they'd lied about buying it and changing their minds. It worked without too many questions. But they knew they'd have to go larger scale and reach industries.

That day they managed to gather several thousand coins, which, after they did another dance of joy, went to buy a very good oil-burning engine with a few leads from Joseph. Of course, Yezh was planning on transforming it into a powered airplane engine from a weaker and simple oil-burning engine.

***

Meanwhile, in a frenzy, Ivan dug a deep hole within a few hours. Like he always claimed about farmer's luck, he did find oil in such a short time. The black gold gushed out of the hole. Katenka had left shortly before to tend to some other important matters around the house and to spy upon their neighbors' return. He hastily yelled to announce to his wife that they really did have oil beneath them, and when she ran out to him, they had their own slice of joy.

"What are we going to do with it?" asked Katenka, all excited.

"We're going to sell the oil for money," answered Ivan, who seemed already prepared for this occasion. "That fool is going to sell some to repair his ship. Meanwhile, we'll put it to better use."

"That Yezh doesn't know how to use his luck. What a pity for him. I don't know why luck is desperately trying to strike him when he is too stupid to know how to use it."

They continued talking in their house after they, too, filled up some buckets. There was so much they wanted to buy and to do with the fortune that they'd have to talk it over for the next few days.

***

It took almost the entire day for Yezh and Marushka to travel and shop. Upon purchase, Yezh paid the company to deliver his engine right away. It was a small engine for a small airplane but Yezh planned to transform it into something bigger. When Yezh got back home, he leaped on his work, and he asked Marushka to make a search for local industries that might buy their oil.

Meanwhile, Ivan and Katenka hurried off to cover their digging with something other than wood planks. This had to be continued tomorrow.

If only that loser had taken more time, thought Ivan.

***

First Farmer In Space

The next day, Marushka dressed her boy for school, and when he went to school, it was her husband's turn. He had that radio interview to do. She carefully picked his clothes, and Yezh looked like anything but a poor farmer. She dressed him casually in more clean clothes, doing her best to make him look good. Yezh left home for his radio station interview around eleven o'clock.

***

This time it was Ivan's turn to visit the local people to sell them oil. Surprisingly, they ran into several customers that Yezh already sold to and were rejected because their supply was full. Ivan knew already that Yezh was playing a sneaky game with him. When he announced to his wife in the car that Yezh was already here, they realized what Yezh did yesterday. He was selling oil. It's okay, thought Ivan. He imagined that he'd have to go to industry. At least they had acquired plenty of coins within an hour. After a long drive, they returned home, where Ivan fell on his couch to rest.

A little bit of news today wouldn't hurt him, either. Maybe they'd be talking about that foolish farmer next door. Ivan didn't hesitate to turn on his television. And why not—the radio too! He couldn't afford to lose a tiny bit of information. Those reporters must have got some more facts.

And look at that! It was his favorite radio station on both television and radio.

***

"Comrades, this is Boris from Red Star radio station. Welcome everybody, and greetings on this marvelous sunny day. We have today a very special guest from Leninsk. His name is Yezh. He is a farmer but also an inventor, and he has a fun story to tell us. Hello, Yezh!"

People from all over Leninsk were listening to their radios, astonished to hear Yezh's voice answering the announcer's greetings. "Greetings to you, Boris!"

Yezh was able to introduce himself properly, telling his background and skills before Boris moved to the important part of story.

"Could you tell us how long you've been doing this hobby as an inventor?"

"All my life I've been thinking and drawing ideas. It started when I

162

was eleven. One day, a generator broke at my parents' house. I decided to make my mother happy by fixing it up with my knowledge. After playing with the wires, I finally fixed the generator. After that I became fascinated by technology and began to have visions of building something new. That must have been my ultimate dream, and it has driven me this far in life."

"Amazing! You must have developed a hand for those things. Are you currently working on an invention?"

"Yes. For a few days now, I've been busy building a ship."

"A ship? What kind of ship is it?"

"It is a spaceship."

"Is it the same object that we saw in the sky yesterday?"

"Yes, it is!"

"Did you hear that, folks?" Boris expressed wonder in his voice. "Yezh is building a spaceship to travel in space."

"We had news that you did not succeed in reaching space. Is that true?"

"Yes," replied Yezh solemnly.

"What went wrong, may I ask?"

"I ran out of water."

"That was unfortunate, but hey—you reached a fair height in that rocket. That deserves some credit, I'd say!"

The fact that someone else told him that fact led Yezh to feel a bit better, as Yezh was ready to accept any and all kinds of praise from the world.

"What drove you to believe that you could fly in space? Why would you think of doing that?"

"It all started with questions that raised my curiosity. Since I wanted to find something to do that would distinguish myself from the others, I thought that challenge would be the best thing ever."

Their interview took about half an hour. At first, he felt uncomfortable with all this, but at the end of their interview, he began to like his fame.

"We wish you good luck in your space travel and hope to hear more from you when you are in space."

"I will get in touch—if I find a way to communicate to you when I'm in the sky."

"That sounds fair enough for a first-time space experience. We could probably reach you with our radio waves," said Boris with enthusiasm.

Yezh wandered off, thinking: If only it could really be possible. Just maybe!

"That might be a good idea," whispered Yezh thoughtfully.

"It looks like our inventor has a new idea. What came to your mind, Yezh?"

"A radio is just what I need to add to my spaceship, but I never owned any such luxury. I was wondering if it's possible that you could spare one of your radios from this station?"

"Spare you a radio? Yezh, my friend, you have come to the right place for a radio," said Boris. "Unfortunately, our radios are still in use. If that's the only thing that's missing on your spaceship, then we wish you the best of luck in finding one."

***

"Ha, ha, he just admitted on radio that he doesn't have any money," said Ivan loudly to Katenka, who was somewhere around the kitchen. "What a bum!"

Ivan found it hard to believe that his neighbor passed on the radio. Strange since Yezh didn't own a radio. His interview was about nothing but his new invention. He even bragged about himself on the air, ridiculing himself in front of the nation.

Ivan had always mocked his idea but hearing Yezh on the radio confess his intention nationwide only confirmed his belief that Yezh truly wanted to reach space with that tin can.

Not only Ivan but nearly all of Leninsk heard the radio. If not, their neighbors passed on rumors, and then it became the only thing that everybody talked about. Yezh's short speech was taken to heart by many people who respected him. That day, many people got ideas about his story. Some who believed what Yezh said formed personal dreams. Young and old, the poor and the rich, the dream-oriented and the dreamless, all were emotionally touched in a way that led them to think big, and perhaps once more to have dreams of their own.

Yezh came back home surprisingly early. Coming through his door, he was immediately welcomed by the smell of cooking. He became hungry on the spot.

Maks was already home from school. Yezh was tired. He only wanted to get out of this good-looking uniform.

"Father!" greeted the little boy with a smile.

"Finally, home?" said Marushka, peeking from the kitchen.

"Sweet little home," Yezh replied, taking off the upper part of his uniform.

He sat by the table across from Maks, taking a breath and relaxing. He scratched his head.

"How was your interview?"

"It was great."

"We saw you on television."

Yezh let out a tired laugh.

"How was school?"

"Fine, I guess," replied Maks. "Look what I did."

There were papers, a pair of scissors, and a few crayons on the table.

"This was my school project today. Look what I drew today!"

He showed what seemed to be a portrait that Yezh couldn't recognize.

"Who is that?" inquired Yezh.

First Farmer In Space

"You don't know who this is?" asked Maks in surprise. "It's Lenin!"

"Oh," said Yezh. "Right. I barely recognized him there."

Now that Maks mentioned the name, he did see a small resemblance from what he guessed was facial hair—a small beard and an old hat of the czarist era.

"And I also made these."

Maks showed his father four letters that he cut from red paper. They were meaningless to Yezh until Maks put them into order, making a word:

CCCP

"That's very nice!"

Maks had been working on the table for his project.

"So, you've been doing something about the Soviet Union in class. A good little patriot!"

Maks was rather proud of the art he displayed on the table.

"We learned history in class. That's why," replied Maks.

Marushka was cooking something in the kitchen. She was making something delicious as Yezh was able to smell it. Tomatoes, peppers, and a few eggs were what his senses were telling him. One of his favorite dishes. He planned to eat first then he'll go to finish upgrading his engine

"Dinner is ready. You can come to the table," his wife called out.

"Well, I guess I came home just in time for eating."

Maks and Yezh stood up and walked to the kitchen. Yezh for some reason thought about Lenin and CCCP. Being so busy, he barely had any moments to see himself as a citizen of such a great nation or to think about their great founding father, the man who was able to change a whole nation, to change the lives of millions of people and the face of history with it.

Chapter 22
Rise of Morale

Nonetheless, Yezh bought it the next day. The money that he earned from selling a few buckets of oil was enough to make a little wish come true. A screwdriver in hand, a tweak here, a tweak there, he made minor improvements to the new radio.

For an hour or two he was entangled in cables and electrical parts. The radio made two-way communication possible. Now he could give feedback to earth and receive questions from his fans.

He went to install one end of the radio on board in the cockpit and left the part meant to be used by ground operators on the table. He was gone from public view for a while until his voice echoed from the speakers that amplified his voice three times louder.

"Communication is operational. Finally, the last upgrade is completed."

The radio screeched loud. Marushka was doing her knitting when she heard it and went to the window where she heard a static screech coming from the radio and the ship, but Yezh was nowhere to be seen.

"Marushka, pick up the microphone!"

Now it was clear: It was Yezh calling her. Surprisingly, he managed to add a radio to his invention. Somewhat confused, she stepped out of the house, came over to the table, and grabbed the microphone. It took her a few moments to find out how to use it.

"You made it," Marushka said happily.

"What do you think of my new space phone? Now you can call me whenever you worry too much."

Marushka felt teased. "Sure, I will."

***

Ivan was startled, sitting alongside his wife in their home. He toppled over from his swinging, soft chair with his newspaper in hand. A loud, omnipresent voice was speaking that demanded their attention. Driven by curiosity toward it, Ivan came out of his house to see that it came from his neighbor. Of course, it did; all stupidities came from there. Seeing Yezh nowhere, Ivan walked out of his domicile for a better look.

It wasn't clear, but he heard Marushka yelling at something she was holding in her hands, and then the same screeching voice sounded back.

He became fascinated again. Ivan pulled off his hat and held it in his hand. Yezh never failed to astonish him with new ideas and perseverance. What he had done this time was but a small victory. He still couldn't believe it. Yezh never knew about radios, and there he was, adding a radio communication device to his new inventions.

***

After admiring her husband's clever work, she told him that she would make him some tea and went back inside.

In the first use of his new intercom, passersby in the streets halted their walk, postponing their destination to look in the direction of Yezh's backyard. Neighbors close by were startled—falling off their leisure chairs or from ladders, having no idea what the loud noise was about. Soon, people from all over the neighborhood gathered around the fence.

Yezh wasn't expecting a crowd to greet him when he exited his spaceship. Nonetheless, he knew he was gaining fame among the neighbors, and he waved at them. Feeling sure that popular opinion had shifted to his favor, he adopted a confident manner when he approached.

"Still working on it?" asked a woman.

"Yes I am. I have done two more upgrades, and now my ship is completed and ready for launch."

"Will it work this time do you think?" said a man gripping a pitchfork.

"I am certain of myself that this time everything is right."

Such boldness struck people's hearts. They looked at each other. unsure what to think.

"When do you plan to launch?"

"I don't know. Whenever the weather permits."

Phoenix Phoenix

Many were seeing it for the first time, and others were eager to see it finished, counting every day that Yezh took to finalize it. Low chatter came from the crowd. They were the beginning of a new legend, still interested in the unusual machine.

"I want to see that machine fly," said one woman.

"Yeah, me too. I don't want to miss that opportunity," said a man in his forties.

"I'm sure you won't. It's hard to miss anything going on in this village," replied Yezh.

"I'll come whenever the launch happens," said the woman.

"It will be a big day for all of us," said Yezh, who was ready for any challenge.

After the greetings, Yezh retreated in his house and was quickly interrogated by Marushka, who had a different opinion about what he said.

"Why are you acknowledging their witness for the launch?"

"Well, if they want to see it, it's up to them. There's nothing to hide from anybody."

"I told you plenty of times: People will talk. This will end up being bigger troubles for us."

"Oh? What could go so wrong?"

Marushka was strictly against high profiles. Rumors always end up as defaming propaganda. She had no intention of living the life of a superstar, especially not one of bad reputation. No matter how many times she preached to Yezh, she found it difficult to make him understand. People don't care if what others do is interesting. They only want to hear and see bad things happening to them.

Yezh stationed himself in front of his spacesuit that hung proudly on a cloth hanger. He relished the display with amazement, feeling uplifted. Marushka knew it was his ambitious curiosity that would send him into space despite any danger that lurked in darkness. She couldn't think about anything except which fate would crush him. She feared for his safety. Slowly she neared him. Suddenly her duties around the house seemed meaningless. Yezh was more important to her now.

"Yezh," Marushka started, gaining his attention. "I think this is a bad idea. I know we talked it over a little, and ..." She paused briefly. "Do you really need to go up there by yourself?"

"Marushka. Isn't there anything that won't worry you?"

"I understand, but I meant couldn't you do more testing before going up there?"

Yezh watched her eyes, trying to figure out the meaning of her words.

"You could send something else instead of you to see what it will happen."

"Like what?" asked Yezh.

"I don't know. Like a camera maybe?"

He hadn't thought of that yet, and the idea was appealing but not very heroic.

"We don't have a camera, and I can't think of anything that can capture information better than the human eye."

She felt helpless to avert whatever might transpire from Yezh's poor judgment. With a quick grip of hands and an outburst of her voice, Marushka spoke her message, sounding angry.

"Yezh! Snap out of your bubble! I know you have your mind over the clouds. Just think about us for once. If you found a cave full of treasures, would you jump right into it, pretending that nothing would jump on you? Whatever you choose to do, I won't stop you, but do think and measure twice before launching."

Marushka turned and walked away.

Yezh needed to be shaken a little bit to realize that what he was doing is wrong. He hadn't considered his family, the effect it would have on them if he didn't return. Dreaming deeply and blinded by curiosity, Yezh understood what he was facing now. He would take precautions for Marushka and Maks, if that was what would make them feel better. This time he wouldn't let those accidents happen.

So how would he manage to make her feel safe? How could he further investigate the void? Would a camera suffice to reveal all that he needs to know? A camera can barely record what it sees, but the temperature, the pressure, the oxygen … all of what will be missed. If a camera survives the void, it doesn't mean a man could. Then how would he do this?

The next few minutes he did a lot of careful thinking. He looked at his space armor hanging on a stand. Would there be any chance he would survive?

Chapter 23
Defective Realization

Yezh gripped his hammer again to start working on the ship. He needed to put in a decent effort to repair his ship completely. He had learned a lot from building and rebuilding, from mistakes and successes. He had a dexterous hand for mechanism, and his brain was well trained to see numbers and logic, considering he was just a poor, stupid farmer. All he had to do now was to test it all.

Only a few components remained to be checked and tested for proper functionality. Some precise details remained, one of them being the functionality of the system. Inspection had devoured an hour. He had worked on his oil engine since yesterday, when he arrived home from the radio interview, and that went well. It became a jet engine now, and its testing was successful.

Everything was fine until he arrived at the psi gauge. Upon studying the complex oxygen input system, he spotted a disturbing defect he let slip by his fingers that could affect life support. There was no way of saying for sure. Some calculations were needed.

Assumptions couldn't be made, but by the looks of it, his invention had to be converted into numbers. He knew the liters of his oxygen, the psi, the flow rate, the volume of the ship, and had plenty of examples.

He needed to know if a space traveler—or whatever he would be called—would have enough air to breathe because he had spotted a small defect in his ship. Numbers take shape in different outcomes. The absence of wind has made it possible to hold onto papers outdoors. The fresh air of a stagnant atmosphere is somewhat helping with ideas.

The oxygen tank's output port could be adjusted to the number of bodies boarding the ship and number of days the missions lasts. The carbon dioxide must be eliminated from the wastes. The tank contained pressurized oxygen that entered the cabin at a rate of slightly under fifteen psi. He used the tank's volume, the hours he intended to keep *Sputnik* in the void, and every important component in an equation designed to assure life support.

Yezh had brainstormed. His long equations running down the paper concluded with a negative number. That was bad. It meant a small defect in the spaceship's makeup produced an unstable oxygen output. For an average person, the oxygen could be disproportionate and could become fatal. The result of calculations was 35 percent—a little bit too low on oxygen in Yezh's opinion. It would be gambling with life just for glory.

Yezh wiped his forehead, realizing the terrible mistake he had made—and at the very last minute. The numbers spoke for themselves. This would be impossible to do. Yezh cursed quietly.

***

Maks arrived from school. He was especially eager to come home since his father told him that he'd be venturing out soon. He lost no time in reaching the space ship, knowing that he'd find his father there as usual. Yezh was wiping his black hands with a handkerchief.

"How's *Sputnik* going?" asked Maks.

"Oh, Maks. Back from school," said Yezh. "I finished upgrading my engine and fixed some problems here and there."

"Awesome. Is it better this time?"

"I'm definitely sure about that. I think this is the upgrade that will make the big difference. I was checking my ship one last time."

Yezh did not talk about the defect he had found near the oxygen tank and the psi gauge. He wasn't too worried about it. His optimism and resilience were too strong.

"Lunch is ready, boys!" Marushka called out from the kitchen.

"Oh, lunch is ready. Let's go to the table before she gets angry," said Yezh, patting Maks' shoulders.

The family sat around the table, where they were about to dig into their meal—a soup with vegetables. They took time to settle over the table, but Maks was hungrier to satisfy his curiosity than for food.

"Are you ready to launch soon, Father?"

Yezh did not answer. He may have tried to find a good answer, but Marushka had no problem answering instead. Trying to be understanding and sympathetic to her son, her soft voice spoke.

"Unfortunately, we had a talk about that not long ago, and …" She paused to choose the right words: "we decided that it'd be too dangerous for him to go now."

"What do you mean by too dangerous? Are you telling me that Father will never launch for space?"

He looked at his mother, then at his father. Yezh showed an apologetic expression and couldn't find the courage to look at his son.

"Maks, I didn't say he'd never launch but that he'll be taking cautious measures to try to find alternative ways," said Marushka.

"Father, you can't do that! How could you? You can't just give up that dream. You promised that you'd be doing it."

Despite being a boy, he knew what his mother was trying to do.

"Maks. Life is more important than fame and money," said Marushka. "We can't afford to lose your father, can we?"

It was true, but for Maks it was the legend that his father was trying to make of himself that was his happiness. It simply excited him to see how big a man could be in a lifetime. Flying to space fitted him perfectly.

"Is there anything that you don't worry about, Mother?"

"I'm sorry, Maks," she said apologetically. "I wish there was another way of doing this. It would be preferable if he would find some alternative to the story."

"That's lame," Maks answered back. "And I thought he'd be the first one to see the moon."

Maks swirled his spoon in his soup, thinking how his father could have been great.

A long silence overcame the lunch, with Maks in a bad mood. Sputnik was probably the noisiest one in the room because he was eating his dog food in his little house. Yezh hated this situation he was in. Being between his wife and his son wasn't the ideal position—a decision that makes one happy and the other sad. His hopes of turning the table in his favor lay with one idea, one that took many hours of his days to be cleverly thought out.

Phoenix Phoenix

"Then I have a better idea," said Yezh.

"I won't go up before knowing more about the void. A camera won't do the trick since it won't record all the information I need. It means we need to simulate a real situation, a real person in flesh and blood."

It puzzled both his son and wife. Maks' face brightened a bit. His father always found alternatives. And Marushka thought that Yezh finally learned to think clearly.

"We may need to prioritize." Yezh watched Marushka's face. She was trying to guess what he wanted to do. "We may need to sacrifice something—or someone."

"What do you mean by *sacrifice?*" Her hope that it would be a good idea was tarnished by one word.

Yezh knew there was no other choice; it had to be done.

"I need someone who will take the glory and risks for me. All I want to know is if it's livable out there. After thinking long hours about who or what to pick, I've come to a conclusion." He took another short pause before continuing to his point. "We'll send Sputnik instead."

"What?" said Marushka in disbelief. "Sputnik? The dog? Why would you send him up there?"

"Sputnik?" said Maks. "You want to sacrifice Sputnik?" Suddenly all the launching talk sounded like doom. It scared Maks, but then he thought that it was supposed to be his father in that place. The adults had instilled fear in the child's heart with this space story.

"Unless you want to risk sending me. I'd be fine with that," said Yezh who had no other resolution. "Nothing will happen to Sputnik if I am sure it won't happen to me." Yezh convinced them both to come back to trust his invention. "The ship is built to near perfection. I have inspected it countless times. Its upgrades were substantial to prevent any failures."

"You disagreed to send a camera, but you'll go with the idea of sending a dog?" Marushka's skepticism couldn't easily be altered.

"A camera is just a camera. It can offer only images, but a dog can prove to us if it is possible for something living to go in space, and if my ship has truly been built to perfection."

"But how would you do that? How can a dog drive a ship?" said Marushka.

That was another problem that he had to face, and he came up with something to solve that problem—without any help from Ivan this time.

"I gave great consideration to that and came up with an idea. I will add one last component that will turn my ship temporarily into a remote-controlled ship."

It was a childish idea that delighted Maks almost immediately.

"A giant RC ship? That's cool!" exclaimed Maks. He turned to the dog, who all this time was listening from his doghouse, oblivious to what they were planning for him.

"You hear that, Sputnik? You're going to fly an RC ship! You're going in space!"

Marushka looked back at him with a lasting gaze, feeling that this could become another horrible mistake that Yezh will commit.

Chapter 24
Sputnik, the First Dog in Space!

After lunch, Yezh had to measure his next modification, hopefully the very last. He went straight to his cockpit, where the main controls were. All buttons and wires were two-way, each meant to send and receive messages from other parts of the ship. The cockpit would serve as the bridge of signal communications. This time he concentrated on one direction, the one that would send signals from the ground to the ship. To accomplish this, he unscrewed and took out the metal panel plate, and remodeled the radio.

The work would have started right away if it weren't for the materials again. He made sure not to forget anything on his list and departed for shopping. All he needed were miscellaneous items such as extra cables, receptor and receiver plugs, small light bulbs, and plastic caps for buttons.

Meanwhile, when Yezh left his backyard to hop into his car, Ivan peeked behind the fence. When he no longer could see the neighbors, he tackled the far end to collect more oil. Yezh's shopping gave them a chance to play a hand on his neighbor. Before anybody saw what they did, a multitude of buckets were ready to store in the back of their car. The last buckets they filled nearly drained the pit. Now all they needed was to find an oil refinery.

Yezh returned home with his tools. Building an RC device on the ship wasn't all that complicated. He needed to know only the circuitry and logic of triggers. The radio acquired another function. It would use transmit signals back and forth. Its conversion was good training. It would also receive information about the *Sputnik*'s altimeter.

A small box with many buttons rested nearby on the table. Each of the buttons were assigned to a different part of the ship. It no longer resembled a radio. Yezh had given it a whole new look.

He grinned happily when his first button triggers were responding. This upgrade took several hours, excluding the walk to the retailer stores to shop.

***

Ivan had searched for a local oil business for hours. It was the first thing he did this morning. Katenka was working around the house when suddenly she heard a shout from the living room.

"Aha! Found it!"

Katenka puzzled over what he meant, but upon looking she realized that he had found something in a booklet of some sort.

"What happened?" inquired Katenka. "What have you found?"

"I found an oil refinery industry outside of Leninsk."

"There is one?"

"Of course. I'm always a lucky man!" said Ivan.

"We should go today if we have time."

"Are you kidding me? For a thousand coins, this is worth losing an entire day!"

"Then we should prepare those buckets while the neighbors are looking the other way. They were locked in their house for a while earlier. Yezh has been working for hours now."

Both knew that when Yezh works on his inventions, he pays little attention to his surroundings. That could be used to their advantage in working on their oil find. So that's what they did, both yesterday and today. "Let's prepare now!" Ivan dropped the book and headed to the car with Katenka. They both had smiles on their faces.

There was agitation on the other side of the fence but nothing that Yezh or Marushka gave any thought about. They couldn't see for sure what was going on, but it was clear to them that their neighbors were once again going out on an errand. What business they had that made them so mobile they couldn't say. But it gave them an opportunity to do whatever they needed without the gaze of Ivan over the fence. When Yezh heard their car leaving their home, he knew that this was the only time he could fill his tank with oil. With a bucket, he went back and forth and slowly did the tank fill.

***

What could Maks do but spend time with Sputnik? He had taken the dog away from the ship and needed a few moments with his friend alone. Sputnik wagged his tail. He had never seen Maks so playful with him, giving him so much affection. Sputnik rejoiced with every bit of love. It had been a while since someone played with him. They were in the quiet of their home, on the couch.

Maks enjoyed playing with Sputnik; the dog always made him laugh. He got licked, and Sputnik's whiskers tickled him. His tail whipping in all direction, Sputnik couldn't remain idle in one place, constantly moving in on his legs. He even wanted to jump on Maks, who laughed. He hadn't had this kind of fun with him for a long while.

"Father is planning to make you a space dog. It won't be too long before you'll be going up. Are you excited?" said Maks. He gave him a short, ephemeral smile.

Sputnik responded only with body language; he was agitated.

"Sput, we don't have much time left to be together," whispered Maks to Sputnik. The dog whined back. "I know. I wish we had more time to play."

Maks didn't know why, but he was sad. His father had told him a while ago to go play with Sputnik. The poor little boy did what he was asked, but he started to wonder why he said that. Maks was a little boy, but he wasn't stupid; he knew what it meant. Suddenly, for the first time ever he looked at Sputnik in a different way—one that showed sorrow and pity on his face, as if he was seeing him for the first time, and the last.

His eyes were seeing Sputnik, but his mind wasn't. He patted the dog mindlessly, but his thoughts were above, among the stars.

The dog licked him out of immense contentment. Obviously, for Sputnik this was all a game, but for Maks it was like a farewell, like a deterrent to crying out loud for the departure of his friend.

"Sputnik," said Maks woefully.

Marushka heard Maks talking with Sputnik from the kitchen and listened. It sounded sorrowful to her ears. She casually peeked toward them without being seen.

Poor Maks. He knows something. He must be getting old enough to understand such things. Poor Sputnik. I feel bad for the little one, too.

It was too sorrowful to watch, and like a strong woman, she turned and walked away.

First Farmer In Space

Nearly three hours had passed. Maks went to have a look at how the RC ship was faring outside.

"Come on, Sputnik. Let's go see what Father is doing," said Maks, and Sputnik barked once.

Maks and Sputnik paid Yezh a visit. He was standing by the box on the table—the radio thing. Maks was eager to see the improvement. His father pushed a few buttons, and to Maks' surprise, something reacted on the ship. The wings moved left and right very slightly. Maks was awed. He was able to control the wings' tilt, the gas input, and the lights. But Maks wondered if his father truly had control over all the ship. He went to sit with Sputnik on the balcony. Both watched his father working on the next step.

As soon as one thing was done, another task presented itself. After making sure that all systems were responsive from ground control, he had to calculate a trajectory. But any trajectory needed to be monitored with accuracy and inevitably would need a computer. There were none in Leninsk, of course, which made things more complicated. He had to bypass that problem. Guessing and doing everything manually was risky and hard, but he was still in the Stone Age. His technology was limited—and so were his financial resources. His brain was the only computer he could have, and he had to depend upon it for all outcomes.

Yezh thought hard for several minutes about how to proceed, how to navigate the ship. Calibrating time and space: That was the key.

He had no books, no expert to consult, nothing that could offer him guidance as to how far the sky reaches out before the nothingness of void continues its extension. That is, if it does.

At last he had everything ready. He had already sold a large amount of oil to various places. He had measured his pit's quantity and had to set a big amount aside for the fuel. He still had no idea how much oil he had beneath his feet.

Let's do one thing at a time. Starting with Sputnik.

There was still no presence of their neighbors. Yezh blamed Ivan and his sneaky evil eyes for contributing to the failure of his first launch. Now that the evil neighbor was gone for a few hours, it was the perfect timing to launch *Sputnik* again.

Phoenix Phoenix

Yezh and Marushka had spoken secretly about the right moment to launch and agreed that it was better when Ivan was absent.

He asked Marushka to give her a big blanket for the floor where *Sputnik* would be. The soft blanket was to protect *Sputnik* from injury if things got a little rough.

She hurried off to get it from the basement while Yezh waited by the living room. He looked at Maks and the dog. All he had to do was to tell him about the moment. It wouldn't be easy.

She came back with the blanket and nearly startled Yezh when she handed it over. Yezh placed the blanket on the floor of the ship. It was pink with dog motifs, a cute theme for our great heroic friend, Yezh thought.

The ship was ready; the control normal; the tank filled with oil; the air compressed within its secondary tank; the ship's cabin was at room temperature. Yezh made sure that everything was as it should be from inside. Next Yezh had also put a thick blanket on the ship's floor to prevent *Sputnik* from being hurt by the impact upon landing. He added some food in case his landing gets delayed.

Maks was both excited and sad, playing with *Sputnik* in a corner while his father was readying the ship.

Marushka, for her part, was simply anxious for the dog as she stood by the door, her arms crossed and a sadness on her face that could tell a thousand stories.

Yezh stepped out of the ship and went to the radio on the table, turned on some switches, and the engine began to whistle. There was nothing else to be done; everything he could have done for *Sputnik* was in top shape. He slowly turned his gaze to Maks, sitting on the balcony.

"Well, it's ready," said Yezh. "It's time."

Yezh tried to keep his optimism up despite his knowledge and the gloomy, sorrowful atmosphere. Sputnik was wagging his tail, still oblivious to what was going to happen to him. He was the only spark of joy around them.

At first Maks was excited about all of this, but the constantly grim facade of his parents convinced his mood and hope to take an alternative course.

First Farmer In Space

"Is he going to come back, Father?" asked the boy with a sad face.

The last hour that he took to reconsider his choice and hope had put Yezh in discomfort from fear and skepticism. Marushka's words and logical thought had gotten a grip on his mind. He felt betrayed by a part of himself, fooled by naivety that God knows where it would have led him in destiny. It was a long, hard moment of silence, and Yezh found it hard to swallow. Accepting the harsh reality, Yezh knew Sputnik might not come back but had no idea how to explain it to Maks. Perhaps it was better if the kid knew less. But it tore Yezh's heart either way.

"I can't decide his fate, but the chances speak for themselves. Everything should go well as planned."

His father's face showed an empathic sorrow that Maks did not trust, and that provided no reassurance. He turned his regard back to his animal friend.

"Sputnik. I love you. Please come back to us safely."

Maks was about done with Sputnik when Yezh spoke up once more.

"Don't you want to hug and kiss him?"

Yezh gave this advice to his son, and he listened, giving a teary kiss to his friend. Sputnik felt the sorrow of his masters and whined quietly, as if understanding their feeling. Marushka neared to give her love to him, patting him on his soft head.

Yezh took Sputnik in his arms from Maks, who couldn't look at Sputnik anymore, his tears uncontrolled. The dog's tail was still wagging from all the intense love that was given to him today.

"Okay, Sput, it's time to go, friend." His voice sounded solemn, a voice that wasn't too far from breaking into a sorrowful one.

Marushka watched how Yezh walked toward his ship. She barely held her tears, feeling like screaming out of pain from a broken heart, and stopping this madness while she still could. No word came out of her. Of course, she did try, but Yezh insisted it would be beneficial for scientific research. Whatever happened to their poor little dog was better to put on him than on Yezh.

Phoenix Phoenix

Yezh climbed the ladder he leaned onto his ship. Each step that he took was like enjoying the final moments with his best friend, one that always accompanied him wherever he needed to go. Shopping, hunting, field cropping, sleeping, bathroom—this dog was always there for them, and they will always be there for him. Their hearts achingly whispered their soft, low blessing of love.

Yezh held the dog high in his hands, close to his face, taking one last look at the pitiful face it had, to remember him well forever.

"Our hope is with you," Yezh whispered softly. "Fly, comrade, with our blessings."

Even Yezh couldn't make himself act normal. It was at this point that he felt like breaking apart, the life-support equation repeating in his head, the numbers flashing negatively, predicting a story with a fateful outcome.

Yezh had forgotten to turn on the lights inside the ship. He gently released Sputnik into the ship, his black eyes sparkling in the gloom of the closed environment with luminosity that seemed to Yezh like some kind of sorrow that Sputnik expressed—that he understood something. The dog knew what this meant. How desperately he tried to show his concern and objection, but nobody seemed to either care or understand his dog language.

Sputnik did not want to stay alone in the gloom when Yezh tried to close the hatch, and he pushed his muzzle outside, emitting a low whine that caused Yezh's heart to ache.

Yezh gently pushed the dog back inside, patting him a little bit to distract him, and in a lucky moment, when Sputnik was no longer blocking the hatch, Yezh closed it. Feeling guilty and like traitor at same time, Yezh found the moment hard to swallow, and to go back to the communication device on the table. He thought how it was supposed to be different.

This was supposed to be you, Yezh. It could have been your victory, or your fate.

In any case, either he had missed his glory, or he had escaped a terrible fate. Sputnik didn't deserve to die. His mind constantly reminded him that this wasn't the way a friend should be treated. This was a death sentence to a friend who had always been loyal.

First Farmer In Space

No, he will survive. He will come back. Just like I was supposed to.

He went to join his family, glancing back at the ship.

"That dog was a genuine friend," said Yezh in an apologetic voice.

A few tears had to be wiped off his face, his sorrowful pity over a whine that could no longer be heard. It was unnerving, but it had to be done.

Yezh manipulated the controls. He turned on the lights inside, and the ship projected fumes and flame. The large ship launched and departed hastily, gaining dramatic acceleration with a space traveler that wasn't even a man.

And so, the man's best friend and fantastic loyal companion was no longer with them on earth. All looked at the ship gaining height except for Maks, who sobbed. He didn't know why he was crying. All this had been a joy that he had supported all this time, only to come crushing on him with a sudden sorrow.

Concentration was an important part of the current situation. Now, if he could go very straight, it should be easier to make the ship drop back to this very same spot it launched from. All he had to do for now was pay attention carefully to the wristwatch until it reached the time frame he dropped from the other day. Based on the information he calculated earlier and what he could salvage from his past experience, he needed to reach at least fifty kilometers. The altimeter, which was connected to the radio as a point of origin, had already begun counting.

Let's hope that all my calculations are right, so we can give our friend a safe ride and a quick one.

Maks got up from the balcony stairs and ran to cry on his mother's dress. She comforted him under her embrace, not knowing who to pity anymore, Maks or Sputnik.

The altimeter climbed quickly to twenty, then reached thirty, then fifty. The speed it took to reach his previous record had been reached with ease in an unbelievably short amount of time. The ship must have been going at the speed of sound. The altimeter was still climbing: eighty kilometers … and then finally it was about to reach a hundred kilometers within a few seconds.

Phoenix Phoenix

***

The department of national defense had spotted another alert, showing a familiar pattern of flight and slightly increased speed.

"Sir. That signal appeared again," said the agent who quickly gained attention from the minister.

"Is it the same one as the last time?"

"The speed and trajectory are quite similar. It has to be the same object."

"It's that peasant's work again," said the minister. "Gather more information, including its location of launch."

This time he knew what to expect. The message from the newspaper was still clear in his mind. Despite of the story that was told on television, he knew that it wasn't a threat of any sort. But ignoring it wouldn't satisfy his scientific interest. A personal feeling pushed him to know more about this mysterious ship and that odd, backward peasant. A moment later he shouted instructions to a worker. The agent worked in a frenzy with buttons, windows popping on the screens.

"Sir, the object has disappeared from the radar."

"What?" Suddenly his mind froze. "How could that be? Where could it have gone?"

They stared at the screen, no red spot to be seen. Could there be a problem with the controls? The agent investigated the matter.

"By the calculation I made," started the agent, "it seems like it … it left the planet."

"Left the planet?"

The screen showed no life. Their gaze betrayed by what sort of trickery had been played. No one could believe that an object of a peasant went into space.

"That's impossible," whispered the minister, astonished by what he had witnessed.

"It seems that it left our planet," confirmed the agent.

First Farmer In Space

Or could it have been alien activity perhaps? It worried the minister.

He moved his attention to another agent and assigned them each a specific task to research more about this object and its whereabouts.

***

The altimeter had reached a hundred kilometers, and something was happening to it: the number vanished on the panel.

What happened to the altimeter? Could it be a malfunction? Or did it reach another zone maybe?

"I'm losing contact with the ship," said Yezh.

Confusion showed on his face as he tried to understand the cause. A long time had passed, and he did not know what had happened to *Sputnik*. The signal cut off as if something happened to it, as if it wasn't up there anymore. From this problematic turn of events, Yezh concluded that *Sputnik* had reached space.

"The panels stopped working. According to the calculation, the ship must have left our planet."

That was the only explanation. Yezh tried to cut off the fuel but didn't know if the signal was sent. Numbers flickered, and Yezh knew that the signal was trying to catch up. He pummeled the button.

Cut off, cut off fuel!

He pressed the button countless times and still didn't know the outcome. *Sputnik* was out of his control. Did it melt? Or did it fly into a zone that no longer exists? Did he just erase his ship from existence?

Maks looked at his father, then on the floor, thinking about poor, unfortunate Sputnik. Did he run out of air? Did he freeze or burn up? The ideas were too terrible for the mind to fathom. How did he fare up there all alone? He couldn't tell. However, he did not give up in his hope because this young boy trusted his father. The lost contact did worry him a lot, but probably not much could be done about it anymore.

***

It was without patience that they waited for any signal to reappear. The minister who thought about it hesitated to give a call to the Kremlin.

He desired more information before doing so, but he figured there wouldn't be anything else to wait for.

"Sir, the signal has returned."

This time the minister was more enthusiastic. The object was slightly lowering in altitude on the screens. They tracked it as he marveled at the accomplishment of the peasant.

"I think we have a hero," whispered the minister. A childish smile took shape on his face.

***

Yezh studied the situation, but there was nothing he could do. Did he pick a cheap radio? Does it need further improvements? Yezh cursed under his breath, his head lowered down.

As promised, people from all over Leninsk gathered around Yezh's backyard. The noise and flare in the sky caught the eye of many neighbors who later came to look. A man with a pitchfork spoke out; his appearance was a surprise.

"How's everything going, comrades?"

"Oh, Vasily. What brought you here?"

"I saw a big glowing light in the sky and came to see." Vasily looked around, unable to spot *Sputnik*. "Where's your ship?"

"It flew up."

Vasily switched the pitchfork to his other hand and was using it to hold his body straight.

"Did you miss your flight or something?" said Vasily with teasing humor.

"Someone else took my place for the first launch."

"Oh, I see. Who's the lucky one you offered the seat to?"

"My dog!"

"Your dog?" repeated Vasily. "You mean that little barker that follows you everywhere?"

First Farmer In Space

"Yes, Sputnik was launched as a test subject."

Vasily nodded slowly in comprehension.

"How long has he been up there?"

"For about half an hour now," said Yezh, his face and tone aggravated by worries. "But he hasn't come back down yet. We're waiting for the ship to land."

Yezh turned to his guest, mindless of the control panel. Three other peasants joined the conversation. Vasily whispered to them what was going on. Soon after, a dozen more encircled them, and they all awaited the delayed landing together. All were curious to know what had happened to the dog. They asked questions, and Yezh explained briefly how he proceeded.

Maks was inside his house briefly. He couldn't contain his sorrow as long he was outside, being tired of falsely hoping, expecting a bad outcome. He returned to his father where neighbors were asking him questions. Looking up, he and saw nothing. Not even a fragment or remains had returned to earth.

After what became too long after the ship was believed to have reached space, it was time for it to come back down, but it took longer than expected. Yezh feared that perhaps it drifted off in the wind or burned up, like Ivan mentioned.

"Where is Sputnik now?" asked Maksimilian. "Isn't he coming back?"

Yezh looked up. "He was supposed to be here by now. I don't know what could have held it up so long."

Yezh looked at the altimeter, which was still blank. No information on the panel could give them any hint regarding the ship's whereabouts. Their hope dwindled once more. Now Maks didn't know what to think anymore about his father's dreams.

"He's not coming back," said Maks after a long silence.

His father looked at him. Hopelessness was in his face. The poor little boy was pessimistic about Sputnik's survival, just as he had imagined. The boy isn't stupid, and he had reason to think like that. Yezh had made another mistake, one that could never be repaired. He must have disappointed his son with his dream. This ship was just another failed invention like all the others.

"It's not over yet, Maks," said Yezh, who wished to at least teach him the meaning of hope. "There is still a chance. Maybe it got taken away by the wind. Anything that goes up must come down."

"If it is true that everything must come back down, then where is it?"

Yezh couldn't answer that, but the search would start soon.

"If the wind blew it away, we will search and find it."

"Poor child, he must have been very close to the little barking one," said Vasily.

"Well, we're all attached to him," replied Yezh. "I'm starting to think negatively about this void thing."

Yezh joined their conversation again while Maks sat down on the balcony, reminiscing about his best friend, who had become the world's first space traveler. He hadn't come back to them, and Maks felt like he'd cry intensely for the next few days because he already started to miss him.

"Sputnik," whispered Maks woefully. "Please come back. You've always come back to us. You've always had good luck in traveling. It had to mean something."

His eyes dropped tears, his head unable to find any strength to hold up.

"Sputnik!"

An unexpected omen passed through his heart. He couldn't tell its meaning, but he felt an urge to look up. A large white object in his sight, moving at a demonic speed, electrified his mind with a sudden realization: It was *Sputnik*. The surrounding conversation had taken Yezh's attention away from his project. It was Maks who made them realize something white was falling from the sky.

"Hey look! Something is falling!"

All eyes peeked above. Yezh suddenly experienced a burst of adrenaline. How foolish he was to forget about *Sputnik*.

First Farmer In Space

"Damn!" said Yezh.

The object had to be his ship, and it was dangerously low. It would crash if he didn't move quickly. His shaky, overstressed fingers found the red button on the communication panel, hoping it wasn't too late. A parachute opened, and the ship decreased in fall speed. They followed it closely as it took a few minutes to reach the ground. The ship came straight down and landed precisely with help of the shock absorbers that he cleverly installed. They did their job properly.

The engine cut off as fumes snaked around the atmosphere-burned machine. Everything became silent. No one was sure what to expect, but the lack of sound was promising. Everybody's eyes were wide open. Yezh shut down his ship and turned off all the lights. The ship needed to cool down.

Fumes escaped from the ship. Did it get cooked by the sun?

Yezh brought his little ladder beneath the hatch of the ship, scared to approach it. He neared the ship with careful steps, his gaze locked on its still-hot, lifeless, aluminum façade. The heat that it radiated was frightening. It hadn't melted, but it surely got well grilled.

He took a handkerchief in hand, stepped onto the ladder, and found the hatch handle. He used slow, precise movements to open the hatch and reveal the darkness within. The hatch handle was still warm under his touch. His heart skipped a beat.

A thumping sound followed the shadowy movement of something that jumped on his face. Yezh reflexively reached out with his arms and closed them over his body with something in his hands. It barked and licked his face.

"Sputnik!" exclaimed Yezh, not believing his own voice.

Marushka had run outside in a hurry. Her and Maks' faces brightened.

"Blessed by the gods, the dog had returned," exclaimed Vasily, amazed.

The people awestruck by the miracle that a minute ago was a grim scene.

Phoenix Phoenix

Yezh rushed down the ladder with his loyal companion. Maks demanded to see him up close. The dog shared his hugs with everybody, his tail wagging with immense pleasure. But he was clearly under stress. The poor thing was shaking a lot.

"Sputnik. You're back!"

He barked once and licked Maks' face. They had never seen him so happy. The audience drew near to have a better look at the dog. He hadn't fried like a chicken despite being so close to the sun. And he didn't fall into an endless pit of nothingness either.

"Look at that, the dog returned after all," said another man to Maks.

"This was truly something today. We have just witnessed the first dog in space."

"How was it up there, little one?" asked Vasily.

"What did you see, Sput?" asked Maks.

Sputnik's tail still wagging in rage, he barked once. Maks didn't understand him, but he was happy to see him safely back on earth. "I knew you would come back to us."

Yezh calculated everything in his head. The odds that things would have gone so bad were small. Perhaps it was a miscalculation or his expectations too exaggerated. It was possible to fly in space, and Sputnik proved it to him, to Marushka, and to the entire nation. For now, it demanded a celebration for the first dog in space.

"Let's celebrate his arrival, everyone. This is truly a great day for humanity."

Smiles, cheers, praises, fists, and hand claps followed. The little dog deserved his accolades and his titles.

"Sputnik! The first dog in space!" exclaimed Yezh.

Those few people from the village who witnessed the launch and return of the dog celebrated the event privately. Sputnik quickly became a topic of conversation and grew popular among children. It was said among children and adults alike that Sputnik was the first dog in space. They spoke his name at school, in the markets, even in the mayor's office.

First Farmer In Space

***

"What a happy ending to a dramatic story, isn't it?" said Rodion, practicing his balalaika.

"Who would have thought to see a dog being the first being in space?" added Kiril.

They had been sitting on their favorite hill for a while. They had the best view in town for the first successful launch in space.

"Well comrades, it seems that we will be having another party to drink at," predicted Makar.

"Yes, nothing is better than a drink to celebrate a good event," said Kiril. "Shall we go? We will give Sputnik our praise for his courage."

"Let's go, comrades. I'm thirsty for some good vodka!" said Bogdan, who began standing up.

And so, the four musicians got up on their feet and marched down the hill to meet their new hero.

***

Moscow was in a hot debate. The minister of the national defense and the president of the science department were called along with many other officials to talk about what people had seen flying in the sky. Phone calls went back and forth for many hours. The department of defense had given every detail of the mysterious launch. The Kremlin was still skeptical. Was it a lucky try? Was it all an illusion? Or a trick perhaps? Moscow demanded more information and asked the minister to spy on this peasant for a while. Their curiosity about the purpose of this launch was their interest.

At least now they knew its location. It took a few trials, but the minister managed to guess its origin.

Chapter 25
First Farmer in Space

That day and the next, people heard only of Yezh's newest intention, and Yezh's promise spread across the village like wildfire. People meeting in markets or visiting friends and even children attending school all talked about how Yezh was planning on flying his ship one more time. Maks hoped that it wouldn't start more laughter in the class.

Even the mayor himself heard the news from his office men. He hadn't spent much time visiting Yezh for he was a busy man. His tourist attraction had failed countless times in the past, and to this day he was still brainstorming on how to improve Leninsk's tourism.

After failing to make a sport stadium to host national cups, and a Ferris wheel park, Georgiy spent hours in his office thinking about his next step.

At least Yezh's story brought him joy. He would have paid a visit today if it weren't for the meeting he was to have with the mayor of Stalingrad—soon to be known as Volgograd.

"I knew that kid would manage to reach space!" the mayor said to his driver.

Yezh turned his efforts toward improving his radio communications and spent extra time to make its waves longer-reaching. He wanted to be able to reach space, and he devoted every inch of energy and knowledge into making it happen. Meanwhile, his fame was growing around Leninsk.

***

Early in the morning, Yezh visited his oil pit. He had to recharge his *Sputnik*. He looked around the fences. No Ivan was in sight. He opened the pit and filled plenty of buckets. Since his last launch hadn't used much oil, he didn't have to work too hard to replenish it.

After that, Yezh went to see Joseph as he had another idea for his inventions. He decided to wear a miniature gas tank on his back and went to ask Joseph for some help.

***

Eagerness was in the air this spring. A little boy was at the peasants' square, waiting to pay for some apples. Some people nearby said something that stole boy's attention.

"Hey, isn't today supposed to be when Yezh will fly in that machine?"

People began reminding each other of the big event that was promised to them. The boy looked around but couldn't make out who was the interlocutor.

"That's true, I completely forgot about that," said another man.

They had been promised, and many were eager to see it. Suddenly, everybody started for a destination. The boy paid the merchant and left in a hurry.

Sir Heartlock was at the market to buy some apples from the same merchant when he saw everybody going somewhere in a group. He had heard something about Yezh and a flying machine but remained dumbfounded. It was hard for him to find any interest in the march as he was forced to go back to his apartment to drop his goods. Perhaps he would find himself among the crowd later. What could it be that drove the peasants of an uncharted corner of the map insane about a piece of news?

***

Yezh did not show stress at all, though his stomach felt it and a malaise obstructed his health. He just arrived from the blacksmith with two gas tanks in his hands. Maks went to school as usual but not without a few words of deception. The boy did not notice Yezh's attention quite accurately.

Our hero took all morning to reflect upon his action. His plan mentally revised and his ship inspected, he couldn't have been more ready than now. His *Sputnik* was ready for a relaunch. As he looked at his ship, he was lost in thought. Marushka brought him back to reality when she called to him from behind. She stood by the backdoor.

"Your lunch is ready. I've made you some eggplant stir."

"Good," replied Yezh, turning toward her. He was coming inside.

She had been impatient all morning. She, too, as a strong woman tried to hide her feelings about Yezh's intention. The spaceflight was still something she'd not recommend. Every second that passed tormented her soul.

"What are you doing now?" asked Marushka with a slight hint of worry in her voice.

"The moment should happen soon."

Yezh went to his armor on the stand and inspected the gas back-pack one last time. He bought it from a local hospital and with Joseph's help was able to bend its appearance to his will.

Marushka didn't like how he was testing everything, double-inspecting every bit of equipment. Why was he so cautious suddenly? He had never been like that before.

There was only silence between them for a short time, and the sudden appearance of voices alarmed their senses. The voices came from the front of their house.

"Who might that be?" whispered Yezh, who went to peek through window.

It was people, the same old neighbors who wouldn't leave him alone for a second. It seemed that people really were interested into this event.

"Well, some people are waking up early for something," said Yezh to himself loudly.

***

Ivan was eager to see Yezh try his chances again. Water and oil—he had channeled all his curses into turning Yezh's famous moment into another infamous, horrible disaster. This time he would have the entire population of Leninsk to laugh by his side. Nothing would be sweeter than seeing him fail in front of all these people. Yesterday was the second time he missed the launch. He started to believe that maybe Yezh was playing tricks on him. This time he would not miss it, he'd make sure of it.

He also had another smart thing to do: to count his coins from his sales yesterday. Ivan and Katenka had been counting them in his living room and laughing as they reached an unprecedented amount of money. Then he left her counting the rest while he went downstairs to finish his armoire.

First Farmer In Space

***

Even Jovani and Anastasia were disappointed they missed Yezh's launch of his dog. Jovani tended to oversleep in the mornings, which gave his partner some headaches, especially since they had arrived too late from Moscow two days ago. They heard the news at the market when they came from their hotel, but to their disappointment had come too late. Luckily, they heard from locals about Yezh's next attempt. The story about the perseverance of a farmer intrigued them enough to participate in it. And this morning Anastasia made sure they wouldn't miss it again.

Anastasia forced Jovani to drive faster. She would curse herself if she missed something else. They established themselves early near the scene-to-be, parking their truck across the street several hours before the event. They readied their camera and set up their equipment around the fence and streets. Crowd began to form around them.

Anastasia went to knock on the door and Yezh answered it. Her smile was bright but not legendary, like Yezh's. He tried to maintain a diplomatic manner with these people. She greeted him and apologized for ringing his bell so early.

"We are patiently waiting for your moment, master Yezh. And I was wondering if you are still going to launch today?"

"Well yes, I was about to dress up when you came knocking on my door."

"Oh really? Then so sorry for disturbing you. We only wanted to be sure. We're set up on the street here. Cameras will be rolling soon. Whenever you're ready, mister hero."

People began to cheer a little bit, some calling his name. One of them was Vasily.

"Thank you for your support, my comrades," said Yezh. "It is much appreciated."

"Yezh!" yelled Vasily. "You'll be the Hero of the Soviet Union."

"If only people all across the world could know who you are beneath that armor," said a woman.

"Well, I think there will be only one space traveler, right?" replied

Phoenix Phoenix

Yezh.

"Right!" replied Vasily. "Only Yezh is our man for this job. We're counting on you."

"Thank you, people," replied Yezh, who checked his watch. "Well, I have to go now. Must get prepared."

People wished him good luck. Yezh closed his door and the crowd in front of his house moved to the sides.

Neighbors who were inspired by Yezh's greatest challenge of all time invited themselves to witness the spectacle that was promised to them. They were counting every second it took for the star traveler to step out from the comfort of his home and embark in the insecurity of his ship on a journey to the unknown.

***

Katenka called Ivan. She hadn't missed a moment of this soon-to-be spectacle of shame. She had been peeking through the window for nearly an hour, and Ivan was finishing his armoire downstairs when he finally came to join her.

"Is he starting?"

"He went inside to get ready. People are everywhere."

"Good," said Ivan. "Let's see how he fares this time."

Katenka couldn't keep up anymore; she had lost too much time already. Her laundry needed to be done, so she vanished from the window.

***

Marushka helped Yezh to dress, making sure every part of the suit was as it should be before putting his helmet on. She helped to connect all the vital parts. They double-checked the gas tank on his back for maximum security. Yezh was very soon struggling against his own new weight and felt more like a scuba diver going on an undersea excursion than a space ship pilot. He could barely move in it. His arms were spread wide.

"How do you feel?" asked Marushka.

"A little bit tight ... a little bit fat."

First Farmer In Space

He looked ready. Nothing was missing, Yezh believed. He took his helmet in his hands and looked at it thoughtfully. Vasily's words that he said earlier echoed in his mind.

How will people know who I am in this armor? Should I write my name somewhere?

He found the idea silly. His name wasn't a suitable part of this armor. He wasn't a dog to be tagged. He continued examining his armor, his mind still away. Last of all, he examined his helmet.

A hero? Me? Hero of the Soviet Union?

Now that he thought about it, what Vasily said was true. This would inevitably make him a nationwide hero. Obviously, this will bring a great deal of fame to his socialist nation.

Fame …

An unrefined idea popped into his head. He could share his fame with this great country. But how?

His sight wandered away from the helmet and into the room, where it fell on the table. Red letters that Maks had cut from hard paper lay there: four of them, meant to represent the USSR. Yezh stared at them.

That's it!

The idea refined itself into something more glorious and dignified.

"Marushka, can you bring me a red permanent marker?"

"A red marker?" She bounded off to fetch one while Yezh continued to stare at those letters, lost in thought.

Marushka was returned from the basement: "I found one."

Yezh grabbed it in his gloves and started to write on the forehead of the helmet. Marushka stood by him but didn't know what he was doing with the red marker as it was in her blind spot.

It took him a few seconds to write it carefully. When he swiped it with his gloves, it didn't meet his expectation satisfactorily. It wasn't permanent on the helmet; it was getting erased easily. Not good.

How could he do it then? His eyes on the table again, he didn't have too much time to think and work out something. With a hint of an idea, he rushed to the table.

He took the four letters and found a bottle of glue at the side. It was all he needed to make it happen. He hastened to finish, his back turned to Marushka.

"What are you doing?" inquired his wife but no answer returned. But Yezh's quick, frantic moves spoke of haste.

When he finished, he showed it to her. She saw four glorious red letters in big, thick outlines on the forehead of the helmet.

CCCP

"Why are you writing that?"

"To glorify our nation. That's why!"

This last-minute detail was sure to change history the way he wanted. After all, he owed Lenin a few patriotic thoughts. The symbol was sure to gain many hearts and much interest. Yezh put his helmet on, and Marushka acknowledged his appearance as elegant.

Sorry Maks, I needed those letters.

His wife made sure he was well tucked in, so he wouldn't catch a cold. They went to the back door, where Yezh stood defiantly against any dangers ahead. Being ready, he knew he was about to put on a show for the demanding crowd outside waiting for his departure.

As soon as he stepped out the door, applause welcomed him to take on his dream, and people began to cheer.

Ivan came out of his home to have a better look. The applause and cheers vexed him already. Where was the mockery? The laughter? The ridiculing of Yezh?

"Hey look, there's Yezh!" said a teenage boy.

Yezh gestured to the crowd with a hand as he stepped toward his ship, waving like he was some kind of legendary hero. Both those who didn't know him and those who knew him learned something on that special day that was yet to become symbolic in human history: that a man is meant to dream. Some would regard him as a teacher who taught them how to dream, how to strive for something higher and better, and to face the hardships of misfortune. Also, they could easily see the gloriously imprinted CCCP on the helmet. This person was planning on becoming a hero.

He checked if the ladder was holding its ground solidly. As Yezh was about to embark on his ship, he slowed down to gather himself together into a solid bundle of confidence. While he was building his courage, a sudden urge from within forced him to take a moment for his natural needs.

What should he do now?

He couldn't go inside again, and he couldn't take off his suit. With a little thought, he knew what he should do.

He went to the side of the ladder—near his ship. Men and women awaited to see his next action. Eyes of wonder gazed at what he would do. He was beside the ladder, and what people saw was somewhat ironic and awkward. Seeing Yezh standing a long moment by the ship and nowhere near climbing it, people began to wonder what he was doing as the cheer dwindled slowly.

"What is he doing?" demanded a woman who couldn't see well with all the pushing around among the crowd.

A boy started to speak. "He's … I think he's … urinating!"

People showed a varied set of grins. Ivan didn't understand why he was doing that but wished that it would be awkward enough to provoke something in the crowd. It was brief but funny, and Yezh felt sorry for what he had shown them, a farmer's lack of social graces.

Satisfying his needs, zipping, and tucking, with a renewed hand wave, Yezh continued his way around along with cheers.

He steeled himself for one final moment before embarking on a wild journey. His gloved hand took a grip on the ladder that seemed to last forever in his mind. He was more than just stressed. Each step he took higher on the ladder was a step higher to the sky, toward a dream that was about to happen, after a long battle, hopelessness, hardships, and frustration. Yezh was experiencing a mixture of emotions.

People's eyes widened, their mouths gaping slightly. Stepping into his ship, Yezh closed the hatch.

Phoenix Phoenix

From now on, only he could witness and live a once-in-a-lifetime experience: what he would feel, what he would see through his amazed eyes, a story of courage that even he'd be telling himself before going to sleep every night.

Other people couldn't see this part of the story; they would never know.

He climbed the steel ladder and carefully sat on his chair placed sideways. It was time to turn on the switches. Lights on the projectors lit on the board in front of him, the engine began whistling outside, and the intercom screeched one time, advising all hearing ears to listen to Yezh's voice, which came next.

"All systems operational. Engine running. Prepare to launch."

Yezh's voice was naturally adapted and suave as he began the countdown.

"Five, four, three, two, one."

A bright light flashed that nearly blinded some people around. Smoke (instead of steam) rushed from the jets, which blasted a large area of soil beneath the ship.

"Launching!"

This time, when the first roaring shakes sent him afloat, he felt power under his hands. This ship must have acquired plenty of extra horsepower just by switching to oil as fuel. The engine roared divinely; the sound was somehow reassuring. Both people outside and Yezh thought: This must be it—the real thing!

The ship trembled as his hands firmly held the shaking joystick. The ship rose higher and higher.

Marushka felt her blood boil from worries, reminiscing about the other day's misfortune. She'd only hope that *Sputnik*—if that's what everyone will call it—would keep him safe. Maybe the name of their favorite dog would bless him with luck.

He remained eager to see his previous height record be reached. The gauge on the panel already showed the altitude in meters.

People's mouths gaped wide open at the rocket that made them hurt their necks and squint at the sun.

Ivan's mouth gaped wider than anyone else's. He took his hat from his head into his hand. He was shocked to see the impossible becoming possible, and it was being done by his worst neighbor, his own rival. For the first time, Ivan saw his curses and evil eye failing to provide a horrible outcome.

Fall, you damn tin can! Break into pieces!

***

Going higher and higher, an airplane was about to intersect his space shuttle's path. American Airlines was written on the sides. Aleksei was on board, heading toward the United States.

One of the pilots widened his eyes.

"What the …?"

His partner looked in his direction and got the same view. He didn't know what it was either.

"What is that?"

The passengers aboard discovered the mysterious unknown flying object. Among their faces, Aleksei's lightened up when he saw it—the only one who recognized it.

His brother-in-law Yezh!

All eyes fixated on the linear trajectory of the odd aluminum alien-looking machine that was nowhere close to colliding with them. It was odd to see that it didn't go straight toward the horizon like they were. This one had a path that aimed upward to the sky. Where was it going? How high was it planning to go? Only Aleksei knew the answer, and he knew Yezh wasn't coming with him to the USA.

Heartlock had just arrived among the crowd. He was interested to see what it was that intrigued people so much lately. He had heard about the ship, heard Yezh on radio, and now he'd seen it. There above his head a fireball challenged the height like a comet going back home, leaving behind a cold trail of smoke frozen in the sky.

During Heartlock's own era of history, when he was still young, he

Phoenix Phoenix

had no way to anticipate the importance of this day. Not until it was made an official day of humanity, and even twenty years later, Heartlock would still have a hard time believing what he had seen.

It was man's first flight in space. But not any mere flight. It had been one that appealed to the minds of people. One that was Yezh's first flight in space!

***

Bogdan was biting on a young wheat blade. All their eyes were locked on the objects up in the sky.

"Yezh finally departed."

"Well perhaps it's a good thing to sing him a song now," said Kiril. "He did manage the impossible."

"Right you are, comrade," exclaimed Makar. "Our friend deserves a song only for him, one worthy of becoming folklore in the next century."

"Alright, let's play him something," Rodion agreed, and the others went for their instruments. Bogdan spit his wheat out of his mouth.

"Ready?" asked Rodion, taking a position behind his accordion and waiting for his comrades to get ready. "For our Yezh!"

"*'Katyusha'*!"

And so, they sang a joyful song, a jingle that will catch minds for centuries to come: *"Katyusha,"* at times a happy song and at other times a sad one. A song so patriotic and so melodiously glorious that it was said to raise fallen Russian soldiers on the field for a second wind. In World War II, the song was sung by girls whose family and lovers departed for war. Young girls would sing a farewell song to the Russian soldiers, hoping for their safe return.

Sadly, despite the blessings, many remained to wait near peach trees whose fathers, brothers, sons, and lovers never returned to their arms.

Such a sad yet glorious song now greeted farewell to space traveler Yezh. And everyone hoped (against the odds of the past), that it would eventually bring the soon-to-be hero back to earth.

***

203

First Farmer In Space

Eyes accompanied the hero and his vessel to the very highest heavens—until their necks were hurting, up to the point above their head where no sound or object could be heard or seen, until they thought there was nothing more to see to this heroic phenomenon.

Marushka heard a static buzzing from nearby and quickly reminded herself of the radio. Hurriedly, she came forth to use it to communicate with Yezh. People followed and gathered all around her, ready to hear anything. Did he manage to reach space? Did something happen up there? When no eyes could find any sign of aluminum or flare in sky, they turned to the radio. People were hungry for information.

"Yezh. Can you hear me?" Marushka called out once.

Only static screeching resonated from the radio, still no response from him. Could it be that the radio he built wasn't working?

"Yezh! Can you hear my voice?" Marushka repeated.

Another screech happened. People began to get worried about this. Marushka's grim look showed her worried sadness.

After what seemed to be another screech trying to form a familiar sound, they finally heard a reply.

"Yezh here. I can hear you."

Marushka's face brightened, and people assisted her with smiles of their own. It was good to know that he was still safe.

"Is everything going fine up there?" asked Marushka.

"Yes! Everything is according to my plan."

That's what she wanted to hear. Marushka smiled, throwing a look at her neighbors standing by her sides.

Yezh's eyes didn't drift from the altitude gauge. Counting the numbers, he realized he had already set a new record.

"I have surpassed my previous records of fifty kilometers and one hundred meters."

Cheers shattered the ear-buzzing near silence. And after barely a minute passed, Yezh's voice echoed through the box once again.

Phoenix Phoenix

"Altitude still climbing."

Ears were straining around the radio. Some wanted to hear repeated what Yezh had said. They were standing too far behind the crowd. Later, his voice again rang through the air.

"Sixty kilometers," said Yezh with excitement in voice. "Still ongoing increase of numbers."

People smiled at the ground level, and after a while, they heard him reach a number that seemed to them to be great and dangerous and record-breaking.

"Eighty kilometers has been reached."

Yezh gazed in front of him and witnessed the discoloration of the beautiful baby blue tone of the sky, turning into an indigo, then dark night. Looking out the window was the only information besides numbers that offered him clues about where he was located.

"I am surpassing my previous altitude, beating my record by double kilometers now," repeated Yezh, who couldn't believe it himself. But the telecommunication was scrambling his voice. "It's getting darker," said Yezh, whose voice began to break up at some points.

"Yezh, I can't hear you well," replied Marushka. But either her voice was too weak, or he wasn't hearing her well. He hadn't replied yet.

Vasily, putting aside his pitchfork, stepped up with his manly voice, and spoke up to his comrade. "Yezh, we are losing you here. We missed a bit of information."

A bit of static boomeranged back to them. And then from the electric noise came a voice.

"This is it. I am getting there. I reached one hundred kilometers," said Yezh. Only a brief silence intervened before he spoke once more: "I'm in space."

This evoked another kind of reaction from people. It somehow excited them and frightened them to think that their comrade was no longer with them on this rock floating through the void.

They all knew that this was the moment of truth, the same thoughts that passed through Yezh a few seconds ago. Marushka, the poor worried woman, could only find solace from Yezh's safe-sounding voice.

"Is everything alright up there?"

"Yes!" said Yezh's voice, which suddenly had a different tone. "Wow!"

He felt gradually lighter in weight, feeling like a feather. He detached his belt and floated upward.

"This …" started Yezh, "is amazing. What is this?"

His senses and orientation were all mixed up, totally confused, and unable to tell what was happening to him. Everything was still dark through his windshield. He had difficulty conducting his movements, feeling like every push of his limbs would be infinite.

Then he thought for a little bit about what Ivan said. He felt no cold, he felt no heat, he had air to breathe, he was nowhere close to dying.

Or would he?

As a farmer herself, Marushka was interested in knowing what he was seeing. Yezh stopped communicating for some reason, and people around were craving for answers.

"What do you see up there?" asked Marushka.

"I can't really tell. Everything is dark. I can see the sun shining on one side," said Yezh. "Let me check my surroundings."

Yezh tried to turn on the lights, but to his dismay saw no results. Not only that, it was dark even though he had flown in daylight, but the directional lights were rendered meaningless. Suddenly Yezh cursed Ivan for lying to him.

Yezh moved his head around to spot something interesting but failed, and to counter the perpetual darkness that seemed to have enveloped his ship, he turned it sideways, as if he was half-way around and going back down. That's when he saw something that took away his breath.

"Oh!" was Yezh's first reply after a moment of silence. People's ears tingled for more sounds. It seemed he saw something.

"Wow! I see something now," said Yezh. His words were sure to engrave themselves on all minds for as long as they will live. "I see earth."

Nobody even breathed for a moment to prevent missing his next words. They feared their voices might drown his out.

"It's beautiful!" said Yezh's voice with sincerity. "I see beautiful colors! The earth … earth is blue!"

There was no doubt that those were genuine words from someone who had reached space. People of all ages were awed by his comment, positively sure that he had finally reached space.

"Wow!" said some people among the crowds.

One of them, a young girl in her twenties with a cute face of a doll, exclaimed her opinion about this, ready to confess the death of her skepticism.

"Yezh is really in space!" she yelled out loudly with a bright smile.

Her voice reached all ears in the back row. Suddenly a wave of crushing strength came from bodies pushing forward to see or hear more clearly from the radio.

Yezh gazed at the glowing blue ball below him. The hymn of the Soviet Union rang in his mind, recalling to himself all the great things his great nation has done and what he had done for it today. This was another glory for his nation, thought Yezh. He'll be a hero in the USSR next time his feet feel the soil again. His senses were missing the soil under his feet, but Yezh wasn't. There was no place for homesickness for this occasion.

Yezh wanted a clear view of the so-called void. The everlasting feathery feeling and the unusual loss of weight and floating ability led him to step out of his chair.

He decided that he could leave his joystick alone for a while and moved. Willing to move to a destination but unable to coordinate his movement carefully, walking on ground was no longer feasible. He was experiencing his very first low-gravity flight. Yezh guessed that suddenly pushing himself in the air would surely propel him forward. But the farmer knew nothing of such a thing called gravity. No law of physics he had ever learned on earth could explain this phenomenon. That slow flight across his ship was something he was sure never to forget, something he had never done in his life. That moment felt like an eternity. He managed to come near his window that was located on the side of the ship, and from there he could witness the continuation of the breathtaking sight.

This time he was in perfect position to enjoy the beauty of the scene: the bluish hue glowing on his face through his helmet visor, his eyes sparkling from the omnipresent luminosity. Earth then suddenly looked smaller to his eyes.   Space and earth—a clear cut between the two and a beautiful mixture of hues from light blue to green, to darker blue and then to coal black. No stars. One side full of life and the other deprived of any—dead. The national hymn of the Soviet Union continued to play in his head. This was a victory of a great nation that would last for centuries.

***

Ivan, who was peeking over the fence, at first couldn't hear anything clearly or see anything that was left of Yezh and his infamous invention. But even he became convinced after he heard people repeating the news by the radio.

No way! That's ludicrous.

Yezh somehow managed to get up there despite his discouraging preaching. Ivan slowly retreated to his house.

His wife, the must-know-it-all person, witnessed Ivan coming from the noisy commotion outside. His wide mouth opened, and his jaw dropped all the way down made him look like he'd seen a ghost in the backyard.

"What happened? What's the noise outside?" inquired the woman, but no response came from him yet.

He walked a few steps forward, trying to process what he had seen and couldn't hear her from his loud thoughts. She approached behind trying to pull some information from her husband.

"Yezh is gone," said Ivan lowly. "He flew beyond the sky."

That was all he said. Ivan trailed away slowly, frightened, leaving behind his confused wife in a state between incomprehension and skepticism.

Chapter 26
Mystery Unveiled

People lingered around a while longer until that they decided that the exciting trip was taking a bit too long and that no further news from Yezh was coming in. It was time to go back to their domiciles and duties. The show was over. Yezh was in space, and there was nothing more they could do now. It would be better to wait for his return. Some even asked Marushka to feed them news as soon as something happened up there. Thus, Marushka gave herself the task to watch over Yezh's whereabouts through radio communication. It was good to know that he succeeded, was safe, and was even having some fun up there.

Worries boiled inside Marushka, making her unable to stay on a chair for too long, needing to walk around to get some fresh air. And occasionally, every hour or so, someone would come knocking on her door.

How is Yezh doing? Where is Yezh now? When is Yezh coming back? Repetitive questions of all sorts came through her door. People were interested in knowing more about it. The lack of information even triggered an outrage throughout the village. It didn't bother her a bit, even if it attracted a lot of attention, something that she always felt uncomfortable with. It was good to know that people cared about him and that they were giving their support to an unearthly neighbor.

Marushka sighed a trembling sigh, but then she couldn't control herself as she had let out a short laugh. She was happy for the news. In her contentment, she thought of doing something to make Yezh happy when he gets back. She remembered something that he told her he liked. The star and moon motif dark blue tissue in the basement came to her mind. She would make him something from that tissue.

I know what to do to make him happy.

***

He had dreamed it, now he had flown to it, but he had yet to find out more about this mysterious darkness that surrounded the ship—despite his proximity to the sun. Yezh's mind filled with thoughts that were a bit too scientific for a farmer.

How big is this place? Why is it dark? What's the temperature outside? What's the purpose of its existence?

Yezh's thoughts drifted for a while, and his eyes roamed all around to see everything seeable. Not even stars were visible, which was strange, and the planet he came from was very bright, like the sun.… No … bright like the moon, actually. From out of the blue he decided that he'd follow the line of gravity and set his ship to take a world tour.

***

The words of Yezh's success reached the ears of the mayor, who, at the great news, almost leaped to the moon to join him out of intense joy. It started when a police officer came in the room in a hurry to tell him.

"I knew Yezh would do it!" said the mayor, his excitement uncontrolled. "There's nothing that Yezh can't do."

At first, Georgiy wanted to launch a celebration, or to call for journalists, but then suggested to himself that since the story was hard to believe, he should first go pay a visit.

These last few days, he had been communicating with his closest officials and the mayor from a sister city in a discussion about improving the city's tourist experience and wasn't able to visit the good, hard-working farmer. After the mayor of Stalingrad's visit, Georgiy found himself free at last. It was about time to pay the poor farmer a visit.

"Get the car ready," said the mayor. "Hurry!"

His assistants bounded off, and the mayor headed toward his wild west hat on a stand.

***

Katenka was constantly watching through the window in the front of their house. She saw countless visitors come knocking on their neighbors' door.

"It seems like Yezh has caught much attention from all around us."

"Let them be! Every minute he spends up there is a minute less in the field," said Ivan, resting on his sofa for a little bit. He had calmed himself after an hour. "He really believes that God will do the work for him. When they see that his crops aren't producing, they will see what an utter failure he truly is. He can't afford his vacation trip to space."

210

Phoenix Phoenix

"I don't know how he managed to fly in that metal box, but he must be very lucky," said Katenka, moving away from the window.

Lucky that he hasn't died yet, thought Ivan, who was impatient to hear negative news from the newspaper tomorrow.

***

Every once in a while, people would gaze up at the sky in hope of seeing any sign of Yezh's ship. That head movement became a natural reflex in their labor, no matter what they were doing. Georgiy drove down the road in his long car and halted in front of Yezh's house. Marushka hadn't gotten any rest since the launch and sewing Yezh's new clothes was at least occupying her mind a bit.

She was startled to hear the doorbell ring several times. Who could that be?

To her surprise—silly that she didn't anticipate it earlier—Georgiy's smile beamed at her when she opened the door.

"Marushka!" the mayor's loud voice echoed within the house. "How are you doing? The news of Yezh's successful launch reached my office."

"Oh, Mayor," said Marushka with a happy tone, feeling better upon seeing it was the good-hearted Georgiy knocking on her door. "You've missed his launch."

"Good to hear that he managed to do the impossible," replied Georgiy. "I always believed in that man, but he never ceases to impress me. Have you heard from him yet?"

"Thanks to his radio he left behind, we are able to contact him once in a while."

"Perfect!" exclaimed the mayor. "Let's see how he fares up there, shall we?"

The mayor insisted on hearing from Yezh himself, so he entered her house casually, leaving Marushka confused.

She brought him in the backyard and showed him the radio. Georgiy had been in the military in his young days, and so he knew how to use a radio like this one. The way Yezh had built it fascinated him when he took the microphone in his hand.

First Farmer In Space

"Yezh! Can you hear me up there?"

Yezh, who was checking his gauges and life support equipment, had been busy studying the statuses of each one. That's when he heard a buzzing from the cockpit. He instantly recognized the voice of the man he'd known for so long, Yezh rushed forward.

"Yezh here," replied Yezh, communicating back.

"Yezh my boy, it's me—Georgiy!"

"Yes, I know who you are, Mayor."

"Yezh, how is it up there?" asked the mayor. "Did you finally reach space?"

"Yes indeed, sir!"

"Great, I knew you'd make it, my dear friend. I'm so proud of you, kid!"

Yezh was happy to hear from his friend, who had always been supportive of his dreams. Yezh expressed his appreciation to the mayor for contacting him.

"Yezh, I want to hear your story when you come back down here. Just stay alive up there! We don't want to lose you, friend!"

Yezh laughed heartily at the comment.

"Sure. I will be back in a few hours or so."

That was it for the mayor. He had finally paid Yezh a visit and had shown him all his supportive admiration.

The mayor was leaving, but Marushka stopped him with a question. She was happy that the mayor believed in Yezh, but she had not stopped worrying about him since he vanished into the blue sky.

"Mayor. Do you think that Yezh will return safely?"

"Of course, he will. If everything failed to kill him all this time, it must mean that he is really a tough little bird," said Georgiy, whose voice consoled Marushka a little bit.

With that comment, he left, leaving Marushka convinced that Yezh would be back to earth very soon.

***

The defense minister visited the Kremlin walls the same day. The successful launch of the dog in space had been viral news nationwide. The Kremlin invited its officials for a speech over what they had observed from the radar and the unknown farmer.

"It is clear that we are dealing with a brilliant man who's father to a very special invention that is due to mark a new day for humanity," said the judge, sitting on his red chair. "What information do we have about this mysterious object that flew up in the sky the other day?"

"The object is some kind of a rocket," said the minister of defense.

"Does it really have the capability of leaving our planet?" asked the judge again.

"Our agents have conducted much research on this mysterious object, and they have concluded that it definitely traveled outside of our planet."

A man entered the room to relate some new information to the red throne. The man, wearing a military uniform, approached the minister's side to whisper. The latter's face changed to one of surprise. He turned to the judge, who remained silent all this time, curious about the nature of this interruption.

"We have received updates regarding this farmer's whereabouts," said the minister of defense with excitement. "We have learned that another trial has just been attempted. As we speak, the farmer himself is in space."

"He launched himself into space?" the judge said in bafflement. "The man doesn't even have any proper equipment and training nor experience to pursue such risky activity. And yet he managed to do it. He's truly a risk-taking man who surely deserves some credit. His actions speak for his invention's success."

Low voices echoed around the room, the voices of people who never heard such news before, never heard of any man traveling somewhere outside of this planet.

"This is exactly why we should move ahead and talk to this peasant.

First Farmer In Space

That new generation rocket is the property of the Soviet Union. Obtaining such technology would be a great asset for our country," said the man who was the president of the Russian scientific department.

The man who was proud to see his Luna project around the moon become a success now found himself fascinated by something that someone else had achieved, a mere peasant. A manned flight had never been seen in history of mankind.

"Then it is concluded," said the judge. "We have enough evidence now. This peasant is our hero, one that will guide the path of the Soviet Union into a brighter future in technology. This is a man that this good nation needs on its side." The judge thought of something and turned his attention to the other decorated man. "You have collected enough information about him, and you know what to do, I suppose, comrade Oleg?"

Oleg nodded. The man had a plan in his mind.

"And what about you, Sergei?" asked the judge to the president of the soviet space agency. "Isn't this worth a few coins?"

"There would be nothing more honorable for me than to meet this man in person. I am sure a little discussion will surely flourish into something most advantageous for both sides."

Both Sergei and Oleg presented their plan in the highest court of the nation. They were ready for action. Enough cat and mouse games. That peasant had been hiding in the shadows for far too long.

***

The trip was shorter than Yezh expected. During the flight, he had seen boundaries of continents and was able to name them from memory: Australia, the Americas, Antarctica, Africa. How small earth was in reality, for he had imagined all his life that it was as large as the void he now got accustomed to.

The trip had been fruitful and a wonderful experience. That's what he did for the next hour or two: he orbited around the planet a single time. He travelled the opposite direction of the earth's clockwise rotation. It was not until he had reached the other side, obscured in nighttime, that he finally saw stars and planets and unknown shooting light spots. Suddenly the darkness had revealed its bright side away from the intimidating sun. It was incredible how many celestial bodies—how many activities are happening in space. Never had he seen so many stars from earth. From this point in the sky, the stars were more numerous, crowding the sky in a chaotic display of flamboyant colors. He spotted some planets that he knew.

In this universe, all stars are aligned to make constellations, all planets are aligned to rotate around the same sun, and far-away stars are clustered in spiral disks. Yezh's mind fathomed its extravagant complexity, and to its beauty he could only marvel.

Order. This void. This space, or universe: Everything makes sense now.

Still, he couldn't call it what it was. It had no definitive name. Yezh believed it was time for it to have a better unique name that wasn't subject to stereotyping a specific boundless location. Should it have a Russian name? Many words come from Greek and Latin origin. That's why from a young age he had studied the Greek language. Then he remembered a definition given by Pythagoras, a famous Greek philosopher, about how the world is orderly. Strange—this void seemed as orderly as the world he came from.

Order—that's what the name needed to define. He remembered the word that the philosopher used and decided that shall be the name for this nameless existence.

"I know now how it shall be called," said Yezh, looking at the wonders. "Cosmos."

Yezh's trip was soon ending its revolution from where he started. He studied the fuel gauge. There was a huge amount remaining of it, and he wanted to try something else: the moon. As he watched it above him, he steered the ship toward it. That was his dream, the purpose of all this flight to glory, where his motivation and inspiration came from.

Now, onto the next adventure!

***

Many hours had passed, and poor Marushka, always worried about Yezh, waited impatiently for him to return. Every so often she'd come to contact him through the radio, and each time he responded back, giving her temporary relief. Sometimes he would not respond at all because he was busy acclimating himself to his new weight and was floating leisurely, experiencing his first low gravity adventure.

She tried to occupy her mind with her duty around the rooms but was unable to shake off the excessive thinking and hoping for his safe return.

"What is taking him so long?" she whispered to herself. She didn't know much about space as a down-to-earth woman and couldn't tell how long a trip in space should last. Hours? Days? Weeks? Would it end up like a vacation for Yezh?

With a firm approach of heavy feet, she came to the radio one more time to try to reach him again.

"Yezh! Yezh!" yelled Marushka.

Yezh was enjoying himself. He never felt so good. During his new zero gravity experiments, he let the joystick stray to take a few swimming laps around his ship. After all, it wasn't like he'd be colliding into anything like a wall or other ships. Space is empty and vast. He was thinking about this mysterious space for a while, trying to come up with a scientific explanation, but Marushka interrupted him. He radioed her back.

"Yes. I'm alright up here."

"How long do you plan on staying aloft up there?" said Marushka with worry in her voice as if she was arguing with him. "Don't you think you've been up there enough long?"

"Don't worry, I am currently planning on coming back."

"Don't play with your life!" Marushka insisted, sounding like she was talking to Maks. "Don't push your luck too far."

"Yes, yes, I know. I said I'm coming back now."

He would have stayed longer if it wasn't due to his wife. He felt a sorrow brewing inside of him. His mind came back to space, this eternal darkness veiling him. Even after long hours, he still couldn't fathom the size of this void, nor could he explain what it was. All he saw was blackness whenever the sun smiled. But at least now he had a vision of it, and to it he gave it a name.

His ship was drifting in space. He had no idea where he was exactly or where he was heading, no way to orient himself. There was only the twilight glowing earth behind blurry clouds as the main and only indicator.

Each time he passed by the window, he'd take long looks at the quiet earth, gazing as if it was his first time … and his last, not sure if this would be his last and only chance to see it.

Yezh felt a sorrowful pity. The moment that felt like eternity was ending too soon for his satisfaction. Marushka was nagging him with frequent static screeches from the cockpit, and he'd feared to run out of air and oil, or simply to drift too far in space. It was good to mention that his ship had drifted and blasted through a long distance in the void. It was time for him to go back home.

For the last few moments he had in solitude with himself, Yezh stared at the moon from his cockpit, feeling pity that he couldn't reach it today. After long hours of flight toward a moon that never increased in size, that never seemed to come, he had just realized how far the moon truly is. It would take more than a few days to reach the moon, if not months. Who knows? Nobody ever tried before.

He looked at the gauge, a device he had installed to see how much fuel he had left in his tank. It used weight and pressure to read its remaining fuel; that's how he could know. The same applied to his air tank. And both gauges were red, with only a few bars that filled the long, empty rectangle. Good that he had thought of that as well.

"Air and oil reserves are low. I should go back to earth."

He did a brief calculation in his mind. He'd been blasting for the moon for two hours now and emptied nearly half of the oil, and the moon was far from his grip. He guessed that he'd need more than triple of this amount to reach the moon. But this will not be a dead dream. Flying to moon will be inspired by today's great flight to wonder. If not soon, then later he will reach it no matter what, even if he must bring two tanks with him.

His eyes were glowing under the radiance of moonlight, making it hard to know if they were watery or not. He slowly raised his gloved fist toward the moon and closed his fist tightly, wishing it to be under his grip so badly. Its glorious radiance somewhat fitted with his inspired courage. Yezh set the course back to earth.

First Farmer In Space

Let's hope it won't take me as long to get back down there.

***

Amiss of the brave adventurous farmer, Ivan's jealousy grew into a burning sensation inside of him. Soon, if not already, people would be talking only about Yezh, how he was courageous to fly to space, how he was smart to build a machine, how Yezh was this and that, when in fact he owned nothing and was nobody special in life. Nothing more than a disillusioned farmer, that's what he was! Ivan's hatred for Yezh found new boundaries.

"Yezh is not back yet. I wonder what's happening up there," said Katenka.

She was arranging decorative statues within the new armoire that her husband finished a few days ago and painted yesterday. The cool night with an opened window was enough to dry the paint.

"I don't think he's coming back." Ivan's voice was stern, as if assured of his hypothesis. He sat uneasily on the couch. His nails were like claws of a wild animal, ready to tear the couch from fury. "He's surely lost somewhere up there."

"You think he must have died up there?" queried Katenka.

"What do you expect? There's no food or air, he could have burned from the sun, or froze in darkness, or maybe one of those shooting stars collided with him and crushed him to star bits. Anything could have happened to him. He is now only stardust!"

The possibilities were branching out. Ivan was never wrong when he predicted something. This is what he used to tell everybody around Leninsk, and people grew respectful of that man. They saw Ivan as an intelligent and knowledgeable person. His prediction had been popular in the village for a decade or two now. Ivan could only adore himself for being good at prediction.

"I only think of how that poor woman must be faring through all of this," said Katenka. "Good thing that I don't have a crazy man who dreams about stars at night."

Ivan looked at her with a grimace, telling her that she couldn't have been serious to have considered that as an option. He was no madman! He knew about these atrocious dangers that the world of void has in store. He'd never think to travel up there for he knew what awaits him. That's why Yezh isn't returning, and he won't anytime soon.

Could Ivan declare victory over his lifelong nemesis rival?

Yezh is dead. His field will never be better than his. He won't be buying anything more valuable than what he owns. Ivan has won. Now there's nobody else to be competing against him. At least he won't be inventing anymore—and being ridiculed and laughed at. He did himself a great favor, thought the farmer. A fitting end for someone who hasn't been killed by curiosity all this time.

***

All the traveling through the cosmos, all the great distances that Yezh burned fuel seemed so small now that he saw how close earth was to him. It was as if he was all along still at the gate to earth from heaven and that he never truly went anywhere too far. Could he even get any farther? Was his ship stuck onto something in the darkness? Was the gravity so intense that it forbade the ship from going beyond a limit of altitude? It was hard to tell. The darkness of space made it impossible to guess easily.

After he had taken his time for temporary farewells, he purposely drifted off course and aimed for the twilight earth. On the return, it would be preferable for him to stay behind the joystick. It would be dangerous to let the cockpit alone for too many minutes. Yezh had been lost in his mind for a while, his sense of time and orientation all mixed up as his eyes looked at the blurry clouds up front but without truly seeing them.

A rock flew by the size of his house, taking aim toward earth—his home. It flew by so close that Yezh was startled to see something nearly hit him. In a race toward earth, the rock exhibited its incredible speed. Never in his lifetime had he seen anything as fast as that object, which seemed to have come from somewhere beyond the darkness of the void. The rock took a direct course toward the bluish, phosphorescent atmosphere. And what frightened him the most was what followed next. The rock began to flare up and suddenly exploded in thousands of little pieces. Yezh briefly saw a bright light sprawling from the crash, but his senses recorded no fire and no sound. Everything happened so fast, in absolute silence and twilight. It was as if it had hit a wall or something.

First Farmer In Space

Yezh's heart rate increased. Sweat shone on his face behind his glassed armored mask where the omnipresent atmospheric light from earth, via indirect radiance from the sun, produced a bluish tint on his visage. Terror was on his face. Yezh connected the fate of the rock to his ship.

Why did the rock explode? The blueness was like a shield. If so, then how was he able to get out from earth's atmosphere? It shouldn't be a problem going back in, should it?

He knew that if he should take the same route as the rock, he'd encounter the same fate. What should he do? No matter what, he had only a few minutes to think about what action he should undertake.

Perhaps it would be better if he'd take a less sharp approach. He suddenly tilted the joystick, and the ship slowly drifted sideways, but it was too slow. He gritted his teeth.

"Come on! Come on!"

He was so close and was heading in a diagonal path into the atmosphere, unsure what was about to happen to him. He was at about the point where the rock exploded. He braced himself for any outcome. If his ship exploded, at least maybe he'd be safe in his spacesuit.

Or would he?

The ship began to shake, his joystick was unsteady under his firm grip. The ship began to glow in a bright red color from its wings and muzzle. His fear remained intense.

Is the ship burning? Flame tendrils and smoke surrounded the side of his windshield—if you can call it any of such—sometimes blinding him from view, but that didn't last too long. Did something go wrong that caused the flames? His brain was overrun by anguished thoughts that ripped him away from freedom of thought. Every moment he descended through the atmosphere gave Yezh assurance that somehow, he would survive this part of his adventure. He had come this far; survived the heights, the coldness and airlessness of the cosmos; and there was no way he'd give up now. He'd gone through too many hardships to die now.

No, Yezh, you will not die now.

Even if he died, his dreams had been somewhat fulfilled, and the moon was just the extension of those dreams. But what Yezh did not know was that, should he die up here all alone, he'd become a legendary hero whose name would descend through the history of mankind. That his ascension to heaven was a great accomplishment of humanity and that people would be talking about him for his greatness and his flamboyant courage that he undertook with pride for his nation, for his dreams.

A flight to death, a flight to glory!

The burning diminished, and the sound of his ship could be heard again. The strong winds and pressure quavered noise from around his exterior ship, which led Yezh to believe that he had made back to the atmosphere. It was a relief; he had survived!

All he had to do was locate his home, which was hard because he hadn't planned for this crisis. He studied the visual layout map, the seas, and lands, and Yezh guessed that he was still somewhere over the USSR.

With the ship's muzzle slightly pointing down, Yezh watched as he descended slowly to earth's surface but knew he had to figure out where his home was located and quickly.

He needed a safe and large wide area to land. His backyard wouldn't be the ideal place; he wouldn't risk the little sprouts that Marushka laboriously took care of. His view of the land that had been so broad got closer and clearer. His eyes were able to identify shapes of trees, telling him that he had reached a risky, dangerous altitude. This would decide the outcome of the landing. He judged it to be the perfect moment to use his special button made for this occasion. After arcing his ship upward near a desired safe place, he cut off the fuel supply, opened the cover, and pressed the button. After arcing, the ship decreased in speed and started falling. Yezh's stomach churned while the parachute deployed itself. The ship slowed down in midair with the muzzle tilted upward, and the parachute expanded near the muzzle. Everything from that point became remote, and he lost the power to guide the ship, depending entirely on the wind and gravity to do their jobs.

His eyes swept the land for any familiar indication, and he spotted something: the peasants' square. He was near Leninsk like he tried so hard to remain in its vicinity. He looked through the window and could see that he was nearly over the peasants' square, and according to his measurements, his ship should be landing right in the middle of the square, where not many people were walking. It was a perfect coincidence, considering its nearby markets. He tried to avoid being so close, but the wind did not ask for his opinion.

Many peasants spotted the object in the sky. They were alerted that it must surely be Yezh coming back. A young man who was walking down the road and who couldn't take his mind off what he had seen earlier about the flying object in the sky saw it drifting slowly. With an explosive voice and raising his finger to point toward the sky, he alerted everybody around him.

"Hey, it's Yezh! He's coming back!"

He started to run toward the horizon. Many who heard him also followed behind, and soon a small army was marching down the street.

***

Even the mayor was impatient. He was sitting with his elbow on his desk and fists on his chin when one of his men came inside his office panic stricken and alarmed him.

"Sir! A strange object is flying down from the sky." He sounded breathless.

"Yeah? What could it be? Many things fall from the sky, you know."

"It looks like a machine. It's big and shiny, sir."

Shiny? Strange object? Georgiy brightened to think the possible.

"You mean it could be Yezh?"

"It's heading toward the peasants' square, sir."

"What are we waiting for? Let's go find that flying machine!"

The mayor jumped to his feet with a great blast of energy as though his great weight were meaningless.

***

Sasha was a local merchant and daughter to a farmer. The flower market was hard as usual. Not many people were in the streets to gather around her small tent to purchase some of the most beautiful flowers in town. She also found life boring in this village. She was arranging her flowers to make sure they didn't wither before their scent caught a client's nose.

Phoenix Phoenix

While engaged in this long and wearying work, she spotted something high in the sky, slowly gliding toward the center of the square, unlike anything she had ever seen. She thought it to be some kind of flying house made of aluminum. Even in daylight, this woman was scared. Her eyes didn't move from the object.

The object slowly dropped vertically and bumped the ground three times before stopping by the statue of workers in the middle of the square where it remained motionless. The tip was pointing toward the sky. The parachute slowly and quietly fell. Sasha looked left and right for anybody around who might have seen it, but nobody who was on nearby streets noticed anything.

She approached with hesitant feet, her heart palpitating in her chest. What could it be? She had heard of some flying by a mere peasant but didn't attend any event. But she had read in the newspaper about scary creatures that appear from the sky. She took a walk to the object despite her fears. Still she saw no movement!

At the same time, many others from the village stopped moving when they saw the object on the ground. The boy from the road wondered at the sight, and many others followed behind.

Soon many people gathered close to the ship. Fear kept them a reasonable distance away.

Then the hatch flung open so suddenly it startled everybody around. Someone stepped out with red clothes covering his entire body and a frightening, huge, bulgy head. But their fear subsided when they saw the CCCP logo written on it in bright red, reminding them that it wasn't an enemy after all.

In a sudden movement, the mysterious man gripped himself on the edge of the door. After staying up there for a moment to calculate the height and options, the man leaped down and crashed on the ground, landing on his backside in a sitting position.

Sasha didn't know what to do. Many of the people watching did not know this man and had not attended his departure. Others who knew him thought it might be Yezh under their widened eyes but weren't sure he was really the same person. For the star traveler did not look stable. He seemed … a little bit dizzy or drunk.

First Farmer In Space

Yezh had difficulty getting up on his shaky legs. Panting slowly, he wiped off the dust from his armor.

The woman approached a bit closer and politely spoke to him: "Where did you come from, may I ask?"

Yezh looked up from his mask. He lifted the glass shield to see her better. It was a human face, and not one of those green or grey creatures from the sky.

"From up there, of course," he started off. He paused to take off his helmet. "I came down from space."

The girl showed a smile on her face. So, the news was real. She had heard from local passersby but never took the time to believe it. When everybody saw that it was Yezh and that he was in one piece, their happiness couldn't be contained.

He was surrounded by people. Many of them knew him, many didn't, and he knew he had to give an excuse for his appearance.

"Don't worry, people. It's me, Yezh! Have you already forgotten about me?"

Someone elbowed himself in the fray. The speaker's voice found him quicker than his feet. Yezh saw him arriving headfirst with wide open arms.

"Yezh!"

It was the mayor, Georgiy, the good old man who never runs short on enthusiasm. Yezh gave him a smile.

Georgiy grabbed Yezh with both hands on the arms below the shoulders.

"You're back! I never imagined you'd succeed in flying up there."

"Well I guess I did the impossible."

"We thought you'd never come back to us."

"I wasn't planning on never coming back," replied Yezh. "I was planning to fly in space. You think I wasn't going to tell you my wild adventure up there?"

Phoenix Phoenix

"I'm sure you'll have plenty to tell, comrade!" said the mayor earnestly. "Come on, let's present you to everybody."

It was with a wonderful, exceptional presentation that the mayor declared their comrade's great deed today.

"Hey everybody, Yezh's back from space! Let's give him a little cheer here."

That's when news reporters gathered around. Jovani and Anastasia finally found their way to Yezh. Their truck nearly tipped over when they took a sharp turn on the street. Occasional flashes of light blinded Yezh. He'd never felt like this—popular and loved by everybody. His farmer's shyness was making his face red. He was living the life of a superstar, unusual for what he truly was.

Anastasia approached the two men and began asking a question. The national television and radio network reporter requested for the mayor to give Yezh a chance to talk about his adventure. The mayor heartily accepted the offer, and before continuous flashes of light and microphones aimed at his head, and before silent voices, Anastasia began the interview.

"Comrade Yezh. We are on the air right now," she said. "Did you really go to space? Did you finally succeed?"

"The mission was a success. I have unraveled the mystery of space."

"Wow, you are the first farmer to go in space. How does that feel?"

"It's magical. I feel like a hero right now."

"Can you tell us what you saw up there? What is space like?"

"That would be too much information for now. Perhaps it would be better if I wrote a book about it. What I can say is that it isn't what everybody expects it to be. Don't always pay attention to what your neighbors say about space. Rumors can be deceiving."

That was a good reply, thought Georgiy, and with the excitement that he couldn't bear to contain, he simply spoke out with all his heart.

"This is a wonderful day for a celebration," said the mayor excitedly. It was so great he had to let everybody know. People showed their interested cheers.

First Farmer In Space

"Yezh, the first farmer in space!" yelled a woman with her fist over her head.

People yelled Yezh's name as shouts that boomed in the streets. Everybody pushed forward, wanting to touch him, to give him a handshake or a hug.

***

Ivan wasn't believing his eyes. He was in front of his television as usual to watch news and reports. He had expected something completely different from this. How could this be? His eyes were wide and blinking from frustration and disbelief.

Ivan believed Yezh was dead, so was sure that he had finally prevailed in his rivalry against his neighbor—his lifelong archnemesis. And yet there he was: on his feet in that red garment, standing by the mayor where he got to have his face imprinted behind the flashes of light.

His wife had been at their neighbors' house across the street when Ivan heard her tumbling in the house all in a hurry, disturbed by something.

"Ivan. Yezh has returned! Did you hear the news? He's back from the sky!"

All she could see was her words passing through the walls, meaningless and ineffective as Ivan stared at the television. He already knew it. She regained her composure.

"Tell us, Yezh, what will be your next goal?" asked the reporter on the television.

"My next goal? I'm planning to extend my dreams to travel farther away. It's not over yet. The best part is yet to come. I still dream of walking on the moon," said Yezh, all too proudly.

Not only that, he got the privilege of being declared a hero by the mayor and got warmhearted hugs alongside abundant attention nationwide, but he's also planning to go to the moon? That would only worsen Ivan's humiliation. For the first time ever, Ivan felt backward compared to his neighbor. He felt technologically back in the Stone Age, and his income, which was greater than Yezh's, rendered meaningless. As if going in space wasn't enough to bring him down, burying him with shame. Not only that, but the comment about not listening to the neighbors stabbed him in his heart like a dagger.

How dare he?

"That man doesn't know when to give up," said his wife, still impressed by Yezh's reluctant nature. "He's going to go to the moon!" Katenka said scornfully as she walked out of the living room. She couldn't stand that neighbor any longer.

"This isn't happening! It cannot happen! There's no way he'll be going to the moon!" whispered Ivan, gritting his teeth. His wife shared the same kind of frustration, but Ivan was way worse. Ivan was left all alone in his corner with his shame and anger.

Then an idea popped out from his head.

"Flying to space was glorious, but flying to the moon is even more glorious," said Ivan quietly, talking to himself. This idea took a more refined shape. He punched his fist on the other open palm with determination. "If he could fly to space, so can anybody else! If I manage to reach the moon before he does … I will be the new hero." His mood was a little more normal now, and the beginnings of a smile tried to erupt from his fleeing vexation.

He looked back at the television. Yezh's smile to the camera was almost as if he was mocking Ivan through wires and lenses.

"Yezh, you're not the only one with big dreams," whispered Ivan with a squint.

***

Most folks departed to their duties, and only a few remained. Yezh realized that his ship was not in a place where it could be stationed. The peasants' square wasn't a good place for the ship, but he had no idea how to bring it back home.

"Now there's a problem," said Yezh who caught Georgiy's attention when the last uproar dwindled. "How am I supposed to bring my ship back home?"

Near silence reigned as deep in thought they tried to find an answer. Some even looked up at the pointy peak of the ship and wondered how this object might fit in any vehicle.

"I don't think there's anything in the Soviet Union that can carry this. It's too big," said one man.

"We'll figure something out. There has to be something to carry it around," assured the mayor.

Yezh had to put his imagination to work again, but nothing came to his mind for a while. Among all the amazed crowd who were in awe at the sky-towering machine, only one man had any good ideas.

"We can put it on a rail or a wheeled board or something," said Pushkin.

The wheeled board was a popular tool for transportation of merchandise, and Pushkin believed he'd seen one around lately. He knew that if he asked loudly somebody might bring one over here.

"Does someone have anything of that sort around here?"

A pastry man remembered he had such a useful tool which he used to transport bags of sugar. "Yes, I have a wheeled platform."

"Is it thick?"

"Oh yeah, it's very thick. I'm not sure if it's going to hold this machine, but it can hold up to two thousand kilograms of sugar bags. I can bring it."

"Sure, yeah, bring it," said Pushkin, and the pastry man hurried to his nearby bakery.

"No, that won't work," mocked Dalan the skeptic, turning his head away.

Yezh used that moment to detach the parachute from the threads. The pastry man returned as quickly as he left, sliding a wheeled board that was five meters wide on each side, enough to cover the entire ship's diameter. Even Yezh was surprised that his ship wasn't that large when he looked at the surface of the platform. Several men jumped on the board to see if it would endure.

"And how are you going to put the ship on the board?" asked a skeptical man.

"We'll lift and carry it over," said Pushkin.

Many eyes widened. They didn't know what to disbelieve more, the existence of such a machine or carrying it around.

"Is that even possible?" asked another one.

"We could always try," replied Yezh, who let curiosity possess him.

Pushkin inspected the ship for any way to grab it easily.

"What kind of spaceship is this?" asked Pushkin, mocking the way it was built. It was so simple in design.

"I know, it looks like a trash can." What Yezh confessed was funny but true.

Dalan interrupted the laughter with a remark concerning safety: "What if we break it in the process?"

"This?" exclaimed Yezh with astonishment, pointing to his ship. "Nah!"

He struck the aluminum wall hard several times with punches that resonated long afterward.

"This can never break! It's hard like the moon."

When Yezh saw that the man was raising his eyebrows with a smile, he knew he had to build his trust. "I think you're underestimating my trash can."

"What can possibly break in the USSR?" asked the enthusiastic man, confident in his nation.

"Right. Made in the USSR!" replied Yezh in a way that raised laughter.

They asked all the strongest people around to gather around the ship to lift it up. There were about twenty people ready to put their muscles to the test.

At the count of three, everybody expended their maximum strength, nearly relaunching the ship back to space. Men quickly realized that they were putting too much strength into it. It wasn't even heavy, as they had expected.

"Hop! Hop! Hop!" said one, guiding the effort of movements over the board. A few others slid the board beneath it and the ship was safely dropped on the board. Their voices did a crescendo and decrescendo like a Russian mountain when the ship landed right in middle of board. It had happened in the blink of an eye. People were laughing at how simple and easy it was.

To carry a spaceship like this by hand? It had never been seen in the world. Only in the USSR!

It was holding well. The cheap-looking board didn't appear to be losing its grip.

"Now what?" asked Pushkin.

"Let's push it to my home."

"What happens if we tip it over?" Dalan's voice warned once more.

"Ha, it's okay! We'll just bring it back up straight and move on," said Yezh with a smile.

And so, the pushing began. A dozen farmers pushed the ship forward. Others held their positions on the sides to guide it. The ropes used to hold the parachute were used by men to stabilize the pointy object. The ship rolled down the street, boldly showing its might like a mobile bomb, a comparison made by some villagers who spoke of its intimidating look.

Sergeant Heartlock, who was walking the street toward the square and looking down at his pocket watch, was disturbed by the laughter and loud voices. He raised his head up, and it nearly fell off his shoulders when he saw a giant pointy object rolling on ...

A wheeled board pushed by local peasants?

"What the ..." Heartlock grimaced in horror, his lips and nose snarling in disbelief.

They pushed it all the way to a rough street, and a sudden movement sent the ship leaning to one side.

"Watch it. Hold it. Hold it!" yelled one, and several people quickly gathered on the other side to push the ship back to the center and pulling on the ropes. It nearly tipped over.

"WOOoooooah!" exhaled everybody at same time.

Phoenix Phoenix

Heartlock froze there as he saw farmers with forks and scythes in hand passing by him, accompanying maybe a dozen more around the ship, pushing the intimidating object to God knows where.

***

As they approached Yezh's house, the commotion stirred the neighbors into peeking through the window. Horrors! Ivan watched carefully as the pointy thing rolled in the streets with more than a few local peasants around it. What greater madness could he witness than to see this thing rolling in the streets? Ivan closed his curtain a little to hide himself from any eye but left a small opening to peek at what was going on. Then Ivan reached his back door faster than a hare to see more from the commotion on the other side of the fence.

The ship was carried to the back. They were more careful on the grass. The same process was done once they arrived at Yezh's backyard and the ship was safely brought back. They made it. The ship was safely dropped in the backyard the same way they mounted it.

Ivan had witnessed everything: the arrival of Yezh, his popularity among people, the machine being picked up by people and dropped in the backyard. He was still trying to overcome his never-ending astonishment.

Marushka was most happy to see him returning home. She had to come out to give him a hug. Yezh looked down at her with the brightest smile that a man can have in a lifetime, his hands around her, and said in a soft voice: "I told you I'd be back."

Sputnik barked madly at the visitors but was more scared than anybody else. Despite the confusion, even Sputnik was happy to see his friend coming from space, a true compatriot of space travel. Maks was eager to see his father returning home. He already had a thousand questions ready for his father—and was still disappointed that they had lied to him about all of this.

Everybody was happy except his neighbor, who, with wary eyes of a wolf, his eyes fixated every bit of his activity within the darkness and silence of his home.

Chapter 27
When Jealousy Has No Limits

Yezh was very tired, not because he worked too hard in his field, but because traveling in space and all the walking around the village was exhausting him. He could go to sleep tonight knowing that he had realized a portion of his dreams. Maks was sent to bed after a few minutes of talking about space. It was hard for Yezh to make him close his eyes, but Maks happily went into slumber afterward, when he could no longer keep his eyes open.

Now it was Yezh's turn. In his indigo pajamas that Marushka made with the moon and stars pattern material, he was ready to snuggle under his blankets. When darkness and silence were established in the bedroom, Yezh was still unable to fall asleep; his mind still throbbed with excitement.

Marushka had her own opinion about all of this. She knew she had some excuses to offer.

"A few days ago, I wasn't feeling very good. I didn't believe anything about space traveling stuff, and I was afraid that something might happen to you up there. When you crashed the first time, I almost died from worries. Even when you succeeded in going to space, I still feared not being able to see you again."

"You know I would always come back for you. I wasn't ready to die up there! Me, too, I couldn't believe everything that happened and what I saw up there."

"What did you finally see up there?"

She was hoping that he was satisfied from seeing things, completing his mission, and witnessing space.

"Nothing special—at first, at least. Everything was dark, but it ended that everything Ivan was preaching about turned out to be fake."

"He tried to hurt your feelings, Yezh," said Marushka, who wasn't surprised at that. "He didn't want you to fly to the sky."

"I know that."

Did Ivan really try to alter his dreams by hindering his courage with petty tricks? Yezh began to judge Ivan to be just another mere farmer like all the rest—still unintelligent and inexperienced. Now that he had seen space himself and enough proof to disprove what Ivan had said, he felt superior to him. Now he knew everything, and anything that Ivan might have to say about space wouldn't make sense. Ivan wouldn't be lying to him anymore, that's for sure, now that Yezh had his experience to rely upon.

"Well I just wanted to tell you …" said Marushka with sincerity that she hoped would reconcile Yezh with anything negative he'd thought about her. "I'm sorry for doubting you."

Silence came over the room as if everything had been solved and ended happily, but Marushka knew it wasn't the true end.

"What are you planning to do now?"

"I still haven't reached the moon, so that means my job isn't fin-ished."

That's exactly what she had feared to hear from him.

"Isn't that going to be more dangerous than what you did so far?"

"I don't know," said Yezh sincerely. The moon was just another thing that everybody knew less about. He remembered what he told him-self on that chair the other day and in the darkness of the void under a majestic view of the moon. "The moon could have all kinds of danger. We don't even know what lives up there."

"You think there are living things on the moon?"

"Maybe. Maybe not! According to the scientists they are trying to find life on other planets, but nobody knows for sure. It's a new map to be explored out there. Each planet is ready to be discovered."

Marushka thought Yezh sounded like Magellan or some kind of pirate in search of unknown treasure. He couldn't find anything to say to sooth Marushka's worries, and he believed that he shouldn't mention that rock in space.

"Who knows, maybe walking on the moon isn't that complicated. What if what I did so far was the riskiest part?"

"You think nothing could happen to you up there?"

"I can't promise anything. Things happened when I flew up there, but now I have more experience. I know how to proceed."

"I'm still worried about this. Do you really have to go to the moon after all this? You know that I was thinking about you all day while working around the house. I couldn't do anything other than walk around thinking what could happen."

"I know you worry but think how great it'll be if I walk on the moon."

"I will always wish you luck. As long as you come back to us, I will be fine. Just don't push your luck. You've seen space like you always wanted. You should be happy with what you have."

A long silence occurred between them. Marushka felt tired and decided it would be better if they go to sleep.

"It's getting late now. Let's go to sleep. Good night, Yezh," said Marushka.

Yezh reciprocated. Their feelings exchanged, they were able to go off in slumber.

***

On their neighbors' side, Ivan had a whole different reason not to fall asleep. His rapid and deep breathing and occasional agitation in bed didn't give his wife a chance for any shuteye.

"What's wrong, Ivan? Why don't you go to sleep?"

"I kind of underestimated that Yezh. All the warnings of danger I offered him, and he still tackled the heights like a stubborn pig. He must have been very lucky to get back to earth. I'm sure of it!"

"You are worrying about that so late at night?" said Katenka with a sigh. She couldn't tell if it was Ivan's insomnia or Yezh's overrated glory that was making her angry. "Maybe he was just lucky. Or he may have en-countered dangers and flew back here."

"He thinks he's always the smart one who knows everything. Any-one as low as him who thinks he could live a better life than anyone else in Leninsk is insane. In any case, I won't let him beat me up that easily."

Katenka was befuddled when she heard him saying that. It was the first time she heard Ivan say that he would do something about it. And he obviously meant Yezh's news about traveling to the moon.

"What do you intend to do about that?"

"I don't know yet for sure, but I got an idea of what it could be," said Ivan, whose voice dwindled to silence as he thought. "I'll do something to beat him."

"What will you do?" she spoke out loudly. "Are you going to build something too? I thought you'd never do stupid things like your neighbor. Don't tell me that you are crazy like he is?"

Katenka was speaking sarcastically when she mentioned building something. Or would he try to sabotage Yezh perhaps? She had no idea what Ivan had in mind.

"Maybe, but I'm not letting him beat me fair and square."

The remark said, Ivan jumped out from the bed and headed to the door.

"Ivan. Where are you going?" yelled Katenka.

It was dark outside. He peeked at the neighbors' windows. It seemed that darkness was established in their home. Yezh was surely asleep. With a lantern at hand, he jumped over the fence and stealthily snuck in silence to reach the spaceship that glimmered by the moonlight of the night.

He checked from all sides, studying carefully every component that was visible to the naked eye.

The engine with four jet blasters must be offering maximum firepower. He had to lean down and get on his knees to have a look beneath the engine. His eyes followed every inch of cables, from where it came from to where it was heading. He didn't really need to know anything about how these must be created. He simply needed to remember everything there is and where it is located.

The body itself was rigid—surprisingly, since it's made of aluminum. Excellent resistance to high temperatures. Explains why he wasn't scorched up near the sun. Ivan thought he'd probably try his luck with these materials.

Sputnik, who was asleep, heard some footsteps in the backyard and woke up instinctively. His ears rotated like antennas to detect any other noise but remained ever quiet.

Ivan was able to identify different parts of the ship and each one's function within the massive machine. He went to the hatch and slowly opened it, and with a lamp that he brought along, lit the way and witnessed the simplicity of the ship.

Just to think that such a remarkable machine exists in this world, and it looks so cheap and so easy to build. *This is a trash can!* thought the farmer. Despite its heroic achievement and lack of originality, Ivan believed that the simplicity and ugliness it showed the world could be beaten with something that only he could create. He observed the interior as precisely as possible.

"Even I can build a better piece of junk than this!" grumbled Ivan on his way out.

Ivan turned out the lamp, so he wouldn't attract too much attention. Nobody was nearby. He stepped out and slowly shut the hatch. It was hard to see through the darkness. Ivan was already concerned how to build his own creation and considered revisiting the surrounding components to be sure to forget nothing, but while being mindful about this and that, his mind lost concentration. His feet stumbled onto something metallic and thin, making an echoing *boing* noise. It was a bowl that Yezh had left behind like he always does with his tools—or toys, or whatever they are. It must have been used for oil dripping or something.

A curse slipped from Ivan's mouth.

Sputnik rose up from his doghouse in the kitchen and barked out loud. Something was in the backyard and he was ready to chase it away if only he'd have a chance to find a gap through the sliding door.

The bark woke up the boy and Yezh, who both got up from bed to go see what had happened in the kitchen.

"What happened, Sputnik?" said the boy, who arrived first.

Yezh came afterward, half asleep.

"What's going on?"

"I don't know. I think Sputnik saw something in the backyard."

Phoenix Phoenix

All three looked through the windowed door but couldn't spot anything of interest or unusual after a few minutes of gazing out.

"It must have been a raccoon. Those nasty things must have started to go after our crops," reasoned Yezh. "Sorry fools, guess you are too early this year."

He moved away from the window, asked his son to go back to sleep, and hushed Sputnik, reassuring him that whatever it was is now gone. The dog instinctively obeyed and retreated to his doghouse by the wall.

Chapter 28
A New Rival

When morning came, the boy was eating his breakfast before going to school. He was reading the newspaper that arrived by the door.

Yezh woke up from a horrible night. He never shut his eyes for a minute and was dreadfully exhausted. It was easy to see from his messy hair.

The boy took his eyes off the newspaper and exclaimed with a great loud shout: "Father! Look at this!"

Yezh wondered what it could be this time. Did Sputnik do something again?

"It's you!" He pointed a finger to the paper. "You're in the newspaper!"

That caught Yezh's attention. Anything about his dreams would stir him up from his half-asleep state. He took a better look. There he stood by the mayor's side with a bright smile accompanying the one on mayor's face.

"Hey, it's really me!"

On the front page in a large, clear, bold font was written: First Farmer in Space! Yezh Kalinin, the Hero of the Soviet Union.

"You are a hero!" said the boy excitedly. Maks was so happy for his father. And now the whole world would know how great the father of this poor little farm boy was compared to the rest of the kids at school. No more laughter and mockery. He couldn't wait to see his friends at school to tell them the great news. He'd make their mouths drop open.

Yezh wasn't the type to read the newspaper. He never liked propaganda and never showed interest in news, but this event was something to celebrate, and to read hundreds of pages about—a great theme to be reading so early in the morning.

Marushka arrived from the cold chamber with a slice of cheese wedge in hand.

"Looks like you're getting more popular every day, Yezh!"

Yezh showed a grin of satisfaction.

Phoenix Phoenix

"Your neighbor must be eating himself alive right now after seeing that in the newspaper."

It was the way she said it so bluntly and mockingly that appealed Yezh's mood. He was never in the mood to think about despicable Ivan, but this occasion was a good time to think about his face and about how it would freckle from anger.

Yezh was having breakfast and was ready to celebrate his success and great achievements with his hands on his fork, his mind on his moon. Yezh couldn't move on from what he had experienced. His heart was over-joyed—so happy, he felt he could tackle a whole acre of field again.

Knock. Knock. Knock.

Something unusual was happening outside. Something familiar to his ears. Something he learned to hear a lot in the last few days. Since the knocking didn't stop, he had to take a look outside. Through the door, he stared left, on the other side of the fence. He was right. The familiar sound was from a hammer.

His neighbor was building something big and tall. Did he finally decided to build a new windmill? Or a new shelter for plants?

He slid the door open. Sputnik launched himself straight at the fence on the right, and Yezh stepped out.

"What are you building there so early in the morning, neighbor?" asked Yezh.

Ivan was on a ladder, nailing wood together. He had to stop to see his neighbor by the door. He was somewhat startled but tried to hide it, though he had nothing to fear since construction of his new creation wasn't sufficiently advanced enough to provide any hint of its purpose—only a vague shape, which could be anything at this stage.

"Something to change my life!" answered Ivan with full enthusiasm as if he had nothing to hide.

Yezh immediately felt a strange feeling of distrust. Not quite under-standing the meaning of it, he decided to let it be for now. It was strange to see Ivan working on something other than his field. What could have convinced him to start building something new?

First Farmer In Space

It was so much easier to duplicate your neighbor's creation than to start one from scratch. Even while Ivan stole information on Yezh's ship, he had a hard time understanding it. He could only imagine what Yezh had to go through with the complications in the wiring system. Either he was knowledgeable, or he was talented. He never could have imagined how easy it was to build a spaceship if one had a mind for it. But Ivan would never admit Yezh to be better in any way. He would claim this creation to be his very own despite the obvious copying.

There were some things he still didn't know how to recreate: things like a radio or the engine, which require dexterity and engineering knowledge. He hadn't spent hours leisurely playing with electricity like Yezh, and there was no way he would waste his time learning. For that there are people designated as professionals, and for a small fee he can make them do it for him. He had just the right people for that, and plenty of oil to back his project up.

While Yezh was having a glorious breakfast with his family, Ivan overstressed himself but did not waver from his hard work. The knocking of the hammer bothered even Katenka as she was waiting for Ivan to come inside to eat. No feet came inside, and she grew tired of waiting, so she stepped out to warn him.

"Ivan! The breakfast is ready. You should come to eat. It's getting cold."

"Just a little bit. Hold on," said Ivan with a grunt, holding and pushing some wood here and there. "I need to finish this."

"What's the hurry? You've worked several hours this morning. What could you even be building now?"

"Ah … uh … Something," said Ivan with hesitation.

"You start to scare me like our neighbor. Come inside to eat and then play."

"Yes—I'm coming very soon."

Knock. Knock. Knock.

She saw how frenzied he was, going up and down the ladder, knocking in maybe ten nails in less than a minute. Why is he rushing? She didn't know what he was building. It must be something for the field, though she hadn't seen him with a hammer like this for a very long time.

After a while, Ivan showed up at the table. His coffee was getting cold, but he didn't mind that. Katenka delivered him the newspaper that came by their door. It was Ivan's policy to read a newspaper every morning. He couldn't start his day without a little dose of news. But he saw in the paper something he wasn't expecting this early. He didn't like what he read in the newspaper. His day was starting badly already. His fingers shook on the edge of paper, and his eyes twitched as he read the font caption where it was written: First Farmer in Space!

Absurd! This cannot be!

He rushed to open the newspaper to inside the first page where there was a big picture of Yezh smiling alongside the mayor.

Ivan read for a few minutes with dismay. Katenka was just arriving from sweeping the front balcony with a broom and came back to see Ivan at the table.

"Your neighbor is getting lots of praise for his flight," said Katenka, mocking the truthfulness of the story. "Who knows where he went? And everybody believed him."

"He won't be shining on the stage for too long."

Ivan took a sip of his coffee, barely swallowing as he was choking on his anger. The warmth of the sip amplified what was already warm: It was feeding the heat of his anger. Next time it will be Ivan, the First Farmer on the Moon that people will read on the front of the newspaper, and Yezh shall be forgotten as a hero, shamefully crushed by his neighbor.

Disgusted by the news, he judged it to be the worst news he had ever read and that this would be the last newspaper that he'd read in his life. He tossed it aside brutally. Unacceptable!

***

Maksimilian didn't want to go to school. He wanted to assist his father in whatever duty he had around his ship. Seeing so many people surrounding his father was exciting. But his parents told him that if he'd become a good student, he'd be smart enough to work with his father in the rocket science field. Maks was happy to hear that, unaware that it was only a pitch to make him go to school. So once again the parents wished their child a good day at school before closing the door.

The phone rang.

Who could be calling so early?

When Marushka answered it, she called Yezh to come at the phone with a serious expression on her face.

"Hello?" Yezh wondered who it might be.

"Yezh!" The mayor's voice was so cheerful in the morning. "Sorry to bother you, but I have something to ask of you today."

"No problem. What could it be that I can do for you?"

Georgiy said, "We have visitors from Moscow here at my office. Very important people, you know, Yezh," He changed his voice to a more serious tone for emphasis. "Very important matters to discuss are on the table. You have been summoned to my office today."

Marushka gave him a look from the kitchen.

"Sure. Understood. You can count on me, Mayor."

Yezh hung up the phone and moved away.

"What was that about?" Marushka asked.

"That was the mayor. He …"

Yezh was interrupted by another phone call.

Who might it be this time?

"Hello?"

"Hello, Yezh. This is Boris from the Red Star radio station. How are you today?"

"Oh, I'm very fine."

"We have heard about your deeds from our news reporters. It seems like you managed to pull it off this time.

"Yes, I did," said Yezh. "I'm a man of my word."

"Fantastic, comrade! How about you come for an interview again?

Phoenix Phoenix

We'll be glad to air you on our show today."

"Sure! Everybody is asking for me," said Yezh with humor and a smile.

Yezh moved to the kitchen, where once again Marushka interrogated him.

"Who was that this time?"

"That was Boris from the radio station. I've been summoned to be on the radio and then attend a meeting with the mayor," said Yezh, emphasizing his next words: "on a very important matter."

She looked puzzled but knew it was about his fame, something they'd be seeing more of. "You're popular, Yezh. If this continues, you'll be more famous than the president himself," said Marushka. "When is it?"

"At eleven o'clock."

"Then you'll have to prepare yourself. Time flies fast. You'll need to wear your dress uniform. You must look professional with those men."

She led him to the wardrobe where she pulled out a military uniform. It used to belong to his father. It looked very handsome on him, and she complimented him on that. It went with the hat as well, providing a complete look of elegance.

Dressing Yezh like a child took its toll of time, and it was already time to go. Marushka nagged him about how to behave in their presence, reminding him of what to do and not to do. When Yezh departed, she promised to herself that she'd work around the house and garden. She hadn't had much time to look at the garden and owed some moments to the sprouts.

When she came out of her home, she witnessed the unusual sight of Ivan—still building something in a frenzy. The knocking was getting on her nerves, but this time she managed to ignore it all. She went to her garden and continued to pay more attention to her little aromatic beauties.

***

The bad news only fueled Ivan's rage over the work. Without blinking or drinking, Ivan showed great stamina in his work. He was very into it until he needed some material for skinning his ship. It had the shape, its bones and its interior veins, and the basic electrical things he knew about, but no skin was visible at this moment, so it remained a mystery what it was going to be.

Before taking off to the store and various electro-engineering services, Ivan blanketed it when eyes weren't looking toward him.

Marushka, who was tending to her sprouts, was absorbed in her work for an hour and didn't look up. When she did, all she saw was a blanket over Ivan's big construction site. She grew doubtful about what Ivan was building after seeing its progress since an hour ago.

Ivan discreetly stepped into his chamber and took his rainy-day funds—all of it, including his oil sale funds. He looked around to see if Katenka was watching. He collected everything and raced to the stores nearby. Then he called a company from another city and ordered what was large and expensive, something not available in Leninsk.

***

Yezh was hired by the authorities at the peasants' square. Special officials from government came to Leninsk from Moscow's Kremlin. Yezh was stressed, not knowing how he would fare in front of important people of this nation. Why was he summoned? What do they want from him? Yezh did not know.

Show some manners, don't be a chicken. Behave yourself! Drop that farmer's uncultured manner, thought the farmer to himself.

He arrived a few minutes later in front of the door to the mayor's office and gathered himself together with a sigh before knocking on the door.

"You may enter!" said a familiar but slightly hoarse voice.

Yezh obeyed the voice. Like a mouse, he presented himself before the official with his back straight in military style, his head held high, and holding his breath before the man spoke.

An overweight man moved away from where the mayor was sitting. He was bold, like the mayor himself. You might wonder if this man was a brother of the mayor. Another man on the other side, this one more built and taller than the other one, also stepped forward.

Phoenix Phoenix

Georgiy stood up to introduce the two men in front of his office.

"Yezh, may I present to you Mr. Oleg Bolshakov. He is the head of the Moscow ministry of defense." Georgiy's hand guided Yezh's eyes to the second man who inclined his head in a greeting. "And this is Mr. Sergei Volkov, the chairman of the national Soviet space agency."

Courtesies were exchanged before one of them began his speech. Yezh saluted both men.

"Comrade Yezh! You have performed a very risky and heroic action. Your great deeds of courage did not go in vain, nor unheard. When we heard in Moscow that a farmer sent his dog and himself into space, we knew immediately that was something to investigate." The man took one more step forward as Yezh listened. "First of all, let me congratulate you on your flight. Of course, you will earn some merit for this, but not now. We still have some work to do. The state has gained interest in your invention, and we desire to see it in action for ourselves. Not only do we want to build a science department based on space, but we'll also want to improve our scientific defenses, and we need your help. We will build a station where we will conduct travels to space, and we want you as the captain."

Yezh was surprised to hear that.

"You're the only one who knows how to fly that ship into space, and we believe that you have important feedback information to give us."

Oleg started anew. "However, the Kremlin has been very doubtful about your background," said Oleg with less enthusiasm. "You see, as a farmer, you are inexperienced in some ways, and the office thought of replacing you with another pilot who has trained for many years in our department."

Yezh's mood darkened. "Why would they do that?" Yezh spoke out but did not cut off the man's speech. "I'm the one who built this machine, and I was the one who went up in sky. Surely that's enough for a beginning of experience."

"Yes, you are right. The office wants to build their own recreation of spaceflight based on yours and to perform their own tests. At the same time, they believe that it would be best to hire another man with the same name as you, someone who would have the proper physical appearance and expertise, like for example someone more smiley, to give a proper image of the Soviet Union. Or better built physically to present a muscular appearance of the nation."

Yezh looked with sadness but the man had to mention the purpose of this change of favor.

"It's for the USSR that we are taking that decision. All we do and choose is to glorify our nation."

Yezh nodded in understanding, his eyes leaving the man's eye contact. He couldn't say anything negative. Still he couldn't figure out why he was called in here, his face showed that expression.

"But I believe in you," said the man, as Yezh regained eye contact. "I was the only one to mention to the office that Yezh is a genuine man. You already went up there, you know what space looks like. It would be a shame to offer that spot of fame to another man. And they have taken my opinion to heart."

"Oh, thank you, sir." Yezh showed a face of appreciation.

"Just be aware that if you cannot accept the post for any reason, we will have no choice but to pinpoint another man for this position. Another Yezh to take your glory. And you'll be considered a mere lost astronaut."

"I understand. As long as a chance is given to me, I will not fail."

Oleg finished his speech and gave a short look at Yezh after a silence as if studying the farmer's potential by his appearances.

"This brings us to our next speech," said the short man, looking at his companion, who had been quiet all this time. He stepped forward.

"The office and the national space agency have decided to buy your model," said Sergei. "Of course, you'll earn your pay and reputation—a fair share for your machine. We are willing to buy it from you for the big sum of sixty million rubles."

Yezh smiled, hardly able to contain his excitement. Sixty million rubles is a lot of coins. It was the way Sergei had said the sentence so slowly that gave Yezh the impression that something fantastic in size was coming. He couldn't afford to ask the amount again. He couldn't believe what he heard and feared they'd change their mind on second thought.

"So, you see, Yezh, you have a great opportunity either way," continued Oleg.

Yezh floundered, not knowing quite what to say. This was like a dream coming true.

"You blow my mind away, dear comrades," said Yezh. "I don't know what to say. Of course, I accept your offer to buy my machine—and to become your captain." Yezh gave a smile, one that would soon grow popular in pictures for perhaps many decades and centuries to come. Oleg found it to be quite a smile, one that would speak for the nation's empathetic and fortifying glory.

"I can already feel a legend coming from within you, my dear Yezh," said Georgiy, who showed him some admiration.

Georgiy gave him a big hug. Sergei mentioned that he would give him more information when the time comes, and that he'd keep in touch. All three men were confident that this machine would be enough to enable them to reach the moon.

The meeting ended, and Yezh left the room keeping his emotions under control. When he left their presence, he had to let his joy out. How was he supposed to behave?

Good, now it's time to go to the other meeting.

***

Yezh was busy with interviews from all directions. He was certainly enjoying himself. Later that day, he arrived at the same radio station that interviewed him the last time. He would have plenty to say, and hopefully Ivan would be listening. This time the story was different. He was no longer seen as a farmer but rather as a hero of the nation.

"So here we have master Yezh back from space," said Boris to the radio audience. "Yezh, it seems you have managed to fly in space, did you not?"

"Yes, I finally did!" replied Yezh with a smile, already growing accustomed to smiling a lot.

"Tell us, how did it go this time?"

"It went exceedingly well."

"What did you do different this time?"

"I switched engines and used a different kind of fuel. I used oil, which did a very good job."

"Interesting," replied Boris. "Tell us then what space looks like. What can you tell us about it?"

Yezh explained about what space was to the extent of his knowledge.

"So, space really does exist then. The rumors claiming that it was the end of the sky turn out not to be correct, am I right?"

"Indeed. Rumors are rumors. The sky itself is finite, but it continues above that as space, which is something else."

"That sounds breathtaking ..."

"Ah! Speaking of which, you want to know what was really breathtaking?"

Boris could only wonder, just like many in the audience who were listening to the radio. "It was our dear planet earth. With its marvelous colorful exhibition, I was able to devour some delicious moments. Earth is blue! It has milky shapes that are clouds, all kinds of colors swirl together, land, forest, mountains, and seas, all harmonizing with each other like a painting on a canvas. I've seen green, light blue, and dark blue until I was seeing only black."

"Well that's not something that we see or hear every day!" replied Boris. "I can only imagine how mind-blowing it must have been."

Yezh continued explaining all the scientific things he learned about this mystical place. He told them his experiences. When he told them how long it took him to reach space, people nationwide gaped their mouths to hear how small the sky layer is in reality. It took him only a few minutes. Yezh was able to explain some mysteries and rumors that Boris pointed out, which made him all the smarter.

It was an exciting day to listen to the radio. People listened from all over the nation. They stood next to their radios, paying full attention to every word that Yezh used to describe his experience. All except of one person.

Phoenix Phoenix

Ivan.

***

The flowers started to show their colors, and their sweet aroma invaded the garden. Katenka was able to enjoy the first hint of summer, a sign of more to come later. She had been working peacefully in the flower garden this sunny day.

Katenka's quiet day changed suddenly when a truck stopped in front of her house. She was bent over her garden in front of her house where she had been watering her flowers. Slowly she straightened herself up. Men in white uniforms with hats came out of it. Another heavy machine assisted their arrival. These men wearing various tools and carrying material made their way to the backyard.

Katenka looked at them wide-eyed.

"What's going on here?"

She encountered Ivan, who assisted the others. He had a smirk on his face and was scrubbing his hands on each other.

"They're here to work for me."

"Work?" She looked at the rushing men with electrical tools. "For what?"

"My ship is almost completed. With these men, my ship will be ready to go by tomorrow."

"What? Ship?" She thought she misheard him. "How could you afford this?"

"I paid a good amount of money for this."

"You spent every coin on that ship? Are you mad like our neighbor? Did you catch his illness?"

"Money is money. It will come back to us. Just imagine how rich we'll be if I manage to fly to space. Besides, we have enough oil to spare some money."

She remained speechless when two other men brought in a big machine that looked like a radio. Then a yellow machine from a construction

249

site carried what appeared to be some kind of engine.

Marushka, upon hearing the commotion outside, went to the window and pushed the curtain aside to see unknown people walking to their neighbor's side.

"What is this?"

Marushka was unsettled by the noise from the neighbors and needed to look at the back window. Upon gazing through the backyard, she saw the visitors, or what seemed to be workers dressed in white. The mysterious object that Ivan had built was unveiled from the blanket, and immediately the men stepped up to work on it like ants.

***

Yezh was proud of his interviews; he did well. He was smiling to himself, his heart about to explode from joy. His emotions were high, and he could only compliment himself as a great inventor and as a new cosmonaut.

As Yezh neared his home by car, what he heard and saw drowned his emotions. His smile vanished. He saw the trucks in front of his house, not knowing what was going on. When he entered his house, Marushka quickly struck him with the news. He knew that it had something to do with what he saw outside.

"Yezh. Did you see what Ivan has been doing?"

"I saw the trucks and people. What happened?"

"He's building something behind the house." She looked panicked. "You should see it. He worked on it all day while you were gone."

Yezh had no idea what it could be since he spent all his day away from home. What could Ivan be building so fast?

He moved the back door and peeked out. What he sees worried him, and he felt a blast of mixed feelings. What seemed to have been only a skeleton this morning was now skinned—to his surprise.

Aluminum, pointy structure, tanks on the sides—this looked to his eyes awfully like his *Sputnik*.

"Do you think he's trying to build something like your ship?" said

Marushka by his side. Both looked through the back window with confusion.

His wife confirmed what he had feared. Her question led Yezh to believe that Ivan was plotting something against him. Again! He always did. Whatever Yezh did, it always affected Ivan in a way that made him try to imitate every move Yezh made.

Everything depended on this confrontation. A diplomatic approach could help Yezh to stay ahead of Ivan and put a halt to any possibility that Ivan might believe that Yezh was jealous. There was no way he'd let Ivan believe he had affected Yezh's emotions. This was no time to allow weaknesses.

He slid the door open and exited. Each step he took toward the fence, he studied the model Ivan was making. But it wasn't really Ivan's work because there were maybe ten more people around the machine who were working very hard. Ivan wasn't wielding any hammer, he was only conducting the building, telling everybody what to do from the back row. His hands were waving, pointing, and conveying body language.

Ivan spotted Yezh by the fence, his noble silhouette conveying heroism and elegance.

"What are you building there?" asked Yezh, his arm on the fence.

"Oh neighbor! What a coincidence!" remarked Ivan. "You are just in time to witness my new machine."

"Unh-huh." Yezh nodded slowly. "I thought you had no interest into space."

"Well you know, neighbor, people can change their minds. When I saw you fly up there, that opened the gate to many of us other people who also have a dream."

"Your dream is to fly up in space?"

"No!" responded Ivan, preparing himself to give the best reply ever. "I want to fly to the moon!"

What Yezh had tried to avoid erupted inevitably. The jealousy and frustration that Yezh had toward Ivan and which he perfectly buried under a bright positive figure sprouted like a vine with thorns. He failed to keep any signs of it buried in him.

Manners, Yezh, manners. Don't let him beat you, thought Yezh.

"I wonder what gave you that dream and motivation to wish for the moon."

"Ah. Your show of courage was inspiring. I decided that I wanted to see the void for myself!"

"Really?" Yezh didn't believe a word from this man. That excuse of "inspiration" that he fed him was a setup story, and Yezh wasn't such a stupid farmer that he didn't realize it.

Ivan was a cunning one.

One of his men asked him a question about one of the components that they were about to install, and suddenly Ivan lost interest in talking to Yezh.

"My ship needs to be finished. My men need my guidance," said Ivan, walking away from the fence. "I'll be communicating with you later through radio."

Marushka was waiting for Yezh to come back inside, and his face did convey how bad things were.

"He's building a ship alright. He said that he always wanted to fly to the moon."

"That's a lie. Since when he has wanted to go to the moon?" argued Marushka.

"He told me that my flight was inspirational for him."

"Inspired by you? That's another lie! Lies after lies," said Marushka. "You'd never see Ivan being inspired by anything other than jealousy. I'd say he spied on you. He copied your work, and now is duplicating it on his own … only different, very different."

Poor Yezh. She could see that the man was exhausted by everything that had been bombarding him. His face was full of expression. She invited him to sit down a little bit, remembering that he just came back from a day of interviews. Marushka joined Yezh over the table. She sighed, and a silent pause lasted. Perhaps she could help him to ventilate his thoughts.

Phoenix Phoenix

"How was your meeting?"

Yezh's mood slightly uplifted as if it convinced him to feel better.

"I met the mayor. He had visitors from the Kremlin. They said that if I prove to them that the spaceship works, they would buy it and they'll pay me for it."

Marushka was happy for the good news. Finally, something that Yezh did was going to be repaid.

"No more field work, no more harsh winters for us if this turns out to be a good deal. My ship works!"

"How much will they pay for it? Did they tell you?"

"Sixty … million … rubles!" replied Yezh, with each word lasting a second.

Marushka had her hand on her mouth. She could hardly believe that such fortune had blessed them finally, after all these years of misery.

"Not only that," Yezh went on. "They want me to fly so they can show the world how the great Soviet Union was able to send a man in space. They also wish to fly to the moon."

Yezh hadn't forgotten about the danger that worried her.

"But things need to be sacrificed for that. I need to do this."

She looked at him and then away, reminding herself of those shocking thoughts that once clouded her mind.

"They even thought of exchanging me for another pilot with more experience, claiming that I'm just a poor farmer with no skills," said Yezh, emphasizing how crucial it was for him to persevere through this dream. "Or if I cannot participate in their next manned mission, then they'll have no choice but to hire someone else. They said that I'll be a lost cosmonaut."

"Lost cosmonaut? What is that?"

"I'm not sure, but I think it means someone who achieves glory but remains unknown to the world."

Marushka didn't know if that was something good, bad, or very bad. There was something about that "lost" term that she didn't like.

First Farmer In Space

"If I stray from this duty, they may think negatively about me and may give this hot spot privilege to someone else. My name may never go down in history and our money would be reduced. We'd be plowing soil for the next twenty years again. Well—we would still have those sixty million rubles, but I could have plenty more. They said they have thousands of skilled pilots who train every day and should be able to find another man with the name Yezh to continue my glory."

She knew Yezh worked very hard for his dreams, and never would she let anything to get in his way of glory. He deserved that money and all the prizes and titles that go with it because he had undertaken great risks for it.

Then she thought about their neighbor who stole his invention and changed its model, thinking he would be able to trick everybody. He'd win the race and be richer than what he is already. That hypocrite propaganda-lover was waiting only for this to happen to Yezh—to be able to fly to the moon to steal the fame for himself. Marushka couldn't let that happen.

"If you fail, Ivan would grasp it for himself."

It was hard not to think about Ivan for a moment in a day. Everything was about him, being more troublesome than a raccoon after his crops.

"So, there's that as well," Yezh acknowledged. All the dreaming had made him forget about that despicable man. "That thief—he must have peeked over the fence to design his replica."

"That's how he has always been toward us." She started thinking, choosing her words wisely, then looked in his eyes. "In any case, you'll be beating him as well. Beat him in the space race! I believe in you."

Yezh was happy that all the challenge he received from everybody was uniting them in the pursuit of this dream, and he was glad to have his wife's trust. It meant a lot to him.

"Don't worry; I will beat everybody."

"I wouldn't want to see another Yezh have your glory. Only my Yezh should be on that television and in the newspaper."

For the first time, Yezh felt support from Marushka. Now he felt stronger and ready to face any evil and obstacles in his new journey.

Phoenix Phoenix

Marushka said, "The main problem here is Ivan. He duplicated your invention. He could try to pull profit from the invention by claiming it's his own. It's not fair. You're the only one who built it, who sacrificed all the crops and money and who risked his life to travel in space."

Yezh frowned and raised his chin, shaking his head slowly. He had let that happen. Yezh was punishing himself over having let his guard down with Ivan.

"He doesn't care about the moon, I'd say. He's after your money," continued Marushka.

Ivan had a lot more money that Yezh ever had. That was the only win he had over him.

"It's not money he wants," he replied.

Marushka looked at him sharply. What did he mean?

"He's after the glory. He wants fame, and the only way to win it is by going to the moon."

"Oh, why is everybody rushing to the moon as if there was money up there?" complained Marushka, rolling her eyes and head.

"By beating me in the moon race, he'd appear in the newspaper, and everybody will praise his heroism and great achievements."

That was it! There was only one thing to do against his plotting.

"Then you will beat him," said Marushka, sounding ever so bold and persistent. "There's no way I will let him win anything that should be rightfully yours. Because he earned no part of it."

"Don't worry, he won't win," replied Yezh, still thinking about how to proceed. The moon race clock was ticking away. For Marushka, it was the technique and economy that were getting in their way.

"It's not fair. He has money and manpower working for him."

"Then I will need to make a deal with the Kremlin to modify my ship accordingly and launch before Ivan does. I will need a bigger tank."

Marushka asked him to call them right away, and that's what Yezh did without losing another minute. Yezh picked up the phone and dialed.

He reached Sergei and explained the situation. The man agreed to help and promised him that they would send him a tank owned by the Soviet space agency. After all, moon travel was the primary goal of the officials. The tank needed to be sent to his residence as soon as it was available.

When Marushka asked him when they planned to deliver it, he answered that it might be in several days. She grimaced at the news. That would give Ivan lots of time to perfect his own ship. All they could do was wait and hope. At least Yezh had a governmental body supporting him. The race had started. If it's a war he wants, he will have it. It was about time for these neighbors to settle this among themselves, once and for all.

Chapter 29
Space Race

Two days later, Yezh peeked through his windows to see how his neighbor's ship was progressing. It took Ivan only two days to build his spaceship, named *Poletnik*, with the help of some of the smartest and most talented people with skill trades, compared to Yezh, who took a week to do the work alone. Yezh learned the name when Ivan came up with it, when a worker asked him about it. Yezh knew that time was running out. Ivan was getting closer to causing irreparable damage to his reputation if he won the space race.

Yezh was waiting for the government to offer him a new tank, larger than his first one, for greater fuel capacity. Ivan, on his side, already bought a big tank, which one of the trucks brought to his domicile yesterday. Yezh didn't know yet when he would receive his new tank, but he figured that the space agency would be launching him back into space around the same time that Ivan's ship would be completed.

"Ivan—that cheap-shot artist!" cursed Yezh through the window, seeing his rival dusting off his hands, body language that meant something was completed. There was no way he would have made it this far all alone, without any help from the manpower. It was his fuel tank that was finished, one that was bigger than *Sputnik*'s, one that Yezh needed and Ivan had. How and where he got it, he couldn't guess.

Yezh had been by the window long enough for Marushka to catch him there when she came down the stairs. She walked to the kitchen.

"Is he still building it now?"

"He's still playing around with it," answered Yezh a short moment later, his eyes not shifting away from the sight. Disdain showed on his face.

"Did he give it a name already?"

"Yeah, he did," answered Yezh. "He named it *Poletnik*."

Marushka found it funny that Ivan named it *flier* without even knowing for sure if it will fly. She mocked the name.

"Did you hear news from the Kremlin yet?" asked Marushka.

Yezh remembered their promise, but he couldn't yet give a positive answer.

"No. Not yet."

"I'd say time is running out. How long do they plan on holding it back?"

Yezh sighed loudly.

It wouldn't hurt to give them a call. Yezh tried to contact the office at the national Soviet space agency, which was gaining strength in Moscow. His new tank wasn't getting shipped any sooner. They were still finishing its design. All they could come up for an answer was the date when they were planning on sending him to space for tests which they deemed crucial for scientific development.

Yezh felt stagnated in his progress. He didn't believe that Ivan's purpose was to help scientific development, so why was he (Yezh) stuck with that problem? It appeared that Ivan took his tank somewhere. He must have left for another far away city.

After trying desperately to think it over, Yezh spent the next hour digging for more information. He still needed more money—and more oil. It would be better not to waste time thinking too much. He would extract more oil instead while he still had some time left. Searching and calling around various contacts that Joseph gave him, Yezh found an oil refinery plant and oil rig near Leninsk that was about a hundred kilometers away. He sighed after wasting lots of energy. Yezh hoped that he at least had enough oil in his backyard for his next flight, so he went to check.

He hadn't come out of his house yet. The fresh air was pleasant. It helped him to ventilate his bad thoughts. Yezh didn't even bother looking at his neighbor's side. Instead, he went straight to the far end of his backyard.

The pit was nearly depleted from his last trip, which leeched a large sum of black gold. Yezh thought the rest of the oil must be underground, and that was the problem. His ideas were becoming disconcerted by a humming coming from the other side of the fence. But he ignored it; he was too preoccupied by the puzzlement of the pit. He needed some way to reach the oil beneath. A bucket and a ladder wouldn't suffice this time. Just great. A big excavation could be fatal to his project. He didn't want it to become a necessity. And it meant more digging.

Phoenix Phoenix

Digging, digging, and digging. That's all he had been doing for a while now.

The humming was still bothering his concentration. Feeling annoyed, he looked over the fence to have a peek on Ivan's side—like Ivan had always done to him. What could that humming be?

A lightning bolt struck Yezh's mind when he saw it: A pit about the size he had dug sat a dozen meters away. From that pit came a long, thick pipe that snaked its way to what appeared to be related to *Poletnik*, Ivan's new ship. The humming came from inside the pit. It was a machine.

Damn that copycat!

He had found oil beneath his soil and had been keeping it a secret. It explained why Ivan had become increasingly quieter than his usual self recently. That also explained how he was able to afford all those services and materials. Sneaky little old weasel! And now he was draining the oil pit with a pump. This realization constituted a setback that vexed him to a culminating point.

It could be worse. What if the oil fields below them were interconnected as one big pool of black gold? That could be the reason why Yezh's pit was emptier. Ivan must be stealing a portion. Which meant he was losing oil every second that Ivan's pump was humming in that pit.

This was a side-by-side race for oil to fuel the moon flight, and Yezh needed to buy his own pump quickly before his neighbor took it all for himself. He'd need lots of it to reach the moon. It would only get complicated now that they both needed that same resource from the same place for one common goal.

***

"Looks like Yezh has a challenger," commented Kiril. All four of the musicians were still hanging around the same old hill.

"He's losing time and fast. If he doesn't find a pump, he'll lose his share of oil," said Makar with a "tch" following it. "That neighbor is very cunning."

Others from the group nodded and agreed.

"Do you think Ivan is going to beat him?" asked Kiril.

"Nah, Yezh is the hero of this story—not someone else!" said Bogdan.

"Still, time is at stake here," said Makar.

"That I cannot deny," said Bogdan.

"Well, no matter what the outcome of this story is," Rodion said after listening to his comrades, "I believe we should praise the true hero as Bogdan mentioned. I believe a good old song could bring fortune to our Yezh."

"What do you have in mind?" asked Kiril.

"Something that speeds up time. Something that ticks off the clock as a reminder."

"Ha, that one!" said Makar. "That's a good one, comrade."

They got to their instruments and readied their army of notes. Rodion looked around him; all were ready for him.

"'*Kalinka*'!"

And so, the four musicians played a rhythmic folklore song. "*Kalinka*" was a popular one among Russians. It was popular because it showed a unique way of playing music—a way that represented Russian culture in general. Its slight acceleration conveys a typical Russian feeling—not to mention moody, too. Emotion is portrayed in the notes. Its ups and downs tell a thousand stories of Russian and Soviet history, from the happy ones of Russian's classical music era to the darkened era of the czarist regime and World War II. Russians have been through a lot in time.

"*Kalinka*" would play as Yezh hastily proceeded to beat his neighbor in a fair battle. As time dwindled for him, the time in music would hasten.

***

Ivan's project did not go peacefully, without interrogation from Katenka. She was concerned about what he was doing with the oil. To her recall, he had promised that the oil would be pumped for the sole purpose of selling it. She did not agree with him and expressed her woeful concern. They had barely pulled any profit from it, and the ship was taking nearly all of it. Katenka began to see a "Yezh" inside of her Ivan. How greatly Katenka tried to wake him up from madness! He retorted that it would benefit them in the end, with results far more rewarding than what their original plans were.

Everything was completed around his ship. Only testing it remained to be done. There was one thing that Ivan nearly forgot during his exhausting work of mind and muscles: His cosmonaut garment!

He politely asked Katenka to make something, and the woman went into action after they exchanged a few arguments. He asked her to be original, and no matter what, it had to be better-looking than that awkward, red, skinny garment that Yezh had. It needed to be thicker and white. Meanwhile, Ivan left his house for his test outside. A few men were supposed to come to give additional support.

***

Ivan's objectives did not go unnoticed. People began to gather again when they heard rumors that Ivan was building something like Yezh did. In the heroic aftermath of the popularity-gaining machine, people's attention shifted toward the other side of the fence, where another form of the same machine took shape.

More brightly colored, shinier, taller, and more sophisticated-looking, the new machine derived from the first one was more than just appealing. People believed that it would surely be instrumental in carrying out one of history's primal achievements. This machine was meant to go to the moon, which was something greater than what they had witnessed previously.

Sputnik was losing fame indeed.

***

Yezh hurried off to the store. There, just as Yezh was about to get in, Radomir caught him. The man had gone to buy some more beers.

"Hey Yezh!"

Yezh wasn't feeling very happy to speak to anybody today but he gave him a neutral wave.

"I've heard that you went to space," said Radomir. "That's amazing!"

Yezh gave a little short smile but not much came out from his

261

mouth.

"How's your *Sputnik* going along?" asked Radomir. "I heard that your neighbor, Ivan, was also building something like you. Is it true? It seems that he wants to go to moon."

Yezh's forehead wrinkled a little bit at the thought.

"Yeah. I've seen that," replied Yezh. "The power of inspiration," Yezh said sarcastically, looking away.

"You're getting popular, Yezh! I think you just started something new in this village. Soon flying to space will be a fad. Who knows!"

They chatted briefly before Radomir decided that he'd leave Yezh to his errands. The man bounded off with his box and a smile on his face. Yezh kept his last thought to himself.

I hope you're not planning to build your own ship, too, with those tin cans from your beers!

But the box of beer Radomir bought contained only glass bottles.

***

Yezh bought his costly pump after losing many hours searching for one in these unreliable Russian stores. There was none in his city and he had to drive to the next city to buy one with his car. In Leninsk there were only few convenience stores, although they had a wide variety of goods, and even if they less fit in the *convenience* definition, they were unreliable. Why even call them convenience store? Yezh made fun of the idea. There're not even enough buckets for everybody in Russia! And yet they were building a ship to fly to space. Russia is a weird nation, thought Yezh.

He started extracting oil immediately after he arrived home. The next few hours left in his day he spent repairing his ship and filling up his tank.

Occasionally he'd go knock on the tank to check on the progress.

At the end of the day, the pump finished extracting what it could. The humming had a different sound. When Yezh went to check, he realized that there was no more oil in the vicinity to suck up. When he went to see his tank, it wasn't full. As he suggested earlier, fearing the outcome, Ivan had taken a lot, leaving him not much for the moon flight. The pool had been a small one.

Yezh cursed.

Tension was in the air. Marushka felt awfully calm, and Yezh was quiet, his smile almost invisible. After running around all morning, Marushka decided to continue knitting her clothes for winter. Yezh was going from corner to corner, unable to sit still somewhere.

"You look overstressed," said Marushka, her eyes on her knitting. "You should sit and rest."

"How can I sit and rest when that Ivan is about to fly up there, and I still don't have any tank? Not only that, but I don't even have enough oil. We can't sell any more for money."

"What? He discovered the oil pit?" But she wasn't really surprised about that. She'd forgotten that Ivan was a sneak.

"There's nothing that weasel wouldn't be able to see. You can't hide anything from him," complained Yezh angrily.

"There's nothing you can do now. You worry too much."

All the talking and stress made them unaware of the roaring outside. Soon after, a knock on their door startled Yezh.

Without glancing through window, Yezh opened the door, and surprise struck him.

"Comrade Yezh! How have you been?"

Yezh's face suddenly broke into a smile.

"Comrade Oleg! I wasn't expecting you at all today!"

"Guess what I have for you!"

Oleg opened the way for a look at the yellow truck behind him. On it was a lengthy and large white aluminum tank, strapped carefully from multiple directions, with cushions added for maximum protection against cracks and scratches.

Yezh was speechless, but Oleg knew that Yezh had to be very happy.

"You thought we'd forget about you?"

Yezh stepped out of his house.

"This one is definitely larger than what I have now."

"Is this what you wanted?" asked Oleg.

"Dear comrade, asking for something bigger than this would be a crime against appreciation," replied Yezh.

It was roughly the same size as Ivan's. Finally, he looked back at Oleg.

"I like it."

"Well then, shouldn't we install it right away?"

"Yes. The moment of glory is just a day ahead of us. I want to be fully prepared."

As soon as it came to his door, they wasted no time installing it. Oleg even brought some reinforcements: two engineer workers who would help Yezh to install the tank on *Sputnik*. These men were highly qualified in circuitry and modern technology—the smartest men in the Soviet Union. Yet they worked now for a mere peasant who had not enough coins to make a living. Yezh couldn't have asked for more indeed.

In the backyard, Oleg spotted another ship on the other side of the fence.

"Another one?" started Oleg, his eyes fixed on it. It took a moment for Yezh to realize what he was talking about.

"That's my neighbor's new ship."

"He has a ship, too? How did you people know how to build these things when not even the state knew?"

"Actually, I was the first one to design it. He simply took 'inspiration' from mine and decided to make his own."

"Are you telling me he stole your idea?"

"I was trying to avoid saying that, but you read my mind."

"I see," said Oleg. "Looks like you have an authors' rights dilemma."

Oleg wondered where he fetched such a tank, but Yezh said that he went far away to buy one. Yezh did not have any more money to spend.

After chatting, Oleg left Yezh to his work. The new tank took a few more hours while Oleg was idle around Leninsk. The oil had to be transferred without causing any spill and the tank was heavy. With a machine they could manipulate those heavy weights.

***

Nothing could go amiss in Ivan's eyes. He stared at the yellow truck in front of his house, stared at the official walking to his neighbor's door, and stared at *Sputnik* receiving its new installation. Ivan was spiteful toward what was happening on the other side.

Why don't you blow up Sputnik and go join your epic failure brothers in the scrap yard? That yellow truck should have exploded with his tank on it.

Ivan's evil eye detested the good fortune of *Sputnik* while his nerves were being eaten deep inside by wrath. Feeling jealousy overwhelming him, Ivan cursed. Ivan tried to spy on their conversation for any news and updates. If by chance Yezh should decide to launch today, Ivan would be more than ready to go change himself and jump in his ship before Yezh does.

***

Oleg went to see the mayor to discuss the event that would occur tomorrow. He remembered when Sergei was talking to him about relocating his agency somewhere more adequate for scientific research. Oleg had grown increasingly fond of Leninsk. There was something about it that had a bit of charm, and for some reason, it reminded him of Sergei's conversation. Leninsk was surrounded by deserts in the south, forests in the north, and vast superficial plains on the sides large enough to host any dangerous activity that needed space. It wasn't very crowded, perfect to keep their laboratory apart from the population. It was a private little territory.

Could outside of Leninsk be the perfect spot to relocate the new Soviet space agency? When Georgiy heard such nice compliments about Leninsk, his happiness and pride blossomed.

The mayor had always struggled to find ways to make his village more centered on tourism, but Oleg's plans did not sound like anything close to tourism.

Georgiy could think only about Yezh and his *Sputnik*, and it lifted his spirits to think that among all villages and big cities around Russia, Leninsk got to be the one to host such fantastic people and events.

***

Oleg had a fruitful conversation with Georgiy that lasted the same amount of time that Yezh needed to upgrade *Sputnik*, and by the time he returned, Yezh and his workers were already done.

Oleg saw satisfaction on his face upon his arrival.

"Can we conclude that *Sputnik* has been fully improved?"

"Yes, comrade," said Yezh, "this was the last improvement that it needed. For now."

"You think it's going to fly to the moon with that tank—and all the rest of the components that it has currently?"

"It will, though ..." Yezh paused to think about what he nearly forgot. "It still needs the key ingredient to reach the moon."

"What is it?" Oleg's face reflected confusion and surprise.

"Fuel. I don't have enough fuel to reach the moon."

But Yezh hadn't mentioned anything about the fuel resource below his soil. Oleg never even bothered to ask all this time how he obtained his oil for his other flights. He eventually supposed that Yezh had found oil somewhere without the consent of the state. It was obvious. When he asked Yezh, the farmer admitted it shamefully. Oleg did not argue, to his surprise. But Yezh had a more serious problem.

"Not only did Ivan steal my invention, but he stole all of my oil."

"Why didn't you ask us to bring you more oil?"

"I didn't know I'd need any. I thought I had my spring all for myself."

"Then we have to order some more for you," Oleg concluded, seeing no problem at all. Despite the good news, Yezh's face hadn't changed from a disdainful and sad one. His face appeared almost worried.

"Is there something wrong?" asked Oleg.

"Actually, yes. You see, my neighbor heard that I intend to fly soon, and so he hurried to build his ship fast. *Poletnik* is finished, as you can see."

Both men looked over the fence, where *Poletnik* stood in defiance of *Sputnik*.

"So, he intends to fly tomorrow. I won't have time to wait another day to get more fuel. There's no way I'm going to let him beat me in the race."

Oleg's face twisted into something ironic.

"A competition isn't it?" said Oleg with a smile. "I understand."

Oleg compared Yezh and his neighbor to the Soviet Union and the United States. The Luna project had stirred the West into action, and the Cold War inevitably spilled over into the space race. Because of this resemblance, he fully understood the reasoning behind this man.

"So, it has to be tomorrow," said Yezh, shaking his head.

"But you said that the oil you have won't be enough to reach the moon. How do you intend to win the race then?"

Yezh stared at the ground. "I don't know."

That day, Yezh had received his new tank and had exchanged the oil from the old tank to the new one. At the end of the day, Maks was happy to hear that Yezh would be launching tomorrow. And Marushka had another talk with him in the bed. Tomorrow would be the big day, and Yezh needed all the sleep in the world to make it right.

Chapter 30
Showdown

The morning came. Leninsk once more grew noisy early. Yezh got up earlier today; his brain was buzzing with space travel. When day began, it was time to make it happen.

Yezh's ship had received its day of repairs. The fuel was transferred from the pit, enough to launch him into space. Unfortunately, it wasn't enough for the moon part. Yezh cursed again by the window. This was bad. He felt like he failed himself, feeling tricked and outsmarted by Ivan's sneaky, cunning copycat mind.

Meanwhile, Leninsk elsewhere was also getting prepared for the great moment. Anastasia and her cameraman could not have overslept this morning. The news was too important to miss. Their truck hit the road from their hotel and headed down the road where people were also gathering. The village knew about it.

***

Ivan's men were still doing tests on *Poletnik*, and when Ivan asked them about the status, they claimed it was not fully tested and needed to be given more time. Ivan stressed that more testing wouldn't be a possibility. Today, Yezh would be launching, and the officials would be looking. It needed to be today. He asked his men to skip the rest of the tests to the great dismay of these professional men. Ivan mocked the warning. At least the most important parts had been tested out, and it worked all fine.

***

Oleg arrived along with the mayor. They spoke with Yezh, and all agreed to make it happen. It was noisy and crowded. Yezh got annoyed by the thoughts, and stress shook his body. Many friends who assisted them wished Yezh good luck and shook hands with him before he went back in his house to get ready.

The cameras were ready; people gathered as an audience, waiting to be pleased; and the officials were present. The officials weren't even aware a few days ago that a second space shuttle was taking shape right away. Now two ships stood side by side, ready for launch.

Yezh was diffident upon seeing Ivan's over-improved ship. It looked more beautiful. It had eye appeal. But Yezh kept reminding himself that it's not the quantity or the beauty of things that makes them better. His *Sputnik* was better off the way it is.

Could it be possible that my creation, which took so long to create, to be defeated by a derivative duplicate that took less time than what I needed to blink an eye?

Obviously, Ivan had attached all the most expensive materials to it. He even bought already-built brand new devices for communications and engines. That wasn't fair, because Yezh had no money. It angered Yezh so much to even think that something as despicable as economics, which he learned to hate so much, could get in the way of a man's dream. Dreams are boundless, guided by the great undying will. They remain the strongest part of life.

***

While Yezh was biting himself for letting his guard down, Ivan was enjoying his beginning fame with Anastasia, who interviewed him.

"Ivan, can you explain what motivated you to build this machine?"

"Lots of dreams," answered Ivan. "In this age of spaceflight, it's time to revolutionize what we did in the past. By flying to the moon, I shall offer humanity a great achievement."

"Does your ship have a name?"

"Yes, I named it *Poletnik.*"

"Wow, what a bold name! This could be the one indeed."

Ivan really enjoyed being interviewed, so comfortable about it that he could spend a whole day talking about himself and his machine, which he considered to be his very own version.

***

Yezh dressed up with help of Marushka and went through all the calculations and procedures in his head. He was shaking a little bit. It was all the fame and money at stake that was unnerving.

Anastasia received the signal from both astronauts that they were dressing up and ready to leave their homes. She rolled the camera in live action.

First Farmer In Space

"Here we are at Leninsk, where two big ships standing behind me are ready for launch. It will happen any minute now. We're waiting for the pilots to step out from their homes and into their cockpits."

More people than ever gathered around the scene, which would soon gain national and global interest. Flashes were going off like a lightning storm as people took as many pictures of the two spaceships as they could before they lifted off. Yezh was panicking in his house, hearing all the roaring voices outside.

Yezh sighed deeply before leaving his house. Marushka supported him from behind, patting his shoulders. The door slid open, and the brave man in a red garment stepped out into the yard.

Applause erupted around him. When Katenka heard it, she knew that Ivan should be going out now.

"Hurry up, Ivan. Its starting! Yezh is heading to his ship."

"I'm coming!"

Ivan took so much time talking and bragging about himself to the cameras that he hadn't taken much time to prepare. But Ivan's appearance also earned its share of applause. This time it was a man in a bulky, white garment that radiated elegance—almost divinely.

Yezh moved to the side of his ship, where he'd urinate from stress. He hated when this happened. For some reason nature always called whenever he felt stressed.

Ivan started for the ladder. Halfway up, he stopped, paid close attention to what Yezh was doing and came back down to deposit his share of urine on the sides.

People had been saying that Yezh's success came from doing what he was about to do. Both men were in position to do nature's work, but only one of them managed to wet his ship. Ivan stood there, but nothing came out. He forgot that he already went to the bathroom before he came out.

Ah, who cares? It's not as if anything bad will happen. I don't believe in fortune anyway.

Yezh finished and climbed up, waving his hand once more. When

Ivan looked behind him, he noticed the hatch that Yezh went through closing, and he hurried to zip up and move up the ladder.

"Hey Ivan!" someone called out to him. He turned away to see his wife holding his lunch in her hand. "You're forgetting your lunch box!"

Ivan hurried back down the ladder, trying to move as fast as he could in his heavy and stiff spacesuit. He walked with his legs spread out as if he did some private business in his pants, or like a penguin missing his dive into the ocean surrounding the frozen continent of Antarctica. He took the lunch box with a snapping grip that could have almost torn Katenka's hand off and hurried back to the ship. People laughed at the funny sight he exhibited.

Meanwhile, Yezh had climbed his ladder, gone inside, closed the hatch, and sat in his chair. He was ready to start counting.

"Engine fired! Starting to count," said Yezh in a robotic voice. "Five!"

"You won't beat me, Yezh!" snapped Ivan, all in a hurry going up the ladder, almost tripping in his boots clinging to the metal.

"Four."

"You won't beat me, Yezh! You won't beat me, Yezh!" Ivan snapped repeatedly while climbing his ladder inside of *Poletnik*, still in a hurry.

"Three."

Ivan took a seat hastily and fired his engine.

"No way, farmer boy! You won't beat me in this race! I am faster. I've always been better and always will be!" Ivan was speaking out loud to himself as he turned on his intercom radio.

"Two," said Yezh.

Ivan began his late counting. There was no time for slow counting like his counterpart. "Five, four, three, two, one!" Ivan snapped out quickly in one breath at the same time as Yezh pronounced his last number.

"One."

Both fingers were on the red buttons, and flames raged from the jets below. People were stepping away from the heat and smoke from the ships' exhaust.

"*Blasting off!*" said both pilots, Yezh still calm and quiet, and Ivan hasty and maniacal.

The ships were blasting away. People were in an awe once more.

"Good luck, Yezh," whispered Oleg.

All his communication devices in the truck were operational; computers were running. Yezh checked his gauges; everything was normal. He checked through his window to see where Ivan was located, if he'd already surpassed him in height.

"You're not beating me, Yezh. No chance!" said Ivan aggressively and gritting his teeth.

Both ships ascended toward the sky for a few seconds like salmons heading upstream. Marushka was ever worried, but Katenka wasn't particularly concerned about it; she was convinced that Ivan was going to beat Yezh in the race.

Poletnik had more firepower. Her components were more sophisticated. Ivan knew already he'd win the race. Yezh concentrated on his course, but he couldn't have missed the drastic but slow appearance of *Poletnik* in his windshield. *Poletnik* was passing Sputnik. Yezh did not react in any way but was surely astonished by the slightly superior speed that the rival ship was displaying in defiance.

Ivan was laughing bitterly. This flight was a comparison to the entire lives of these two farmers—with Ivan being always an inch higher and forward from his archnemesis rival.

But in the heights of the blue sky, red lights began to light up on *Poletnik's* gauge.

"What?" Ivan snapped, his eyes bulging out of his eye sockets. "What's happening now?"

His joystick was shaking under his firm grip. A large sound echoed in his ship as his jets choked with dying flames.

"No! No!" yelled Ivan, his heart palpitating.

Phoenix Phoenix

Poletnik ceased to climb in altitude. Ivan's engine wasn't producing any more energy. He was losing height; he was falling. Yezh saw *Poletnik* going to his blind spot.

"No, this can be happening. I was *soooo close!*" Ivan's loud voice echoed in his aluminum walls.

His voice was so loud that even people on the ground could hear him cursing through his intercom that was made to echo louder than *Sputnik.*

"Look, something's happening to *Poletnik,*" said a man.

"Um, guys," said one kid with terror on his face. "It's falling down. It's going to fall on us if we don't move right now."

It was good that the kid spoke out. Because of his alarming voice, people pushed into the fray and out of the way.

"It's falling, get out of the way now!" yelled a man.

Ivan tried his last resort, which was to open the parachute. Suddenly cursing the workers, he felt like urinating on their professionalism.

Some professionals they were! Can't even make things right!

He lifted the cover of the button and pressed it, but nothing happened. That's when he realized the greatest of maledictions: He had forgotten to install the parachute!

Why? Because he had built it so fast, bypassing security, and guaranteeing that it worked. He was so into beating Yezh that he was blinded by jealousy and rage and had forgotten the most precise and meticulous details on *Poletnik.* The ship suffered engine failure because it was built too fast, without proper testing and verification.

Nobody saw it happening. They were fleeing for their lives when *Poletnik* came crashing down. A loud noise banged on the ears of the frightened audience. An explosion was imminent, smoke blinded the scene, and people saw themselves needing to run farther away from the choking smoke.

"Ivan!" yelled Katenka, who got out of her house as soon as the smoke dissipated.

First Farmer In Space

Poletnik was totally wrecked, and the hatch was barely holding itself onto the ship when suddenly it flung open and flew to the side somewhere, revealing Ivan inside sitting on his back. He had kicked the hatch with his foot.

"Look what happened to you!"

He took off his helmet for air and threw it aside violently, choking on ashes, his face blackened by smoke, his hair messy, and his spacesuit ruined.

Katenka began to cry, her hands in praying position.

"Ivan what have you done?"

The woman wasn't crying for Ivan. She was crying for the sprouts which had caught fire. Their crops were burning and crushed under the weight. The tank fissured, and oil leaked in abundance. Because of this, their soil wouldn't be producing for at least the next five years.

"Our peppers! Our cucumbers!" Katenka cried in great dejection.

Ivan had difficulty escaping his wreckage.

"I almost lost my head, and she's crying for her peppers and cucumbers," complained Ivan, still choking smoke.

Chapter 31
Aftermath

The mission was carried out safely, as Yezh had hoped. When he looked on the side, he no longer could see *Poletnik* in competition. Yezh knew what it meant.

"Looks like Ivan met a terrible fate," said Yezh to himself. "A flight to glory, a fall to shame!"

Once more, *Sputnik* left the atmosphere. The cameras installed by the scientist from the Soviet space agency was capturing many pictures. His voice was heard through the radio. The officials recognized this as another success for the farmer. His ship really worked. Man can fly to space!

Oleg smiled. Sergei, conducting his observation live from Moscow, was delighted, too, knowing that the mission went well. He'd have no problem writing a check for the peasant. His machine was worth millions!

The moon was in his sight. At first, he was launching toward it. Yezh was paying attention to his gauge. He tried to measure the distance and probability of reaching it. Oleg contacted him, telling him that Sergei wished to talk with him through his radio.

When Sergei's voice reached the cosmonaut in space, the man gave his feedback and valuable insights from ground control on his mission. Sergei discouraged Yezh from continuing to waste fuel heading toward the moon. Sergei already knew how far away the moon was and the liters that Oleg mentioned gave him a good idea of how far *Sputnik* could go.

Yezh showed disappointment in the news, but Sergei was right. He spoke of the kilometers between earth and moon, and it made sense to Yezh. He had figured it out by himself. Too bad for his neighbor. *Poletnik* would have reached it easily with the stolen supply. Or maybe not! Perhaps they both needed bigger tank on their ships.

This was his second flight, and still no moon walking would occur in the near future. Instead, Sergei asked Yezh to make a trip around earth, and to that, Yezh found no objection. It was aired internationally, and people from all over the world saw him flying. The mission was live on television.

Even the Americans were awed at the success of a farmer. They,

First Farmer In Space

who had hoped to surpass the Russians, found out that they had lost the race.

***

The mission lasted for a few hours. Then the ground operators were able to guide Yezh through the sky when he had to re-enter the earth's atmosphere. The entrance in atmosphere was easier than he had experienced before. The synchronized fall and operation in his ship were accurate with the help of Sergei's guidance. The peasants' square was the perfect spot they thought. Yezh was lucky. He had a lucky habit, and probably Leninsk was a lucky spot for launching and landing.

That day thousands of people came from all over Russia to witness the spaceflight. People were seen marching down the streets toward the red peasants' square. Police were barricading the perimeter for security of landing.

The ship landed safely, and Yezh opened his hatch safe and sound. His reappearance turned into an uproar of cheers from all around him as they saw their hero after four hours of absence. His hands were on the rails, but when he stepped out of his ship, he lost balance and nearly tumbled down the stairs. Yezh didn't know what was going on, but did feel a bit dizzy and nauseated, and the change in gravity made him feel like he forgot how to walk. Unable to stand on his feet, Yezh fell on his back.

People came to assist him. Hoisted by two broad-shouldered men in military uniforms, Yezh waved at everybody and decided to take off his helmet. It took him a few minutes to get re-accustomed to the gravity, and he was able to stand by the mayor when Georgiy came rushing in to give him a warm hug with a bright smile.

"Well done, my Yezh. Our hero!"

Somewhere from the rear, Oleg spoke out to his agents. "This is it. I think we have a champion and a first farmer in space!"

Cheers, smiles, familiar faces—everything was so fantastic. He had proven himself to everybody. He managed to uphold his title.

And he proved that dreams can come true!

***

Phoenix Phoenix

"Now that's a happy ending to a legendary story!" said Bogdan.

"Indeed, not only did he do the impossible to reach his dreams, but he defeated his archnemesis."

"How epic!" said Kiril as a compliment.

"He had come from a long way, just like we did," said Makar. "I'm glad I met this peasant. I feel inspired to sing new songs."

"That's exactly what I've been doing, my Cossack friend!" replied Rodion.

"Should we play one last song for our hero?" asked Makar, who turned to look at Rodion.

"One last it is!" said Rodion. "One that I've been composing for a while now: Yezh's very own theme song."

Rodion started the music. Its vibe gave hints to others on how to join in. He sang a song of legendary praise. In musical lines, he defined what difficulties this man had to go through. They sang about his misfortunes and the challenges he had to overcome.

They loved it! A masterpiece it was, cleverly thought up by Rodion. And now they had nothing else to do in this village. Only a sorrowful silence remained, with wind and leaves singing their own ballads.

"I think our job here is done," concluded Makar.

"You're right!" said Rodion. "Our journey will continue toward other cities."

"Come on, comrades!" said Kiril.

"Let's go," said Bogdan.

The four musicians stood up and began their journey anew, walking away from the hill that they grew acquainted with, this time, with one more new song added to their ballads. They would visit from city to city, crossing all the Soviet Union to sing an inspirational song that defines dreams, one that tells the legendary heroism of a great man that they had once met.

***

After Yezh's second glorious flight to space, documents were delivered to the minister of space science. They summoned Yezh to Moscow several days later, to the Kremlin's Red Square. More people gathered in the streets.

A red car with an open roof drove down the street surrounded on both sides by fans. Yezh was seen from his waist up on the ride.

He waved his hands at the crowd amidst a rain of colors and masculine music played in the background by top musicians of the state. The ride ended at Red Square, in front of the presidential palace, where he descended and moved along near the steps.

There he recognized some people he met back in Leninsk. Sergei, Oleg, Georgiy, and the president were applauding as well. There was silence when the president approached to speak to Yezh in person.

"Dear comrade Yezh: In a world and time where uncertainty made us doubt the possibility of flying in space, a challenge which no man ever dared to take on, you—Yezh—have undertaken that challenge and succeeded. You have shown the world a great deed and have proved to everybody that a man can indeed fly in space. Humanity has received a lot of advancement in technology with your spaceflight. And for that you have our appreciation and praise."

The president, dressed in white, turned to his side, where a man stood with a red cushion in his hand. He picked up a medal and turned back to Yezh.

"For that show of bravery and talent, you have earned not only the title of first farmer in space but also this medal. I congratulate you with this gift to honor your courage."

He took a few steps and attached the medal onto Yezh's military uniform. When Yezh looked closely upon it from above, he knew what it was. He never thought he would acquire such a prize. It was a medal that defined him as a hero of the state.

Yezh looked back at the president with amazement in his eyes. The leader of the socialist state was reaching to him with a handshake. Both smiled as people cheered once more.

Marushka and Maksimilian were present. Even Sputnik was with them. She couldn't keep herself from crying, and when Yezh spotted her among the crowd, she stepped up from the perimeter to assist Yezh and hug him. Then he patted Maks' hair, messing it up. Of course, there was also Sputnik, his friend who helped him to build his spaceship and gave him motivation. Such a brave dog deserved applause, too. Yezh picked him up and held him high to show him to the camera.

"Look, Sputnik. You're popular now. You're going to be on television!" said Yezh.

Smiling, decorated, and united with his family, that moment was forever immortalized in newspapers and books to come. His name would go down in history as Yezh Kalinin, the first farmer in space.

Epilogue

Meanwhile, poor old Ivan, the man who claimed to be superior to Yezh in all ways and whose riches were unmatched by any other resident of Leninsk, found himself reconsidering his title. For the next few months, Ivan was forced to sow new sprouts. After clearing out the oil spill and adding some good compost, he could only hope that winter wouldn't catch him without a reserve of food.

Ivan cursed all day long, sometimes for days and days. Plowing his field again, he kept telling himself how close he was to flying into space, how close he was to becoming popular and rich. He could have succeeded if he had listened to his engineers and gave it an extra day for testing. Maybe his failure had come from a curse. His gut feeling told him that he should have emptied his bladder on the ship when he had to. Maybe that would have brought him the good fortune to walk on the moon.

He not only lost money in that wreckage, but he had gone for all or nothing with the funds he accumulated from the oil sales. Now he began to regret spending it all on *Poletnik*. He lost both ways.

Ever hateful toward his neighbor, he never abandoned his competitive and jealous nature.

If only I had urinated on my ship! If only!

***

As for Yezh: As promised, the state rewarded Yezh with a large sum of money for the machine he invented, and soon the state had its own spaceship. The state began building the first cosmonaut facility south of Leninsk and hired Yezh as a spaceship pilot for future spaceflight. But this time he had a team appointed under his command. Yezh saw his life gaining a whole new look.

***

But somewhere around the world where fame was missing, others had their own dreams and feelings of jealousy toward their rivals.

The United States of America also drew inspiration from the Soviet Union and built their own space science station. It prepared to conduct its own manned spaceflights, and soon the space race began anew, this time among nations rather than neighbors.

A man with slick blond hair arrived at the entry of the large edifice and read the logo on the establishment's welcoming board. It was the American space agency. After uttering a few prayers and wishes, and the young man entered the building.

Inside, it was crowded. People from all over America were training as pilots. It was busy in the recruiting office, because it was a national day for hiring astronauts and selecting the few men for space missions.

A room was dedicated specifically to interviews. Various candidates were around the room, filling out papers on tables.

"Who's next on the line? You may approach!" the recruiter said out loud.

When the slick-haired young man walked in, eyes turned on him from all over the room. Among the faces that showed confusion, stress, or happiness, his face was the only one that was relaxed, as if reserved.

"What do you want?" asked the recruiter, the intensive interviews he had all morning already showing in his voice.

"I wish to become an astronaut."

"Great. Do you have your papers with you, sir?"

"Yes, I do. How could I ever forget such an important thing?" said the young blond man, who handed over his papers.

The recruiter looked at them in a fast glance.

"A farmer?" Surprise was on his face and in his voice. "Okay," said the well-decorated military officer. "Tell me, farmer, why do you want to join our space missions?"

The young man didn't hesitate to reply with great confidence, as if that he'd never regret it.

"Because I want to fly to the moon. I want to be the first farmer on the moon, and I'm here to collect my rightful title."

"First farmer on the moon?" repeated the man, showing a smile on his face, pointing his pencil at people around them, who burst into laughter. "Everybody here has dreams of walking on the moon one day."

After a moment of joking around, he came to a more serious question, expecting an equally serious answer.

"What makes you a special candidate?"

That day, in front of dozens of witnesses, the blond man said something that convinced them to stop their laughter, something that the recruiter and soon the director would remember for decades to come. Soon the entire nation and its history would memorialize the man.

"Because," said the blond man, holding himself straight and adopting a serious expression, "my name is Flynn Hammerfall."

(To be continued in First Farmer on the Moon …)

Phoenix Phoenix

About the Author

I am a beginner in book writing, a young novelist. I began writing in 2011. It was by mere coincidence that I started writing seriously. I was doing some cinematic projects as I wanted to make my own 3-D animation movies at home by myself. I must have written several hundred pages of manuscript when I learned to fall in love with writing. *First Farmer in Space* is one of the first books that I have written and is my first published book.

As a writer with a good imagination, I tend to start writing something only to abandon it after a while when complications arise. Therefore, I acquire countless stories that are nowhere near finished. I do not intend to let go of my dreams but will finish them as they could offer a great deal of entertainment to my audience. I will continue pursuing this avenue of writing in hopes of changing my tasteless career into a fun one, all the while improving my skills in English and in storytelling and offer to my audience great entertainment. If you like what you read, please take a few moments to leave feedbacks on social media and help us to spread the word about this book to others who might be interested. A new writer like me would be so appreciative to you all.

Thank you for reading my book, and I hope you enjoyed it like I did writing it.

Also from Phoenix

Please check out the website,

www.phoenixphoenixbook.com

www.ingramcontent.com/pod-product-compliance
Lightning Source LLC
Chambersburg PA
CBHW051410050726

47595CB00010B/4011